Electric guitar chords send throbbing chills up the spine. The spotlight moves from man to man in the band.

The man in the shadowed balcony neither understands nor enjoys. His last encounter with British rock was "Penny Lane." He does not know that Harrison, Lennon, McCartney, and Starr have gone their separate ways. He has never heard of "Crackerbox Palace," Yoko, Wings, "No, No, No, No" . . .

He wouldn't care if he had.

The spotlight roams. The spook lifts the silenced Weatherby. Through the sniperscope, after all these years, the target's face is that of a stranger . . .

The bass guitarist's brains splatter the organist.

The assassin is half a mile away before anyone can begin sorting the screaming mob in the hall.

A Matter of Time

GLEN COOK

ACE SCIENCE FICTION BOOKS
NEW YORK

A MATTER OF TIME

An Ace Science Fiction Book / published by arrangement with
the author

PRINTING HISTORY
Ace Original / April 1985

ISBN: 0-441-52213-0

Ace Science Fiction Books are published by
The Berkley Publishing Group,
200 Madison Avenue, New York, New York 10016.
PRINTED IN THE UNITED STATES OF AMERICA

I. On the Z Axis;
12 September 1977;
At the Intersection

Total darkness. Silence broken only by restless audience movements.

Suddenly, all-surrounding sound. A crossbreed, falsetto yodel/scream backed by one reverberating chord on the bass guitar. A meter-wide pillar of red light waxes and wanes with the sound.

Erik Danzer is on.

Nude to the waist, in hip-deep vapor, he rakes his cheeks with his fingernails. He is supposed to look like an agonized demon rising from some smoldering lava pit of hell.

Light and sound depart for five seconds.

Owlhoot sound from the synthesizer.

Sudden light reveals Danzer glaring audience right. Light and sound fade. Repeat, Danzer glaring left.

Harsh electric guitar chords, with the bass overriding, throbbing up chills for the spine. Mirror tricks, flashing, put Danzer all over the stage, screaming, "You! You! You!" while pointing into the audience. "You girl!"

The lights stay on now, though dimly, throbbing with the bass chords. Danzer seems to be several places at once. The pillar-spot moves from man to man in the band.

The man in the shadowed balcony, whose forged German Federal Republic passport contains the joke-name Spuk, neither understands nor enjoys. His last encounter with British rock was "Penny Lane." He does not know that Harrison, Lennon, McCartney, and Starr have gone their separate ways. He has never heard of "Crackerbox Palace," Yoko, Wings, "No, No, No, No"...

He wouldn't care if he had.

The pillar roams. The spook lifts the silenced Weatherby. Through the sniperscope, after all these years, the target's face is that of a stranger.

The bass guitarist's brains splatter the organist.

Spuk is a half mile away before anyone can begin sorting the screaming mob in the hall.

II. A Pause for Reflection

Sometimes the balloon is booby-trapped.

Grinning little vandal, full of pranks, you jab with your pin. Ouch! It isn't a balloon at all. It's a Klein bottle. The pin comes through behind you, butt high.

If you're obstinate, you play Torquemada with yourself for a long time.

Take a strip of paper. Make it, say, two inches (or five centimeters if you're metrically minded) wide and fifteen (40 cm is close enough) long. Give it a half twist, then join the ends. Take a pencil and begin anywhere, drawing a line parallel to the paper's edge. In time, without lifting your pencil, you will return to your starting point, having drawn a line on both sides of the paper.

The little trickster is called a Moebius Strip. You might use it to win a beer bet sometime.

Now imagine joining the edges of the strip to form a container. What you would create, if this were physically possible, is a hollow object whose inside and outside is all one contiguous surface.

It's called a Klein Bottle, and just might be the true shape of the universe.

Again, you could begin a line at any point and end up where you started, having been both inside and out.

There is always a line, or potential line, before your starting point and after, yet not infinite. Indeed, very limited. And limiting. On the sharply curved surface of the bottle the line can be made out only for a short distance in either direction. You have to follow it all the way around to find out where it goes before it gets back.

III. On the Y Axis; 1975; The Foundling

Norman Cash, line-walker, began to sense the line's existence at the point labeled March 4, 1975.

It was a Tuesday morning. The sneak late snowstorm had dropped fourteen inches.

"It's killing the whole damned city," Cash told his partner.

Detective John Harald packed a snowball, pitched it into the churn of Castleman Avenue. "Shit. I've lost my curveball."

"We're not going anywhere with this one, John."

At 10:37 P.M. on March 3, uniformed officers on routine patrol had discovered a corpse in the alley between the 4200 blocks of Castleman and Shaw.

Ten-thirty, next morning, four detectives were freezing their tails off trying to find out what had happened.

"Hunch?" The younger man whipped another snowball up the street. "Think I got a little movement that time. You see it?"

"After twenty-three years, yeah, you develop an intuition."

As a starting point the corpse had been little help. White male, early to middle twenties. No outstanding physical characteristics. He had been remarkable only in dress, and lack thereof: no shirt, no underwear, no socks. His pants had been baggy tweeds out-of-style even at Goodwill. He had worn a curiously archaic hairstyle, with every strand oiled in place. He had carried no identification. His pockets had contained only $1.37 in change. Lieutenant Railsback, a small-time coin collector, had made cooing sounds over the coins: Indian Head pennies, V nickels, a fifty-cent piece of the kind collec-

4

tors called a Barber Half, and one shiny mint 1921 Mercury Head dime. Sergeant Cash had not seen their like for years.

He and Harald were interviewing the tenants in the flats backing on the alley. And not making anyone happy.

They were pressed, not only by the weather but by fifty-two bodies already down for the year. The department was taking heat. The papers were printing regular Detroit comparisons, as though there were a race on. The arrest ratio pleased no one but the shooters.

"That's the way it is," Cash mumbled. He shivered as a gust shoved karate fingers through his coat.

"What?" Harald kneaded the elbow of his throwing arm.

"Nobody wants to help. But everybody wants the cops to *do* something."

"Yeah. I been thinking about taking up jogging. Getting out of shape. What do you think?"

"Annie grew up on this block. Says it's always been tough and anti-cop."

"She married one."

"Sometimes I think maybe one of us wasn't in their right mind."

The flats had been erected in the century's teen years, to house working-class families. The two- and four-family structures had not yet deteriorated, but the neighborhood was beginning to change. For two decades the young people had been fleeing to more modern housing outside the city. Now the core families had begun to retreat before an influx from the inner city. Soon the left-behinds would be people too poor to run. And landlords would give up trying to stave off the decay of properties whose values, they felt, were collapsing.

"I thought we'd get some cooperation 'cause they know us," said Harald, after having been cold-shouldered by a high-school classmate. Cash lived just two blocks away, on Flora; John had grown up in the neighborhood.

"Badge does something to people. Puts them on the defensive no matter how hard you try. Everybody's got something to feel guilty about."

The entire morning had been a no go. People had answered their questions only reluctantly, and had had nothing to tell. No one had seen or heard a thing.

Not that they cared, Cash thought. They just answered fast and true to get the cops off their doorsteps.

Cash had met a girl once, Australian he now suspected, who had had a strange accent. That had been a long time ago, college days, before he had married. He no longer remembered who had introduced them, nor what the girl had looked like, just her accent and the fact that he had mimicked it, thinking she had been putting him on. He still felt ashamed of the incident.

Little things like that hang with you, he thought, and the big things get forgotten.

The memory was triggered by the old woman at 4255, Miss Fiala Groloch.

Miss Groloch's was the only single-family dwelling on the block, a red-brick Victorian that antedated everything else by at least a generation. He found it odd and attractive. He had been having a love affair with stuffy, ornate old houses since childhood.

Miss Groloch proved more interesting still. Like her house, she was different.

He and Harald grumped up her unshoveled walk, onto a porch in need of paint, and looked for a bell.

"Don't see one," said John.

Cash opened the storm door and knocked. Then he saw the bell, set in the door itself. It was one of those mechanical antiques meant to be twisted. It still worked.

MISS FIALA GROLOCH was the name printed in tiny, draftsman-perfect letters on a card in a slot on the face of a mailbox that looked as if it had never been used. Miss Groloch proved to be *old*, and behind her the interior of her house looked like a hole-up for a covey of old maids.

"May I help you?" Her accent was slight, but the rhythm of her syllables conjured visions of tiny European kingdoms perishing beneath the hooves of the Great War.

"Police officers, ma'am," Cash replied, tipping his hat. That seemed compellingly appropriate. "I'm Detective Sergeant Cash. This's Detective Harald."

"Well. Come in. Is very nasty, yes?"

"Sure is. Who'd have thought it this late?" To John, whispering, "Knock the shit off your shoes, Hoosier."

They followed the woman to her parlor, exchanging frowns. That curious accent. And she talked slowly, as if trying to remember the words.

"It has been a long time since company I've had," she said

apologetically, clearing a piece of needlepoint from a chair that, Cash suspected, had been an antique before his birth. She brisked to another, woke a fat tomcat and shooed him. "Tea I will have in a minute."

"No thank you, ma'am," said Harald. "We've only got a minute. Sorry to bother you like this, but we've got to visit everybody on the block."

Cash chuckled. John was trying to be genteel. It was the contrasts. Harald's contemporaries had all the gentility of Huns in rut. But that house, and that woman, demanded it.

"Oh, fooey. What bother? Already the pot is hot. Just time to steep it needs. You *Jungen* are always in so big a hurry. Sit. Just sit. Be comfortable."

What could they do? The little lady rolled along like a train. They hadn't the heart to derail her.

She was tiny, under five feet tall, all smile and bounce. She reminded Cash of his wife's great-aunt Gertrude, who had come from England to visit the summer before. Auntie Gertie had been a hundred-fifty pounds of energy jammed into an eighty-pound package. Except in terms of spirit she was indescribable.

They exchanged shrugs and glances in her absence, but neither voiced his fear that they had been shanghaied by a lonely old woman who would use them as listening butts for slice-by-slice accounts of her seventy operations.

Cash studied his surroundings. Everything had to be older than Miss Groloch herself. It could have been a set for an 1880s drawing room, crowded as it was with garish period impedimenta. Most moderns would have found it distressingly nonfunctional and cluttered. Cash felt comfortable. Something in him harkened back to good old days he had never lived himself. But, then, as his sons had often told him, he was an anachronism himself. He was an idealistic cop.

There was no television, nor a radio, or a telephone. Incredible! The lights were the only visible electrical devices. Gas jets still protruded from the walls. Would they work? (He was unaware of the difference between natural and lighting gas.) An old hot water heating radiator stood in a corner, painted silver. Had her furnace been converted from coal? There were still coal burners around, but he couldn't picture Miss Groloch running downstairs to shovel.

She returned with delicate, tiny china cups on a silver tray.

And cookies, little shapes with beads of colored sugar like his wife had made for Christmases before the boys had grown too old for productions. There was sugar in lumps for the tea, with tongs, and cream. And napkins, of course. Luckily, she came to Cash first. John was too young to know the rituals. Cash had had maiden aunts with roots out of time, leap-frogging a generation into the past. Harald did a credible job of faking it, though, and left the talking to Norm. He nibbled cookies and waited.

"Now, then," said Miss Groloch, seating herself primly at the apex of a triangle of chairs, "slowed you down we have, yes? You won't be having a stroke. But busy I'm sure you are. That last gentleman, Leutnant Carstairs, the criminals said were taking over." There were little soft *z*s where the *th* sounds should have been. And *Leutnant*. Wasn't that German? "Relax that man could not."

"Carstairs, ma'am?" Cash asked.

"A long time ago was that. Years. Now. I can do for you what?"

Accent and rhythm were moving more toward the Missourian, though her compound and complex sentences remained confusing.

There were concepts of feminine delicacy which went with the age into which they had plunged, concepts especially strong as regarded little old ladies. But in their business they weren't accustomed to dealing with murder delicately. "Our officers found a man in the alley last night," Cash said. "Dead."

"Himmel!" One tiny hand covered her mouth momentarily.

"We're asking everyone if they heard or saw anything."

"No. Though Tom was restless. The weather it was, I thought."

"Tom?"

She indicated the cat, who sat at her feet eying the cream pitcher.

"I see. Just one more thing, then. We have to ask you to look at this picture. . . ."

"Not to be so apologetic, young man. Please to let me see it."

Cash handed it to her, said, "No one knows who he is."

There were a lot of things the department didn't know, he reflected. Like how the guy died. Forensics, the coroner, and fingerprint people were all working on him.

She stiffened, grew pale.

"You know him?" Cash asked, hoping he had struck oil.

"No. For a moment I thought . . . He looks like a man I knew a long time ago. Before you were born, probably."

Indian Head pennies and a corpse that was an utter mystery to everyone except, possibly, an old lady who said he looked like someone she had known before he was born. Not much to go on.

"Well, thanks for your time and the tea," Cash said. "We really do have to get on."

"Welcome, Sergeant." She accompanied them to the door, an aged but spritely gnome in Cash's imagination.

"You think she knows something?" Harald asked as they approached the four-family flat next door.

Cash shrugged. "I think she told the truth." But he had reservations.

John glanced at her house. "Spooky place."

"I sort of liked it."

"Figured you would."

They struck out everywhere.

"The prelims are in," Lieutenant Railsback told them when they returned to the station. "We've still got a John Doe."

"Give them time," said Cash. "FBI won't even be awake yet."

"Christ, it's hot in here," John complained. "Can't you turn it down? What ever happened to the energy crisis?"

Railsback was one of those people who set the thermostat at eighty, then opened windows.

The lieutenant ignored Harald, one of his favorite pastimes. "You ain't going to believe the coroner."

"What'd he say?"

Railsback lit up. It had been two years, but Cash still lusted after the weed.

"The guy was scared to death. Ain't that a bite in the ass? And he was dead less than an hour when they found him."

"Any marks?" Harald asked.

"On his back. Maybe fingernail scratches."

Cherchez la femme.

"Eh? Damned college kids. . . ."

"Means find the woman. He was a Jody. Somebody's old man got home early."

"And scared him to death?"

"Maybe he was the nervous type."

Cash intervened before the dispute could heat up. "I don't think it'll hold water, John, but it's an angle. Let's see what Smith and Tucholski got." The detectives who had worked the Shaw side of the block, he saw, had been back long enough to get the red out of their cheeks. Long enough for Tucholski, who looked like a slightly younger Richard Daley, to have fouled half the office with dense blue cigar smoke. Smith defended himself by chain-smoking Kools. Officer Beth Tavares, who was little more than secretary-receptionist for the squad, coughed and scowled their way.

"You guys get anything?" Cash asked.

"Pee-pneumonia."

"Frostbite, maybe."

"John thinks maybe he was visiting somebody's wife. Any possibles?"

Tucholski exhaled a stormcloud. "Broad at . . . shit. Middle of the block. Kid's got it in the book. What was her name?"

There were two Kids in the squad. Harald by Railsback's designation, Smith by Tucholski's. Both were in their late twenties.

Smith, a black, was the smartest of the new generation coming into the department. Cash figured he would go far even without affirmative action. He stayed even with Tucholski by having a Polish joke for every occasion.

"Gobielowski. Wouldn't you know it? All we have to do is find the bowling shirt the guy left behind."

Smith and Tucholski bickered constantly, yet were close. Their feud was entirely in honor of tradition.

It was lucky, Cash thought, that neither had a hair-trigger temper.

"John?"

Harald, too, had to keep the notes. "A Mrs. McDaniel. Looked the type, too. In the upstairs flat in the first building east of the old lady's."

"Put them down for a followup."

"Gentlemen," said Railsback, "it's almost shift's end and I know you want to finish your paperwork so you can get home and shovel the sidewalks, so we'll start in the morning."

"Shit," said Tucholski. "He's had one of his brainstorms."

"Tomorrow," Railsback said, "you guys are going to take the pictures around to the coin shops. Somebody'll know him."

"You want to bet?" Cash asked. "I've got a hunch we imagined this guy."

"It's too early for pessimism," Smith observed. "The body's hardly cold." The investigative machinery had barely started rolling.

"FBI will ID him," said Railsback. "They'll find him in the military files."

"Or we might get a confession from a wife with a guilty conscience," said Harald, without conviction. "Or a witness might pop up like a genie out of a bottle."

"We might find an illegally parked car come sweeper day," Cash suggested. "Wednesdays and Thursdays are street-sweeping days over there."

"A thought," Railsback agreed. "I'll have a car check it."

Fifteen minutes later Cash finished his paperwork and left.

Annie had haddock on for dinner, because of his cholesterol. On the bad days, if it were not for her, he would break down and hit a dozen pork chops like Attila the Hun. He had a little sign on his desk at work, one of several homespun gems: You know you're past it when a doctor, not the law or church, takes away everything you like. He was supposed to shun coffee, alcohol, cigarettes, and cholesterol. He did all right on the latter two.

Sometimes it was a pain in the butt. He managed with cussing and little self-reminding notes about having to hang on long enough to collect the pension he had been getting ripped off for all these years.

"Bad day?" Annie guessed.

"The worst." He explained. She had a good head. Interested in his work. He told her what he could. But she was a little drifty about it. She was a mystery buff. Any given time there would be ten to fifteen paperbacks scattered round the house. She came up with some weird suggestions.

"He wasn't dumped? There's that drug war on the North Side."

"No. The doctor says not. The scene agrees. With the snow and everything, they got it pinned. He died where they found him when there was an inch of snow on the ground. He was barely cold when they spotted him. This fish isn't bad. What'd you do?''

"No tire tracks or anything?" Her quick little mind was cataloging possibilities from mysteries read. She had the memory of the proverbial elephant, though it was as cluttered as a scrapyard.

"Not even tracks for him past three steps. They claim they went over that alley with everything. It's like he stepped out of thin air, walked a few steps, then croaked."

"Kaspar Hauser," she mumbled. "How about a fall?"

"Nope. Nothing he could've fallen from. No bruises or anything, either. Just some passion scratches on his back." Her eyebrows arched. "That's what John thinks."

"There goes my helicopter idea. Eat your broccoli."

Ech, he thought. Especially broccoli. But cauliflower was worse and he would get that tomorrow if he didn't eat up today. He was the only baby she had now.

"Matthew called," she said, and was off with the latest from their youngest, who was at UMC and costing more than some of Uncle Sam's earlier wars. His major was Criminal Science. He wanted to follow in his father's footsteps, he said. Cash was not sure why, did not understand, but was pleased. Most kids weren't interested in their old man's work. Especially cops' kids. They all wanted to make a new world and a million bucks. Cash wasn't against doing either. It was just that the youngsters apparently believed in witchcraft, that somewhere, maybe in Washington, there was a magic button. If you were to push it, all the bad guys would get good, all the poor people would get rich, and all the starving would be fed. But the Powers had hidden it, because for some obscure reason that was to their advantage.

Talking about Matthew inevitably led to their other son, Michael. Obliquely, Annie asked, "When are you going to have John and Carrie over again?"

John Harald and Michael had grown up together, gone to college together, and had been in the war together. Vietnam. That had been "The War" to them. To Cash it was that nearly forgotten playground squabble with the Madman of Berlin. To each generation its own, he thought.

Michael Cash had not come home from his. He was still technically MIA. It was a thing between John and Cash that sometimes made them uncomfortable with one another, though they had few differences over the war itself.

"Did you hear me, Norman?"

"Sorry. It's the case."

"I asked what block."

"Eh? Oh. Forty-two hundred. Four or five places west of where you used to live."

"Ech. Good place for it. Right behind old spooky Groloch's. Is she still there? Did you meet her?"

"Yeah. Nice old lady. Reminded me of Auntie Gertie."

"We thought she was a witch when I was little. Took a dare to get us to go past on her side of the street."

"She's been there that long?"

"Was I born in the Dark Ages? Just because little Mike thinks I polished cannonballs for George Washington . . ."

"You know what I mean. Nobody stays around over there. She's probably the only one on the block that was there five years ago."

"Another murder mystery at Miss Groloch's," Annie mused. "What do you want to watch tonight? There's a Tony Curtis movie on Channel Five. An original, one of those pilot things. Or 'Hawaii Five-O'?"

"Cop shows, cop shows, that's all you get on Tuesday. Let's watch the movie. What do you mean, another murder mystery?"

"Oh, a long time ago, before I was born, they tried to get Miss Groloch for murdering her . . . lover, I guess. Only they never found the body."

"Warm up the time machine. I'll send them mine. Then we'll all be happy."

"That's not fair. I think she was innocent. He probably ran off with her money. He was a rat."

"If you weren't even born . . ."

"Mom told me about him. Even if she was guilty, she should've gotten a medal. When I was a kid, people still talked about how rotten Jack O'Brien was. Most of them did think she killed him, but they were on her side. They said he was a liar, a thief, a cheat, that he never worked a day. And that the only reason he would've hung around an older woman was to use her somehow. But nobody ever figured how she could've done it. That's how come we were scared."

"How old is she, anyway?"

"I don't know. At least eighty-five. That was in nineteen twenty-one. . . ."

"Twenty-one?" Cash echoed, startled.

"Yes. So?"

"This guy . . . he had a pocketful of old coins. A twenty-one dime was the newest."

They stared at one another.

"A practical joke?"

"Annie, people don't kill people for a joke. But I'll check it out. See if anybody's got it in for her, or if there's any bodies missing. . . ."

"You never did say. You think it's murder?"

"I don't know, hon. When we get bodies in alleys, we have to dig. He could've escaped from a funeral parlor."

"You said he died there."

"Yeah. So let's do the dishes and watch the movie, or something. Before it drives me crazy."

Next morning, before beginning the rounds of the coin shops, Cash cornered Railsback. "Hank, you ever heard of a Lieutenant Carstairs?"

"On the force?"

"Yeah."

"Can't say that I have."

"He'd go back a ways."

"I can ask the old man. Is it important?"

Old Man Railsback had retired in 1960, but still hung around the station more than home. He lived with his son, which Cash felt was explanation enough.

"Not really. Just curiosity."

The old man seemed to know everything that had happened since Laclede's landing. Apparently, he had been there. Or so his reminiscences made one think.

Cash shifted subjects. "Annie thinks our John Doe might have been lowered from a helicopter."

"No way," Railsback said. "I thought of that myself, Norm. I called Lambert Field. They said not even a nut would fly a chopper in that."

"I didn't think so. But Annie—"

"Annie should write mysteries, not solve ours. Now, if you've got the time, find John and do the coin shops. Maybe we can wrap this up before the next one comes floating belly up. Here's your list."

It was no go. They got shrugs, blank stares, and a few definite negatives. They wasted half a day. But that was the nature of the job. You always played out every chance.

"What I think," said John, around his Big Mac at lunch, "is we should put his picture on the wire. Guy's probably got a wife and seven kids in Little Rock, or someplace."

"Maybe. But you've got the feeling too, don't you? This one's going in the files unsolved."

"Yeah. It's weird. Like in Nam, you could tell Charlie had an ambush set without seeing a thing. . . ." He turned it off because of what he saw in Cash's face.

Funny how it keeps on hurting, Cash thought.

He had had an uncle who had gotten it in Italy, 88 mm in the chest while standing half out of his tank turret. That had never bothered him the way Michael's loss did. He supposed it was this not knowing for *sure*, this perpetual half-suspicion that the boy was alive somewhere in the Asian jungles. And it was worse for Nancy and the kids. Their lives were drifting away while they marked time.

"Maybe FBI will find something."

"They're running out of places to look. What do we do then? Call the CIA? Interpol? Or put his picture in the papers?"

Cash got a new angle on John there. This case was bothering his partner as much as it was him. He thought he understood why. It did not seem right that a man should die, murdered or not, without so much as a memorial in a police record. A man should have a monument, like maybe: "Here Lies the Unknown Victim, A Casualty in the Cops-and-Robbers War."

They were remembering Michael, that was why. Michael would have no memorial either. His war had cast him into a limbo where there were no monuments, no eulogies, no benefits for his survivors. . . . Only their memories would ever show that he had existed. And here they had the mirror image, a corpse that was the only proof that a man had ever lived.

One wake without a ship, and one ship without a wake.

"Maybe Tucholski got something," Cash said.

"Want to bet?"

"Not a doughnut hole."

John was right. The women on the reinterview list had iron-clad alibis. One had a mother, and the other a boyfriend very

much alive and kicking about being hassled. And of the cars illegally parked on the Wednesday side of the street only one
could not be accounted for. That was a junker without plates
the neighbors said had been there for months.

Dead ends. It was all dead ends. They still had nothing from
FBI. Missing Persons across the country had come back with
nothing. Lieutenant Railsback got growly when he heard his
brainchild had been stillborn, grumbled about putting the case
on a back burner till something concrete turned up.

It had begun bugging them all. Nobody wanted to do it slow
and by the numbers.

"I talked to the old man at lunch," Railsback told Cash
later, as he and John were about to go home. "He said there
was a Colonel Carstairs on the Board of Commissioners in the
late thirties. Came up out of Homicide. That's the only
Carstairs he remembered."

"Probably the same man. Thanks, Hank."

"What was that?" John asked on the way down to the
parking lot.

"Just checking something the old woman said the other
day. About a Lieutenant Carstairs. You and Carrie coming
by?" Annie had insisted that morning so he had extended an
invitation.

"Yeah. We'll bring Nancy and the kids, too. Carrie called
Nancy and Nancy said Annie had already called. . . ."

"I get the picture."

It was nice having people around sometimes, Cash
reflected, though the children made him nervous. And Carrie
and Nancy, who were cousins, made these evenings together a
sort of wake. Michael's body might be gone, but his ghost remained very much among them.

Following dinner the children established squatter's rights
to the TV while the women caucused in the kitchen, so Cash
and Harald retreated to the rathskeller.

"Something bothering you?" John asked, letting Cash pour
him a scotch and water.

"The case. The damned John Doe." He repeated Annie's
story about Miss Groloch and her mysteriously missing lover.

"Coincidence," said John. "Or a grisly joke."

"That's what Annie thought. Wanted me to check for body
snatchings."

"No go. Front page."

"That's what I told her. And how to get it there still warm, during a snowstorm, without leaving a trace?"

Against one wall stood a crude set of shelves, boards on cinder blocks, that Cash had erected for his wife's old mysteries. Somehow, when Michael had gotten married, a lot of his science fiction had migrated into them rather than out of the house. Nancy's people were stodgy. He had preferred to hide his reading tastes the way his father's generation had hidden their *Playboys* from their wives in the fifties. John pulled out a couple and tossed them onto the bar.

"Tried to read *The Time Machine* once," Cash said. "Didn't grab me. Never noticed this other one before." It was *The Corridors of Time* by Isaac Asimov. Its dog-eared look suggested that it had been one of Michael's favorites.

It was Cash's fault that his son had gotten started reading that stuff. He had brought home a book called *The Naked Sun*, same author, given him by someone at the station who had thought Annie would like it. "But I get your drift."

John looked expectant in the way a pup does when his master catches him peeing off the paper.

Cash shrugged. "There's a more reasonable explanation."

"Tell you what," John replied. "Let's check the files. See what the reports have to say."

"John, I wouldn't know where to look. I mean, sure, they keep the files open forever. Supposedly. But where? We'd really have to dig. First just to find out where they keep records of where they keep records from fifty years ago. And on our own time. . . ." The case bothered him, yes, but twenty-three years of homicide investigations had put calluses on his curiosity. He had not worked on his own time for ten years, since the bizarre rape-murders around Mullanphy School.

John seemed disappointed. "All right. I'll do the digging. If I locate the file, I'll have it sent over."

"Railsback would crucify us just for thinking about it. No imagination, old Hank."

Cash was saved John's stronger opinion of Railsback by Carrie.

"I'm sorry, Norm. We're going to have to go. It's my head, John."

"Didn't you bring your pills?"

"I didn't think . . ."

"We've got aspirin, Carrie," said Norm.

"No. Thanks. I'm sorry. With aspirin I have to take so many I make myself sick at my stomach."

"Okay," said Harold. "Get your coat. I'll be ready as soon as the kids are."

Carrie's headaches were genuine, but Cash suspected they were a psychological convenience. Judging from the past, she had gotten Annie and Nancy going on Michael, real soap-opera stuff. Cash had been through a few of those sessions himself. Carrie was good at starting them. But she didn't like being around the people she made unhappy or depressed.

"All right," he said. "I'll see Nancy and the kids get home. John, we'll talk about it tomorrow."

Thursday they got another negative on cars illegally parked and more silence from Missing Persons around the country. FBI produced nothing. Railsback decided to release photos for television and the papers. John got on the phone and started trying to locate Homicide records for 1921. Friday lunch he disappeared, turned up late with a crusty file, thick, handwritten, almost illegible.

They never got into it. The new case, that had held off longer than seemed believable, finally broke. It was a holdup-murder. Two partners in a cheap used-furniture store had been killed, and an officer wounded. One freelance socialist was dead and two more were fleeing on foot, one of them hit. The whole division was on it till dark, and by then they had another. The weekend had begun. It was Tuesday again before Cash had a chance to worry about the mystery corpse.

On Sunday the story hit the papers. On Monday the Channel Four evening newscast mentioned the case in passing. Tuesday morning, at 8:30, Cash got a buzz from Tom Kurland on the booking desk.

"Norm? Got a live one down here. Voluntary confession on that John Doe stiff from last week."

Ah. The genie from the bottle. Cash brightened. "Hey. Good. Bring him up. You made my day, Tom."

"On the way." Mysterious laughter lurked round the fringes of Kurland's voice.

"Hey, John. . . ." he called from his gym locker of an office.

A florid, gray-haired man with the build of an athlete long gone to seed, who looked like he ought to be traveling in a cloud of flies, pushed through the main door. " 'Lo, Beth," he said.

"Winehead Andy," Cash muttered. "The Prince of Hungary. I'll get you for this, Kurland."

Officer Tavares tried stopping the man. He just grinned and kept coming, with a little wrist-flick of a greeting to Old Man Railsback, who was snoring in a chair in a far corner.

"It's all right, Beth."

" 'Lo, Sarge."

"Hi, Andy. What is it this time?" As if he didn't know. The man, who claimed to be a deposed Prince of the Austro-Hungarian Empire (he was neither old enough nor, insofar as Cash had been able to determine, did he speak a word of German or Magyar), was, with a blush, going to admit that, in a fit of madness, he had slain the mystery man. Andy swore that he was the Jekyll-and-Hyde type.

"Can't live with it anymore, Sarge. Had to turn myself in. . . ."

The man had confessed so often that Cash no longer found him amusing.

Neither did Lieutenant Railsback. "What the hell is that wino doing in my squad room?" he thundered from his office.

"The usual," Beth replied, returning to her work.

Rather than come out looking for trouble, Railsback slammed his door.

"All right, Andy. You know the routine," said Cash. "How'd you do it?"

"Knife. In the back. Grabbed him from behind and stabbed him in the heart. . . ."

"Wrong-o, Andy. You lose again. Think it out better next time. That's hard for a right-handed man."

"Just testing, Sarge." He stopped smiling. "I really strangled him. . . ."

"Missed again." Cash shook his head. He didn't understand. Andy's sole ambition seemed to be to get himself put away.

There had been a time when he was a semipermanent resident in the holdover downstairs, especially in winter, but these days every room with a lock on its door was packed with genuine bandits.

"Shot him?"

"Andy, here's two bucks. Go over to the Rite-Way and tell

Sarah I said to give you the breakfast special.''

Andy took the money. "Sarge, one of these days you're going to catch me red-handed. Then you'll believe me. It's my mind, see. I can't remember afterward. . . ."

"I know, Andy. Till I do, you'll keep getting away with it. Meantime, I've got to go by the book. Now do me a favor. Go eat breakfast.''

Andy stood tall as he left. A wino, yes, but he walked like a prince.

"Beth, remind me that Tom Kurland is one up on me.''

"Us." Her dark eyes sparkled mischieviously. "I'm working on it already.''

"Make it vicious." He walked to a window. "He's out the door already.''

Below, Andy scampered through traffic.

"Liquor store?''

"You must be part Gypsy. Anything on my corpse?''

"No. No ID. No claim on the body. FBI says they've given up trying to locate prints.''

"Norm," said Railsback, "you get rid of him yet?''

"He just needed the price of a bottle, Hank.''

"About your mystery corpse. 'Bout time you got it certified nonhomicide, isn't it? Get it off our backs? I don't like it. I want it pushed back, out of the way.''

"Not yet. Maybe in a couple days.''

It's really bizarre, Cash thought, the way this is affecting us. Railsback would not have let go of any other case for weeks or months. But with this one even the marginally involved people, like Beth, were behaving strangely.

Once Railsback did get it shoved back, little happened.

Events elsewhere devoured Cash's attention and emotions.

IV.
On the X Axis;
Lidice, Bohemia, 1866;
A Minor Event during the
Seven Weeks' War

A wise man once observed: The past is a foreign country. They do things differently there.

Fiala . . . Marda . . . Fiala tossed her head violently, battered her temples with her fists. What was happening? Was it the Prussians?

The pain broke the grip on her mind.

Father lay sprawled half in, half out of the doorway. Mother knelt before the Virgin, moaning.

Fiala was having a fit. He heaved on his pallet, shrieking.

Her brother? She was an only child. . . . And her mother had died in the Uprising.

Couldn't be the Prussians. The armies were north of Lidice.

Lidice? What the devil was Lidice?

Who was Marda?

"Uncle Stefan. . . ." Oh, Lord, her mouth wouldn't shape the words right.

Mother whirled, stared in horror.

Where am I? What's happening to me? Who are these people? What's wrong with my mind?

What's wrong with my mind? God help me! Something's in my head. Possessing me.

German. That was it. Only no one spoke German anymore. Not outside a classroom.

It was a strong demon. "Mother. . . . Priest. . . ." Mother ran from the house. Would Father Alexander believe her?

What was this mumbo-jumbo? Only recidivist subversives believed that nonsense anymore. Only stupid, ignorant country people. . . .

21

"Oh blessed Jesus, help me!"

Slap! "Marda!"

The blow floored her. And terminated the contest. The terrified thing in her mind twisted away with a fading shriek, as if sliding off round the treacherous curves of a Klein bottle.

Who was this ragged brute? The man who had been lying in the doorway.

"Father?"

"Yes. Come on. Get up."

The words were butchered by lips and tongue that had never spoken Czech.

"What happened?"

"I'm not sure. There's no time to worry about it now. Just accept it. Help me with Stefan."

His absolute calm enveloped her, included her. The thing inside her, the other, momentarily gave up trying to reassert itself. Numbly, she seized the feet of the hovel's remaining, now silent tenant and helped swing him onto the rude table. He was just a boy, yet his face was a land on which several bad diseases had left memorials.

No one outside a labor camp lived this way. Dirt floor to sleep on, a pallet stuffed with straw. Only furniture a homemade table. . . . No, there were a few crude pieces in shadowed corners. No water. No toilet.

This wasn't her world.

"The woman. She went for someone."

Then she studied herself.

And received a greater shock.

The body she wore, beneath the crudest peasant clothing, was tiny, emaciated, just entering puberty. It was the female counterpart of the boy on the table. "Oh. . . ." It couldn't be a labor camp.

One of those places, only rumored, where they experimented on enemies of the State?

Outside, the sun was rising. On a morning like this, the spires of Hradcany Castle would be visible from the church belfry.

A scant sixty miles to the northwest, men named von Bismarck and von Moltke were defining her history with words spoken by the mouths of cannon. Already the troops were moving at Königgratz.

She had come to a land more alien than she could believe.

Its name was July 3, 1866.

V. On the Y Axis; 1975

The collapse of South Vietnam had begun in January, a slow, snowballing thing that had not seemed serious at first. But when Hue and Da Nang went and the North Vietnamese started whooping down the coast routes like a juggernaut, it became obvious that the end had finally come. Those with an emotional investment in the country could, like watching the football Cardinals go into the second half down by seventeen, hope for a miracle, but that hope was wan.

One night Cash woke to find Annie sobbing beside him. He pretended not to notice.

Later that week he found her sniffling in the kitchen when he returned from work.

"What's the matter?"

"Been a rotten day. Everything went wrong. And now I burned my finger."

She was lying. The stove wasn't hot. But he let it slide. Even shared griefs had to have their private facets.

"Nancy's bringing the kids over tomorrow."

"Yeah? Second time this week. What's up? I thought she didn't like us that much."

"People change."

"I guess." They just could not get it out in the open.

The worst cruelty, for Cash, was the indifference of the people he encountered. But they were dead-tired of Vietnam. Most would have been pleased to see the damned country follow Atlantis's example.

Cash was angry and unapproachable most of the time.

During the downhill plunge to the fall of Saigon he remained utterly distracted. Nothing could draw him out of the netherworld to which he had retreated. He had little time for murders or murderers. His thoughts all revolved around that one little country, that pimple on the ass of the world, where his oldest son was still missing. . . .

He did not really care about Vietnam *per se*. He was no rabid anti-communist. The system had done wonders in China. Through the later years of the war he had been critical of United States involvement, though for reasons at variance with those vocalized in the streets. Those he could not comprehend at all. They had no apparent relation to reality, only to wishful thinking about how the world *should* be. He felt that, like a too cautious coach, the United States had gone, at best, for a draw. He felt the military should have been allowed to go for a victory with everything but nuclear weapons, and to hell with futile arguments about the propriety of being there in the first place. Once you're wet, you should go ahead and swim, not cry about falling in, he thought. But he kept his opinions to himself, being rational enough to know they *were* opinions and not something Moses had brought down from the mountain in his other hand.

He had greeted the January, 1973, news of United States withdrawal with relief. The Kissinger "peace" had seemed a last, comic punctuation to an era of futility. He had predicted the disaster even then, and had tried to school himself to live with its inevitable consequences.

Vietnam was dead. The people who had buried it wanted everyone to forget. That would be nice, Cash thought. He wished he could. If he had known for sure about Michael, he might have been content to stick his head in the sand with the rest. But he knew the other side wouldn't forget. They knew, now, that they had carte blanche in that end of the world. They knew, from peasant to premier, that the fall of Saigon symbolized far more than the culmination of years of warfare. It marked the east's watershed victory in World War III. Solzhenitsin had pointed it out: the west had been fighting a halfhearted and half-assed delaying action since 1945; Vietnam had marked the beginning of the end. From the fall of Saigon onward the collapse would cease to be gradual. The west, whether good or evil or whatever, was about to come apart, and at a rate which, historically speaking, would be precipitous. Cash supposed he would live long enough to see the barbarians at the gates himself.

But, from a historical perspective, it would not matter much. Life would go on. The big change would be in which gang of mental cases would be running things.

Times were when Cash grew extremely cynical. Especially about government and the people in it.

Annie, in her anger, in her passion to show others her feelings, volunteered to adopt an orphan. There weren't enough to go around. After the collapse, she decided they would sponsor a Vietnamese family. Cash acquiesced, hoping she would not start blaming them about Michael, expecting she would forget the whole thing when she calmed down.

Mayagüez put everyone on an even keel again. It was silly, being such a small incident, not well executed at all, and likely to be nothing more than a fix for the national pride.

Yet next day Cash was able to get back into his world, to work by more than the numbers.

John Harald was more perceptive than Cash had suspected.

During the grim months he had not said a word about the mystery corpse. That morning after *Mayagüez*, quiet because even the bandits were home following the news, he strolled into Cash's office and dropped the ancient file onto his desk.

"Want to glance through this?"

"What?"

"Carstairs's file on the Groloch investigation. The missing man."

"That again?"

"Just have a read. I'll be catching up on my paperwork."

They had been a lot less formal in the old days, Cash discovered. Carstairs's report contained a lot of opinion and suspicion that was hard to separate from evidence. The story was much as Annie had described, though Carstairs had been convinced that Miss Groloch *had* murdered Jack O'Brien. Good riddance, he had observed. But the extent of the report indicated that he had put a lot of hours into hunting a solution.

Initially, Cash's strongest reaction was an eerie feeling of *déjà vu*. Carstairs's emotional responses had been identical to his own.

Atherton Carstairs had felt *driven* to find out what had happened to O'Brien. And had faced the same reluctance to push it on the part of his superiors. They had wanted to write it off as a simple disappearance after only two days—despite the fact that there had been a dozen witnesses willing to testify that O'Brien had been seen entering Miss Groloch's house, that later there had been the screams of a woman being beaten, then a masculine voice pleading for mercy. And O'Brien had never come out.

The file included a thick sheaf of letters. For years Carstairs had kept up a correspondence with friends in other cities, hoping someone would stumble on to O'Brien alive. A search of Miss Groloch's house, in a day when such things need not be done so politely and proper, had produced nothing. He had not found a doily out of place, let alone bloodstains or evidence of violence. For weaponry the woman had possessed nothing more dangerous than a few kitchen knives.

Carstairs had made his final entry in 1929, on the eighth anniversary of the case, and the eve of his assignment to the Board of Police Commissioners. He had left best wishes for anyone who became interested in his hobby case.

He had finally surrendered.

Pasted to the last page was a snapshot of a man and a woman, in the style of the early twenties. Penned on the yellowed sheet was "Guess who?" in John's hand, with an arrow indicating the man.

The resemblance was remarkable. Even to the suit. And the woman was undeniably Fiala Groloch.

"John!" Cash thundered. "Get in here!"

He appeared quickly, wearing a foolish grin. "Saw the picture, eh?"

"Yeah. You didn't fake something up, did you?" John and Michael, as teenagers, had loved practical jokes. John had once gone through a camera stage. He and Michael had made some phony prints showing Cash and a neighbor woman leaving a motel. There had been virtual war with Annie before the boys had confessed. Cash had never forgiven them.

Because he really had been guilty, his feet of clay had been innocently, accidentally exposed, his darkest secret had been hauled, bones rattling, from its casket by children who knew not what they did. The experience had made him suspect there might be something to the law of karma after all.

John's smile faded. "Not this time. You want to run tests?"

"No." Cash believed him. He didn't want to, though. "Wait. Maybe. This's impossible, you know. It can't be him."

"I know." Harald seemed proud of his little coup, but frightened. As was Cash, who felt like a wise Pandora about to open the box anyway.

"There're no prints in the file," Cash observed. "Did they use them then?"

"Got me. I don't even know how to find out."

"They started in the eighteen hundreds, I think. Didn't Sherlock Holmes use them?"

"Shee-it, I don't know. Never made any difference to me."

"Okay. Okay. We got a problem. How to prove our corpse isn't Jack O'Brien. We need something concrete. Dental records?"

"No way. You saw the coroner's report. No dentist ever saw the inside of that mouth. Perfect teeth."

"Yeah. Wouldn't find anything medical, either. It'd be here in the file. Scars and things. Carstairs doesn't mention a one. You'd think a guy with O'Brien's street record would've gotten cut up a little. Must've been a lucky bastard. Bet you couldn't even find a birth record. . . . Wait! O'Brien. Catholic. . . ."

"Got you." John started to leave.

"Hold on here. Let's have a plan. All we can do is find out if he was born here, maybe if any relatives are still alive. . . . Yeah, that'd help. Find somebody who really knew him besides Miss Groloch. Wouldn't be conclusive, though."

Cash paused, thought for nearly a minute. "We need to get ahold of something with his prints. You think any would still be around?"

John spread his hands, shrugged. "They found pterodon bones in Texas a couple months ago."

"Okay. Anything's possible. Slide out when Railsback isn't looking and start checking parish records. I'll cover for you."

"But Railsback is looking," the lieutenant said from behind Harald. "What're you up to now?"

"Not much. A little hobby case, you might say."

"Yeah," said John. "Just a check on a birth certificate. It'll only take half an hour."

Railsback spotted the file. And picture. "Hey, the John Doe. Where'd you get this? Who is he?"

Harald and Cash exchanged looks.

"Well?"

"Name's Jack O'Brien," said Cash. "That man disappeared in 1921. This is the file on the investigation.''

"Eh?" Railsback frowned. "What the hell? You're shitting me.''

"Nope." Improvising, Cash added, "We thought the John Doe might be a relative.''

"Really?" Railsback gave them both the fisheye. "You got the Donalson thing straight?''

"He's in the can, ain't he?''

"Sure. But for how long? Judge'll probably release him on his own recognizance.''

They had brought Donalson in for a double murder. He was an enforcer for one of the drug gangs, had been on bond awaiting trial on two previous murder charges when they had grabbed him. One case had gone more than a year without disposition. It was the sort of thing that made them wonder why they bothered.

"The paperwork's current," said Cash. "Won't be anything more till the prosecuting attorney asks for it.''

"Okay, you want to chase some crackpot time machine notion, go to it. Just keep in touch, huh?''

John disappeared before the lieutenant changed his mind. Once he was gone, Railsback exposed a bit of his normally hidden human side. "You feeling better now, Norm? Maybe if you get into something really zany like this . . . ?''

"Yeah, Hank. I think we got it worked out now. It hit Annie pretty hard, though.''

"I heard she wants to sponsor one of the families.''

"We've talked about it." From there they let it slide into shop talk. Railsback had lost his idealism in the trenches of the Us-and-Them War of their business. He had worked his way up from patrolman, and patrolmen often became disillusioned early. They began seeing their lives in terms of cops against the world. Sometimes the people they protected became indistinguishable from the predators. An Alamo psychology developed. Guys who understood what was happening to them usually got out. The others stayed in and exacerbated the profession's bad image.

After fifteen minutes Railsback wandered off. Cash wondered if he were having family trouble again. He had seemed distracted. He did not socialize much on the outside. No one really knew the private Railsback, though it had long been apparent that he and his wife lived in a state of armed truce, which explained why he often worked a double shift. The one time Cash had met Marylin Railsback he had come away wondering what Hank had ever seen in her. The ways of love were as strange as those of the Lord.

What with keeping up on the daily casualty list and not making much headway with parish records, John didn't find anything for a week. Cash's own workload, which now included covering for Harald where he could, gave him no time to get involved. And on his own time he had private problems. Annie kept fussing about taking in a Vietnamese family. For reasons known only to herself, Annie had asked for a police official. Cash wasn't sure he would be able to handle that. Some of them, surely, had earned their reputations.

But John eventually came rolling in. "I've got it: a sister. Twelve years younger than O'Brien, but she's still around. All his other relatives have moved or died. What took so long was, she was married, then her old man got blown away in World War Two, then she went into a convent. Lot of name changes."

"Which one?"

"Saint Joseph of Carondelet."

"Hell, that's right over on Minnesota."

"Yeah. Thought you'd want to go along."

"Damned right. So let's hit it."

They slid out while Railsback was on the phone home, arguing. That didn't bode well for their return.

"Think we ought to take her down to the morgue and spring it on her?" John asked while on the way.

"What for?"

"To look at the corpse."

"You mean they still got it?"

"Yeah. I checked this morning. Since nobody ever claimed it, they just sort of forgot it. Sloppy, leaving a stiff laying around the meat locker like that."

"Isn't that against the law, or something? I mean, there'd have to be all kinds of screw-ups. Should've been an inquest, should've—"

"Probably. Anyway, they're talking about doing something with it now that I reminded them."

"That's the weirdest thing about this guy. Everybody's in a rush to get rid of him, if only by forgetting. Even us. Look how long we let it go. It's like he don't belong and everybody can feel it just enough to want to ignore him. How'd you stop them this time?"

"Told them I thought we'd found a relative."

"John . . ."

"So I fibbed. Just wanted to see what she thought."

"This is an old lady, John, a nun. Maybe it's too rough. . . ."

Sister Mary Joseph was no aged but delicate flower. A glance was enough to show them that she was a tough old bird. Had to be. She was a first-grade teacher with twenty years service in the witch's cauldron walled by children, parents, and superiors in the archdiocese.

"Sister Mary Joseph? Norman Cash."

"You're the policemen?"

"Uhm. This's Detective Harald. John Junior. His dad was a competitor. Episcopalian."

"Why'd you want to see me?"

"Just to ask a few questions."

She seemed puzzled. "About what? Will it take long? I have classes. . . ."

"This man?" Cash handed her the picture of the corpse, the same one that had gotten a reaction from Miss Groloch.

She frowned. Her breath jerked inward. One hand went to her mouth, then made the sign of the cross.

"Sister?"

"He looks like my brother Jack. But it can't be. Can it? He died in 1921."

"Disappeared," Harald corrected. He presented the picture from the file.

"Fiala Groloch. The heathen foreigner." This time she made a sign against the evil eye, then reddened when Harald and Cash looked puzzled. Cash had never seen an embarrassed nun.

"Sorry. There was a lot of animosity. Would you explain now?"

Cash took it, kept it simple, did no editorializing. "We're playing a long shot. Hoping this man might be your brother's son or grandson."

John added, "We hoped you'd be willing to view the corpse. To let us know if you think that's possible."

"Well, I suppose. Sister Celestine won't mind an extra hour with the children." She smiled a delightfully wicked little smile.

Cash couldn't help observing, "I think you'd like my wife's

aunt, Sister Dolorosa. She's a Benedictine. At a convent in northwestern Pennsylvania."

"Oh? Well, I'd better tell Mother Superior. Be right back."

Sister Mary Joseph returned while John was on the phone to the morgue. "I've always had a feeling this would come back on us. Fiala Groloch should've been burned for witchcraft."

Cash didn't respond verbally, but his surprise was obvious.

"I know. That's not charitable. Not Christian. But if Satan ever sent his emissary, Fiala Groloch's it."

"That much bitterness? After all these years?"

"Oh, it's not Jack. I was too young to understand at the time, but he was the devil's disciple himself. He probably deserved whatever he got. Did you meet her? I hear she's still there. And strong as ever."

"We did. She seemed like a nice old lady."

"Old? I wonder how old she really is."

"About eighty-five, I guess. She only looked about sixty, though."

"At least she's aged some."

"I don't understand."

"When it happened . . . whatever happened with Jack . . . she looked about forty. . . ."

"Early thirties, I heard, but you're the only one I've talked to who knew her then."

"About forty. And even then there wasn't anybody who remembered when she didn't live there. Her house was built when that part of the city belonged to the private estate of a Mary Tyler. When I was a child, the old folks said it'd been built right after the Civil War."

"I figured the eighteen eighties, just guessing."

"My grandparents came over in eighty-three. She and the house were there then, and had been for a long time. My grandmother told me she'd heard that there'd been a man who was supposed to be Fiala's father. He disappeared too, I guess. Miss Groloch told people he went back to the old country. Nobody ever heard which one it was. She used to get out and around in those days. Didn't lock herself in till after Jack disappeared."

"The name sounds like eastern European." He wasn't really hearing the sister. That Miss Groloch might be 130, or even older, seemed so ridiculous that her words just floated across his consciousness like unsinkable ice. His only reaction was to make a note to tell John to check the tax and building records on the Groloch house.

Harald returned. "Okay. All set, Norm. Got to hit it now, though. The morgue people are spooked about having the stiff around so long."

"Sister?"

"I'm ready."

During the trip downtown Cash tried to draw the woman out on her feelings toward Miss Groloch. He failed. She retreated into a shell not at all in keeping with the warmth and spirit she had shown earlier.

Sister Mary Joseph made the sign of the cross again when the attendant rolled the corpse out. Several times. Cash feared she would faint.

But she got a grip on herself. "Do you have his clothes?"

Harald spent a half hour hunting them up. Then the Sister merely glanced at them. She found a chair, sat, thought for several minutes. Finally, "You'll think I'm crazy. And maybe I am. But that's Jack. Those are the pants he was wearing the day he disappeared. I remember. I was sitting on the front steps with Colin Meara from upstairs. Jack gave me a dime and told us to get a soda before the old man heard about us holding hands on his own doorstep. He winked at Colin and went off whistling. He had his lucky tam on, and his hands stuffed in his pockets. Sergeant, it's him. How can that be?"

Harald grinned like a Little Leaguer who had just pitched a no-hitter. Cash just sat down and put his face in his hands. "I don't know, Sister. I don't know. This thing's getting crazier and crazier."

"How did he die?"

"Scared to death, the coroner says."

"Is that possible? I mean . . . ?"

"It's possible. Not common, but possible."

"But how'd he keep so long? They didn't have freezers."

"He died March third. About 9:30 P.M."

"This March? That's impossible."

"I know it. You know it. But that there Jack O'Brien don't know it. Didn't know it. He was barely cold when they found him. His body heat had melted the snow. . . ."

"But it's impossible. Fifty-four years . . ."

"I know. I know. I know."

John continued to grin—with worry beginning to nag around the edges as he recognized more and more improbabilities. Cash and the sister sat in an extended silence. Finally, she said, "I think you'd better take me back now." To the puzzled attendant, who had been hovering about all along, "What do I have to do about the body? About arrangements?"

She was convinced.

Railsback was at his foulest when they returned. He looked, Cash thought, like a tornado about to pounce on a trailer park.

"Cool it, Hank," Cash said. "Sit down and shut up till we're done. We just bought a time bomb."

Railsback recognized distress, was reasonable enough to realize a tantrum was inappropriate. "Talk to me," he said.

"We got a claimant for our John Doe. Guy's sister. Positive ID. Absolutely no doubts. But . . ." And Cash gave him the buts.

As was becoming more common, Railsback thought before he growled. But he growled anyway. "Norm, I don't want anything to do with it. Get it out of here. There's got to be some way we can dump it on somebody else. . . ."

"There's still a murder file open."

Railsback pulled a bottle of pills from a drawer, gobbled a couple. "Who knows? You and Harald. Me. The sister. Anybody else? This hits the papers and TV, they'll clobber us."

"Not today's developments. I guess the wives are current through yesterday. Oh, and there was the attendant at the morgue, but he didn't know what the hell was going on."

Railsback rubbed his forehead. He got headaches when the pressure was on. He was an ulcer man, too. He ate Valium like candy. "Too many. It's going to leak somewhere. All right, you guys dug it up, you bury it. One way or another, you get out there and prove she's a nut. Maybe we can't find out who he *is*, but we damned sure better find out who he *isn't*."

"How?" John asked.

"I don't care. It's your problem. Use your imagination. Roust this Fiala Groloch. Way you describe her, she's got trunks full of mementoes. Look for prints. Do whatever you have to, but do something."

VI. On the Y Axis;
Through 8 August 1964;
The Chinese Puzzle

A man named Huang Hua, whose true name was something else entirely, spent the years 1956–1973 in virtual self-imprisonment in a two-room office in a basement in Peking. He was a veteran of the Long March and the engineer of the POW defections during the Korean War.

One room was living quarters. It contained his bed and toilet. The other contained cooking facilities and a small desk with a single telephone. Along one wall stood a bookcase containing numerous looseleaf notebooks of western manufacture, each filled with the tiny, precise characters of his pen, plus several hundred books, mostly in English. Along the base of another wall were cartons of office supplies, more than Huang could use in two lifetimes. He was a hoarder.

Only four men knew why Huang had gone into hibernation: himself; the chairman; Lin Piao; Chou En-lai.

In 1971 Lin would feel compelled to let the Muscovite revisionists in on the secret. Air Force fighters caught his aircraft over Mongolia on September 12.

Huang's telephone linked directly with a small underground establishment in Sinkiang. It was the only regular connection. Security was more strict than at the Lop Nor facility.

Huang's life and project reflected the Chinese character. He had failed in Korea. Certain that other chances would arise, he had kept his project going and growing. Not once did the policy-makers ask him to justify the expense or necessity. Tibetans, Indians, recalcitrant regionalists, old Nationalists, even a few Russians from the 1969 clashes on the Ussuri River, and Burmese from the border skirmishes there, came to his facility. He learned. He polished. He refined. He persevered.

August 8, 1964, provided one of the great moments in his life. That was the day the Chairman himself phoned to give him the news about the Gulf of Tonkin Resolution.

All things came to the man who was patient.

VII. On the Y Axis; 1975

Cash and Harald were in the station parking lot when John said, "We can't prove a thing even if we do find prints that might've been O'Brien's."

"Why?"

"How do we prove they're his? How do we date them? If they match the John Doe, all we prove is that he was in the house. Not when."

"Yeah. Well, shit. At least we'd have a reason to ask Miss Groloch *some* questions."

"If she cooperates. We haven't got a warrant, you know."

"Whose side are you on, John?" Cash slammed the car door. "Can you see what the court would say if we applied?"

But they went on in hopes she would cooperate. Carstairs had noted her willingness to do so several times. That had fed his suspicions.

On the way Cash told Harald what Sister Mary Joseph had had to say about Miss Groloch. With a sigh, Harald replied, "I'll dig through the records. This's getting to be a lot of work for no return, Norm."

Miss Groloch, of course, was in, and remembered them. "Sergeant Cash. Detective Harald. Just in time you are. I just put some cookies out to cool. Tom!" she shouted toward the rear of the house. "You get down!" Cash could not see the cat. She explained, "On the table he will be getting now. We know each other well. Sit. Sit. The tea I will start." She bustled toward the kitchen.

Miss Groloch's parlor had not changed since their previous visit. Cash began wondering about the economics of her life. Annie had said no one could remember her having left the

36

house since the O'Brien incident. He and John had caught the mailman on the way in. The man claimed that all she ever got was junk mail. No personal letters, no Social Security checks.

"What about tax forms?" Cash had asked.

The man had not been on the route that long. But then he did remember that she sometimes received packages from a health food firm in New Jersey. He had seen nothing that might have been a tax refund or rebate check.

At Lambert's, the little market a block north, the manager had told Cash that his boy delivered twice a week, in small amounts. She always paid in cash, and always gave the boy a list for next time. Her tastes seemed a bit old-fashioned, but not as much as might be expected of a refugee still steeped in the last century.

Cash wanted a look at her kitchen, to see if she had a refrigerator.

A thousand questions piled up every time he thought about Miss Groloch. And he had barely scratched the surface. The questions came like those little metal puzzles you take apart, then can't get back together, only in a chain a hundred puzzles long.

"Now," said Miss Groloch, the amenities performed, "What can I do for you this time?"

Sometimes Harald had the tact of an alligator. He did it on purpose. "We've got a positive identification of our corpse: Jack O'Brien."

When you look into a kaleidoscope and turn the barrel, patterns shift. Sometimes, after the flicker, the change seems undetectable.

That happened with Miss Groloch. She was pallid for an instant. Her teacup rattled against her saucer. Terror lightninged across her face. Then, so quickly her reaction seemed imaginary, she was the cool old lady again. "No. Seventy-five Jack O'Brien would be. The photograph you showed me, it was that of a boy." Her pronunciation altered subtly, moving toward the European.

"His sister identified him. She was so sure she claimed the body."

The woman seemed to wander off inside. The tomcat came and crouched nervously against her ankles. Finally, "The Leutnant Carstairs, he said you would never stop. . . ."

Cash tried to get a handle on the accent. German? Somehow, that didn't seem quite right. His duties in 1945–46, as a sergeant attached to Major Wheeler of the Allied Military Government, had kept him hopping through the Anglo-American Zone. The accent, he was positive, wasn't North German. Too soft. Nor did Bavarian or even Austrian seem quite right.

John was playing it too heavy. It was time he stepped in. "You'll have to excuse John. This case is frustrating. We're sure the man's not Jack O'Brien, too. We came because we hoped you could help us prove it. It's indelicate to mention it, I know, but you knew him best."

"It is that. But if I can help, I must." She was in such rigid control that her accent and structural stumbling all but disappeared. "There is so little to tell. He was like a—what do you call those spring storms?—like a tornado. Here, there, gone before he left a deep hurt. I know what people thought. But love him I never did. . . . Does that surprise you, Sergeant?"

"No." But it did. He had fixed notions about his elders and their times. Casual affairs then? No, not till later, once Prohibition had reached its absolute nadir.

John horned in. "Would you be willing to look at the body?"

"For what?"

"To tell us how it can't be O'Brien. So we have something to go on."

That flustered her. It meant a trip downtown. "I . . . I don't know. To going out I'm not accustomed." Her accent thickened again. She slowed her speech as she groped for words.

Cash groped too, for the high school German that had been the army's excuse for sticking him into the AMG operation. Maybe he could catch her off-guard.

But no useful phrases would come.

What about maintenance? he thought. A big house like hers, so old, had to have paint, tuckpointing, and repairs all the time. The plumbing had to be crankier than a '47 Ford. How did she manage upkeep without going out? And, if they did find someone who had made repairs, would they learn anything?

Harald softened his approach. "I know. I don't think you'd have to if we could find some other way. Say, fingerprints."

She frowned, turned to Cash for an explanation. He tried, showing her the difference between their thumbs. "The natural oils leave marks," he told her. "I'm sure you've noticed, housekeeping. No two people's are alike. We hoped you'd have something around. . . ." Her housekeeping habits did not appear the sort that would leave fingerprints lying around for fifty years.

Cash was fishing for an invitation to see the rest of the house.

She was cool for having been so long alone. Panic scrambled around behind her eyes, like a roomful of mice with a cat thrown in, but she did a good job of controlling it. Time had made her timid, but she refused to be spooked when the world assaulted her privacy.

"Is no chance, I think. No. But look we can. Where do we begin?" She rose, patted her skirts down.

"Any souvenirs?" Cash asked. "Something glass might have taken a print. Or paint if he touched it while it was tacky. Or a photo."

"Was a photograph once, yes. Just one. Your Leutnant Carstairs never gave it back. I do not remember any painting doing then. Everything has been painted since. Many times. I would not leave a dirty glass sitting for fifty years."

"We're grasping at straws," Cash admitted.

Her spectral smile informed him that she was aware of that fact.

For a moment he felt he and John were being manipulated, that her cooperation was a subtle form of mockery.

"Well, come then. Upstairs we'll go and see."

Cash didn't know what to expect. A locked, dusty room, memorially closed in respect for a withered love? Something like that. He just couldn't take her no love claim at face value.

What he did see was pretty much what an ordinary visitor would expect: just an old lady's house.

Cash stuck close. He was briefly bemused by her spryness on the stairs. John hung back, sticking his nose everywhere. With another of her quiet smiles, Miss Groloch pretended not to notice.

"Where to look I really do not know," she said, leading Cash into a bedroom. "But this seems the best place to start. It's a mess. I'm sorry."

"My wife should be so slack."

"Most of his time he spent here. Or in the kitchen. He was that kind."

Despite her ingenuous claim, the room had been kept with

the care of a woman who had little else to occupy her. Cash picked up a perfume bottle that looked old enough, but which was of cut glass. "Any presents?" he asked. "He ever bring you anything?"

"Presents?" She looked thoughtful. "Now that I think, yes. Once. A porcelain doll. From Germany. Dresden, I think. He stole it, probably."

She went to an alcove off the bedroom which seemed to function as storage space, though it had probably been meant for a nursery. She opened a wardrobe which showed flecks of dust, rummaged around the back of a cluttered top shelf.

Cash noted four dresses hanging inside, all in styles a woman might have worn shortly after the Great War. They appeared to have hung undisturbed since their proper period. Miss Groloch wore appropriate old lady clothing now.

She might live outside it, but she was not unaware of the world.

It just keeps getting weirder, Cash thought.

"Here it is." She brought out something wrapped in yellowed tissue paper that crumbled when she tried to unwrap it.

"Hold on." John appeared genielike, a doily in hand. "Lay it here. You'll ruin any prints if you handle it."

"Fah!" she said. "Filthy it is. Laziness. No excuse is there. Someday to clean this, I will come." She stirred through the wardrobe, muttering to herself. "Sergeant, your force. It has the . . . *vas ist?* . . . charity?" She held up several sound but ancient shoes.

"We do." He forebore saying that he didn't think anyone was desperate enough to accept something fifty years old.

John slipped away with the doll, carrying it in front of him, on his palms, as though it were a nitro bomb. Miss Groloch abandoned the wardrobe in disgust, continued giving Cash the tour. John rejoined them as they were about to look into the attic, which proved to be a vast, dark, dusty emptiness. Miss Groloch refused to go up.

"Up there Tom gets sometimes," she said. "Filthy he comes back. I maybe should get one of those vacuum sweepers. . . ."

"Don't you go climbing around up there," Cash told her. "If you fell over a joist and broke a leg, who'd come help you?"

She smiled, but didn't reply.

Cash was satisfied. He did not bother going into the attic. As Carstairs had noted so long ago, she was too smart to leave any evidence. If ever there had been any.

But Harald asked to see the basement. He seemed determined to push till he found the limit of her cooperation.

The basement had to be entered through the kitchen. Miss Groloch did have a refrigerator, Cash noted. It was so ancient that it had the round radiator stack on top. Ammonia coolant? he wondered.

To Cash the basement looked as innocuous as the rest of the house. Already certain they would find nothing, he remained at the foot of the steps taunting himself with Miss Groloch's accent while Harald prowled. What little looking he did was for his own curiosity's sake.

As he had suspected, the furnace was a conversion, coal to gas, probably with fuel oil as an intermediate step. The electrical wiring was the old exposed single strand, heavy guage copper wire. He noticed several places where the insulating fabric had become frayed.

"You see where the cloth on the wires is getting ragged? That could cause a fire someday. And this floor joist. You see where the insulator goes through? By the knot. It's cracked. You should have a carpenter scab on a sister beam before it settles and ruins your floor."

"This house and I, we are alike," Miss Groloch responded. "Getting old. Coming apart. Nothing lasts forever."

It was odd, the way she said that. Her wistfulness caused Cash to examine her expression. For a moment she wore a faraway look, then gave him that ghostly smile. Once again he had the feeling he was being manipulated.

"Tear it down they will when I'm gone, I expect. A pity that would be. It is a good house. Love and attention it needs, is all. Houses, they are like people, that way."

Before she could pursue this unexpected line, Harald said, "Well, sorry to take up so much of your time." He seemed disappointed. "We appreciate your cooperation." He made it sound as though he would have appreciated a confession a good deal more.

"I am happy to help, any time. You will be back, yes?"

That had the ring of accusation. Harald shrugged.

"You are always welcome. To being alone one never grows accustomed."

John grunted, took a last look around.

Loneliness. Cash wondered why she had never taken another friend after Jack O'Brien. Or had she? He would have to double-check with Annie.

Back in the car, after another round of tea and cookies, Harald asked, "What do you think?"

"What's to think? It's perfect. We've got to find another goddamned angle."

"Something's out of kilter. Something's not straight."

"How so? I didn't see anything."

"I don't know. Petty shit, I guess. Maybe it was the basement. You notice anything queer?"

Cash tried to visualize. "No."

"Probably nothing, but there were a couple things I noticed. Like, it wasn't a full basement."

"So?"

"So the end that would've gone under the rest of the house had a wall that looked like it was built a long time after the other three. The stone was different. And it was laid on top of the floor. And the floor was poured a long time after the basement was dug. It looked like it was done in sections. Like somebody mixed and poured it by hand."

"So? What can we do about it? Never mind the buried men and the secret rooms. You think Carstairs wouldn't have found them? Think we should cite her for not getting a building permit? Even then you'd have to *prove* she violated the building codes. They probably did it before there were any."

"You're no help, Norm. Not a damned bit. We already know Carstairs wasn't infallible. And there were other anomalies."

"Ooh, college words. Like what?"

"A washer and dryer. And water heater."

"That's a crime?"

"When the rest of the house is so old-fashioned?"

"No, now hang on, John. You might think you've got to have a telephone, radio, and TV, but somebody who grew up without wouldn't. The stuff she's got is practical. And she had an icebox. I mean refrigerator. You take a bushman out of the Kalahari, offer him one modern appliance he could take back, I bet you he'd want a refrigerator. . . ."

"Okay. Okay. So that explains some of it. Maybe. But not where she gets the money."

"You're bound and determined to nail her for something, aren't you?"

That was an aspect he kept worrying about himself, though, technically, it did not relate to their case. "Look into it if you want. Go down to the IRS. Maybe they've got something."

"If they'll let me have it." They swung into the station lot. "But they've probably never heard of her."

"Take care of the car, hear? I'll haul the doll upstairs."

"Got one for you, Beth," Cash said, opening the door with his rear while keeping both hands on the doll.

"What?"

"Print evidence. Lab stuff. Want to take it to them for me? Okay? You got a box, or something?"

"Kleenex box okay?" She fished one from her wastebasket.

"Fine. Anything. Give it to George, all right?"

"Special?"

"The Groloch thing."

"Your wife left a message. I put it on your desk. I'll take this over while I'm remembering it."

He studied her behind as she left. Not bad. Someday he might give that a try. . . . He returned to his desk.

His *In* tray had had a litter in his absence. It was all routine stuff that could have been handled by a semiliterate, patient chimp. Mostly revenue-sharing record-keeping that no one would ever look at once it left his *Out* tray.

Cash got less done than the chimp would have. His mind refused to stay off Jack O'Brien, Miss Groloch, and the certainty of Sister Mary Joseph. Somehow, something had to add up. But it just would not.

The puzzle of Miss Groloch was, more and more, displacing that of O'Brien's death.

And the clock kept capturing his eye. Beth had left the memo, in purple ballpoint, square in the middle of his blotter.

Norm (in wide, looping script): Annie says she went ahead. A man from the Relocation Board will visit you tonight. Try to get home early.

Beth

P.S. I guess this is a surprise.

It was. Despite her talk, he had expected Annie to fold.

While he was trying to make up his mind whether or not to leave right away, a voice said, "You've done it this time, Cash." Lieutenant Railsback appeared before his desk.

"You look like Rip Van Winkle the day he woke up. What's happening?"

"Your china doll. They got a print off it. Already. Right thumb."

"No."

"Yes."

They stared at one another. All Cash could think was that this was impossible. But if it were true, there was a hole in Miss Groloch's defenses. She had made a mistake.

"Hank, I saw that doll come out of her wardrobe. I can't *prove* it, but it sure as hell *looked* like it'd been in there for years." He recalled impressions of being manipulated. Had the old woman known they would find a matching print? Was she mocking them? No. That would mean too much attention. She wouldn't want that. "The tissue paper . . ."

"I already told them to work on it. Told them to run every test they could think of, and to go to FBI if they had to." He dragged a chair up to Cash's desk, flopped in. "There's got to be a hole. Somewhere, there's got to be a hole. Or we're up against a Fu Manchu."

"Uhm. You remember Doc Savage?"

"The old man never let me read that crap. So I read his after he goes to sleep now. Yeah, I know him. Even went to the movie. Too campy. What about him?"

"Just think it'd be nice if we could put in a call to New York, have him clean this up. You notice how he always gets the job done in a couple days?"

"Don't pay any attention to the rules, either. Just busts people up." He snorted. "Long as we're wishing, why not go for a psychic? There's that fat English broad out in the County. . . ."

Cash thought about it. It was straw-grabbing time, and there were precedents. Then it struck him. "We wouldn't dare. We'd be up to our necks in reporters. That's their meat."

"Norm, I'm getting close to retirement. I don't need this."

Close? Cash thought. More like five years. Matter of viewpoint, he supposed. "I didn't ask for it either."

"You sure as hell did. You had to keep poking and poking."

What was keeping John? Cash had wanted to talk to his partner, but did not feel like listening to Railsback while waiting around. He also wanted supper and time to put his heels up before the refugee placement interview.

"Look," he said, "we've had it this long and nobody's popped a cork. Why don't we just keep it canned? There's no pressure. Meanwhile, put a hold on that stiff. We've got a print from the old lady's house now. We can put some heat on."

"Yeah? All right." Railsback was unimpressed. "Wish we could just bury him. That's what I'd do with most of them if it was up to me. Often as not, they need what they get." He rose. "Give my best to Annie. Have to have you over sometime."

"Right. Same to Marylin." Cash hoped he would never receive a more definite invitation.

The lieutenant left without responding. Toward the end of the day he always grew depressed and remote, especially when he had no work to keep him overtime.

Annie got to Cash sometimes, as all wives do to their husbands, but, he felt, if she came on like Marylin Railsback, he would have bailed out years ago.

John wasn't going to show, Cash decided. He left.

"Fish again?" he grumbled as he walked in the door. "I could smell it clean out in the street."

"You were expecting maybe filet mignon?"

"Bad day?" He stalked Annie across the kitchen, put his arms around her from behind.

"Not really. Just nervous."

"Second thoughts?"

"And thirds and fourths. What's your problem?"

"You can still back out." Then he explained about the case.

" 'Curiouser and curiouser,' as Alice said. I thought you'd given up on that one."

"We never give up. We just put it away for a while. Getting sorry we came back. Oh. Don't tell anybody about it. Hank told me not to tell you."

"Okay." She twisted free, commenced setting the table. "What do you want to wear?"

"You going through with it?"

"All the way. A little buck fever, that's all."

He was not sure she understood the relationship of Michael to refugee in her own mind, but asked no questions. He never would. It was hers to work out.

"When's this guy supposed to show up?"

"Around eight. They were real nice when I told them about your job."

"Sure."

"What's that supposed to mean?"

"Just that they're having trouble finding people. You know me. Always the cynic. Bureaucrats don't make things convenient to be nice. They got a Moses somewhere who brought down a tablet telling them to be horse's asses."

"You're right. You are a cynic. Don't get going tonight."

The bell rang a minute after eight.

"That's them already!" Annie exploded in a frenzy of last second seam-straightening and hair-patting. "They're early."

"It's eight." He went to the door. Startled, he said, "Yes?" to the man he found there.

"Jornall Strangefellow. From the Relocation Office."

"Oh. We've been expecting you." Someone, anyway. But not a six-foot-four-inch, roly-poly black man with a bizarre name. Cash tried to cover his reaction. "Come in." He led the way to the living room. "Annie, this's Mr. Strangefellow. From the Board. My wife, Ann."

She did a less competent job of concealing her surprise. Strangefellow stirred uneasily while pretending not to notice.

"Well, sit down. Let's see what we have. Can we get you anything? Coffee?" Cash flashed Annie a look. What will the neighbors think was all over her face. This, probably, was part of the testing pattern.

"Tea. If I may. Plain."

Miss Groloch flashed across Cash's mind.

"What we have," Strangefellow said, after making small talk till Annie, composed once more, brought coffee and tea, "is a family of four. A major of police from Saigon, Tran Van Tran, is interested in your offer. Our backgrounding suggests you'd be compatible."

"Uh? . . ."

"Mr. Cash?"

"Well, to be honest, I'd be a little worried about his record. You know, the Fonda people were always talking about the police over there. If they were on our side, they were concentration-camp guard types.''

"I see. Understandable. Some probably were. You needn't worry, though. This guy's as straight as Jack Armstrong. Educated here and in France. He was liaison between the Saigon police and our MPs for two years. He had no connection with the secret police. Oriental politics operating the way they do, though, he probably did have some political responsibility on paper.''

"No, that wouldn't bother me. Even here we've got trouble keeping City Hall from using us. I just didn't want any SS-types.''

"None of that. Tran's a genuine Audie Murphy, Vietnamese-style. Squeaky clean war hero. Remember the Tet Offensive in sixty-eight? He won their equivalent of the Medal of Honor during that one.''

"Oh?" Cash was beginning to grow distracted. Strangefellow was so thoroughly educated and bureaucratized that he seemed like a white man in blackface. His failure to conform to *any* racial stereotype was flatly disconcerting.

"Seems that, even with a bullet through his liver, he singlehandedly stopped a Viet Cong suicide squad from reaching a packed ARVN hospital with their satchel charges. And later, when the end came, he stuck it out till the last minute. He was one of the last people they brought out.''

"Have you met him?" Annie asked.

"No. I'm sorry. Not yet. Except through the paperwork. The book on him is this: he's thirty-eight, his wife, Le Quyen, is thirty-four, his sons, That Dinh and Don Quang, are fifteen and twelve. There aren't any extended family complications. This is Tran's second time on the run. Just after he got married, he and five brothers had to scoot out of North Vietnam. They were Catholic, and Ho had just given the French the boot. Their parents and most of their relatives still live in the Haiphong region, they think.''

"It sounds good to me,'' said Cash. "Annie?''

She nodded. "Go ahead.''

"We can handle our part, then. Might have some trouble finding him a job, though. Things are tight here. But we're ready to go to the next step.''

Annie nodded again. She did not trust her mouth much tonight.

"No hurry on decisions," said Strangefellow. "This is just a preliminary interview. We won't get started on the details till the Board reviews my field report."

"I see." The whole thing hung on the impression they had made tonight.

"There're some personal questions I'm supposed to ask. If you think the answers aren't any of my business, just say so."

Yeah, Cash thought. And Annie can kiss her pet project good-bye. "Go ahead."

"You lost a son in Vietnam?"

"Missing in Action," Annie replied. For her, and thousands like her, the distinction between KIA and MIA was critical.

"I see. Thank you." Strangefellow smiled thinly. "I'm trying to determine if there's any resentment of the Vietnamese because of your loss."

"No sir," Annie said.

Damned right there is, Cash thought. "Maybe a little," he confessed. "You can't help thinking some strange things sometimes. Especially what if this or that had happened differently. You don't have to worry about us taking it out on Tran, though. We're not that petty."

"And your daughter-in-law?"

"I can't speak for her. I think she's mostly mad at the government, though. Kissinger especially."

"Friends of the family?"

"We don't move in a large circle. There'd be more curiosity than anything."

"Mrs. Cash?"

"I guess they're mostly the sort who'd try to make them feel wanted."

"Good enough. I think that's all for this time." He began assembling the few papers he had brought.

"That's all there is to it?" Annie demanded.

"For tonight. There'll be paperwork if the Board gives us the go-ahead. I don't foresee any difficulties there, though."

"Oh. I see." Annie always felt more secure when bulwarked by paperwork.

"Thanks for the tea. And I'm sorry I took up your evening."

Norm glanced at the clock. The man had been there less

than a half hour. Amazing. He walked Strangefellow to the door, said good night.

"I should've expected it," Annie grumbled when he returned.

"What's that?"

"That they'd send a black man. Or someone different."

"Well, it don't matter now. I think we got through all right. It kept me from worrying about O'Brien and Miss Groloch for a while, anyway."

He switched on the TV, but mostly thought the thoughts he wanted to avoid till the ten o'clock news came on.

That was the same old noise. Two more of the people he was supposed to protect had gotten themselves killed. It seemed like the department was always too busy picking up the bodies to indulge in any prevention.

Next day, long before his evening escape rolled round, he began wondering if he should not just spend the rest of his life locked in his bathroom.

VIII.
On the X Axis;
Prague, 26 August 2058;
Agency for State Security,
<u>Que Costodi Custodes?</u>

"Thought you should know, sir." Sergeant Helfrich's voice sounded tinny, crackled. His picture kept twisting away into a dark, slanting line.

"We'll be right up." Colonel Neulist severed the connection, glared down at the page for his stamp album that he had been hand-lettering. He had smeared the black ink in a little feather that obscured several letters. "Damned phones. Even the agency can't get ones that work."

"Yes sir," his aide, Lieutenant Dunajcik, responded, thinking the quality of service at home was far worse. At least here in the agency building one had reliable sound.

"That was Helfrich. Good man. He's been with me since the Uprising." Neulist's fingers showed none of his rage as he used a white-out solution to conceal the smear.

"Yes sir." The lieutenant had been twelve the summer rebellion had swept through Central Europe like the fury of an avenging god. Like the fury of a god betrayed, Dunajcik thought. The People, the Party intoned reverently in every statement. Who _were_ these People being deified? Certainly not those who had thought their last hope was to take up arms against Party and State.

Neulist held up a stamp with a pair of tongs. He peered at it this way and that, with the wonder of a child examining a butterfly. "Look at it, Anton. A work of art. The engraving. . . . As fine as any banknote."

The lieutenant could not begin to understand his boss's love affair with the little bits of paper. There were as many stamp albums and medical journals on the disorganized shelves as there were accepted agency materials. Albums and catalogs always lay open on the colonel's desk. "Yes sir."

Dunajcik had been with the agency three years, mostly in Neulist's cluttered office. The man often made him wish the rebels had succeeded.

As he often did, the colonel skipped tracks without warning, shifting emotions as he did. "Let's get moving. The Zumstegs are up to something. They brought the girl with them. Today."

This was a crisis point in the agency's history. Perhaps the State's. This was the unexplained limit date of the Tachyon Displacement Data Transfer System on which the agency had built its remarkable record. Everyone in the building knew Time Zero was approaching, that the Central Committee was watching closely.

"Yes sir." Dunajcik eased the colonel's wheelchair into the corridor and started toward the elevators. His heart fluttered as they passed the emergency stairs. Dump the bastard down there someday, he thought. ISD could requisition a power chair for its director.

Internal Security Division's primary responsibility was ferreting out enemies of the State hidden within the agency itself. It was the agency's most powerful, shadowed, and feared division, and Neulist made an erratic guiding spirit.

The colonel was a dreaded man. His whim could terminate lifelines anywhere in Prague Zone. Dunajcik was one of a tiny handful of Central Europeans who did not hold the man in absolute terror. He just hated Neulist.

The colonel's current obsession was nailing the Zumsteg brothers for the anticipated failure of the TDDTS. But his motivation was spite, not service to the State. Otho Zumsteg's physician daughter had rejected the colonel. And Otho had had the nerve to threaten personal violence after having learned of the advance.

Dunajcik had witnessed that confrontation. He had come away with his hatred reconfirmed.

The colonel would not tolerate rejection, much less threats. He seemed to feel he was a god, above any rules or control.

Dunajcik's greatest failing was that he took as *ex cathedra* every encyclical published by the Central Committee.

By their officially published guidelines, Neulist was guilty of gross abuse of power.

Dunajcik had therefore pursued the only course he had seen as open to a minor cog in the State machine. He had approached Committeewoman Bozada, who was known for her dislike of the colonel.

Was Neulist aware that he had become the woman's creature? The bastard was slick as a greased snake. He wriggled out of every trap.

In the Zumstegs the colonel had met a match. They had patrons on the Committee. Their subdivision, a cornerstone of Security, Economic, and Agricultural Directives, was absolutely critical to the welfare of the State. Only Neulist had ever questioned their loyalty. And their genius was such that the TDDT System could not function long without them.

Neulist had chosen a hard nut.

Three floors up, Sergeant Helfrich managed his electronic sorceries from a room hardly larger than a closet. Dunajcik and Neulist were compelled to remain in the open doorway.

"What're they up to?" the colonel demanded.

Helfrich glanced at Dunajcik.

"Go ahead."

Was that a signal of trust? Or of imminent termination? At one time, before the Uprising had radically altered his life, Neulist had been an outstanding medical experimentalist at one of the secret research facilities. It would suit the man's sense of humor to condemn his aide to human guinea pig service in such a place.

Helfrich was as near a friend as the colonel had, and even he walked on eggs.

"They're setting up to transmit the final program. With triple fail-safes, all recorders going, like that. Frankly, I think the girl's with them because it's the one place you can't reach her."

Neulist smashed his good fist against the arm of the wheelchair. The lieutenant and sergeant exchanged looks, anticipating one of the colonel's fits. Dunajcik reached back to make sure he still had the hypo kit attached to his belt.

"What the hell's wrong with that picture?"

"Static from the tachyon generator, Colonel. When my laser beam bounces off the back theater wall . . ."

"Doesn't anything work in this place? Give it more power."

"I can't, sir, without giving them interference readings that would tell them we're watching."

"All right. All right. Damn you, Dunajcik. You brought me up here for nothing."

Always his fault. Why hadn't they given him pilot's training the way he had asked? He swallowed an observation concerning the colonel's own stupidity. Any fool could have seen this was pointless, today of all days.

"Hell. I'm going in there. Those bastards have been getting away with this shit for too long. Dunajcik. The programming theater."

"Sir?" He could not stifle a sharp intake of breath.

"You heard me. Wheel me in there where I can watch while those traitors sabotage the system."

He was further gone than Dunajcik had suspected. He had begun to confuse his own interests with those of the State.

No one—and there was an unexplained Special Advisory specifically banning Neulist—was allowed within the main programming theater without clearance from the Committee itself.

What to do? Dunajcik wondered. He had his ass in a sling now. If he conformed to security directives, Neulist would devour him. If he did not, he would be explaining why to Committeewoman Bozada.

He flashed a look of appeal at Helfrich.

The sergeant nodded slightly. One finger tapped a nervous tattoo near his phone.

Take a chance. Maybe Helfrich could place the State ahead of his old master.

Dunajcik fingered a scrap of paper from the hypo kit, let it fall where the sergeant would see it.

There was a number on it. The one Bozada had given Dunajcik.

Helfrich acknowledged with a slight nod.

Relieved, Dunacjik wheeled the colonel into the corridor. Now, if he could just stall. . . .

There was no way to restrain Neulist long enough. Even if Helfrich reached Bozada immediately, it would take time to poll the Committee, and to advise the Ministry. Then word would have to reach General Kulage, who would have to trace and convince Neulist's number two, Major Votruba. . . . With the comm systems in their present state, an Emergency Executive Action might take an hour.

The lieutenant ran out of stalls and time-consuming stupidities much sooner.

They pushed through a door guarded only by dread and respect for the importance of the work carried out behind.

Today, of all days, Dunajcik thought, you'd think there'd be a sentry.

"Stand by," Otho Zumsteg was saying. "It's coming. Marda, watch that. . . ." He whirled. "Neulist. You idiot. What're you doing here?"

Beyond him, his daughter's face reflected a lightshow of colors from the winking lights of the programming console.

"Zumsteg, you traitor. . . ."

"Oh, damn. Now I see. Lieutenant, get that fool out of here! Don't you know what you're doing?"

For an instant Dunajcik hated Zumsteg. Here was a man who could say what he thought and get away with it.

He didn't know what to do. He was in the meat grinder now.

He did a thing that was treason by everyone's standards. He said a silent prayer that Helfrich had indeed called Bozada. Then he began backing the colonel from the room.

Neulist produced a pistol, obviously with the intent of using it. Dunajcik fled. Shots pursued him. One smashed into his right shoulder, spun him, hurled him to his knees in a half-faint.

He did not feel the pain, only the horror of failure.

"Oh, god," Stefan Zumsteg moaned. "Otho, this must be what the Neulist message meant."

"You're right." Otho stared into the muzzle of the colonel's weapon. "Override and send the warning. Try to be more explicit this time." He stepped carefully toward Neulist, his intention to soothe the man. "Marda, help me. . . ."

Stefan managed exactly the same message they had received six months earlier, jammed into the weekly weather/agricultural program: "Neulist in theater. . . ." It was the only explanation they had ever had for the fact that the future ended on 26 AUG 58.

The colonel resumed firing.

A bullet shattered the heads that recorded the information

to be impressed on the tachyon stream. The result would be, or had been, a burst of white noise on January 4, and every point subsequent when an intercept of the particular program had been attempted. Messages received after that date had all been transmitted prior to the final program.

Dunajcik recovered, staggered toward Neulist. Tape heads could be replaced. The installation and Zumstegs could still be salvaged.

"We're all fools," he muttered. "We protect the State. . . ." But who could prevent the State from destroying itself?

One bullet had changed him, or compelled the admission of changes that had been coming on since his assignment to the colonel. He could now indulge his heresies, his seditions. He no longer had anything to lose. Even his life might be forfeit.

He had failed. Both himself and the trust of Madame Bozada.

The Zumstegs retreated into a frightened huddle. Neulist now wore the mad-gleeful expression that had become so familiar in Uprising news tapes, at those moments when he had personally dispatched rebel ringleaders for the camera. That had been before the reactionary bomb had rendered him permanently disabled.

Neulist had come to his position in an oblique manner. Strong rebel mobs had hit the agency building early, very nearly destroying the agency's ability to react. Then director of a nearby medical research facility, Neulist had led his staff in counterattack, had picked up the reins while the Central Committee remained stunned, and had acted so well in the crisis that he was allowed to continue prosecuting the Uprising's suppression. The ISD Directorate, once the bomb had rendered him an invalid, had been his reward.

It was one the Central Committee often rued giving.

Dunajcik hit Neulist. The wheelchair rolled toward the Zumstegs. Dunajcik clung, unable to aim it in the direction he wanted to go.

The colonel emptied his weapon.

One bullet penetrated the tachyon generator. Another shattered the governor on the tiny fusion plant that provided the theater's independent power.

A hitherto only theoretical tachyon storm raged for nanoseconds. Then the generator blew with the force of a satchel bomb.

Luckily, the fusor didn't go, didn't take out the agency's headquarters. Instead, it just died.

Major Votruba arrived as fire began gnawing at the cabinets containing the master programming disks. They, and the Zumstegs, were beyond salvage.

For an instant he forgot everything the State had taught him. "Mother of God!" He crossed himself.

For the first time in seventy years the State and agency would have to meet the future head-on, without foreknowledge.

Despair soon gripped the Party hierarchy.

IX. On the Y Axis; 1975

Cash arrived early, but found John in ahead of him. Harald looked as though he hadn't gotten much sleep.

"What'd you get?" Cash asked.

"Christ. I fought it out with a whole battalion of clerks down there, for almost nothing." He opened his pocket notebook. "About the house. They started building it in 1868 or 1869, depending on who you ask, for two guys named Fian and Fial Groloch. Brothers? Anyway, these guys contracted the whole thing from New York. Never even came out to look at the land. Nobody knows for sure how they got Mrs. Tyler to let them build on her estate. Some people think that Henry Shaw arranged it, that he met them in Europe. If you want, I'll dig into that. Shaw's pretty well documented. Fian Groloch came out in sixty-nine to move in. He brought a man named Patrick O'Driscol with him. O'Driscol may have been wanted both in Ireland and New York. He seems to have been a Fenian, and a draft dodger during the Civil War, as well as hooked up with some shady people in New York. Fian also brought either a daughter or niece named Fiala. . . ."

"Where the hell did you get all this?" That wasn't the sort of information kept in city records.

With a sarcastic stress on the *O* in official, he said, "From the official historian of the Shaw Neighborhood Association. Old dingbat named Mrs. Caldwell. 'Virginia, if you please.' You might know her. She lives on Flora too. Her old man, a doctor, died in fifty-nine, left her a bundle. Keeping track of this kind of stuff is all she does. She's got about three hundred diaries and a ton of papers and letters. Thrilled as hell when I showed up. The way she talks, she's got enough to tell us every time a Groloch farted. She's going to dig it up for us. They were great Groloch watchers in the old days. But don't go to her house unless you got a good excuse to get the hell out again quick. She'll drive you up the wall. Thinks she's still nineteen. . . ."

"What else?"

"Taxes are current. Paid in cash every year. I had a hassle with the IRS, but they did break down and admit she's up to date with them. Pays quarterly estimates, by money order, on stock dividends that come to around twelve grand a quarter."

Cash whistled softly.

"Yeah. Sweet. That's about it, except they said she doesn't collect Social Security. I'll try to get a handle on her finances next. Banks and brokers. Utilities. Stuff like that."

He flipped his notebook shut, stared into space for a moment. "One other thing. O'Brien wasn't the first disappearing Irishman."

"Eh?"

"O'Driscol. He and Fiala had a thing going on for years, then he disappeared. I'm not sure this's the same Fiala, by the way. Maybe her mother. I hope. Mrs. Caldwell didn't say.

"And what about this Fian, you ask? Just dropped out of sight, apparently sometime in the eighteen eighties. And a guy named Fial apparently never made it out from New York."

Cash had the feeling he had ridden the carousel too many times around. "Railsback put a hold on the corpse."

"Yeah? So?"

"So I thought we'd take her down. Spring it on her. While she's off balance, we hit her with questions about the prints."

He hadn't heard. Someone had slipped up. Or maybe not. It was Railsback's style to play games. "The doll. They got a matching print."

"Oh, shit." The vinegar went out of Harald. He dropped into the chair Railsback had used the previous afternoon, gripping its arms like an old person flying for the first time. Like me, Cash thought, screaming inside all the way, *It's going to crash, it's going to crash.* His face grew pale. His lips trembled. "That old. And now prints."

He changed. "Norm, somebody's set this up. Somebody's gone to one hell of a lot of trouble to cover a trail." He had reached the limit of his credulity. His features became set. He wanted an alternate theory. Cash suspected that from now on he would edit all the facts to fit one he liked.

That had to be aborted. The attitude could leak over into more mundane cases.

"You were the guy who brought up the science-fiction angle to begin with."

"Yeah. Yeah. But I never thought we'd get backed into a corner where it was the only explanation left."

"It isn't. Not yet. That print just proves she knew the guy. Hell, it doesn't even prove that, really. It just proves that something he touched ended up in her wardrobe. He could've been a burglar. But it is circumstantial evidence that she hasn't told us everything. Hey! Here's an angle. Suppose he really is a descendant of the original Jack O'Brien? Say he came back to check on Grampa's old flame?" The possibility had occurred to him on the way to work. "Or, if you want it bizarre, he could be her son and she's kept him locked up since he was born."

"Come on, Norm. She's fruity, but that'd take a genuine *National Enquirer* basket case. Anyway, his age isn't right."

"Just a hypothesis. He could be her son but O'Brien's grandson. How's that for off the wall?"

"There would've been rumors. You can't keep babies a secret. They yell all night." He said that bitterly. Cash now knew why he looked so haggard. His youngest had had a bad night.

"Just trying to make the point that there's still lots of possibilities. Probably a lot we haven't even thought of yet. When we find one that fits all the physical evidence, we'll have it whipped. Meanwhile, we just keep plugging."

That summed up Cash's philosophy of detective work. No grandstanding, no Sherlock Holmes ingenuity. Like the ram, just keep butting your head against that dam. Sooner or later, something would give.

"You dig some more this morning. I'll arrange a viewing for this afternoon. Say around two."

"Okay." Harald left in a hurry, as if glad to escape the speculations. Cash would have liked to have escaped himself. Miss Groloch and Jack O'Brien had driven his thoughts into some truly bizarre channels.

He did not understand why, for sure, that everyone, even he, assumed the old woman was guilty . . . of something. If

she were really as old as she seemed, might there be an alienness which could be sensed only subconsciously? A natural
resentment on the part of the ego?

"Heard you guys talking," said Railsback, replacing
Harald in the chair. "I think you ought to follow up on your
theory."

A glance told Cash the chance that incest and/or genuine
murder were involved seemed, to Railsback, a piece of spider's
silk thrown to a drowning man. He wanted logically neat, if
morally outrageous, answers.

Even if the evidence at the scene hadn't suggested any direct
connection with Fiala Groloch. Cash cautioned himself
against grabbing for scapegoats, for easy outs.

He dithered a while, pushing papers, then checked out and
went to the convent.

Sister Mary Joseph kept him waiting fifteen minutes, then
appeared with a curt, "What is it this time?"

Cash was startled. But even nuns had to have their bad
days, he supposed.

"A favor."

"And only I can help."

"We're going out on a limb. If you'll help, we're going to
try jarring some information loose from Miss Groloch. Seems
like it's the only way to get the whole story."

She crossed herself. "What would I have to do?"

"We figured we'd bring her in to view the body. And have
you there to see what happens."

"You should take her into the room with the rubber hoses."

Cash shook his head. The sister seemed to have an overpowering, irrational hatred of the old lady.

"All right. But these interruptions are getting to be a
habit."

"I'm sorry. I really am. If there were some other way . . .
Well, my partner, the young officer, will pick you up about
one-thirty. I'll try to have him call ahead so you'll know
exactly when."

"Do that."

Cash beat a hasty retreat, involved himself in some unre-
lated legwork, a call home, and his daily Big Mac.

During the drive to Miss Groloch's he caught himself listening to the dispatcher with a grim intensity, as if subconsciously

hoping something would interfere with his complicated, makeshift scheme.

Among other maneuvers, just this once, he had decided to bring Annie into the game.

Miss Groloch no longer appeared pleased to have company, though she remained a polite and fussy hostess. She even asked if he would like to see anything special on the television she had been watching.

The change was more marked in the behavior of her cat, who watched him warily, tail lashing, while he sipped tea, and sneaked amazed glances at the television. It had materialized overnight.

"It's my boss. Lieutenant Railsback. The woman claims the dead man's her brother. He says that, being's you're the only other one we can find who knew him, you'll have to come down and take a look too."

The woman was no fool. From her four-feet-ten she looked up and smiled a thin, I-don't-believe-a-word smile. Well, so much for poor Hank, he thought. For once the horns and tail couldn't be sloughed off on him. My turn in the barrel.

But she didn't call him on it. He suspected she had already decided that it would come to this and had elected for continued cooperation. Even if she *were* guilty of something, the net he was drawing closer had holes big enough for much larger fish to slip through.

"Just let me get my hat and coat," she said. "I'll only be a minute."

To his surprise, that was all it took. As she returned, she said, "I hope you will understand if I'm nervous. I have not been anywhere in so long."

Her stepping-out togs, which included a parasol, confirmed her claim. Coat and hat were ancient, and looked it, though they weren't threadbare. Cash thought his mother, at thirty, would have looked stylish in them. He hoped no one laughed. He was causing the woman enough distress as it was.

"I look how?"

His pause gave him away.

"Behind the times, yes? I can see out my windows, Sergeant." Her accent thickened. She smiled nervously. "Maybe, for my trouble, around the shops I should make you take me."

He groaned inwardly, dreading the chance. Annie was a window-shopping terror who drove him squirrely, and her wardrobe was up to date. Shopping with any of the women he knew sent him up the wall. His style was to decide what he wanted beforehand, get in, grab it, and get the hell out.

His dread showed. "Not to fret," she said. "Force you I won't. Well, let us be off." Her nervousness grew more intense.

Cash glanced at his watch. He was running early. He led the way to the car, making sure he held doors and gates. Neighborhood children stared. Some ran to inform their mothers. Miss Groloch pretended not to notice.

Cash was about to pull out when a truck stopped alongside him. A boy ran the afternoon paper to Miss Groloch's door. No big thing, Cash thought, but proof she wasn't completely out of touch.

Cash's home was just two blocks south and two east. He had to kill time. Miss Groloch had gotten ready far faster than expected.

"This's my home," he told her as he rolled to the curb. "I'm going to pick up my wife. I thought you'd be more comfortable if she went with us."

She did not respond positively or negatively. All during the drive her gaze had been aflutter as she devoured the changes time had wrought on the neighborhood.

"Is possible I can wait inside? Meaning no imposition."

"Of course." She would feel exposed, Cash thought. He hurried around to her door, saying hello to a neighbor's child on her way home from some special event at St. Margaret's School. Another dozen children were in sight. Miss Groloch paid them no heed.

He hoped Annie would be as slow as usual.

She was, the mindreader.

Miss Groloch prowled his living room like a cat in a strange environment, saying, when he offered her a chair and tea, "I'm too skittery. You don't mind?"

"No. Go ahead and look around."

She examined the television, apparently comparing it to her own, the telephone, a clock radio, and other impedimenta that had been developed or refined since she had gone into seclusion, and seemed especially intrigued by the concept of a paperback book. Several lay scattered about. Annie couldn't work on just one at a time.

"The kitchen? May I look?"

"Sure. Sure. I like to show it off. Did it over myself, about five years ago. It was a real antique. Same icebox and stove as when we moved in in forty-nine."

Miss Groloch seemed amazed by the smooth, coilless surface of the electric stove, and by the freezer compartment atop the refrigerator.

"So pretty. And convenient. And reliable? But wasteful, I suppose."

"Up here, someday, I'm going to put a microwave oven."

In moments he was doing all the talking, revealing plans of which even Annie was unaware. Time whipped past. He might have conducted the grand tour had Annie not decided it was time to go.

Miss Groloch had not, till that moment, seen Cash's wife. When she did, she peered at her queerly for a moment, then snapped her fingers. "The pears. Ripe pears from the tree beside the carriage house. I never did catch you, did I?"

Annie's eyes got big. One hand fluttered to her mouth. She grew more red than she had when Cash's Uncle Mort, drunk as usual, had gone further than usual with his off-color remarks at Michael's wedding reception. "Oh. . . ." was all she could say, then and now.

Cash frowned at each in turn.

"Oh, she was a demon," said Miss Groloch. "Bolder than any of the boys. They thought I was a witch, you know. She would climb the fence and steal the pears. The boys would hide in the alley behind the carriage house."

Cash looked at his wife, trying to picture her as a tomboy child. He didn't doubt that she was guilty as charged. He decided not to tease her about it just yet, though. She looked frightened.

A memory that good did seem witchy.

Annie valiantly tried playing hostess all the way downtown, but couldn't get into the role. She kept lapsing into long silences. For Cash's part, he was thinking about carriage houses. Miss Groloch's, and any neighboring pear tree, was gone now, but its location was interesting.

He had seen Miss Groloch's backyard. There was room for

a carriage house in just one place. Against the alley where the body had been discovered.

Had the carriage house been there still, there would have been little mystery in most of the physical evidence. The man could have stepped out and collapsed.

The bustle of downtown did nothing to settle anyone's nerves.

John met them in the hallway outside the morgue. He looked grim.

"Problems?" Cash asked.

"I feel like a Fed trying to make a tax case against Tony G. The trails are invisible. And none of them lead anywhere anyway." He then shut up. Miss Groloch was perturbed enough.

Sister Mary Joseph, in full habit, was with the body, which could not be seen from the doorway. The same nervous attendant hovered nearby. He was a young black man who, likely, had gotten his job on patronage. He was clearly uncomfortable with his work. If he remained a good party man, though, he would soon move to something better.

He was having trouble waiting.

So was Sister Mary Joseph, in her way. She crossed herself when Miss Groloch entered.

Cash wasn't sure how he had expected the old woman to react. Certainly with more emotion than she showed. But she had been forewarned, hadn't she?

"I will say this," she said. "It certainly looks like Jack. Paler, thinner, and shorter than I remember him, but memory plays tricks. Uhm?"

John removed the sheet, exposing the entire body.

"*Himmel*! Is this a bad joke, Sergeant? He could pass as Jack's double."

Cash and Harald turned to Sister Mary Joseph, who had been staring fixedly at Miss Groloch since her entry. The nun could not bring herself to speak. John signaled the attendant. The man produced the plastic bag containing the clothing and effects that had come with the corpse.

Miss Groloch examined them carefully, but with distaste. Finally, "Sergeant, I think I am going to contact my solicitors."

Harald grinned, thinking they had her on the run.

"Either you men, or his baby sister there, or someone you know, are doing what, I think, you Americans call the

frame-up. Sergeant, I think you better take me home now."
She was cool and hard.

John's grin evaporated. Now she was an extra step ahead.

"Is this, or is this not, Jack O'Brien?" Cash asked, using
his official tone. "I'm afraid I have to insist on an une-
quivocal answer."

"If this were fifty years ago, I would say yes. But this is
1975, Sergeant."

"Miss Groloch, there're a lot of things here that look impossible. And I think you know what I mean. If this isn't Jack
O'Brien, then who is it?"

"Sergeant, I don't know. If you have any more questions,
wait until I talk to my solicitors."

"Miss Groloch, we aren't accusing anyone of anything. We
don't have to wait on lawyers. Now, it doesn't seem possible
to me that you can't identify the man. You yourself gave us a
doll that had his fingerprints on it. That, you have to admit,
gives us some justification for asking questions."

Her face registered shock. She turned to the corpse once
more, hardly listening as Cash kept on.

"Now, we don't know that any crime has been committed.
We're not saying one has. That's what we're trying to find
out. You see? If we do find out, and you've been holding
back, then you'll have been an accessory. Do you understand
that?" He paused a moment for it to sink in, though he wasn't
sure she was listening at all. "Look, I don't like this any more
than you do, but the man died weird. We have to find out how
and why. And who he was. And you're our only lead."

She remained stubbornly silent. She now posed defiantly,
hands on hips.

"Don't be upset," said Annie, fussing round the older
woman. "They're not trying to crucify you."

Her reassurances had no effect.

Harald didn't help. He played the bully. "The rest of you
can be nice if you want. Me, I've got questions. And she has
the answers."

"John. . . ."

"Just can it for a minute, Norm. Let's get the shit cleared
away. Like, how old are you really, Miss Fiala Groloch? If
that's really your name. Where were you born? Are you really
human? Whatever happened to Fian and Fial Groloch? What
about Patrick O'Driscol? And Jack O'Brien? Too many

disappearing men, Miss Groloch. Too many arrows pointing to you, Miss Groloch. And I, for one, mean to find out what they're pointing at. Talk."

"John, you're being an ass. . . ."

"Annie, I'm up to here with this old witch. One way or another, the truth's coming out. All of it."

Not one question elicited a response, nor did Miss Groloch seem much surprised by any of them.

"John, shut your mouth," Cash snapped. He sent a look of appeal to Sister Mary Joseph. She was the one who was supposed to apply the pressure.

But the nun had folded in the crunch. She seemed too terrified to do anything but alternate between signs against the evil eye and crossing herself. The few words that crossed her lips were incantatory Latin.

Miss Groloch spoke but once, to amplify Annie's point. "Young man, you are a boor."

Cash wondered, again, at the improvement in the woman's English.

"We're just getting mad at each other," he finally observed. "Let's cut it off here. Let it rest awhile. Miss Groloch, I'll take you home now. John, will you take Annie?"

As he pulled to the curb before the old woman's home, Cash apologized for the third or fourth time. "I'm truly sorry we upset you." She had ignored him all the way. He wondered if John and Annie were getting anything from the nun.

"Sergeant, stop the pretense. Although it is impossible, you think I murdered Jack O'Brien. Without leaving a mark. Then I transported him fifty-four years." Her accent was thick enough to slice, yet the improved sentence structure persisted. "You've made up your mind. Now you are looking for ways to prove your convictions. Let me assure you that, even if I had a way, and wanted to scare a man to death, I would not drop the body behind my own house."

"I'll grant you that much sense. I'll even confess that I *haven't* made up my mind. In fact, there's no evidence indicating murder. I'm trying to tell you. This isn't a murder case. Not yet. Like I said downtown, all we're trying to do is find out who the man was and what happened."

"I wish you luck. But you will gain nothing by hounding me."

"Maybe not. But I'll remind you that there's a connection,

a provable connection that'll hold up in court, between a dead man and a porcelain doll found in your possession." It would not hold up, really. A good lawyer would get the whole thing laughed out before the prosecutor went before the Grand Jury. But the old woman didn't need to know that.

"That'll have to be explained," he continued. "Really, what makes your position difficult is your mysteriousness."

She started to let herself out. Cash reached over, gripped her left hand with his right. "Please. You read the paper. You should have an idea what would happen if the media got ahold of a story like this. We're trying to keep them off, but if we don't get it cleaned up pretty quick, they'll get their hooks in. They could make a circus out of you. We're trying to protect your privacy as much as anything."

She wasn't mollified. "Thank you. And good-day, Sergeant." She took care of the car door and gate herself, leaving Cash with one foot still inside the vehicle as she stamped up her walk, a diminutive Fury.

Glancing round, Cash saw several neighbors watching. A teenager with ragged hair and beard spat, mouthed a silent "Pig."

Halfway to her door Miss Groloch stopped, turned, said, "If you want to find out what happened to Jack, look into the Egan Gang. Carstairs would not."

"Egan's Rats? He was connected?" But she was on her way again.

Carstairs's report hadn't mentioned Egan's Rats at all. But the gang had been powerful at the time, with Torrio and Purple Gang alliances, and O'Brien's belonging would explain how he had supported himself. Cash made a mental note to look into it.

He frowned the long-haired youth into his flat, then dumped himself into the car.

X. On the Z Axis; 21 June 1967; A Company Scale Action

Whang! Whang! Whang!

The bullets did more damage to nerves than to the Huey. The AK47 couldn't punch through the ship's armor.

Michael clutched his M-16. John's fingers were white on his M-79.

Twenty-two was too young.

Then Wallace, who was at the open hatch talking back with the M-60, said, "Huh?" and stiffened. The machine gun kept firing, muzzle climbing.

John staggered over to help Sergeant Cherry drag the dead giant away from the weapon that had been his closest friend. Through the black man's nap he saw the rotor wash whipping the up-rushing grass of the landing zone.

The chopper shuddered, shook, flipped. Its main rotor played power mower for a fractional second.

"Ahshitmyarm!" John screamed as men and equipment piled onto him.

"Not again!" Michael yelled.

"Get the fuck out before the fuel goes!" Cherry ordered. "Come on! Move it! Cash, take care of Harald."

Oblivious to the gunfire, the men hauled one another through the hatchway. Michael got an arm around John and, crouching, firing with his left hand, dragged his friend away from the wreck. "Medic!"

Gunships ripped across the sky, sending their best to the little brown brothers behind the treeline. Air cavalrymen poured from the uninjured craft.

Wham-whoosh!

The force of the explosion threw them forward.

"Damn!" Michael snarled. "We didn't get Wallace out."

"He don't care. He was dead already."

"Lyndon Johnson, I love you, *mein Führer*. How's the arm?"

"Hurts like hell. I think it's broke."

"That was a good coon. A bad motherfucker."

"Yeah."

"I hope the lieutenant does it. If he don't, I will."

"Write the letter?"

"Yeah."

Wallace had said, if he got skragged, send the announcement to his next of kin, George Corley, care of the Governor's Mansion, Montgomery, Alabama.

"What the fuck are we doing here, Michael? We had wives. We had deferments." Incoming mortar bombs crumped like a beaten bass drum with a loose head.

"You was the one who wanted to quit school and join the army." Cash peered into a cloudless sky so bright it hurt. "Here come the navy birdboys."

"I wasn't the one who said let's volunteer for Nam. I wanted to go to Germany. Remember?"

Napalm sunflowers blossomed among the trees. They only perturbed the brown brothers more. The volume of fire doubled.

"Them bastards were laying for us again."

Cherry came snaking through the grass. "How's the arm, Harald?"

"Okay, except a little broken." John groaned when the sergeant made sure the bone hadn't broken through the skin.

"Where's the grenade launcher? Lieutenant's got a machine gun that company says needs skragging."

"In the chopper."

"Shee-it. Great. Well, Cash, it's you and me hand-delivering it, then."

Michael unconsciously fingered a grenade. "What about John?"

"He'll be okay. All he's got to do is lay here and jack off. The dinks will be hauling ass out of here in fifteen minutes. They don't, the navy's going to splatter them from here to the Cambodian border. And the Arvans are coming up behind them."

The ADs began a second pass, this time firing rockets.

"So take it easy, John," said Michael, examining his weapon. It had a tendency to jam.

"You be careful. I need somebody to bring me flowers in the hospital."

"Hell of a way to get the Purple Heart." Cash's smile was a pale, nervous rictus. "What I'll bring is that little Le girl you liked so much. The one that works out of the Silver. . . ."

"Never mind the pussy. Let's go." Cherry slithered toward the treeline. Cash scrambled along in his wake. Bullets whipped the grass, harvesting clippings by the pound.

The gunships took over from the ADs.

You got to hand it to the dinks, Cash thought. They've got balls.

Cherry waved him forward. "They're in some kind of bunker, else they'd have been skragged already. I want to come at them from the side, so they don't spot us."

All around the company's perimeter similar little stalks were underway, driving the Cong back. That he wasn't the only one crawling into hell did nothing to calm Michael's nerves, though. It was becoming a very small, very personal war.

"I'll put the grenade in. You cover."

"Don't be a hero. . . ."

"Hey, man. Not me. This here's Chicken Charlie Cherry talking. If I was in the navy, they'd call me the Chicken of the Sea. But if we don't get that gun, a lot of guys are going to be dead when the Arvans get here." He resumed crawling, more cautiously now that they were near the trees.

Michael crept along behind, remembering his company commander in infantry school, Master Sergeant Heinz Krebs.

Michael had invariably grandstanded the exercises. And as inevitably, Krebs's softly spoken admonition had been, "You goddamned idiot. The idea's supposed to be to make the *other* jackass die for his country."

Krebs had always had an illustrative tale to show his pupils what they should have done. His father had managed to survive six years of the Second World War, most of them in the hell of the Eastern Front. He had been one of few enlisted men to win the Knight's Cross, Oak Leaves, and Swords to the Iron Cross.

His son *had* made an impression on Michael. Cash remembered his lessons once he found himself in a place where the bullets were flying.

Three dead men lay just behind the treeline, surrounding an American-made 57 mm recoilless rifle. They were so tiny and skinny that they resembled children. And in years, they were. The oldest might have been seventeen.

"No shells," Cherry observed.

"Shit. Think this's what got the Huey?" Several spent casings lay to one side.

"Could be. Let's go."

The snarl of the machine gun was loud now. It sounded like one of the Czech jobs, not the Russian. It was arguing with an American counterpart out in the grass. The American fire was all way high.

"Sixty meters," said Cherry. "Let me get about fifteen ahead before you follow me. They surprise me, you surprise them."

It went like an exercise. Everyone in the area, except the gun crew, seemed to be dead or gone. The ADs and gunships had done a good job.

Cherry made it to the flank of the low earth and log bunker, prepared a grenade, tossed it through the personnel opening in back.

Oblivious to the bursts from the American weapon, Cherry sprinted toward Michael.

A rifle cracked.

Whump!

Several hundred secondary explosions followed as machine gun ammo went.

Michael put three rounds into the guerrilla who had shot Cherry in the back, then killed the two who, miraculously, staggered from the bunker.

His weapon jammed.

As someone tried for a homer with his head and helmet for a ball.

Feebly, he rolled onto his back, stared into the hate-filled eyes of the fifteen-year-old about to bayonet him.

An officer in North Viet uniform seized the boy's rifle.

Michael fumbled for his own bayonet.

The officer kicked it away. And allowed the boy to punt his ribs a half dozen times while he ended Cherry's misery with a pistol round through the brain.

By the time the ARVN battalion arrived and the body counting began, Michael Cash was three miles into an odyssey that would pause only briefly in a grim little camp in North Vietnam.

From one point of view, he could be considered lucky.

He was still alive.

XI. On the Y Axis; 1975

It was almost quitting time when Cash reached the station, returning from Miss Groloch's. He was near distraction with the case.

It had taken Harald as long to dispose of Annie and Sister Mary Joseph. They arrived at the same time. Cash told him about the Egan lead.

"Egan's Rats? Don't think I ever heard of them."

"Predecessors of the Syrian Gang, more or less. Goes way back. Bootleggers, train robbers, like that. Some supposedly were the trigger men in the St. Valentine's Day Massacre. I was thinking. I know a couple of the old Syrians. They go back far enough. Tommy O'Lochlain in particular might remember O'Brien."

The Syrian Gang, with most of its members in their dottage, was probably the last of the Irish outfits. Cash had never learned the reason for their name. Perhaps because there were a number of Lebanese connected.

They moved into the office. From behind his desk Cash asked, "How'd you do with the sister?"

"She went completely drifty. Kept babbling about witchcraft and Satan was going to get her. She's scared to death of that old lady. It's weird."

"What about this morning?"

"Oh." He took out his notebook. "Didn't get much that's solid. She ought to launder money for CREEP."

"She's got a lot of stock. Old stuff, in rails and arms, A, T and T, companies that have been around as long as she has. She's also got a growth portfolio that she's done good with.

73

Like Xerox. Her income, about fifty thousand, is all from dividends. She puts most of it back in. Her brokers have a power of attorney. They pay her living money into an account managed by an accounting company. Those guys take care of her bills, taxes, and things. I couldn't find out if she has a savings or checking account anywhere. Depending on what she's buying, she pays cash at her door or has the accountants send a money order. Twice a month they send a messenger with cash and any paperwork that needs signing. She sends back written instructions for the accountants and brokers.

"The brokers are a little scared of her. They've had her since the thirties. She never loses money. She doesn't move often, but when she does she's always right. When she shakes something out of her portfolio, they pass the word to their other clients. But she's no Getty. I think because she's careful. Doesn't want to attract too much attention."

"Maybe Annie and the sister are right. Maybe she *is* a witch. What about everyday things? Maintenance on the house, appliances, like that?"

"Per the letters of instruction. The accountants let me look at their records after I started to make a scene. They wouldn't let me see the letters without a warrant, though. Anyway, she's had them on retainer since forty-seven, when they took over from another outfit. Since then, nobody's done any work inside. But she's had wallpaper, paint, and stuff like that delivered several times. Outside work, even gardening, she contracts. Lawn mowing and stuff is probably done by neighborhood kids. The furnance was converted to oil in fifty-four. The washer and dryer came in sixty-three. On a trade-in. Probably some real antiques. And a TV just the other day."

"You said nobody got inside."

"Not to paint or anything. But the gas company did the furnace conversion. The appliance dealer did the delivery and installation on the washer, dryer, and TV. You think we could find any of those guys now? She might be Hitler in drag, but there's no way to pin her down. She's stayed so insulated that it's unreal."

"On purpose?"

"Hell, why else?"

"So why's she hiding? From whom? Goddamn, John, if she's really the same Fiala Groloch who came here a hundred years ago, she's already outlived anybody who could've been after her in the old days. Unless they're some of those two-hundred-year-old Russians.''

''Or the Secret Masters?''

''What?''

''Just joking. Haven't you ever heard about the secret society that runs the world? Sometimes they're supposed to be immortals.''

''Yeah. And sometimes they're Communists, Tibetan monks, Rothschilds and Rockefellers, Jews, Masons, Rose-crucians, combinations thereof, or the gang in this Illuminati book Smith was on about the other day. I don't believe in vast secret conspiracies, John. Not even real ones if I can help it. Wouldn't it be nice if Patty Hearst and the SLA, or the Manson family, were just some cheap writer's gimmick? I'll stick with the time machines, and thank you.''

''Whatever you want, Norm. But you got to admit that her being a spry hundred-and-thirty-plus takes some explaining.''

Everything about Fiala Groloch took some explaining, Cash reflected. He was beginning to wish that he had let Railsback bury the whole thing. ''You find anything about a demolition contract?''

''A who?''

Cash explained about the carriage house and pear tree.

''No. But that's something we should be able to trace at City Hall. I was going down tomorrow to check out the house anyway.'' He put the notebook away, rose. ''But right now I'm getting the hell out of here. Don't want to think about this anymore for a while. Maybe I'll take Carrie to see *Jaws*. They say that'll blow anything out of your head.''

''Yeah, me too. I keep finding myself wishing these were the old days and we could just drag her down into the dungeon and get the answers with the whips and chains. The good old Iron Maiden. . . .''

Just then he spied Railsback backing from his office while arguing vehemently with someone inside. Beth made violent signals indicating they should use the door. ''Time to make a break, old buddy. Hank's going to have somebody's ass on toast in a minute.''

Harald made it, but by the time Cash had gone down to his personal automobile, discovered he had left his keys in his

desk, and had returned for them, Railsback was a thunder-
head on a course to intercept him at the door.

"What the hell kind of clown's festival did you and the kid
put on today?" he thundered, startling every eye into looking
their way. "I thought I told you to keep it quiet."

Cash put on his puzzled-but-curious face and asked,
"What's the matter?"

"I got some bozo from the *Argus*, of all goddamned things,
in there bugging me for an old-fashioned scoop, and I don't
even know what the hell he's talking about. He's got more
imagination than you and the kid combined."

The *Argus* was a small but highly respected newspaper, the
oldest black business in the city. The source of the leak was
obvious. The morgue attendant. Equally obvious was the fact
that the major dailies and electronic media would be on it by
tomorrow.

Cash shrugged. "We just took the old lady in for a look at
the stiff. She claimed we were working a frame. Where's the
hassle?"

"There was this attendant, see? And he listened to everything, see? Maybe he didn't hear so good, but there was this
spooky old lady, this hysterical nun, and these two weird cops
claiming the stiff was a guy that got croaked fifty years
ago. . . . I got to say more? Can you see it when it hits the
Post? They'll go the 'Cops roust little old granny lady over
science-fiction theory' route. And that bleeding heart jackoff
McCauley could turn it into the biggest show around here
since the World's Fair."

Over the past ten years, the *Post*'s editorial stance had become ever more left-radical, and Railsback's opinion of it had
declined proportionally. There were times when he mumbled
about driving a stake through the heart of Jason McCauley,
especially when that worthy did one of his columns bemoaning
the plight of some prisoner it had taken city and state years to
put inside. Cash suspected that his superior lived in terror of
being discovered by the newspaper. It had ruined careers
before. Cash had his own differences with the *Post*, but remained amused by Railsback's pointed fingers and endless
cries of "Anti-Christ!"

"They wouldn't go that far."

"The hell they wouldn't. Stay away from them, Norm.

Don't give them anything. Let them dig it out without any help from us. Maybe *they* will come up with a rational explanation. Now get the hell home before I blow a fuse. Best to Annie.''

"Yeah. 'Lo to Marylin, too.'' Cash made himself scarce.

"Honey,'' he said as he pushed through the door, "you started supper yet?''

"Got some hamburger thawing.''

"Put it back in. I'm taking you out. Movie, too.''

"What brought this on?'' Being taken out to dinner was an event so rare it called for some questioning.

"I just need to get out. Away.'' He described the encounter with Hank.

"What if Nancy calls? The kids might need something. . . .''

"She should be able to cope for one night. Come on, get your purse. Don't even bother fixing up.''

She went with great reluctance, and dinner was no success.

"What's worrying you?'' Cash finally demanded, after his second and third choices of movies elicited flat refusals.

"I just think we should be home in case. . . .''

"Christ! How come you're so all-fired sure. . . .''

"I ran into Martha Schnieder at Kroger yesterday. She told me her daughter has been baby-sitting for Nancy.''

"Huh? So?''

"So lately it's been three or four nights a week. Nancy has been hanging out at the Red Carpet Lounge in Cahokia. Sometimes she doesn't come home till three or four in the morning. . . .''

It finally sank in. And for a minute his emotions rushed this way and that. Finally, he took her hands in his. "Honey, there's a fact that we've all got to face. Michael's been gone for eight years. And Nancy's still young.''

"Norman, that's enough. I know it all by heart. Every damned argument: 'It's time we accepted the fact that Michael's dead'; 'Nancy has the right to a sex life'; 'She has the right to find a new husband.' And on and on. Anything you can think of, I've thought of already. And it's all true. But dammit, Norm, it *hurts*. She and the kids are all that's left.''

He knew she was describing a battle he still had to fight. Not yet engaged, he could observe, "I don't think she'd cut us out. She's still family. The most she'd want is for us to mind our own business. It *is* her life."

"What if she married somebody who had to move somewhere else?"

"We'd just have to live with it."

"I don't *want* to live with it!"

She was getting loud enough to draw curious glances. "We'd better go. Come on, I'll take you to Baskin-Robbins." She loved ice cream. A cone had smoothed over many a rough spot.

They spent the rest of the evening in front of the TV. As Cash had predicted, the phone didn't ring once. Instead of watching Carson, he turned in early.

He didn't sleep well. Michael's ghost hovered over his bed whispering about time machines.

The media did get hold of the story next day, but didn't play it up. Cash supposed it was because they could get nothing to sink their teeth into, though Railsback offered the opinion that reportorial imaginations bogged down when wandering outside the traditional bounds of business, politics, and crime. Harald claimed it was because the department itself was for a time diverted.

The entire department became embroiled in a series of crash priority cases, a hectic mishmash of murder probably due, in part, to the torrid weather. There was the killing of an off-duty patrolman during the holdup of an evening church service, then the rape-murder of a ten-year-old girl, followed by the molestation-immolation of two young boys by a gang of teenagers, and a homosexual jealousy homicide involving the scion of a prominent family. Next came a flare-up in the ongoing struggle for control of heroin traffic in the heavily black central and north wards. There, every time a big fish got sent up, the medium fishes shot it out for the top spot.

It was busy busy busy. If not hunting down a convicted murderer who simply bolted from the courtroom as the verdict was delivered, or beating the bushes in a panicky search for two teenage girls who had run away from the School for the Blind, Cash and Harald were continually in court. Their cases seemed to be coming to trial all at once. Most were disappointing in result. The fifteen-year-old who had gunned down a retired lieutenant, in the course of a robbery witnessed by the forty-three passengers aboard the bus from which the victim had just descended, was found guilty of assault and robbery, but the jury couldn't agree on the murder charge. Cash, being an officer, had never done jury duty. He couldn't begin to fathom the workings of the juror's mind. He sometimes wondered how anyone got put away.

But they both managed a nickel-dime investigation in spare moments. Harald continued doing the donkey work, discovering that the Groloch house had started construction early in 1869, and that the carriage house had been demolished in 1939. He actually located one of the workmen, but the man barely remembered the job, and had seen nothing out of the ordinary. No one remembered Miss Groloch ever having possessed either car or carriage.

And Harald discovered that large quantities of sand, gravel, cement, and building stone had been delivered to the house in July 1914. Presumably these were the materials used to pour the basement floor and wall off part. Cash went back to Carstairs's report several times, but there was nothing in it to indicate that he had thought the basement unusual.

And again he returned to the report. He had copies run off and took one home with the notion of musing over it while watching TV, and of letting Annie worry it instead of why they hadn't heard from the Relocation Board. Somewhere in the report, he thought, overlooked by everyone, was the key.

He had to keep reminding himself that he and Carstairs weren't working the same case, only cases with a coincidental connection spanning fifty-four years.

Cash passed another birthday. Each seemed more miserable than the last. Somewhere around twenty you began the downhill slide, he reflected, though you didn't realize it till years later. Around thirty you tried to stop looking forward. There was one bad ambush up there that you got more and more reluctant to approach. No matter what you had accomplished, you felt like a failure because there was so much more you should have done. By forty you were moving along looking backward, engrossed in might-have-beens. You remembered the girls who were willing when you were too chicken, opportunities that went begging because you dithered when you should have dashed in, alternate branches of the road you didn't even recognize at the time. You cried a lot inside, and died a little more each day. Maybe you fought the hook a little that decade, but by fifty you had surrendered.

Sitting at his desk, before going home to a "surprise" party put on by Annie, Nancy, and his grandchildren, he did his silent dying and penned a fragment of a poem:

> *Time wanders into oblivion, gentle as a rose*
> *A traitor only too late revealing, had I but known,*
> *The perfect moment.*

There were times when, even more than immortality, he wanted a time machine with which he could go back and adjust. . . . Or, at least, use to send an admonitory message to his younger self.

XII. On the X Axis;
3-6 July 1866;
Travels

"You know the cruelest jest?" Fian asked. They were walking eastward, tending a little south, toward the Bohemian-Moravian Highlands. "This little cosmic joke rips a vital organ right out of the corpus of State philosophy." It was his first remark in hours.

The roads were awash with refugees and stunned imperial troops. No one paid any heed to three odd peasants.

"How so?" Fial responded.

They had decided they would be less conspicuous using the names of the bodies they wore. Neither the people of Today nor Tomorrow would pick them out as easily.

And, of course, Neulist was a consideration.

Who could guess when, or where, the colonel was?

Father was so damned calm about everything, Fiala thought. "Yes. That bears explanation."

She remained balanced precariously on the knife-edge of a scream. The Other wouldn't die. Temporarily defeated, it lay back in the deep shadows, wounded, hating, a savage thing waiting with reptilian patience.

"Souls. I'm talking souls. Or something so much like them that it makes no difference."

He and Fial, immediately, became hounds on the scent of the connections between souls, tachyons, and Dialectical Materialism.

Fiala (Fial was her twin in this incarnation) remained intellectually numb. She just couldn't surrender to belief in the evidence surrounding her. She tried ignoring it all, even her companions, who strode through this alien time as though they were on foreign sabbatical and going home was a matter of traveling kilometers, not years.

She coped with the impossible by concentrating on the one thing with a reality too unrelenting to be denied.

The soul-eater waiting in the dungeons of her mind.

Father and Fial had decided that they had to remove themselves as far from their own pasts as possible. Who, more than a Zumsteg, could imperil the future? Who knew but what the State might never be born because of a chance remark by a peasant from a village on the outskirts of Prague?

It was ludicrous. Loyalty to something not yet dreamed?

But there was Neulist.

Fiala understood Neulist.

If the colonel *had* come back, he would haunt them. He had the soul of a demented terrier. He never let go. And, should he locate them, he might wound the future far more in achieving his sick satisfaction than ever they could by shifting three supremely unimportant peasants out of Europe.

Fial had argued for Brazil. Armies, even nations, could vanish into that vast South American wilderness.

But that nation would not be tamed, really, till the end of the twentieth century.

Fian had decided they should lose themselves, instead, in the witch's cauldron of post-Civil War United States. The nineteenth century was primitive enough. No need to overdo the pioneer thing. America offered an opportunity to wait out the future with some prospect of comfort, and little chance to alter the destiny of the State.

So why were they traveling eastward?

The day after tomorrow, on July 6, an Austrian official, fearing capture by Prussian cavalry, would bury nearly a hundred thousand florins in gold and silver near a tortoise-shaped granite boulder at the edge of a meadow on the western slopes of the Bohemian-Moravian heights. It would remain a lost treasure till workmen unearthed it the spring of the year before the outbreak of the Uprising.

Fian planned to borrow that treasure long enough to establish his family in America. With a little capital and Fial's historical knowledge, waiting in style shouldn't be difficult.

"Marx is in England now, isn't he?" Fial mused. "I wonder. . . ."

"I have a feeling that the most important thing we can do here is shun our shrines and saints." Fian had always been irreverent of political holies, but his dedication was beyond question. Two centuries out of his own time, and still he was sacrificing for the good of the State. "The disappointment could be too much to handle."

Fial chuckled. "For us or him?"

"Both, probably."

Fian was also a realist. The State wasn't the workers' paradise Marx had envisioned. Nor, he was sure, would Marx be the ivory tower Messiah created by generations of State information officers.

"Father," Fiala asked, "do you really think Neulist is here?"

"There's no way of knowing. We've seen no proof that he isn't. For our own welfare we've got to act as if he is. Still, I don't think it's likely. He was quite a ways from the focus. But nothing about this seems likely. Anticipate the worst, hope for the best, survive, take the warning back the only way we can. That's what we have to do."

"That lieutenant. I feel sorry for him."

"Yes. Dead or blown back, he's better off. Seldom has a man been in a tighter spot. We'd better speak Czech for a while."

They had been forcing themselves to use German. It was a minority language in Bohemia, but the official language. It would be decades yet before Masaryk could elevate Czech to equal status. Even then, Czech would not take over completely till the fall of the Third Reich and the evacuation of the German minority.

Now, coming to a crossroad where an endless column of Austrians were moving south, they had to take care lest they were overhead.

The battered, dispirited vanquished of Könniggratz wouldn't give three ragged Bohemians anything but a hard time. Ordered to wait, they spent hours reviewing that parade of defeat. Fial and Fian debated the possible courses of history had the Empire beaten the Prussians.

For at least the twentieth time Fiala relived the final scene in the hovel at Lidice.

What had gone wrong?

The woman had returned with a priest, the pair chattering at one another crazily. The cleric hadn't believed a word—till he entered the hut.

Whatever it was about them, he had sensed it without a word having been spoken.

Mama! . . . the Other had screamed. . . . And had slammed into her, out of mental nebulae, coming within a micron of shattering her control, of betraying all three of them.

The creature would babble the last gram of truth if ever she got the opportunity.

She knew, then, that there never would be peace between them. They were too alien.

The priest's eyes had widened startlingly. He had thrust the woman behind him, shielding her with his body, and had compelled her retreat while brandishing his crucifix. He had stammered something about bringing in the bishop and an exorcist.

Fian had grimly chuckled and said they had best depart before villagers gathered with torches and wooden stakes.

They had grabbed a few things and had gotten out immediately, before the villagers could react. Fial they had had to support between them till he recovered. Only after they were a half-dozen kilometers from the village did they begin planning, once Fial, with his historical background, had recovered enough to make them fully aware of when they were.

Where was no problem. Fial explained that Lidice had at one time been a national shrine. Later, the Central Committee had chosen it as the site of the headquarters, Agency for State Security.

There had been no spatial displacement.

Fial and Fian would invest man-months trying to develop a mathematical model of a chronon field capable of linearly linking a site despite all the motion of a planet, solar system, galaxy, and universe over two centuries.

Fiala concentrated on medicine. It would be critical if they were to survive this medically primitive era. At least they hadn't come in their own bodies, to a world where all the viruses and most of the bacteria would be alien, deadly, able to overwhelm their bodily defenses in no time.

XIII. On the Y Axis; 1975

The drug war flowed into the West End for one violent evening and, while in the area following up a lead linking the activity to a case in his own district, Cash stole an hour to drop in on a physicist at Washington University.

Dr. Charles DeKeersgeiter seemed awfully young for the high-powered reputation his secretary imputed, though he was sneaking up on forty.

Cash had never heard of him.

The age thing had always bothered him. Even now, though a grandparent, he unconsciously expected successful, powerful men to be much older than himself. During his early thirties he had gone through a bad crisis in which he had suffered deep depression and self-doubt each time he had heard of, or read about, someone who had become a substantial success at an age younger than he was then.

But the whole race couldn't consist of Alexanders or Napoleans, or even Al Capones. In time he had made a shaky peace.

"I'm not sure I understood why you wanted to see me, Sergeant," said DeKeersgeiter, after Cash had been shown into his office.

"I'm not either. What I want is for you to tell me about Time." Briefly, he presented the apparent facts of the Groloch-O'Brien case. "The only handle we can get on it is an impossible one: time travel."

"What we call the least hypothesis." DeKeersgeiter showed more than the polite interest Cash had expected. "That's the simplest theory that'll include all the known facts. Sometimes you come up with something outrageous. This time, though, I submit that the facts aren't all known." He made a steeple of his fingers beneath his chin, stared at the ceiling. "Time: The popular view is that it's like a river, flowing one direction at a steady pace. In physics we know this isn't necessarily true. Time's a phenomenon associated with space and matter. And motion. Velocity and the shape of space can cause differences in observed time flow. Especially in the matter of motion. It's my own feeling that matter, or the mass thereof, also directly correlates to time in any given frame. We know it does at the event horizon of a singularity. With better math, we might find gravity even more important than commonly thought."

He spoke slowly, pedantically, as if unsure he could express himself in terms Cash could understand.

"That is, time flow on the surface of a neutron star should differ significantly, not only from here but from current mathematical predictions, because of the proximity of disparate masses." He glanced at Cash as if to solicit an opinion. When none was forthcoming, he went on.

"A few years ago there was a flap over a hypothetical particle called a tachyon. At first it was supposed to move faster than light and have negative mass. Then it was supposed to have positive mass and a velocity below that of light, but was supposed to be moving backward in time. Some of my colleagues also feel there's a movement of mass backward in time from a black hole or singularity to a white hole or quasar, extremely violent stellar events so far away that what astronomers see are events which took place almost back at the beginning of the universe. But I was talking about tachyons. Since nobody's been able to detect them, and their proponents have been heavily criticized by their opponents, the excitement's pretty well died down. I haven't heard a thing recently. But I'm so damned busy pushing paper—federal grant, you know—that I don't have time to keep up with the literature."

DeKeersgeiter's mind seemed to jump tracks for a minute. He treated Cash to a critique of federal grant practices that would have endeared him to Lieutenant Railsback. Then, as suddenly, he skipped back, leaving Cash momentarily bewildered.

"We have fads in physics, too. Tachyons. Gravitons. The latest is the Hawking Black Hole." As the physicist sneered at the impossibility of BB-sized or gram-weight singularities left over from the explosion of the primal egg, Cash began to wonder if he were going to get any sense from the man at all. Then the man's mind skipped another track.

"There's only one way your corpse could've moved in time, so far as we know. The usual. Unless . . ." He steepled his fingers and studied the ceiling once more. "I almost overlooked something. Fell into the obvious trap. When you think time travel, you always think of going back. It's a powerful, almost archetypal human drive, to go back and put things right. But your man came forward. And that's possible. There's a shortcut.

"The mechanism is that of Fitzgerald-Lorentz. When an object with mass nears the velocity of light, its time reference relative to slower objects grows retarded. If we could put a man into a spaceship and whip him up to ninety-nine point-nine nine percent the velocity of light and send him off to, say, the nearest star and back, to us it would seem like it had taken him about nine years to make the trip, but for him only a few months would pass. Of course, that's not *humanly* possible. But the theory's sound. It's been proven with atomic clocks in satellites and fast planes."

Cash caught the stress of "humanly." "You mean a flying saucer could've gotten him?"

Embarrassed, DeKeersgeiter nodded. "It fits the least hypothesis as neatly as your time machine. There's more evidence that they exist. And it doesn't conflict with physical law."

All Cash said was "Thanks," but thought, A whole new can of worms. What else would he come up with before they closed the case? Suspended animation? Perpetual motion machines? How about deals with the devil? Sister Mary Joseph had suggested that one already.

He got the hell out. Politely, but out.

And got hell.

The dispatcher had been trying to get in touch. Annie had called. Major Tran was on his way in from Fort Chaffee to look them over. She wanted Cash to meet him at the bus station. She was afraid to handle it herself. But Railsback, because he hadn't let the dispatchers know where he would be, wouldn't let him go.

Cash caught John leaving as he himself went into the station. They hadn't seen much of each other recently. "You heard?"

"About the gook? Yeah."

"Hey!"

"Sorry. Railsback's been on my ass."

Beth was trying to get his attention. He held up a finger in a wait-a-second gesture.

"I just wanted to know if maybe you could come over tonight. Maybe ease things a little. You know these people better. . . ."

"Now who's doing it?"

"You know what I mean."

"If he spent time over here before, he can cope. Probably better than we did over there. But I'll stop over." He started on. "Oh. I'll come by myself. You'd better keep Nancy and the kids away, too. Let Annie get settled before you sic the whole gang on him."

"Right. Good thinking." Cash didn't think his daughter-in-law would cause a problem, but the grandchildren might.

"Cash! If your personal life can stand it? . . ." Railsback. The way he had come on all week, life at home must have become hell.

Cash glanced at Beth, who just smirked and mouthed, *I tried to warn you*.

Once he turned, before he could say anything, Railsback snapped, "What the hell have you been up to this time?"

Cash thought he was still pissed about not being able to get in touch. Wrong. As soon as he started to explain, Railsback interrupted.

"You shook a nut tree is what you did. I got a bunch of goddamned flying saucer freaks coming in here tomorrow. Here. They didn't even ask, they told me. Why can't you just write this creep off? You have to put our careers on the line over him? And don't bug the old lady no more, either. Last time you did I had a whole platoon of ambulance chasers shaking my phone off the wall."

Surprise and surprise, Cash thought. DeKeersgeiter had moved fast. Cash hadn't suspected the man was that interested. And this was the first the lieutenant had mentioned the lawyers. Which meant that he had gone to bat for his troops. He wasn't as bad as he pretended.

"Look, Hank, there's got to be an angle on this thing. And Miss Groloch's in it up to her pointy ears. And covering up. You don't haul out the legal talent if you're not feeling guilty, not just 'cause you got a little pressure from a cop. Not if you're an old timer. Kids these days are something else. And we got prints, remember? With that we might be able to get a search warrant. Speaking of prints, whatever happened to the paper that came off of that doll?"

Railsback looked thoughtful, then sheepish. "I sent it over to FBI."

"That old, huh?"

"Looked like."

"Well, I'm not letting go. Not even if I have to bring in Gypsies with crystal balls."

Railsback was less angry than he pretended. He grinned, made a dirty crack, said, "Norm, I read the Carstairs file, too. The sonofabitch didn't let go for eight years. And he didn't get anywhere. How come you think you'll do better?"

"Because I already have, Hank. I've got a print, and I've gotten a rise out of Miss Groloch. She gave me an angle herself, but I haven't had time to follow it up." He explained the connection with Egan's Rats. "Hank, it might get tough, but I won't give up. It doesn't *seem* rational, but I think there's a connection between a 1921 murder without a victim and a 1975 victim without a murderer. I'm not saying Miss Groloch had anything to do with it. I'm not saying this is O'Brien from twenty-one. I'm just saying there's a connection. And she's holding out on us."

"Personally, I think you're full of shit, and ain't got a snowball's chance. You won't get her to talk. She's tough, Norm."

"Maybe not. But maybe I'll find the right lever. You've got to keep plugging."

"I hope you've got a guy like you for a sergeant when you've got my job, Norm. Like Harald. Tied to you like a can. But you're a good cop most of the time. Go on. Haul ass before I find something for you to do."

Cash got out of his way, and out of the station as soon as he could. Beth's bemused smile pursued him all the way.

Major Tran turned out to be a friendly, energetic little man who resembled Marshal Ky in Ben Franklin glasses. He wore them perched on the tip of his nose, peering over their tops.

Cash's first impression was Walter Mitty, bookkeeper, not the hardnosed hero-cop on record.

Tran had the language pat and the customs near enough to get by. Cash supposed he could have passed as Nissi had he so desired. They shook hands, started feeling one another out while Annie mixed drinks. She had gone to the bus station after all, and had arrived home just as Cash was getting out of his own car. He had paid the cab for her.

"I'm a martini addict," said Tran. After a sip, "Your wife mixes a good one."

"Rum and coke man myself, when I break doctor's orders. And tonight I need one."

"Bad day?"

"Aren't any good ones anymore. Just some not as bad as others. We're under siege."

"Ah. The Great American Lament. Overworked and underpaid."

Cash chuckled. "Overworked, anyway. I don't know. It just seems like everything's coming apart. And nobody cares. Not enough to get off their butts and do something."

"Norm," said Annie, "I don't think Major Tran is ready for that." She had put on the warning frown usually reserved for grandchildren.

Tran had been westernized. He didn't blink at the interruption. He held up a hand, smiled, said, "Rather say it's a problem I knew too well. It's not uniquely American, though it seems to come with Americanization."

Cash frowned, wondered if the man were being critical. Flashes of old news clips rambled across his mind. He saw the man's point. Saigon, in part, had become cardboard America, a cheap imitation of the cultural exporter's already tawdry features.

"Don't mind my grumps," Cash told him. "I've got an especially frustrating case."

"Miss Groloch again?" Annie asked.

"Still." The doorbell rang. "That'll be John." He started to rise.

"I'll get it." Annie hurried doorward, presumably anticipating feminine companionship. While she was being disappointed Tran asked about the case and Cash sketched it for him.

"Most curious," he said. "And interesting. Amidst a war

one hasn't time for such delicate investigations. I've always been fond of the *outré*. Have you read Conan Doyle?"

"Sherlock Holmes? A little. His cases didn't seem that unusual."

"In the context of his times . . ."

John came in trying to placate Annie for not having brought Carrie. Cash made the introductions. "I was just telling Major Tran about the O'Brien thing. Might as well fill you in. Railsback didn't give me a chance this afternoon."

When Cash finished describing his visit to Dr. DeKeersgeiter, John said, "Hank'll really love you now. Flying saucers!"

"Oh, he does. What he wished on me was to have you as my second for the rest of my life." They chuckled together, then Cash asked, "I take it you like UFOs better than time machines."

"A hell of a lot. I can believe it. Only it's just as hard to prove."

"I don't." Just thinking about it made him queasy. "Too many late shows, I guess. Bodysnatchers, like that." Then, "John, what're we doing? Dammit, I'm sitting here taking it seriously when we should be trying to figure out what really happened. But I'm going to let those saucer nuts work on it. It'll keep them out of our hair."

Said Harald, to Tran, "One of the problems with being a cop over here is you've got to be nice to everybody, good guys, bad guys, and nitwits."

"You are, perhaps, too much intrigued by the exotic," Tran replied. "If one unfamiliar with all the details may speak? As you outlined it to me, Norman, you haven't yet gone to conclusion with the critical question."

"Eh? What?"

"The nature of the connection between woman and corpse. That appears to be the critical element. It would seem that all else would fall into place once you discovered what she and the dead man were to one another."

"True," said John. "Thanks, Annie." He sipped the drink and avoided her eyes. Though he had been around the house since childhood, he still wasn't comfortable using her first name. He had had the same problem with Cash when he had come into the department, but had outgrown it. "But American law, like God, moves in mysterious ways. We can't go into her house after proof till we can prove it's there. I'd love to tear the place apart. But we couldn't get a warrant with what we've got.''

"John," said Cash, "we might. I've been thinking about that. Judge Gardner's moving from Juvenile to Criminal. He might take the chance."

Gardner had the reputation of being a hard-nosed, old-fashioned jurist. His three years on the Juvenile bench had been accompanied by storms of controversy—and a dramatic decline in juvenile crime. He might take a chance on the print—if they could argue convincingly enough.

"Maybe. I've got court again tomorrow. I'll try to see him. Did you check the gang connection?"

"Haven't had time."

"Norm. John. Major Tran's come a long way, and not to listen to you two talk shop."

Cash started to apologize. She was right.

"Not to be concerned," said Tran. "I find it relaxing. It's been months since I've worked myself. This matter, so intriguing, stimulates my mind. Should the chance arise, I'd like to meet this woman. She sounds most remarkable."

"She is that," Cash responded, then steered the conversation to more immediate matters. "But Annie's right. We should be talking about *your* problems. Maybe I haven't been looking as hard as I could, but I've been asking around about jobs. Can't say I've had any luck."

"Not to worry," Tran replied. "I have an offer. Waiting tables in a place called The Mainlander, with a chance for my sons to work part-time."

"It's a name restaurant," John said. "Good tips." He didn't seem surprised.

Cash and Annie were. "You sure that's the sort of thing you want to do?" Annie asked.

Tran was surprised by their surprise.

"There is pride and pride," he said, trying to explain. "In America a man is too proud to work below his station. This is true of some of my countrymen also. But there is another pride. It refuses to allow one to live off the good will of others when one is physically capable of working. This is a peasant philosophy, perhaps. In the country everyone must work. Only the city rich . . . I'm sorry. Perhaps I should say it thus: Your country has done enough by permitting me to escape the

Viet Minh once more. Now it's up to me to care for those who have joined their lives to mine. Perhaps someday I will move to better work. They have begun making arrangements for retraining doctors already."

"I don't know how you'd get back into your own line," said Cash. "Residency, citizenship, all that crapola. And physical requirements. You'd have to get a height waiver."

"Not to mention good old-fashioned prejudice," Harald added. "There're a lot of bitter people here."

"We might wrangle a retainer as a consulting expert in Vietnamese affairs," Cash mused. "Enough refugees have settled around here that there's bound to be some problems."

Tran shrugged. "There will be difficulties. I expected them. I survived them before. I will again. I did my thinking before I boarded your helicopter. My problems this time, likely, will be less than before."

Cash didn't understand, but Harald did. "You haven't seen real prejudice till you've seen it over there, Norm. They aren't a bunch of pussy-footing Archie Bunkers. Everybody hates everybody. A refugee from the north, especially if he was Catholic and fell in with Buddhists, would have had a bad time. Though less so than, say, the Black Thai."

Tran nodded, smiled. "On that everyone agreed. Everybody hated the Black Thai. Looking at it from here, I begin to wonder why."

"You'll have to excuse my ignorance. You don't get to see much of that from the home front."

"No matter," said Tran. "Those are all problems for the PRG now. May they get their bellies full."

Annie had grown restless during the discussion and had begun drifting back and forth between kitchen and living room. Now, from the kitchen, she called, "Supper." She scowled at Cash for not having warned her about John.

The sum of the evening was that Cash and Tran found one another acceptable.

"I think," said Tran, "that I'll bring my family here as soon as I can. Unless you change your minds. Fort Chaffee is . . . well, it's not comfortable. We'll be as little trouble as we can, and out as soon as possible."

The man, Cash reflected, was positively embarrassed.

Tran became more so when he asked, softly, "Your wife. Why is she so tense? So strained?"

"We lost our oldest son in Vietnam. Missing in action. We still don't know anything for sure. . . ."

"If this will work an emotional hardship, perhaps I should look elsewhere?" Tran, of course, would have been briefed. Cash supposed he was just making sure all the cards were on the table.

"No. No. There'll be no problem."

"I think I understand. My father, mother, sisters, brothers . . . It's been more than twenty years since I've heard anything from my parents. And only my one brother, Trich, got out this time. He's in San Francisco. The others were all army officers too. There are nights when I get no sleep wondering what has become of them."

It helped. Especially when he told Annie the same things, after insisting on helping her with the dishes—an eventuality which left John agog.

The major's return bus was a late one. Cash didn't get to bed till after three o'clock. Next morning he was in no mood to take crap from anyone. He went in to work almost hoping Lieutenant Railsback would pitch one of his infamous fits.

The man had a sixth sense. He stayed out of sight even while the saucer freaks were stamping up dust in the outer office, driving Beth to distraction.

XIV. On the Z Axis; 24 December 1967

"Shit, Mike," said Caldwell. "They're making an early start this week."

"Eh?" Cash glanced up as Snake lowered himself painfully from the crack in the barracks wall. Dawn shoved a broken finger inside.

"Bashful's making his rounds. Got the colonel, Captain Richards, and Commander Wainwright already."

"Shit." Cash tried to shrink into his pallet, to twist himself into a fetal ball too tiny to be found. His turn would be coming up again soon. He had stopped hurting. Except around the hunger knot in his stomach.

"Going to be a big show. Dopey, Doc, and Sleepy are with him."

Michael shuddered. "I can't take much more, Snake." The polite, smiling, nameless little brown men never let up. They looked like comic opera or movie gooks in their baggy uniforms, carrying their antique rifles, but their humorousness ended in interrogation. "What the hell do they want?"

Any military information they possessed was far out of date. And any forced confessions to imaginary war crimes would be believed by no one.

"It don't make sense, Snake."

"Shut up, you guys," Koester growled from his pallet. "And for Christ's sake quit whining, Cash."

He was getting a reputation for that, and for malingering. But what could he do?

"They're just trying to get even," said Cantrell. His eyes

were questioning as they rose to meet Michael's.

Did he suspect?

Michael had just about decided to cooperate.

The door creaked inward. Bashful made a black silhouette against the pale light. "Caldwell. Cash. Koester. DeLosSantos Zachary." He needed to say no more. The prisoners knew the drill.

The dwarves had collected twenty-three men already, including all the senior officers.

"Big party," Cantrell observed, as he and Michael fell in at the rear of the column of twos. Dopey made a threatening gesture with his bayonet. "Stick it where the moss don't grow, asshole." Snake said it like, "Good to see you again." Bashful was the only dwarf who spoke any English. "Hey, group, what say we have a little Bridge music?" He began whistling.

Michael turtled his chin down into his filthy collar. Snake just wouldn't learn.

Captain Richards quickly took up the tune, and the other navy flyers followed his example. Bashful's shoulders tightened, but he didn't turn around. He couldn't club them all. Not right now. Soon even Michael was whistling.

"Sesu Hayakawa he ain't," said Snake when the party, swollen to forty of the camp's eighty-plus inmates, halted before a strange, bespectacled little man. The commandant hung around him like a nervous puppy anxious to please.

"A Chink," said Cantrell. "And a wheel. Maybe if I kiss *his* ass, he'll get me a guitar. Or let me have the harmonica back."

The drill resembled an inspection. Spectacles passed through the ranks. The commandant and a translator followed, playing Pete and Repeat before each prisoner. The dwarf called Grumpy hung around with a stack of file folders, some of which Spectacles inquired into when examining lower grade officers and enlisted men. In most cases he just grunted what seemed to be Chinese for yes or no.

Once he finished, Bashful called names. There were fifteen. Michael Cash was the fourteenth.

"Shit. What the fuck? Snake. . . ."

"Just hang tough, Mike. It'll be all right."

"I'm scared shitless, Snake." He eyed the battered Russian-made bus coughing toward them.

"Probably just a working party. Fix a road or power station the airedales blew away. You better move out. The dwarves are getting restless."

Bashful reassembled those who had made the cut and herded them aboard the bus.

Four men in regular North Viet officer's uniforms, with AK47s, watched over them. None, apparently, spoke English. They didn't try to control the murmuring of their charges.

It *had* to be something new, something special. This was the first time Cash had been taken anywhere without having to walk.

The journey north had nearly killed him. He still hadn't recovered completely.

The bus rumbled through hills, jungles, and paddies for two hours, till it reached a deserted airstrip. Four MiG 21s lurked beneath camouflage netting at one end; two SAM sites and several AA positions could be discerned. Base personnel were remarkable primarily by their absence.

Spectacles had arrived already. He stood at the foot of a ramp leading to the passenger section of an old Ilyushin with Chinese markings. The four officers shepherded the prisoners into the aircraft. Spectacles took the weapon from one officer while he and the bus driver pulled the cabin hatch shut.

The ship's engines roared.

The confused Americans sought seats. No one said a thing. Their guards took predetermined posts and, one by one, exchanged their Viet tunics for Chinese.

The Ilyushin grumbled and shuddered down the runway, staggered into the morning sky. One engine coughed and sputtered uncertainly at times. Loose rivets rattled. There were places where Cash could look through cracks in its skin.

Michael felt a brief moment of hope when navy F4s slid in on the quarters to see who had the balls to fly their sky in broad daylight. The Chinese pilot just kept heading for the border. Navy eyeballed the plane's markings, then departed in search of prey on the politicians' approved list.

The Ilyushin was old and slow. The flight, including a fuel stop at another deserted airstrip, took sixteen hours. The thoughtful Chinese had provided a bucket which, when the pressure became unbearable, had to be used in full view of all aboard. There were no meals.

Cash missed Snake. They all could use a little of his irrepressible defiance here.

It was deep night when the aircraft reached its destination. The pilot did not kill his engines, remained on the ground only long enough to discharge his cargo. The passengers never saw him, nor he them.

"Merry Christmas," Captain Richards told each man as he descended into the chill air of an apparent desert. The pilots and navigators studied the skies as if seeking a guiding star.

Michael Cash was too frightened to give a damn what day it was, or where he had been taken.

XV. On the Y Axis; 1975

It was a Friday, but an unusually quiet one. For once Norm didn't have much paperwork. He suspected that it was his temper. It was so foul that the gnome-god who spat blizzards of blank fitness reports and law enforcement assistance forms had been intimidated. The easy load and a quart of Beth's virulent station house coffee had brought him around to semi-human by ten o'clock. He called Tommy O'Lochlain, his man in with the Syrians, and made a lunch date.

O'Lochlain was what the papers called "reputed *consigliere*" of the gang. His own people didn't call him that, nor did Cash, who had never heard the term before *The Godfather*, but that was or had been his function. Number Two among those of the gang age and infirmity hadn't yet claimed. They still had their hands in amusements, vending, and gambling, but were no more than a ghost of the old mob. The Italians had begun displacing them as early as the middle thirties. Now the Italians were giving way to blacks, at least on the street level, as time and the IRS depleted their ranks. But such transitions were long and slow and never as bloody or complete as movies and television would indicate.

But that was unimportant to Cash or O'Lochlain.

They were old acquaintances. During his rookie year, when the Syrians had had far more pull, Cash had made the mistake of stopping O'Lochlain for speeding, then had arrested him on a concealed weapons charge. The man had gone in with Cash grinning, chatting amiably, giving advice on what he saw as good police procedure, then had glad-handed it with his company fixer, who had beaten them to the station. Cash had felt, and had looked, so pathetic that O'Lochlain had laughed and promised him better for the future.

Even then the man had been old, a gray-topped mop who had looked like he was dying of cancer.

Though Cash had remained perfectly straight, O'Lochlain had adopted him as his pet cop. The relationship hadn't become friendship, but they respected one another. Both had profited, though Cash had also come by his share of grief. People asked questions, especially when O'Lochlain gained as much as the department.

The trouble with meeting O'Lochlain, even for lunch, was that someone would notice. Even a hood so old that he looked like an oversight in the Reaper's bookkeeping remained a hood. Neither man, from viewpoints on both sides of the law, had any business consorting with the enemy. There was no way to escape watchers. So their meetings were infrequent, always public, and on neutral ground.

Even so, Cash expected some static. He thought it worthwhile when balanced against what he might learn.

"O'Brien?" O'Lochlain asked around a mouthful of expensive spaghetti. "Nineteen twenty-one? What the hell you digging that far back for?" The neutral ground was a restaurant indirectly owned by the man John affectionately called The Head Wop. The clientele were often a mixture of mafiosi and the crime-busters watching them. By meeting there the two announced to these observers that business wasn't on their agenda. There was a ritual and formality to such things, though it was being destroyed by the barbarisms of the sixties and seventies.

"I'm not sure. We've got a stiff that, by every test we've applied, comes up O'Brien. Yet he was supposed to have been killed back then, though the body never turned up. The one we've got is the right age, for then. I heard he ran with the Rats. I thought maybe you knew him."

O'Lochlain did his Fifth Amendment face.

"Hey, look, it's ancient history. And I'm not asking for names."

"I'm not holding out, Rookie. Just thinking. Sure, I remember the guy: wild, scatter-brained; didn't care about anything but himself. What you'd call a security risk nowadays. Couldn't trust him with your money, your secrets, or your woman. If he'd stayed around, he would've taken the ride. One way or another. He was a punk. The top boys were watching him."

"Why?"

"They had him running the bag to the precinct houses and collecting cash and slips from the betting shops. Donkey work, the kind they used for breaking in new fish. It looked like he was skimming, a few bucks every run. Nothing big, but enough so that they wouldn't trust him with a big bag. There was some talk about breaking a bone or two to straighten him out."

"Did it get done?"

"No."

"Ah?"

Playing a game of suspense, O'Lochlain downed mouthful after mouthful of spaghetti, chasing each with huge drafts of steaming coffee. A large pot had been brought to the table for his convenience, without his asking.

"Thing came up where they were short on men. They decided to give him the acid test. They palled him with Fred Burke and sent him to Torrio with some new girls. They were doing a triangle with Torrio and the Purple Gang, with Maddox in Chi directing the thing. Girls recruited here usually went to Chi for training, then Torrio would wholesale them to Detroit for Canadian whiskey. Detroit girls came here, then went to Chi. And so on. Sometimes they went the other way. Clothing factory work was usually the hook. Sometimes they got suspicious. That's why they needed a couple of guys along.

"This time there was merchandise both ways. Torrio's people had gotten onto some good counterfeit. They were going to bring back twenty Gs to, what you might say, test market. If it went, they'd buy in. They didn't tell O'Brien. Wanted to see what he'd do around that much cash."

While O'Lochlain paused for more spaghetti and coffee, Cash reflected that the man's *they*s were sometimes hard to follow. But Tommy had always been reluctant to name certain names.

"What he did was knock Burke in the head and jump the train while it was pulling into Union Station."

"And?"

"They put a thousand on him; a G and a half for recovery."

"Anybody collect?"

"No. Not even when they went to twenty-five and opened

the contract. Not a whisper. The G-men never got him either. Their people on the inside were watching for him. He just disappeared, Rookie. Like Judge Crater. They figured his girl friend got him, same as the bulls."

Cash asked the date. Perfect fit. O'Brien had jumped the train in the morning. The screams at Miss Groloch's had been heard that afternoon.

"Did you know him well enough to finger him if he walked in here right now?"

"Yeah. I'll tell you, Rookie, I was hoping I'd be the guy who collected on that one. I owed him." But he wouldn't go into detail.

"Want to come look at the stiff we've got?"

"No."

"Hey. I paid. Give me a break."

"Sure you did. On the expense account. Okay. But I don't like morgues."

Cash grinned, thought, I can see why. You're afraid they'll realize they've overlooked you and yank your card out of the living file.

"Good," he said. "Maybe we'll stir something up. I haven't had a row about being on the pad for years."

"Rookie, I'm out of it. Everybody knows that."

"And you were saying that before I was born."

O'Lochlain smiled, downed another cup of coffee. "Kojak you're not."

The lean black attendant was getting used to it. "Twenty-three again?" he asked, pulling the card.

"Right."

"How long's this guy been there?" O'Lochlain asked.

"Since March fourth."

"Christ."

"They pumped him full of something. They're kind of in a tight spot. Can't get rid of him."

"Oh, Christ!"

The attendant had rolled out the corpse. Cash glanced at O'Lochlain. "What?"

"It's him. The sonofabitch. Only it can't be, can it?" He stared, stared.

Cash felt like the *Hindenburg*, after. Down in flames. There was just no way to keep that bastard from being Jack O'Brien. "You know anybody else that might remember him?"

He shrugged. "Looking for an out, Rookie?"

O'Lochlain was quick. He had seen the whole problem without being told.

"You won't get it from me. I know it's impossible, you know it's impossible, but you park my butt on the stand, I'm going to say it's him. That's how it hangs. Sorry."

"You're sorry? You don't have to live with it."

"Are you finished with me? I'd better make a Mass. I feel the need coming on. You know, when you called, I figured you was going to be after me about Hoffa."

"Hoffa?"

"Sure. Every cop in the country is after every guy that's ever been even remotely connected, trying to make a name by being the guy who finds out what happened. Going to be some heat on over that one. Hope the guys who did it got paid off in suitcases full of money."

"I haven't been paying much attention. He asked for it."

"Yeah."

As they walked down exterior steps to where O'Lochlain's driver had parked his limo in a No Parking zone, the Irishman asked, "You got any angles?"

"Not that I can believe. Either it's O'Brien and he's been moved fifty-four years, without damage, or it's not, and nobody in the whole goddamned country knows who he *is*."

"Maybe he's a Russian spy."

"Maybe." Cash chuckled, didn't bother giving details which made that answer less than satisfactory. He said goodbye and returned to the station, where Railsback was waiting with the third degree about consorting with known hoodlums. The lieutenant was sorry he asked.

John came in later, looking glum. "Gardner won't help."

"Why not?"

"I laid it all out. He only asked one question."

"What?"

"Did we have any evidence that a crime had been committed."

"Yeah. I should've figured."

"But I do have a new angle." And suddenly he seemed frightened and nervous. Cash was puzzled by it.

"Norm, if I tell you something personal, will you keep it quiet?"

"Eh? Sure."

"I mean really. Not even tell Annie. Especially not Annie. Or anybody."

"Hey, if you're that worried about it, you better keep it to yourself. That way nobody can tell."

"Well, if I tell my news, I have to tell the other thing too."

What the hell? Cash thought. He had known John since Michael's second day of grammar school, didn't think there was much he didn't know about the younger man. "It's up to you. But I'll keep it under my hat."

"Well, there's this girl. We went to high school together."

A ghost of a smile fleeted across Cash's lips. So John was messing around. He almost confessed his own secret, in the matter of the doctored photograph, but remembered his own advice. There was no way he would risk getting that stirred up again.

"She works at the *Post*. In Classifieds. I had this wild hunch last night, see, so I called her and asked her to do some checking."

He had turned a startling red. Cash began to suspect a name: Teri Middleton. John and Michael both had pursued her during their senior year, and, Cash suspected, had caught her. They had vied for her weekends while in college. She had gotten married somewhere along the way, about the time that Nancy and Carrie had come into the picture, and had dropped from sight. Cash thought he remembered Annie saying she had gotten a divorce after two and a half years and two kids. For a while there, the girl had been as much a part of the family as John.

"Anyway, we had lunch and she gave me this." He offered a pink, scented bit of stationery covered with numbers. "She's going to check some more."

"I can't make anything out of this. What is it?"

"Dates and codes. These first numbers are the dates they ran classified ads for a certain party."

"Miss Groloch?"

"I think so. They were put in by her accountants. And get this. When she showed me this, I asked her to check her subscription file. She got back to me a few minutes ago. Sure enough. They've got one to Rochester, New York, in the name of Fial Groloch, that's been going out regular as long as they've been keeping track."

It was a breakthrough of sorts, proof that there was more than one Groloch, and pinned him or her to a specific address.

"Kind of corny, don't you think? And clumsy. And slow. But secure, I guess. Lucky you thought about it."

"Carrie's fault, really. She was reading the paper and asked me what I thought some Personal meant. You know how cryptic some of them are. Anyway, I started thinking about spy stories where they sent messages that way. And Sherlock Holmes. He was always putting ads in. Then I remembered you said she took the paper. Decided to check it. But I never thought I'd find anything."

"Serendipity, that's what you call it when you get something good when you don't expect it. Still good thinking, though. You get any of the ads?"

"Not yet. She's going to check through their file copies. She has to do it on her own time. You won't say anything, will you?"

Cash tried for a bemused expression. "About what? I haven't heard anything yet. I can't tell what I don't know."

Harald relaxed a little. "I won't hear anything more at least till Monday. . . ."

"It's another piece in the puzzle, but it probably won't get us anywhere. All we found out is that Fial Groloch, or somebody using the name, is alive and well enough to subscribe. Doesn't help us with our dead man."

"Maybe not, but it makes me wonder if we shouldn't bring in the FBI, or somebody."

"What the hell for? Don't we have problems enough?"

"Norm, don't it bug you that we've got a woman a hundred and thirty years old hiding out here? And she's got a relative in Rochester who might be even older? Goddamned, they must be some kind of Draculas. And you keep worrying about the dead guy. I'm starting to think maybe he shouldn't matter so much, that we should be worrying about the ones that're still alive."

"John, there's people in Russia that old. There's even this old guy down in Florida that was in the army during the Civil War and can prove it. Anyway, we don't have a shred of proof that these people are really that old. They don't have to be the same Grolochs. . . ."

Harald looked at him. Cash looked back. "You're ducking it," said John. "I don't believe it's that simple. And I don't think you do either. Only you're scared of the can of worms. . . ."

"*I'm* scared? Anyway, what right do we have? We can push about the corpse, but the rest really isn't any of our business."

"Yeah?"

"All right. Look. I know a guy in New York. We did the FBI course together, years ago. I'll call him Monday. Maybe he'll dig something up. Give me that Rochester address. And I'll try Immigration on the name Groloch. I don't know if their records go back far enough, but it's worth a try. The Feds never throw anything away."

Harald settled himself in a chair and put on his stubborn look. Maybe he was right, Cash thought. Maybe it was time to get some government agency involved. Somewhere in Washington, with its numberless bureaucrats, and bureaus, there was bound to be an outfit that investigated people like Miss Groloch.

"You get anything more from your Mrs. Caldwell?"

Harald shrugged. "Been trying to stay away. But she should have her stuff ready sometime next week. She called about it the other day. What about your saucer people?"

Cash had almost forgotten. "Nothing. They made copies of everything we had, then disappeared. One guy said they wouldn't bother me till they got something."

Harald's expression grew more stubborn. "Norm, I'm getting some really bad vibes from this thing. If we can't give it to the Feds, maybe we should let it go."

Where had his enthusiasm gone? Cash wondered. It was just minutes since he had been excited.

"How? The way I see it, we're riding a tiger. People have started to notice, to watch. Might be some difficult questions if we turned loose now."

John nodded, looked more glum, glanced at the clock. For an instant Cash saw another Hank Railsback foreshadowed in the younger man's face.

"You and Carrie having trouble?"

He seemed startled. "Is the Pope a Catholic?" Then, "It shows, huh?" He remained silent so long that Cash decided he would go no further. But, finally, "Norm, you've been married a long time. Can you figure Annie?"

"Whenever I start thinking I do she surprises me. Like this

refugee business. I would've bet anything she wouldn't have gone through with it.''

"You know how Carrie gets when she's pregnant?"

Cash didn't know the woman as well as Annie did or his daughter-in-law, but recalled that during each of three pregnancies she had made life hell for those around her. And the nearer full term, the worse. The last time it had carried over postpartum, and had come close to taking the marriage to court.

On the surface it seemed she hated John for causing her condition. For the final four months of that last pregnancy they had slept in separate bedrooms. Cash had once overheard Carrie telling Annie she would castrate John if it happened again.

"Yeah."

"Well, she's started yakking about wanting another kid."

"Oh, shit."

"Is right. Norm, I had a vasectomy after the last one. I never told her. I don't know what she'll do if she finds out."

"How'd you manage that?"

"I lied. Told them I was divorced. They never checked."

Cash pursed his lips and exhaled thoughtfully, slowly shook his head. "I don't know what to say. Sounds like you're between a rock and a hard place. If it was Annie and she got the way Carrie does, I'd just keep my mouth shut and make like I was trying. Way she was before, she'd probably change her mind as soon as it was too late."

"I know she would. And I know I couldn't go through that crap again. That's why I got the operation. But she might get to be hell on wheels anyway."

"Uhm." And there's Teri, too, Cash thought. He wondered how much she had had to do with the operation. He didn't ask.

"You know, Norm, lately I've been asking myself a lot what the hell am I doing here. Why I bother. You think it matters? You know what I keep thinking? I could just jump on my cycle and head for the coast. Let her have everything. You can live on the beaches around L.A. . . ."

" 'Vanity of vanities, all is vanity,' " Cash quoted. " 'What doth a man profit? . . .' "

"What the hell?"

"Ecclesiastes. The Bible. You aren't the first. Everybody

feels that way sometimes. Especially if you step back and look at your life and you see it going by and you're not really doing anything with it. The things you wanted to do before you had to spend all your time coping with babies and bills. I know I do. Mostly I just hang in there and hope something will come up to make it worth the pain.''

" 'The majority of men lead lives of quiet desperation.' "

"Something like that."

Cash was not sure he had made any impression. John could be hard to reach. But, at least, he had matured enough not to sneer at the voice of experience. Cash smiled, remembering John and Michael and their self-certainty, what seemed just a few months ago, when they had been in high school. As one local wit had been heard to observe, there *is* a substitute for experience: Being sixteen.

"Maybe. Maybe. But sometimes I just get so depressed. . . ."

"If it's that bad, maybe you'd better see the departmental psychologist."

Harald didn't become defensive. Cash considered that a good sign.

"I've been thinking about it. Maybe I will. But I don't think it's that bad. Not yet, anyway."

"Then maybe you should put in for vacation. I know for a fact that you haven't taken one since you came to the District."

"That's an idea too. And when was the last time *you* took off, Norm?"

Cash shrugged. "A long time ago. A week when my mother died." Michael and John had been eight, Matthew newly born. Cash started getting antsy if he were off more than a weekend. "Don't go copying me, John. There're better models."

He had a sudden, frightening intuition, and hoped he was wrong.

John was an only child. His father was a minister. His mother had divorced the man when John was nine. That had been a hard period for both John and Michael, neither of whom had understood. Since, till his marriage, John had lived with his mother, who had never remarried.

Within a year of the divorce, Harald had begun calling Cash "Dad." At the time, Annie and Norm had thought it both cute and pathetic. The behavior had faded when Cash had refused to reinforce it with a positive response.

Could that still be in John's mind, down deep where he didn't recognize it?

Harald always had been nearly as close as Michael, but Christ, Cash thought, this was a responsibility he didn't want. I never did that good by Michael or Matthew. How dared John put that load on him?

It was terrifying.

But flattering.

"You're not that bad, Norm."

"Crap."

"Except maybe you're too private. Know what I wish there was? A machine where you could go right inside somebody's head and figure out what they *really* think and feel."

"I'll tell you what I really think about that. It sucks, that's what. If some guy ever invents one, and you don't blow his brains out before he can tell anybody, bend over and kiss your ass good-bye. The Gestapo would be lining us up to find out if we're reliable or not."

"Yeah. Probably."

"You better believe."

"I never thought about it. I just thought, like, you could get to know people who mean something to you, because everybody hides from everybody, a little bit. Like, I could understand why Carrie gets the way she does. But, yeah, we could use it too. Round up all the bad guys and ship them out before they hurt anybody."

"We're Gestapo enough, John. And I don't think we could resist the temptations. Get thee behind me." How did we get on to this? he wondered.

"Probably be no more reliable than a lie detector, anyway."

"Yeah. Even if you could get Carrie to be honest right now, I bet you couldn't get her to explain herself. She probably doesn't know either. Hormones."

"Bull. She's just trying to get to me."

"Bull to you too. Bet the way you're feeling right now has to do with hormones too."

"Yeah? Maybe."

"I'll tell you what I think. You and Carrie should probably get away from each other for a couple weeks. I mean, every time I see you together and one of you says black, the other one hits the roof screaming white. I don't say you're planning it, but both of you are picking fights. Whatever you do, John, don't end up like Hank.''

"Hey, come on. It ain't me. . . .''

"Crap. You think you try. You say you do. So does Carrie. But you don't, not really.''

"Hey, this's getting a little heavy. . . .''

"You're both lying to yourselves. What you're really doing is setting each other up to take the blame. Like this guy on the radio was saying the other day, you're not fighting fair. That's why I say get away from each other for a while. Let the scabs heal, think about the real issues. Maybe write them down and trade lists without talking about them.''

"You know how jealous she is. . . .''

"Right.'' Cash now wanted to end the discussion, so made no comment at all about Teri. He had said too much already. He was no Dear Abby. Lifting the lids on the trash cans of others' lives made him too damned uncomfortable. His concern for John had taken him past discomfort to outright embarrassment this time. "What about the case?''

"Why don't we, for Christ's sake, just shitcan the damned thing?''

"Not a viable option. And you know it.''

"You threw Bible stuff at me. How about this? 'Sow the wind and reap the whirlwind.' That used to be one of my dad's favorites, whenever a spanking was coming on.''

"Okay. I already know you don't like it. Some of them I don't like either. But we don't get refusal rights. We have to go by the rules. You have to go after this one just the same as one you did like. I mean, you came up with some good angles already. We get a few more, we might start getting a picture, something that'll give us a handle on it.''

"Yeah. We could get lucky.'' Harald responded with all the enthusiasm of a man asked to fly off a cliff by flapping his arms. "But what you want to bet we don't?''

XVI. On the X Axis;
1866-1914

The Austrian treasure lay exactly where Fial had predicted it to be. He took a small silver coin from the hoard.

"Fian, I'll flip you for who goes back to that last town."

"What for?" Fiala asked.

"We need pens, ink, and paper. To list the coins. Dates, values, mint marks, wear, like that. It'll be years before we can replace any of them. Memory won't do. And it'll have to be right, else it might change something."

"What about economic changes? Won't putting that money in circulation make changes? You didn't think about that, did you?"

Neither man had. Fian responded, "We have to take the chance. We need the capital. I can't see how a few thousand florins would effect history much anyway."

Fiala pursed her lips. They were compromising their resolve already. They would be able to rationalize their deviations any time convenience demanded it.

It was pretty much what she had expected. Anyone who attained any standing in the State machinery learned the trick early.

Fian lost the toss.

"Well, take a fistful," Fiala said. "I'm starved. And I could use some decent clothes. This thing must've been made out of a potato sack."

"She has a point, Fial. We'll end up in prison if we go flashing a fortune looking like this." He took a handful of small silver, studied the coins.

"Don't spend it all in one place. The more you scatter it, the less attention it'll draw."

"I know. Can you remember these till I get back? To check me?"

"I'll have to, won't I?"

"What's your size, Fiala?"

"Think about that, Fian," said Fial. "This is eighteen sixty-six. You don't buy things off the rack here. You make your own. Unless you can afford a tailor. Just say yea by so. That'll be good enough till we get out of the country and find a tailor."

"I suppose you're right again. I'm beginning to think you burying your nose in books all the time wasn't such a waste of time after all."

Thus, by degrees, they upgraded their apparel and story as they stole westward across Europe.

Neither Fian nor Fiala could get over how little real control governments maintained over their citizens. Contemporary social organization, from their viewpoint, was only slightly more structured than anarchy.

And the amazing thing was that the political movements of the time, even those antecedent to their own, all seemed to espouse *more* democracy and anarchy.

"That Bakunin is a madman," Fian said of one of the State's minor saints. "He wants to destroy everything. Something must have been lost in the translation."

Fial just chuckled. "Maybe it *is* a good thing we decided not to look any of them up. But hang on, brother. It'll get worse."

It was in Paris that they encountered and charmed the Americans. The people were even more naive and generous than their fool descendants.

The Atlantic storms were terrible during a December crossing. Their ship was a day late making New York.

"Damn, I wish they'd hurry," Fian growled from his place at the promenade rail. "I'm supposed to meet Handy today."

"Use the English, father," Fiala admonished remotely. She was captivated by the huge, rude new land rearing behind the piers, so different from the New York she had seen in her own time.

"Too slow, the strange tongue," said Fial. He still fought

mal de mere. A nineteenth century steamer was a far cry from a twenty-first century SST.

Fiala regressed to German herself. "Look at them. Swarming like rats." Hundreds of men crowded the piers. Less than half appeared to be stevedores, or otherwise employed.

"Unemployment problem," Fial observed. "The country hasn't successfully changed over to a peacetime economy yet. Plus immigrants. Looks like we'll be able to go ashore in a few minutes."

Fiala rushed to be first.

Minutes later, "Top o' the morning to you, young miss."

Fiala turned.

The redhead, about twenty-five, cut her out of the mob with consummate skill, and established some proprietary right immediately acknowledged by his competitors.

"And won't you be needing someone to manage the plunder?"

She frowned in perplexity.

"Ah, me manners. O'Driscol. Patrick Michael himself. . . . Ah, it's not me manners. Ya sweet thing, ya don't speak the language."

"I do. But do you?"

"Ah, she's got the tongue, don't she, Patrick Michael? Aye, it's the Queen's Own Anglish I'm talking. Her Majesty just hain't the proper use of it yet."

And thus O'Driscol drifted into their lives, initially as a porter helping with their baggage, and later as a guide. And later still, as a bodyguard when, quite unaware of what he had saved, he drove off three would-be robbers while Fian was carrying twenty thousand dollars.

One morning, a year later, they went to see Fial off to his new home in Rochester.

As the train pulled out, Fian asked, "Patrick, what's haunting you?"

The Irishman was forever looking over his shoulder and starting at the passage of unknown people. Hitherto, though, he had been completely uninformative about his past, except to proclaim that he came of the Kerry O'Driscols and not the Kilkenny, which made all the difference.

Patrick glared. Then grinned. "I'm an Irishman, ain't I?"

"That might be explanation enough to another Irishman.

Maybe even to an Englishman. But we lesser races . . .''

"Ah, the Anglish. They'd know, yes, but they'd never understand. A stubborn, thick-headed race.''

"So. Maybe you left home after some ill-starred attempt to educate them?"

"You know the Fenians, then?"

"No. But I understand the cantankerous nature of the human beast. You really think the Queen's men would chase you this far?"

"No. But there's them here what would be pleased to lay hands on the genuine Kerry O'Driscol. Them as put down the draft laws during the recent brouhaha with the South. And there's them from Washington City worried about what the Fenians might be planning for Canada, and them on the other side o' the law what feels O'Driscol owes them.''

With those points as arguments, and Patrick's growing interest in Fiala to tilt the balance, Fian did not have a great deal of difficulty convincing O'Driscol that he should join their move west. The Irishman had lost virtually all taste for the life of a political activist.

It was a romantic era. With no State to demand her total devotion, Fiala enjoyed a postponed adolescence. Her life became a masquerade, she a tourist enjoying a foreign time. Even Fian succumbed, somewhat, to the Mardi Gras spirit.

Without duties or obligations, the soul was at liberty to chase butterflies of personal happiness.

Diversion was a necessity. Two centuries could make a long, boring walk home.

That making it was possible was beyond doubt. Fiala didn't abandon herself completely. She researched contemporary medicine with the same intensity given play. And she quickly developed substitute rejuvenation courses that would see them into a more medically enlightened age, where the real thing could be obtained.

Fial's job was to twist the tail of the tiger of capitalism till it yielded up enough danegeld to finance Fian in the creation of a primitive tachyon communicator. Fian was driven by a need to warn his future, or past, of Neulist's imbecilic actions.

"What I'm trying to do," he once told Fiala—she had just rendered a professional opinion, warning him that he had begun showing obsessive-compulsive tendencies—illustrating with a piece of string in which he had tied a loop, "is use the machine to snip out this backward loop, so, and have a straight line again."

"Too many paradoxes for me."

"Such as?"

"If you were going to be successful, we would've gotten the message already. We wouldn't be here now."

"Not necessarily. There's still a knot in the string. Anyway, without computers, all I have to go on is intuition. My feeling is that there's an oscillation. A duplication. Where it happens both ways. And going either way makes the other happen."

"Isaac Newton?"

"Or thermodynamics."

But Fian erred in his topological analogy, though he was on the right track. The string and loop were too linear. He should have been thinking of a Klein bottle, where the loop could go any of a thousand directions, inside and out, and still come back to the same starting point.

"It's . . . elegant," Fiala decided. They were viewing the St. Louis house for the first time. "Period. Definitely period." She descended from the carriage. Patrick helped, then ran to open the gate. She had captivated the Irishman completely.

Fian followed with an amused smile. For Patrick's peace of mind he pretended ignorance of what was going on.

"It's remote enough." The nearest house was a quarter mile away, on the Shaw estate. "Come on, Father! Let's see what it looks like inside."

"I'm glad you're making the best of this. I never gave you much happiness before the accident."

"You were all right. For our times. Anyway, it'll all get tiresome. It's a long time to wait."

"Have a good time while you can, then."

Fian's obsessive work on his communicator persisted for a full two decades. He was compelled, to all practical purposes, to create his own technology, and that was a challenge worthy of an Einstein. Patrick made an invaluable, if ignorant, assistant.

Fial, from Rochester, made it all possible.

Patrick's eventual disappearance finally murdered the little joy left in the working vacation.

There was nothing mysterious about it. He had found a woman interested in marrying and raising children. He hadn't the nerve to explain in person, so just left a note.

"And I taught him to read and write!" Fiala spat.

"He was a good Catholic man," her father replied. "His conscience got to bothering him. It had to happen someday. Be glad you got as much as you did."

Fiala would not be consoled. She had loved O'Driscol in the silly, romantic style of the time, and insisted that she was desolate. In a month, though, the hard-headed twenty-first century doctor returned and the decades with Patrick slipped into perspective. An amusing, diverting episode along the long road home. Nothing more.

The absence of the Irishman's perpetual optimism made itself felt in Fian's work immediately. Fian had never realized just how much donkey work there was. But he kept plugging for another two years.

"That's it!" he shouted disgustedly one morning. "There's no way to build the thing using tubes. I can't create a pure enough vacuum. It'll be another seventy years before I can go solid state. Fiala, I'm going home."

"Where?"

"Back to Prague. Just for a year or two. It's time those coins were replaced anyway. Fial can spare the money now."

The new land held no more excitement for Fiala, either. "I'll start packing. Are we going to sell the house?"

"No. I want you to stay. You'll be safe. Neulist could be prowling Europe like some vengeance-mad Wandering Jew. Damn. Wouldn't it have saved a lot of trouble if that bomb had killed him?"

The argument ran for days, but Fiala finally had to accept her fate, to remain behind.

Thus did the lonely years begin.

For one reason or another—his excuses always *sounded* good—Fian never got around to coming back. Eventually, Fiala resigned herself. He never would.

There was the occasional lover, when she encountered a man who, like Patrick, couldn't sense the *difference* about her. She tried making friends with the new people building nearby, but few of them were immune to her alienness.

The loneliness became unspeakable for one raised in the crowded communal life of the densely populated State. It was broken only by occasional letters from Fial or her father. And those, ultimately, only depressed her more, for their loneliness leaked through their cheerful words.

The past was indeed a foreign land.

Maybe the Christians were on the right track. There was a hell. And this was it.

Over the first twenty-seven years—as long a time as she had lived in her own era—Fiala gradually forgot the thing in the back of her mind. Fian and Fial had annihilated their predecessors in the flesh within hours of reaching the new age, and she assumed hers had perished as well, though more slowly and quietly.

She was to be unpleasantly surprised.

The first attack came the evening of April 12, 1893, as she was about to retire.

She barely survived.

The thing had lain back all those years, studying, learning, abiding the opportune moment.

After four attacks spanning the next three years, Fiala finally determined the pattern. The assaults came only when she was tired and deeply depressed.

The Other wasn't stupid. It wouldn't attack when she wasn't vulnerable. . . .

So many years to wait and battle for existence.

And Fian just wouldn't come to help.

The woman who had been her mother's body had died. Those who remembered Fian as a peasant had all passed away. Shortly after the turn of the century, he re-established himself at Lidice. He hoped, he explained in his letters, to have more luck contacting the Agency from that site.

He even intended pursuing the obvious in crosstime communications by burying a warning note with the Austrian treasure.

Fial visited occasionally during the decades straddling the century's turn, and Fiala made several journeys to Rochester. These vacations did little but make the loneliness worse after separation. By 1914 they had restricted communication to the occasional letter.

Populations were exploding near both homes. The St. Louis neighborhood, especially, was in the grip of a building boom. It seemed wise to retreat from public view lest too many questions be asked about their apparent agelessness.

Fiala invested that summer in concealing Fian's machine with a wall and beneath a new basement floor. For several months that kept her too busy and too tired to be lonely.

An attack, a week following Fial's final visit, came closer than ever to destroying her. Her haunt did seize control for a few minutes, driving her body into the street, where she shrieked for help in Bohemian German. Her Irish neighbors decided she was insane, but took no action.

The thing, fortunately, had no strategy for maintaining control. Fiala fought her way back.

Now it was she who lived in terror. The next episode, or the one following, might be her last. She was certain she could not destroy her unwanted companion. The thing had made itself invulnerable. She was much less confident of the reverse. Each assault educated the Other a little more, highlighting her weaknesses. She feared that, if it successfully supplanted her, she would suffer the fate of the spirits that once had occupied the bodies now inhabited by Fian and Fial.

Once the Other had been an ignorant peasant girl with severely restricted horizons. Barbarically ignorant. But it was smart, savagely crafty, and making full use of its advantages.

It had complete access to Fiala's memories, thoughts, and emotions—while revealing none of its own. It knew what Fiala knew, could do what Fiala could do. Fiala, on the other hand, had gotten almost nothing from it since leaving Bohemia.

One thing she did know. The need to break out, to reassert control, to extract a revenge, had driven her mind-companion completely mad.

It was like living in the same head with a Colonel Neulist.

And someday, if she didn't make it home first, the Other would win the one victory it needed to reach its goals.

XVII. On the Y Axis; 1975

It began to move. Monday morning Cash called his New York friend.

"Come on, Frank. You owe me. Big. The Jackson brothers last fall? I wore out a pair of shoes on your account. Come on, don't try to snow me. What about that bond-skipper? Branson."

Frank seemed to be a one-way favor man. He argued.

"Hey, I know Rochester's out of town. But it ain't in Poland. I ain't got time—or the evidence—to go through channels. And you're my only connection back there. Why don't you get your state police to check it?"

Frank bitched and moaned. Cash remained adamant, going so far as to show a little temper. "Look, One-way, you owe me clear back to the Gallo War. And you're going to want something again someday."

As soon as the man folded, Cash yelled, "Beth, be a darling and see if you can't get ahold of somebody in Immigration who knows their history and record-keeping."

The woman materialized in his doorway. "The Groloch thing again?"

"Yeah. Still. You look sexy this morning."

"Well. You're getting frisky, old folks. Good weekend?"

"I guess. Matthew turned up. We had a barbecue. . . . Yeah. It was okay. Made it to the ballgame too. I think they're going to start winning, they keep playing that good. What'd you do?"

"Cleaned house and watched TV."

"Thought you and Tony would—"

"He had something else come up."

Cash thought her fiancé was a first-class prick. The only time he came round was when he couldn't get screwed anywhere else.

"Beth?"

"Uhn?"

"Oh, never mind. I keep my mouth shut, I won't have to taste my dirty sock."

"Oh." She smiled weakly. "You might as well say it, Norm. Everybody else has. My mother . . . God. Must've spent an hour yesterday trying to get me to move back home. It don't hurt anymore. Much. I know I'm a fool."

One more minute and the tears would start.

"You deserve better."

Beth was extremely shy, and, apparently, subconsciously convinced that whatever happened to her was the result of her own shortcomings. She was extremely vulnerable to the Tony-type of predator, who knew all the right things to do and all the right things to say to snare the shy ones. He was so arrogantly self-certain that girls like Beth surrendered even while aware of what was happening. The man's complete lack of self-doubt was, even more than his lack of concern for the feelings of others, the reason Cash loathed him. Cash envied that certitude.

He had seen Beth get dumped on before. He had been her crying shoulder more than once. In one way she was right. It *was* her own fault—because she kept letting it happen.

"Norm, I . . ." She took a tentative step into his office.

He later suspected that she would have said something important and difficult for her had she been allowed the opportunity.

It had taken her four years to feel safe enough to play their everyday game of office banter, a game she engaged in with no one else.

Hank Railsback shattered the fragile crystal moment.

"Norm, I got it."

Beth closed up like a poppy at sunset.

"What?" Cash snapped. Hank was startled. But only momentarily.

"A whole new angle on your damned Groloch case. I think it's the answer."

"Excuse me," said Beth. "I'll start calling."

Bulwarked by anonymity and long distance, she could sometimes be a dragoness. It was too bad she couldn't live her life via the long lines.

"Thanks, Beth. So clue me, Hank."

"I got the idea watching the Bijou on four Friday night. Know something? I can't even remember the name of that turkey now."

"I don't care what it was."

"You don't have to bite. What it was was, there was this private eye who had a problem something like yours. Couldn't get the facts to add up."

"So?"

"So, in the end, it turned out that the cop who supposedly found the body was really the guy who did it."

Cash raised a hand, asking a chance to think.

He grinned. The rattle of his head machinery must be shaking windows throughout the building.

Of course! Hank had to be right. Or on the right track, anyway. Not once had he bothered counterchecking the evidence itself. Nor had he questioned the reporting officers, nor the evidence technicians, nor the man who had done the autopsy. There was plenty of room for error or outright lying. . . .

"Goddamned, Hank! After all these years I've got to admit I was wrong about you. You just keep your genius hidden. Hey! How much pressure can I put on? Could I use a polygraph?"

A phone rang. Beth, with receiver in hand already and another call on hold, said something neither shy nor ladylike.

"I thought I'd dump it on the inspector's office."

"My ass. This's mine, Hank. You start the ball rolling. Soon as Beth finishes what I've got her on now, I'll have her dig up the names and current shift assignments."

Beth called out, "Your wife, Norm."

"Eh?" He went to take the call at Beth's desk.

"Not that one. The other one. I've got Immigration on hold there."

Cash grabbed the receiver. "Yeah?"

"What happened to the twenty thousand?" Annie asked.

"Huh? What twenty thousand?"

"The counterfeit money O'Brien snatched. I think you said it never turned up. I thought maybe he might have left it at Miss Groloch's."

"She would've gotten rid of it. . . ." The wheels were turning again.

"She hung on to that doll. And she probably wouldn't have known it wasn't any good."

"Could be. Could be. I'll talk it over with John."

Harald had been in and out at start of shift almost too fast for "Hello." He was rushing his legwork because they had a court appearance that afternoon. Cash was to meet him in the civil courts building at one o'clock.

Hopefully, jury selection would be complete and they would spend just the one afternoon testifying.

"Beth, be a doll and, when you get a chance, see if you can get me a meeting with Judge Gardner during lunch."

She sighed into the phone she was holding. "More Groloch?"

"Of course."

"You really *should* let go."

"No way. Annie?"

"Patiently waiting."

He couldn't think of a thing more to say. Norman Cash would never win prizes as a phone conversationalist. When on he would speak his message, then wait, first nervously, then impatiently, for the other party to end it. He was completely aware of what he was doing even while doing it, yet could never smooth over with small talk. Even with a wife of half a lifetime.

"Anything else?" he asked, knowing she would resent it, yet totally unable to think of any better course.

"No. Bye then." Her tone was disappointed. It always was. Damned, but he wished he knew how to give her more of whatever it was she wanted. Or that she could understand him a little better.

"Bye." He hung up with the inevitable feeling of relief.

Beth still watched with those big brown eyes. They seemed to stare right down inside to those shadowed parts of his soul that were alien even to him. His own gaze slid away.

Another bad habit. How come he had so much trouble meeting a woman's eyes?

Maybe *he* was the one who should make an appointment with the departmental shrink.

"Uh . . . I'm going out. To see O'Brien's sister."

Beth merely nodded. Then, as he was moving out the door,

"Norm, I've got to have your LEA paperwork today."

"Aw, shit. Okay. I'll get it when I get back. Oh. Do me another favor. See if you can track down Tommy O'Lochlain. So I can give him a call."

Beth sighed again. Cash went out thinking he should do something special for her. He had been dumping on her a lot this morning.

Sister Mary Joseph was openly hostile this time around. Cash pretended not to notice. Maybe he should do something for her, too.

"Just a couple questions this time," he said. The answers should have been in the Carstairs file. The lieutenant must have carried on a remarkably narrow or uninformed investigation.

"The day your brother vanished he stole twenty thousand dollars from the people he worked for."

He really needed go no further. Her surprise answered his question before he put it into words.

"I wondered if he'd been home that day? If he had a package or briefcase or anything?"

"Yes. He was there. For half an hour. To change and eat. He'd been away for three or four days. I told you that before. But he didn't bring anything home. I don't think. But I remember he was real happy. Excited."

"Tch. Yeah. Pretty much what I expected." He took a deep breath, plunged. "I'm really sorry about all the trouble I've been. Can I do something, a gesture, you know, to make it up? Maybe have you to dinner some night?"

Damn, it was hard making the feelings translate.

She was surprised. Then a ghost of a smile flickered across her lips. "Thank you. I might take you up on that. Just to get even."

"Well, you're welcome. Annie would love having you. Just give me a call at the station when you make up your mind."

"I will." She reached out and touched the back of his hand. He returned to the station feeling good.

"Mr. O'Lochlain is waiting for you to call him at home," Beth told him, handing him a note. "Your friend from New York called back. He's set it up with the state police, and he'll get back to you in a couple days." She handed him a second note. "I told him to ask them to check back a ways, that we have at least one other crime involving our Groloch here."

"Good thinking. Thanks."

"John called too. He says he'll be getting the texts of those classifieds come lunch, and he picked up the historical research from Mrs. Caldwell." She passed him another note, then a fourth. "Judge Gardner will see you in his chambers. Eleven-thirty."

"Ha! It's moving. Beth, we're closing in. I can feel it."

"Crap, Norm. Bet you dinner—you pick the place if you win—that none of this gets you an inch closer."

"You're on," he replied without thinking, turning toward his office.

"And get on that LEA stuff. You've only got an hour."

"All right. All right. Why don't they hire somebody to take care of that crap?" Then he muttered, "Christ. Starting to think like a bureaucrat." Paying someone to handle LEA paperwork would absorb half the district's grant, making the whole thing just another exercise in governmental futility.

He whipped through in time by faking half his data. Lieutenant Railsback was supposed to double-check and countersign before sending the stuff on for the captain's signature, but Cash knew Hank would never see it. Beth would forge his John Hancock for him, with his blessing.

Someday they were all going to get their tits caught in the wringer.

"On my way out, Beth." He tossed her the papers. "Don't check them too close."

"Who gives a damn, Norm? They just file them. Remember that bet. I mean to collect."

Railsback shoved in the door. "Oh. Sorry, Norm. Well, I got what you wanted. Captain says we can polygraph everybody who had anything to do with the stiff, long as they're willing. Only, you ain't going to like the arrangements. Says we've got to do it on their time, meaning second shift, which is where most of them still are."

"Gah. Annie's going to love that. When can I start?"

"How about tonight? I want this done with. Oh, one other thing. If you start this, the captain says you have to go with it all the way. Meaning you, the kid, Smith, and Tucholski got to take the test too."

"O joy, O joy. All right. I'll show the troops how. Be the first victim. Beth . . ."

With one of her long-suffering sighs, she replied, "I'll find the people and set it up, Norm. You want me to call your wife?''

"No. I'll handle that. No point you taking the shit for me. Look, Hank, I got to meet Judge Gardner at eleven-thirty.''

"Okay. So go.''

"Norm,'' said Beth, "did you call Mr. O'Lochlain yet?''

"What're you doing messing around with that hood again?''

"Damn. I clean forgot. I'll do it from downtown.'' Cash patted his pockets to make sure he had his keys and Beth's notes.

"I get tired of explaining about O'Lochlain,'' Railsback grumbled.

"He said he'd only be there till one.''

"Okay. Okay. Bye, all.'' He sailed down the hall with Hank glaring after him.

He had trouble finding a parking place, so was five minutes late. The judge didn't mind. "They've turned half of downtown into a parking lot the last ten years,'' the man observed, "and still there's no place to park. I have a theory that says building a parking space spontaneously generates two cars to compete for it. Sit down. Tell me about your case. The girl who called was pretty vague.''

Good girl, Cash thought. "Probably nerves. She's shy.'' He began a quick outline while studying Gardner, whom he hadn't seen for ten years.

The man had aged well. He looked and sounded like a fiftyish Everett Dirksen. The most amazing thing about him, in Cash's opinion, was that he refused to use his bench as a springboard to political office.

Only the unicorn is more rare than the lawyer without political aspiration.

Perhaps it was because he was so controversial. He had as many liberal enemies as he had conservative cheerleaders. And there was some sort of fiscal foul-up in his court which, while due only to clumsy administration, didn't look good in the papers.

"Hold it, Sergeant. Seems to me there was another officer here with the same story a while back.''

"My partner. And you turned him down. But there's been a new development.'' He explained about the counterfeit money and outlined his other plans.

"You're coming out of left field and I think you know it. You want me to let you go looking for the money because you hope you'll find something else. You know perfectly well that anything you found would be constitutionally questionable."

"I know. What I'm really after is a gap in the old lady's story. She knows a lot more than she's telling."

"They all do. That's not the point. To be frank, I think you're getting damned near harassment. I can't do anything the way it stands. Suspicion of possession of counterfeit is a federal thing anyway. And I doubt if they'd be interested. First, statute of limitations. Second, you couldn't pass one of the real bills nowadays."

"Well, if you can't, you can't. Thanks for your time." Cash rose.

"Hang on. First run out your other leads: O'Lochlain; these polygraph interviews. If you come up empty, and only if—no, if you get something supportive, too—call me back. I'll see how I feel about it then. I go by intuition sometimes. But you make damned sure you've tracked that money, that you've eliminated all the other possibilities. You'd better check with the Secret Service, too. See what their attitude is."

"Yes sir."

Cash couldn't help whistling as he waited for a down elevator.

He grabbed a quick lunch at a chili joint four blocks east. His stomach didn't know how to take it. It had grown accustomed to an endless progression of Big Macs. After browsing through a bookstore, picking out a couple mysteries as a peace offering to Annie—he had wanted *The Dreadful Lemon Sky*, but the clerk told him the paperback wasn't due till September—he called home. Annie was more understanding than he had expected, though still irritated.

"Norm, you're scaring me."

"Eh? Why?"

"Because you're getting so involved in this. Almost obsessed."

"Hey. Not to worry, Hon. We're just getting close. Smelling the kill. Anyway, it's a lot more challenging than your usual family murder or gang killing."

"You're making excuses."

He knew it, and had begun worrying a little himself.

He said good-bye with a smile. She seemed to be having a

good day. That was encouraging. She had so few anymore.

"Norm! Hey!"

He was stalking back to the courts building when John hailed him. He waited as Harald and the woman slipped through traffic, jay-walking.

"Hi. You're looking good, Teri." She was. She had turned into a damned sexy woman. He envied John. "I appreciate what you're doing for us. How have you been?"

Trying to cover what he suddenly perceived as a tactical error, John interposed himself and began flashing papers. "Mrs. Caldwell's stuff."

"Jesus."

The woman had done a hell of a job, typing everything up and inserting it into an Accopress binder. It ran more than fifty pages.

"She really must be lonely."

It didn't take much sensitivity to feel the scream for notice implicit in so much hard, unnecessary work. He would have to show his appreciation somehow.

"She is. You got to feel sorry for her. But she comes on in a way that makes you look for excuses to get out."

"I know the type. Lot of old people get that way. You know, we're piling up some debts on this one."

"You are. I haven't been making any friends. In fact, I've about run out of angles."

"Yeah?" Cash grinned. "I'm just getting started. Got so much going today that I won't have time for it all. Been driving Beth crazy."

He glanced at his watch. "Fifteen minutes. And I've still got a call to make." He had come near forgetting O'Lochlain again.

"I'll catch you in the courtroom, then. It's twelve, in Kiel."

"Right. Nice to see you again, Teri." He chuckled as John hurried her away before she could strike up a conversation. She began giving him hell before they were out of earshot.

The Fates were conspiring to make him late today. After finally getting change from the blind couple who ran the courts building canteen, he found the phones tied up. He got through to O'Lochlain barely in time.

"Hey, Rookie. I'd given up on you. I'm on my way to the club now."

Couldn't be too bad, being retired, Cash thought. Phone in

his car yet. "I won't tie you up long, Tommy. Remember what we talked about last time?"

"O'Brien?"

"Right. I wanted to go over some things again. Especially the twenty thousand. That ever turn up?"

"No."

"Not even one bill?"

"Not a one."

"How much looking did they do?"

"Plenty. They covered every step he took from the train to the girl friend's house. It disappeared when he did."

It seemed to Cash that, for twenty-thousand 1921 dollars, rough riders like Egan's Rats would not have balked at man-handling Miss Groloch. "Anybody talk to the woman?"

There was a long silence.

"I take it they did. Come on, Tommy. What's to worry now?"

"I wasn't in town, so I don't know the details. The bet was that they got the cash and decided to vacation."

"Who?"

"The two guys they finally sent in a couple weeks later. Only, when they never turned up, they sent a couple more to make sure."

"Four men? You mean a whole gang disappeared there?"

"Five guys if you count O'Brien. It was so spooky that after that they couldn't get nobody to go ask the questions."

"Four more. Jesus. How come you didn't tell me before?"

"You didn't ask. You got to ask, Rookie. Anyway, you was just interested in O'Brien. Look, we're coming to the club. I got to go."

"Do me a favor. Just one more. Drop me a postcard. Just four names on it. Okay?"

"I'll think about it. Watch yourself, Rookie." He hung up before Cash could respond.

Norman first ascribed the disturbance to the chili. Then he remembered a time when his stomach had felt the same with nothing in it at all.

He was sitting in a peasant shack in eastern France on December 17, 1944, supposedly safely behind the lines. He had been in France just two weeks. Somehow, during the night, he had lost his first patrol and himself. Exhausted, he had decided to hole up till morning before trying to find his unit.

The only evidences of war were an abandoned German field telephone and a tiny wood stove the Krauts had made from a fuel can.

A nagging sound from afar wakened him, a growling, metallic cling with overtones of squeak. Twice he tore himself away from the stove to look out across winter at nothing but skeletal, distant woods. The sky was so heavily overcast that nothing was in the air, and few shadows stalked the earth below. The third time he looked he saw the vague shapes of the winter-camouflaged Tigers and Panthers. The Fifth Panzer Army was on the move.

The feeling was terror. Stark, unreasoning terror.

Five men had vanished without a trace. He and John could have gone the same way. . . .

"Hey, buddy, you going to fart around all day?"

He realized he had been staring into nothing for several minutes, reliving the past. He glanced at his watch. "Shit." He was late already and still had two blocks to walk. "I'm really sorry."

"Yeah. Sure."

The assistant prosecuting attorney scowled as Cash slipped into the pewlike courtroom bench next to John. The man was one of the young firebreathers, bound for political glory. The judge, defense attorney, and court staff barely glanced his way. The jury and other witnesses paid him no heed either.

"Anything happened?" he whispered.

"Still making speeches." John handed him a manila envelope. It contained two-dozen Xeroxes of classified pages, Personals. The key item on each had been circled in red magic marker.

Most began with a cryptic, "Thanks to St. John Nepomuk for favors received," and a date, followed by two or three vaguely religious and completely uninformative lines.

Nepomuk? Wasn't that a Czech saint? Cash asked himself. There was a Czech Catholic church at Twelfth and Lafayette dedicated to him. Why would a German, especially one who showed no religious inclinations in her home, be invoking a Czech saint?

Wait. Parts of Czechoslovakia . . . the Sudetenland, Bohemia. That had been Hitler's excuse for invading Czechoslovakia—to liberate the German minority. People who spoke German, anyway. In fact, Czechoslovakia as a country only went back to the First World War, didn't it?

What was it before that? Part of the Austro-Hungarian Empire. But the part called Bohemia had been an independent kingdom once. Prague was the capital. Hadn't there been a Mad King Ludwig once? No, he had been king of Bavaria. Hadn't he? Or was that Leopold? No, that was in Belgium. . . .

There were times when he wished he knew more. About everything.

"The dates are important," John whispered.

Teri had gone to the bother of typing up a catalog list. Most of the dates, the earlier ones, were at regular six month intervals. But since March there had been four, at erratic intervals. Cash reread those ads. He couldn't see where they varied significantly from the others, but their publication seemed timed to his encounters with Miss Groloch.

"How'd she put them in?"

John grinned. "Through her accountants. I did a little number on them this morning. Had to stretch the truth a little and hint that we were on a narcotics case. The boss finally admitted that he got his instructions by phone."

"But she doesn't have one."

"There's an outside pay phone at the service station at Russell and Thurman. Only two blocks. She called the man at home, late at night."

Cash laid a hand on John's arm. Both prosecutor and judge were eying them in irritation. "Later."

He began browsing through Mrs. Caldwell's report, which told him almost nothing he really wanted to know. It was thick because the woman had reproduced the entirety of dozens of letters or diary entries which mentioned the Grolochs only in passing.

During the first few decades, when there had been few neighbors, there seemed to have been a great deal of traffic to and from the Groloch house, mainly the coming and going of tradesmen. Letters of the period remarked on the odd bent of the Grolochs' interests. They were believed to be inventors, working with telegraphy, telephonics, or electricity. But Miss Groloch also seemed immensely interested in things medical.

She received dozens of journals, many from Europe.

Was invention the source of their fortune? Cash wondered. Was he going to have to undertake a stalk through patent records?

There had also been the air of mystery still felt today. Perhaps it had been even stronger then. More than one letter mentioned an irrational dread of the foreigners, who were universally admitted to be perfect neighbors.

Only the Fenian, O'Driscol, seemed to have been comfortable in their presence.

Of the Irishman there was little mention. The man seemed to have maintained a low profile, which fit his hypothetical revolutionary and draft-dodger background. His disappearance had caused so little comment that Mrs. Caldwell hadn't been able to pin down the exact year, let alone a specific date. Sometime in the eighties, probably late.

His departure loomed important only in retrospect, in the minds of a handful of people who had still been around at the time of the O'Brien incident.

Cash penned a marginal note: *What was happening in Ireland?* The man might have gone home to take part in one of the periodic uprisings.

Then he noted, *How has Fial been responding to ads?* And, *Miss Groloch to take lie detector? Ask Hank about her lawyer.*

The departure of Fian, also, had slipped by with little notice, though it was better documented. June 14, 1889, aboard an eastbound train from Union Station. Explanation, a death in the old country, an estate that had to be settled.

Cash made another note: *Passport issued?* Then, *U.S. citizenship?*

Suppose the Grolochs were illegals? . . . No, no leverage there. Every ten years or so Congress passed laws exculpating long-term illegals.

There seemed to have been no animosity toward Miss Groloch during the Great War, either because no one knew of her origins or because St. Louis's vast German community had remained completely, demonstratively loyal despite countless family ties in Europe. There had been little trouble.

Cash closed the folder little wiser. Just with more questions. Always there were more questions.

And don't lose the forest for the trees, he cautioned himself.

Jack O'Brien had a crafty way about him. He kept trying to disappear among the distractions. And he, or whomever the dead man might be, was what this case was all about.

He opened Mrs. Caldwell's report to the page where he had made notes and added, *Any other mysterious corpses on record?*

Digging into that ought to keep John busy for a while.

Harald poked him. Everyone was rising. Court was recessing without their having been called to testify.

"Damn," John complained as they departed. "There's tomorrow shot all to hell. Christ, it's hot out here. Hope Carrie bought some beer."

Cash told him of his evening plans.

John was furious. But he didn't say a thing.

Cash brought him up to date on the morning's work. John began to get that hungry hunter look again.

"Maybe it *is* starting to go. Maybe. You'd better let Gardner know about those four hoods. If we could just jam *her* into the damned lie detector. . . ."

Cash had a sudden thought. "John. That mailman . . . let's find out if her mail has changed since we've been pushing her. Also, you might ask your friend if there's any chance of tracking down classifieds from the time when she was having trouble with Carstairs."

The look of the hunter faded. "Norm, this's getting to be a pain in the ass."

"You don't like it, get out and drum up some alternate business. Me, I'm determined to nail this one shut."

"That's what Carstairs was going to do, remember? For eight years."

"Yeah. I remember." And he thought about it all the way back to the office.

XVIII. On the Z Axis; 1973-77; Homecomings

The most striking thing, Thorkelsen scribbled on his note-pad, as the former prisoners descended from the transport—*and it is the same every time I come out here—is not their gauntness, nor their confusion about the changes that have taken place in their absence, nor even the mechanical way they greet their families and respond to our questions. It is something I cannot quite put my finger on.*

He wrote all his notes longhand, laboriously. His handwriting was so bad even he had trouble reading it if he hurried.

He turned to Cameron, who had been sent down by the *Sacramento Union*. "They're all the same. You see it?"

The second reporter grunted. "Hunh? Nope. What do you mean?" But he wasn't listening when Thorkelsen tried to explain. He was wondering if he would have time to slip into Frisco and catch a hooker before he had to go home to a wife he detested. The girl named Fay knew exactly how to get the damned thing up, and had the patience to do it right.

"Big ones, little ones, black, white, commissioned or enlisted, they all look like the same guy designed them."

Thorkelsen knew only the air was listening. But he persisted. He could order his thoughts by talking, and might get through just enough to stimulate some sort of insight.

This was his fourth planeload met. He was now certain he lingered on the edge of a story. But the damned puzzle pieces wouldn't fall into place.

"It's not looks, though. They look pretty much alike because they've got to meet the same physical requirements and go through the same training. The pilots, anyway. No, it's something else. Something inside."

There were enlisted men on this flight. Just a handful, but only the second group he had seen.

They were the same too.

"Hey, Bob, I'll catch you later." He had noticed a tech sergeant who *didn't* have the nameless air.

"Yeah. Sure." Cameron resumed pursuit of his interrupted fantasy. What Fay could do with her dark little hands smothered in soap lather was a certifiable miracle. She ought to be canonized.

The sergeant's nametag read CANTRELL, A.O.

"Excuse me, Sergeant Cantrell. Nils Thorkelsen, *Fresno Bee*. Got a minute?"

The man stopped, but did not reply. He stared through Thorkelsen, did not bother dropping his travel bag.

Thorkelsen tried to explain the feeling he had gotten about the returning prisoners of war, and that he had sensed something unique about Cantrell. "Could you tell me why that is?"

"I'm uneducable."

"Eh? Could you try again?"

"I can't be programmed."

Debatable. The man's a zombie, Thorkelsen thought. He stood as still as death, the weight of his bag unnoticed.

"And the others can be?"

"Yes."

"Have they been?"

"Yes."

A fountain of information here. "How? For what? Would you explain?"

"Brainwashing. The best ever. Their mission is to resume positions in the imperialist armed forces and society, assuming positions of control as available, and await orders. Some will enter business or politics. Most are unaware of their status. They will be activated by a post-hypnotic key at the proper time. One thousand Trojan horses."

Cantrell spoke without emotion or inflexion, as if repeating a message he had often rehearsed for this one telling.

"Not that many prisoners are being returned."

"Some must be retained for other employment."

"How can you tell me this? If the others can't?" There had never been a hint of such a thing, though it was clear the Pentagon was covering something. That, it was pretty clear, was simply a prohibition on discussing maltreatment while interned.

"I couldn't be programmed. They couldn't break me."

Debatable, Thorkelsen thought again. Not much of a man remained here.

He had his major story. A story of the decade. A sure prize-winner.

If it could be proven.

Prisoners of war returned as Communist agents. . . . Nobody would believe it. "How come they let you go, if you're beyond control?"

A frown twisted Cantrell's face. "Bureaucratic error. The kind of screw-up that happens whenever people saddle themselves with the idiocy of a government. I didn't set them straight." He began to show a little animation delivering that remark.

"What do you plan to do with this knowledge?"

"Nothing. I've done it." He seemed puzzled by the question. "You ask. I have to tell. They succeeded that much. I talk. I talk. I talk."

"Shouldn't somebody be warned?"

"Why?"

"I don't understand. Why not?"

"Because I don't give a fuck. The Chinese did this to me. But you put me where they could get their hands on me."

The Chinese? "A pox on both our houses?"

"Yes."

Certain he was interviewing a madman, Thorkelsen shifted his questioning to the mundane. "What're your plans now? What're you going to do with all that back pay?"

"Buy me a guitar."

"Eh?"

"Buy me a guitar. They wouldn't let me have a guitar."

"That's all? That's your only ambition?"

"Yes. It's been six years. I'll have to learn all over again."

Thorkelsen was convinced. This pot wasn't just cracked, it was shattered. Maybe the VA could put the man's head back together again.

"Thanks for your time, Sergeant. And good luck." He was so sure it would draw belly laughs he promptly forgot the whole thing.

It didn't come back to him till, three years later, while working for a Los Angeles paper, he noted an AP wire-service story about a navy captain, ex-POW, who was resigning his commission to run for Congress.

"Hey, Mack," he called to his editor. "You see this about this ex-POW running for Congress in the Florida primary?"

"Yeah. Need more like him. 'Bout thirty of those men in the House, we might start getting this country back to what it's supposed to be."

"I don't know. . . ."

"What do you mean? A few real patriots up there . . ."

"I mean he might not be a patriot."

"What? After what he went through for his country? The camps, the—"

"Exactly. No, wait a minute. Let me tell you. When I was with the *Bee* they used to send me to Beale every time a planeload of prisoners came in. The third or fourth time I interviewed this army sergeant. A really spooky guy. He was a nut, but he had a good story."

"Such as?"

"Such as the Chicoms brainwashed all our prisoners before the North Viets returned them. Turned them into agents. He claimed most of them wouldn't even know they were agents till they got their orders from Peking. All they would know was they were supposed to get into important positions in the Pentagon, and in government and business. They were sort of, like, hypnotized as well as brainwashed."

Thorkelsen's editor hailed from Orange County, Bircher country, and could believe in seven more outrageous communist plots before the first edition every morning. And his strongly conservative paper was in dire need of something that would catch the imagination of a predominantly liberal market.

When the man's jaw finally rose and his brain had at last finished pursuing the germs of a hundred new conspiracy theories, he asked, "What about MIAs? Did he say anything about them?"

The man was planning a campaign, Thorkelsen saw. Allegations of a plot wouldn't get him the attention he desired. He had made a career of crying wolf. But an apparent break in the MIA question . . . that would grab national attention. While he had it, his message could be delivered. The nation could be awakened.

"Find that soldier, Nils!" Mack ordered. And he meant it. "Find him and drain him like a spider would. Every detail. His whole story, from the minute he was captured. You get the name of just one MIA, we can hold the whole world by the nose while we pound it with this other thing."

And for the next hour Thorkelsen endured a harangue damning the eastern Jew liberal press and the investigative reporting that had toppled Richard Nixon. Now those self-righteous hypocrites were going to get a shithouseful dumped right back in their laps.

But Cantrell had left no trail. It took Thorkelsen more than a year to identify and trace his man, now the bass guitarist of an obscure British rock group.

Long before Thorkelsen could make contact, before, even, he had located his man, Mack had begun trying to hype circulation with editorials hinting at a forthcoming blockbuster of a story, one that would send the blade of the guillotine plummeting toward the neck of the left-wing clique destroying the country.

Unfortunately, he named and told too much about Cantrell.

A Chinese agent included the articles in his routine reports. The story took months to percolate through the Peking bureaucracies, but it did, and eventually entered the ken of the man called Huang Hua.

An order for executive action went out immediately. Hua had the confidence of Mao's successor, Jua Kuo-feng, who had an even greater interest in the project than had the Chairman.

A race was on.

And Thorkelsen, plodding along in his spare time, drawn on only by drifty visions of a Pulitzer, convinced he was hunting one crackpot at the behest of another, never knew he was running with other horses.

XIX. On the Y Axis; 1975

Cash found Lieutenant Railsback in the process of departing when he reached the office. "Hang on a minute, Hank." Beth had already left. An envelope addressed to him lay centered on her desk. "I need a couple things. Mainly, a shot at the old lady's lawyer. To see if he'll let her go on the lie detector. When he says no, I want to show him what we've got."

"What you've got? You've got to be kidding. You ain't got shit."

"I've got four more mysterious disappearances, in her house, and a missing twenty grand in counterfeit that also looks like it ended up at her place."

"What kind of crap are you trying to feed me now?"

Cash outlined his day.

"Look, let me think. I'm just going to the Rite-Way anyway. I'm going to hang around for the polygraph session."

"Bring me a couple large Cokes and one of Sarah's special cheeseburgers then, okay? Here." He handed over two dollars.

John came in while Cash was opening Beth's envelope. He had a cold six-pack. Two cans were missing. "Bribes," he admitted. Bringing beer in was a violation of regulations.

"Hank's coming back." Cash popped a top and drained half a can.

"I know. He's got dibs on a can too. If I'd have known this was going to happen, I'd have got a case."

"Let me see what Beth has to say here."

It was a lengthy letter. She meandered. There had been something beside business on her mind. The gist was that she had begged, cajoled, or bullied everyone concerned into appearing for the polygraph test, and Immigration would be no help. The government hadn't gotten seriously involved until 1882. Their suggestion was to appeal to immigrant societies of the national group to which his subject belonged.

Well, he hadn't expected that angle to pan out.

If he wanted her to take notes during his evening extravaganza, he should call her at home.

"What do you think about Beth, John?"

"Huh? Nice ass. Tits ain't bad either. But she's cold. Something drifty about her."

"Not really. She's just not sure of herself. You remember how she was when she first came here? Quiet, goosey?"

"Still is with most of us. Got to whack her up side the head just to get her to say hi. Except you. You she treats almost normal. Guess maybe because you're a safe old father figure."

All I need, Cash thought. Another part-time kid.

"You know her number?"

"Huh? That's the best-kept secret since the atom bomb. Why?"

"She says to call her."

"Then you must have it somewhere."

"Not that I know of. Maybe it's in the book."

He looked it up. Sure enough.

She had just gotten home. She begged five minutes for a shower.

"God, I'm a rotten old bastard," Cash told her when she arrived. He was feeling loose. Hank had gone out after more beer. "I saved you a Coke, though. And dinner when you're done. All right?"

"Getting pretty feisty for an old man, aren't you?" John asked. "I mean, hustling young girls. . . ." Beth blushed, stared at the floor, then tried to cover by searching for pen and dictation pad.

"I already called Annie and told her," Cash responded defensively. Annie hadn't liked the idea, even when he had invited her to go along. She had refused on grounds that Nancy might need her.

"Some other time?" Beth asked. "I think everybody's down there now. They all got here early. Guess they want to get it over with."

As they descended the stairs, Beth observed, "Everybody was so cooperative, we probably ought to call the whole thing off."

"I'll buy that," said John.

"You know we've got to go the whole route, John. Step by step. When I'm done there ain't going to be a hole big enough for a roach to crawl through."

"You're just painting yourself into a corner."

"Beth! Who *are* all these people?"

"Reporting officers. Evidence technicians. Ambulance driver and attendant. Emergency room staff. People from the coroner's office. From the morgue."

"Jesus."

Twenty bewildered pairs of eyes watched the polygraph operator set up his equipment. Hank Railsback leaned against the wall in a shadowed corner, an amused smile playing across his lips as he listened to the captain.

"What kind of story did you feed them, woman?"

Beth just blushed and studied the floor.

"Uh-huh. A line of bullshit."

It was eleven-fifteen before they finished.

John was right. Beth was right.

Nothing.

Nursing a headache, Cash watched the polygraph operator pack his gear. Beth kept flexing fingers sore from gripping a pen. John, and everyone else who could, had taken off long since.

"Too bad Hank didn't stick around. But he hates to see his brain-children stillborn."

Beth moved behind him, began kneading his shoulder muscles. It startled him, but felt so nice he didn't ask her to stop.

"Where do you want to eat?"

Her grip tightened. She started to say something, choked on it. Her fingers quivered. "I still think I should take a raincheck. We've got to be back in here at eight."

"Yeah. Right. Well, I'll walk you to your car."

Leaning in her window, he said, "Thanks again. I really don't know what I'd do without you, Beth. You shouldn't put up with the crap I dump on you. That we all do."

"I don't mind. For you. At least you . . . Well, you know. You're nice about it. I'd better go."

"Sure. Thanks again. Bye."

He thought about Beth all the way home.

More and more, he suspected something was happening. It was flattering, tempting, and terrifying. If he formally recognized the condition at all, there would be pain and trouble no matter what course he followed. The wise thing, he supposed, would be to cool it by completely ignoring it. That would minimize the potential for pain.

Annie had fallen asleep watching Johnny Carson and rereading MacDonald's *The Girl in the Plain Brown Wrapper*. He wriggled himself a seat and gently woke her, presented the books he had picked up downtown.

"Struck out again, huh?" she mumbled.

"Yeah."

"Keep plugging, honey. It'll come."

"I'm beginning to wonder."

Cash's depression carried over into Tuesday. Lack of sleep was no help, and spending morning and afternoon being bored or angered by lawyers badgering witnesses or protesting one another's antics was a classic downer. He kept stifling an urge to stand up and scream, "But what about *justice*?" The concept seemed to have vanished from the American courtroom completely. All that remained was a highly ritualized barristry.

There were moments when he wished the Good Lord would send down a plague able to take no one but ambulance chasers. They were a pestilence themselves, a pustulant wound on the corpus of humanity. Directly or indirectly they controlled everything.

These dreary courtroom passages often brought on moments of paranoia when he felt as intensely about attorneys as had Hitler about Jews. He fancied very similar conspiracies.

Beth had but one bit of progress to report when he returned to the station. Railsback had contacted Miss Groloch's attorney about the possibility of the old woman undergoing a polygraph test. The man had refused. Of course.

John had completed his courtroom purgatory by noon recess. He had spent his afternoon digging. He now arrived, looking sheepish.

"Got an idea," he said. "Illegal as hell. Well, shady. You got your contacts in the outfit. I thought maybe you could get them to help."

"I don't think I'm going to like this." Cash guided Harald into his office, closed the door.

"Suppose we jump the old lady?" John asked. "Anything, just so we get her to move. We got a good idea she'll make it down to that pay phone. Maybe some of O'Lochlain's people could snatch her for a while. And some others toss her place. Like with metal detectors and stuff. We could loan them the gear."

"I knew I wouldn't like it."

"What about it?"

"In a word, illegal. John, something like that could get us crucified."

Cash was tempted. Unbearably. Otherwise he would have responded with a simple *no*.

"Only as a last resort, of course."

"Of course."

"You'll think about it?"

"How can I help it now that you've brought it up? But I guarantee you I won't pull anything like that unless Judge Gardner keeps turning me down. He doesn't, we can do it ourselves, legal. Subject closed."

"Okay. You don't have to bite my head off. Now, how about your little brown brother?"

"My who?"

"Major Tran. When's he coming?"

"Not sure yet. Sometime this week. Why?"

"Carrie and Nancy have had their heads together. Near as I can figure, they want to come over and do the welcoming party cooking for Annie. As a surprise."

"I don't know."

"Know what you mean. If they get going on Michael. And the kids making like Indians . . . Maybe we could get sitters."

"Maybe. Their hearts are in the right place, anyway. Let's worry about it when the time comes."

"Okay. I'm heading home now. Oh. We're having a barbecue Sunday, if it doesn't rain. Bring your own beer and pork steaks. And if Annie wants, she can make one of those green cakes."

"The pistachio?" Cash's stomach lusted. He loved barbecued pork. "Me, I'll have to make it with the all-beef hot dogs again. Sounds good, though. I'll see if I can't come up with a watermelon for the kids. Hey, all right if I bring Matthew? He might come down this weekend, to meet the Trans."

"You have to ask?"

As John left, Cash noticed Tony something-or-other Spanish, Beth's guy, in the outer office. What a loser, he thought.

He examined the reaction for the taint of jealousy. It wasn't there. But there *was* a lot of envy in it.

Desirable as Beth might be, his feelings seemed primarily paternal, protective. His reaction to *that* was both one of relief and one of mild self-deprecation.

Next morning the card with the four names arrived. He hadn't encountered a one of them before. He slipped the card into his desk, on impulse dug out the phone number of the man conducting the UFO investigation.

Those people had found nothing, though the man spent a quarter of an hour getting around to the admission. Cash told him of the additional disappearances. Then he rang Judge Gardner's court and left the same information. Not pressed with any other business, he then spent an hour playing bureaucratic double shuffle with the local treasury department people. The Secret Service proved to be very uninterested in fifty-four-year-old counterfeit money. The attitude was much the same as that expressed by Judge Gardner Monday. The stuff couldn't be passed anyway, so who cared?

He found Beth in his doorway when he hung up.

"John called while you were on the phone. He said he talked to that mailman. He says the old lady has gotten three or four real letters the past few months. The reason he noticed was because the sender used all real old two- and three-cent stamps. Postmarked in Rochester, New York. No return address."

"Hmm. We're getting something stirred up, then. Wish we could spook her into giving herself away."

"Norm, how come you want to get her so bad? You used to get on John. Now I think you don't care anymore. Not even how, so long as you take her down. How come?"

"Beth, I wish I knew. I worry about it too. Really. And I don't much like me for it. But I'm sure I'm right. I *have* to do it. I think part of it comes from everybody else being so damned eager to kill the case."

"Phone's ringing." She darted out. A moment later, "It's your wife."

"I'll take it in here. Yeah?"

"Mail came. There's an invitation."

"Huh? What to?"

"A funeral."

"Come on, Annie. . . ."

"Really. From that Sister Mary Joseph."

He was silent for a long time. Then, "Beth, when did Hank release my stiff?"

"Early Monday morning. I thought you knew."

"Son of a bitch. Me and him are going to have words over this."

"Norm?" Annie was trying to get his attention again.

He snapped his fingers. "Honey? Where? What time? Let me get a pencil here."

"You're going?"

"Damned right. I'll bet Miss Groloch was invited too. And I'll bet she shows. No matter what part she's played, she's got to be damned curious about this thing."

He wrote demonically as Annie relayed the information. "Thanks, love. I've just got to run. Love you. Bye. Beth! Put out the word for John to call me."

A half hour later they had it set up. John was able to confirm, from his chat with the postman, that Miss Groloch had received an invitation that morning.

Cash parked a half block short of the Groloch house. Castleman was one-way, eastbound. Any cab would have to pass them if already called. They had arrived, they judged, forty minutes before the woman would have to leave to make the funeral.

"This's crazy," Harald insisted. "I just don't see why you think she'll go."

"Call it a hunch." The sun beat down. The car quickly ovened up. He didn't feel communicative.

"How's she going to get a cab?"

"She's going to walk down to that pay phone. If she hasn't already."

Passersby gazed at them curiously. The neighborhood hairy youth appeared on his front porch, stared, ducked back inside. Even plainclothes cops were easily recognized by their suits, semi-military haircuts, and blackwall tires.

"Bet that jerk thinks it's him we've got staked out."

"Want me to go roust him?"

"What for?"

"He must've done something."

"Shit, John. Probably got a little pot put away. What's the dif?"

Harald shrugged, changed the subject. "What the hell do we get out of this even if she does go?"

"I don't know. It just seems to me that, long as we can keep her breaking her pattern, chances are she'll slip up. I want to be there when it happens. You ever see a dog go after one of them little box turtles you find in the woods? That turtle is safe . . . as long as Rover don't con him into sticking his head out."

"Shit. Can't we move up? That sun's murder."

"Soon as somebody pulls out from under a tree."

"How about I walk over to Lambert's and get us a couple of Cokes?"

"You really got the fidgets, don't you? Yeah, sure. Here. I'll buy."

"Hang on. Here we go."

Miss Groloch was on the move. She was brisk, businesslike, as she strode eastward, quite alert to her neighbors' reactions. Few of them had ever seen her. Those who had been out surreptitiously eyeballing the cops now watched her.

"Now?"

"No. After the cab comes. We'll follow her now. Make sure she uses that phone."

"Norm, I'm beginning to think this maybe isn't such a hot idea."

"It was yours."

"Yeah. That's why. No. Only sort of. And it's not legal. I'd rather have crooks do the crooked stuff. What if somebody spots me and calls the cops? Lot of people out here. Could we talk our way out of it?"

"What do you mean, 'we,' white man?"

"Norm, if it was anybody else sitting over there, I wouldn't admit it. But I'm scared. Last time I had the shakes this bad was the day Michael . . ."

"Want some outside backup?" Cash started the car, began creeping down the block. "Smitty might do it."

"No. Shit no. We can't get anybody else involved. Even you shouldn't be. Twenty-three years is a lot to risk."

"Nah. No problem. We can bullshit our way out." But he,

too, had begun to feel that peculiar twisting of the guts re-membered from the Ardennes and several occasions when he had approached women with less than honorable intentions. He dithered at the intersection with Klemm till another vehicle rolled up behind him.

He turned right, went over to his own street, then east a block to Thurman. He parked beneath the huge elm on the corner. In the distance, Miss Groloch turned on to Thurman and strode purposefully toward the service station.

Cash said, "Guy that lives here on the corner is going to run for alderman next year." As John grunted his disinterested re-sponse, Norm turned to peer out the back window. They had parked in front of the house next to his own. He wondered if Annie had noticed. "Maybe you knew him in school. Name's Tim Schultz."

"It's the service station all right. She's crossing over. You going to cruise past?"

"No. She might make us. Don't want her changing her mind now."

Miss Groloch vanished behind the bulk of the station.

"I figure you should have a good two hours," Cash con-tinued. "Plenty of time. I'll leave you off, then head for the funeral. Soon as you finish, hoof it over here. Annie'll be home. She never goes anywhere anymore. I'll pick you up when I get back."

The funeral was small and quiet. The priest didn't have much to say. He, Cash, and two men from the funeral parlor did the pallbearing. Sister Mary Joseph was accompanied only by two nuns. No one else came.

Except Miss Groloch, who watched from a distance, from the shadow of a grove of young maples. Her cab awaited her on a cemetery road behind her.

After depositing the casket next to the grave, Cash positioned himself so he could observe the principals. Sister Mary Joseph showed neither warmth nor coldness. Earlier, she had greeted him only with a curt nod. Miss Groloch seemed more interested in the surrounding cemetery than in the funeral, though there was no one in sight except an old man, off among the fancier monuments, who appeared to be a caretaker.

Once the casket had been lowered and he had deposited his

handful of earth, Cash started the old woman's way.

"Sergeant?"

He stopped, turned. "Sister?"

"Thank you for coming. Even if you had to."

"Had to? I didn't. It just seemed right."

"Did *she*? . . ."

"Miss Groloch? Yes. She was in those trees over there."
The cab had departed while his back was turned.

The sister squinted.

She was nearsighted, Cash realized. No wonder she hadn't
noticed.

"She's gone now. Do you need a ride back to the convent?"
He cast a sour look at the gravediggers. They were sidling
nearer already, not trying to hide their impatience. Didn't
anyone have any respect anymore?

"I'd appreciate that. We came out in the hearse. There's
something I want to tell you anyway."

But she could not seem to get started. After a half mile,
Cash asked, "I've always wondered. How come Miss Groloch
upsets you so much? You seem to have adjusted to . . . to . . ."

"Jack's disappearance? It's all right, Sister Carmelita," she
told the younger of the nuns in the back seat. The woman had
placed a comforting hand on her shoulder. "I liked Jack,
Sergeant. Even when I knew what he was. He was that way.
Nobody could really hate him.

"I had no illusions. I knew something would happen, the
way he lived. I think I was used to the idea before it did.

"No. I don't hate her for Jack's sake. It's Colin that did
it."

"Colin?"

"My boyfriend. Colin Meara. If you can have a boyfriend
when you're that young. The kid I was with the last time I saw
Jack."

"I remember now. But I don't understand."

"The whole neighborhood knew about Jack. Because of
the yelling and screaming and all that. Well, Colin decided
he'd play detective. So he snuck into her house one night.
And . . ."

"And?" Cash prompted after fifteen seconds.

"He never came out. Never. Nobody ever knew what happened but me. His parents thought . . . his dad was really

rough on him. Because he was afraid Colin would be like
Jack. He adored Jack. They said all sorts of crazy things, but
mostly they just thought he ran away. He was an only child. I
never could tell them the truth. Not even his mother when she
was asking for him when she was dying. Couldn't ever tell
anybody. Till now.''

Sister Carmelita patted her shoulder.

Cash almost ran a red light. ''Why?''

''I was waiting outside. We stayed awake and snuck out
after everybody was asleep. I remember it so clearly. It was
after midnight, almost a full moon. Not a cloud. The stars
were so beautiful. . . . We were going to do it together. Only I
got scared. So he told me to wait outside. And he never came
back.''

A silent sob racked her thin frame.

''Sergeant, fifteen minutes after he went in . . . that woman
came to the door. Then she came outside, all the way out to
the gate. I couldn't run. She just stood there and stared at me
for maybe five minutes. It was like looking the devil in the
eyes. Then she just smiled and nodded and went back inside.''

''She didn't say anything?''

''Nothing. Not a word. God in heaven. I was scared.
Of her, of my father, if he found out I snuck out nights, of
Colin's father. . . . I'm still scared. I can still see that evil
smile. . . .''

Lord, another one, Cash thought. The Groloch place was a
slaughterhouse.

''I thought you'd come today. I prayed you would. Last
night I wrote it all down. I borrowed a school typewriter and
put down everything I could remember, all the stuff I didn't
tell you before. Maybe it'll help.''

''Everything's a help.'' Something akin to elation coursed
through Cash. It was starting to come. Finally, the information was breaking loose.

He had been home a half hour and had read the sister's
deposition twice before he thought to ask, ''What happened to
John?''

''I haven't seen him,'' Annie replied. ''Was I supposed to?''

''Yeah. He was supposed to meet me here. Hey. Maybe he
found something and grabbed a cab back to the station.''

''Found something?''

Cash evaded by ducking back into the memoir. It was richly detailed, yet told him nothing Sister Mary Joseph hadn't covered orally.

"Honey, you ever hear of Miss Groloch having another boyfriend after O'Brien?"

"I don't think so. Why?"

"Just curious. Been wondering, off and on." He phoned the station. Old Man Railsback answered. "Is Beth around? Well, have her call me when she gets back. At home. Never mind what I'm doing here. Just do it."

Hank's father was making himself useful, more or less, while Beth was in the can.

The phone rang within five minutes. "Beth? Yeah. Do me a favor, will you? Check the O'Brien autopsy sheet and see what he had in his stomach." He wasn't sure, but didn't think the report jibed with the sister's statement. She claimed his last meal had consisted of cold roast beef and cold boiled potatoes, washed down with homemade beer.

Beth took another five minutes. Then she asked, "You still there?"

"Gathering cobwebs."

"Hank's kicking up dust about something. I was helping his dad calm him down. Norm, this thing don't look right. It says there wasn't anything in his stomach. Except almost indetectable traces of what may have been pureed beef liver, and what may have been applesauce."

"No potatoes? No roast beef? No beer?"

"No." She sounded puzzled.

Cash let out a whoop. "We did it! We proved it! The guy ain't O'Brien."

"What the hell are you talking about?"

"Babe, I'll tell you all about it when I get there. Don't let John get away. He'll want to hear this too." He hung up, wrapped Annie in a powerful hug.

"Norman, will you please calm down long enough to explain?"

"Honey, I just made a breakthrough. It'll put Hank on Cloud Nine. The dead guy can't be Jack O'Brien."

"I heard. So how can you prove it?"

"He ate meat and potatoes before he disappeared. The dead guy ate liver and applesauce."

She smiled, sharing his joy. Then, "You'd better sit down. You forgot something."

"Like what?"

"Like you only proved that he wasn't run through the time machine right away."

"Hunh?"

"Those meat and potatoes wouldn't stick to his ribs forever. Fifty years is plenty of time to digest them."

"Oh." He slumped against the back of the couch. "I went off half-cocked, didn't I?"

"Looks like." She took one of his hands in hers. "It'll be okay. You'll get to the bottom of it."

"Shit."

"Norm!"

"Okay. Look, I got to get back. Hank's pissed enough now, we spend so much time screwing around with this thing."

"Don't let him keep you too late. Major Tran called. They'll be here in time for supper."

"Damn. I don't know if I'll be able to cope. Unless John's got something to cheer me up. There was another one, honey. I found out today. Besides O'Brien and the four hoods."

"What?"

"Another victim. A kid. Twelve years old. Carstairs never found out about him or the hoods. But he must've felt something. That had to be why he was so stubborn about letting go."

"Evil. I told you. . . ."

"I'll be home as soon as I can." He kissed her good-bye. They still did that, after all these years.

"What happened to the high?" Beth asked as he slouched through the office door.

"My old lady shot it down." He explained. "Where's John? What'd he get?"

"I haven't seen him. I thought he was with you."

"But . . ." What the hell? John had had plenty of time . . . Teri? The sonofabitch was making whoopie on company time. He grabbed a phone, then thought better of it. No point stirring things up, or playing Typhoid Mary with his depression. Let John enjoy till he decided it was time to come in.

A thump startled him.

Old Man Railsback had dozed off. A book had fallen off his lap.

Hank's door was closed, but the sound of his feet as he paced could be heard.

"Beth, see if you can get Judge Gardner for me. If you can't, just leave a message saying I dug up another disappearance. With a witness."

"At the Groloch place again?"

"Yeah. I'll be in here shuffling papers."

Quitting time arrived. Still no John. This was going to have to stop. Sooner or later, Cash decided, Harald was going to force him to take official notice.

Irked, he returned home. He had been counting on John to give the day a bright ending.

It was just the day that had him down. John had been vanishing without explanation since before Christmas.

A cool shower did wonders. Norm felt human by the time Tran and his family arrived.

XX. On the X Axis;
1889-1945;
A Bohemian Physician

Neulist arrived May 12, 1889.

The crone of a midwife strained cataracted eyes—and screamed. "Another one! Another devil!"

No one listened. She had been going on this way for twenty-five years, since the flight of her husband and children. Her warnings had been so fervent for so long that even the most compassionate villagers shunned her as a madwoman.

Those same villagers shunned the growing boy. His approach stirred irrational loathings. Even his parents barely tolerated him.

He had spent years in isolation, hated by millions. The antipathy of a few hundred superstitious peasants troubled him not at all. What bothered him was being a child.

Children in this age were little more than slaves.

He found the midwife's past overwhelmingly intriguing. All that talk about her husband and children, about possession and flight. . . .

The other villagers were bored with it. Possession? By now they believed she had driven them off with her shrewish ways.

The mayor once mentioned having received a letter all the way from America, from Fiala, asking after her mother. The boy broke into the man's home and stole it when he was seven.

It gave him an address.

He mulled that letter, and the old woman's story, for years. And knew were his destiny lay.

As a child he had no more rights, and little more power, than a bondservant. Till he turned thirteen he hired out to work in the fields. Then he joined his father in the mines at Kladno.

There was little he could do till he became a man.

Except study. The village priest overcame his revulsion and helped a haunted but brilliant child find the navigation markers of life in that age.

Those were the years when he learned patience. He had no choice. A strapping was the inevitable consequence of the slightest rebellion.

His mother died when he was nine.

His father loathed him almost as much as did the midwife. His childhood became one long exercise in discipline. He learned, without coming to understand, what it was like to live on the receiving end of dictatorship.

In time he became perfectly willing to invest decades in his vengeance. And absolutely determined to carry it out. For these years of hell the Zumstegs would pay in agony and blood.

The summer of 1908, finally, saw him fleeing his hell for Vienna, taking his own, his father's, and his church's savings. There, through applied gall and a talent for forgery, he enrolled himself in the Academy of Fine Arts, where his work as a sculptor was just good enough to keep him in. Two years later he reverted to old habits, began studying contemporary medicine with a Dr. Mayer in Leopoldstadt, Vienna's Jewish district.

Despite, or perhaps because of, his background in twenty-first century medicine, he was an abysmal failure as a medical understudy. Students weren't permitted to contradict the common wisdom of their teachers, nor to promulgate crazy medical theories. Mayer endured him for two years. The doctor was a patient, tolerant man, completely oblivious to any aura of the alien. His cause for dismissing his apprentice was, in fact, personal. He learned that his *goy* pupil had been bedding his daughter—and had gone so far as to abort their love-child.

Mayer expelled his protégé from his practice with that air of great sadness characteristic of the career long-suffering European Jew.

There had to be, Neulist thought at the time, laws of temporal inertia, or laws of chronological thermodynamics, that refused to permit the introduction of changes or new ideas.

He could not comprehend the importance to these people of being *goyim* or Jew, nor the intense revulsion the period's habitués bore abortion.

His response to the dismissal was blind despair. Medicine was the only field he knew—since people in this age had little need of a chief of secret police whose duties were to maintain the purity of the party ideal. Not even his obsession with the Zumstegs could break through. When the depression at last lifted he was left with nothing but indifference and a bottomless well of self-pity. His social condition slipped from bad to worse—he made his few kronen performing abortions—and to worse still, till in January 1913, so destitute that he no longer possessed a winter coat, he pawned his shoes for enough money to spend a week in the Männerheim. The Männerheim was a five-hundred-bed dormitory maintained for the not-quite-indigent, a sort of Viennese YMCA.

Even there, among outcasts, he remained an outsider. It was as if he exuded some alien scent that kept most everyone at a distance. There was just enough human contact to start him on the road back up.

His one friend, a man as alienated as he, was one he had long admired, in historical retrospect. Even though marooned in this desert isle of time, he had never hoped to meet the fellow. Certainly not among the down-and-outs of Brigittenau district, where Jews were thick as flies.

At that time, though, the man was just a young, directionless crank and third-rate artist, possessed by no political ideals and certainly not obsessed with the Jewish Question.

"Things must be different this time," Neulist mumbled to Hitler one morning, when they were alone in the writing room. "Unless I'm more ignorant of your biography than I thought."

The skinny, homely youth glanced up from his watercolors puzzledly. This was the sort of mysterious, never-to-be explained remark that had first drawn him to his companion, this Michael Hodzǎ. That and a shared feeling that they were trapped in a foreign world.

Over the months, the vague remarks included such cryptic admonitions as, "Finish Sea Lion before you start Barbarossa," and, "Don't trust Count von Stauffenberg."

After each remark Hodză became embarrassed, as if he had spoken out of turn.

Neulist, aka Hodză, no longer worried about altering history. His experience with Dr. Mayer had convinced him that he could not. So he did as he pleased, spending his little energy scrounging a living, and for a time completely forgot the Zumstegs.

His latter days of poverty and impotence were, paradoxically, among his happiest in two lifetimes.

Yet he remained the Avenging Sword of the State. It was his duty to pursue traitors even here in the backwaters of Time.

But the State, to all practical purposes, did not exist. How could he presume to act in its behalf?

In this age, in a whole body, he suffered none of the pain, physical or mental, that had driven him over the borders of rationality in his own time.

The friendship with Hitler never deepened, though they became traveling companions. On May 24, 1913, they set off together on a railroad adventure which ended at the cradle of the Führer-to-be, Munich.

The piling international crises of the time, the Balkan Wars and the separatist movements in the imperial Hapsburg hinterlands, brought Europe to a simmer. In June 1913 the men separated. Hodză returned to Prague. Using forged credentials, he established himself as a physician. He met Hitler again briefly in 1936, when he was physician to the Czech Olympic team. Hitler didn't recognize him.

But the Führer did remember him later, on July 20, 1944, at about 12:35 p.m., when the Count von Stauffenberg entered the conference room in the Lagebaracke at the Wolfsschanz with a fat black briefcase.

Hitler puzzled the vague memory till it was too late to flee. The bomb went at 12:42. . . .

But this time it didn't kill.

The colonel had effected a major alteration of the past.

By 1936 he suspected things *could* be radically changed. There were subtle little differences in this history and they seemed to be accumulating. He continually wished he had studied his history closer so he could identify their nature. The big, shaping changes then still seemed improbable.

Those Prague years, more than a score of them, hurried

past. He made only halfhearted attempts to fulfill his duty toward the Zumstegs. He was content with his life.

Contentment and happiness expired late in 1938. They perished on a day when Hitler and Chamberlain were meeting at Munich.

Because he made a delicious, exciting, entirely coincidental discovery. A vagary of Fate fanned his mad anger till it became a raging, possessing demon.

On that ill-starred September morning he had decided to visit Isador Neumann's tiny philatelic-numismatic shop. A tall, rugged, hard-looking man jostled him at the door. Their eyes met. Both frowned, paused as if trying to remember the name of an old acquaintance. Hodză watched the man walk on while trying to fathom his sudden excitement. Finally, he went inside.

"Ach, Dr. Hodză," said the gnome of a Jew with the incredibly merry eyes. "Buying or selling today?" And, "What're the English and Germans doing to us now?"

"I'm selling, Isador. And so are the English. But they'll get no joy from their thirty pieces of silver." He opened the special wallet to reveal the stamps within, then glanced toward the door perplexedly. "Who was that man?"

"Him? One of my oldest customers. Not a very talkative sort. You really want to sell these? Hold them another year. They'll go up."

Neumann was a good fellow. His advice was well-meant. But in a year the market would be dead. The fate of Czechslovakia, and of Europe, was being sealed this very day. "Yes. Only the forty-eight copies known. But I want to sell. That man?"

"I have his card here somewhere. He always buys the old Austrian coins. Long ago he gave me the list. Two, three times a year he comes to see what I've found. You're *sure* you want to sell?"

"Absolutely."

These stamps would explode in value after the war. All these copies, twelve of the forty-eight known, would be destroyed when a misguided Resistance fighter, under the misapprehension that any free Jew must be a Gestapo agent, would, in 1943, throw a bomb into this shop. Hodză planned to gather the surviving copies in 1945, once the Russian occupation had destroyed the value of everything but food.

Hodža had been riding the highs and lows of the stamp market since the close of the Great War, often obtaining future rarities at issue. He had developed a vast but portable fortune in tiny bits of paper, and in Switzerland, in a vault in Zurich, was material with a potential worth in the hundreds of millions.

"Here we are. I'm going to have to get this place organized someday."

The colonel-doctor laughed. The crowded little shop hadn't changed in decades. "You said the same thing the first time I came in. That was fifteen years ago."

"And I meant it. I just haven't found the time."

Hodža took the card, it said in two lines:

FIAN GROLOCH
LIDICE

He nearly collapsed.

"Is something wrong, Doctor?"

"Right here under my nose all the time," he murmured. Off and on, he had had a dozen private detectives tearing up America for as many years, and no amount of money had been able to unearth more than one Groloch, the Fiala whose address he had obtained from a letter written fifty years ago, to the then mayor of Lidice.

He surged toward the door.

"Doctor! Without your hat?"

Neumann's question reestablished his link with reality.

German troops were already over the border at Eger. They had been for days. In hours the full might of the *Wehrmacht* would roll. It was too late. There was no time to do a proper job. Right now.

He resumed his business with Neumann, a plan already shaping in the depths of his mind. Its success would hinge on two eventualities: his own ability to escape Czechoslovakia before the iron grip of the Third Reich tightened, and Fian Groloch's known unfamiliarity with his nation's early history.

Had Fial been there in Lidice, Neulist's trap could never have been sprung.

His escape route led through Poland, and along the way a Czech patriot named Josef Gabiek lost his papers, identity, and life.

*   *   *

The night was pitch. The air moaning through the hatch was chilly. Kubis shivered so much his teeth rattled. But that had nothing to do with cold. He had been doing it since takeoff.

For the first few hours he had worried aloud, constantly, about the Luftwaffe, but the endless silence and absolute confidence of his companion, the man who called himself Josef Gabiek, had compelled him to retreat into a fear-filled shell.

How *could* Gabiek be so certain? So sure that he had been able to sell the British and the government-in-exile?

Gabiek was not certain. This time around he had moved the operation up five days in hopes of taking Fian Groloch by surprise. Also, there was the fact that the real Josef Gabiek, in the operation of his own past, hadn't survived.

The light came on. The RAF men shoved the equipment bundle to the hatchway.

"Time to go," said Kubis, more to himself than to his companion.

Gabiek rose slowly, tightened his chute harness. "It's changing, Jan," he muttered. "I can feel the difference now."

A minute later the soil of their homeland was rushing toward them from the darkness. Gabiek tracked the equipment chute. Kubis searched the upsurging forest for a sign of the SS men he *knew* would be waiting. . . .

Gabiek was right, just as he had been all along. It went perfectly.

Morning. May 29, 1942. The open-topped green Mercedes sports car and escort were right on time.

Couldn't Gabiek miss?

The older man jumped out and began firing. Without effect.

Kubis threw the bomb.

The Mercedes disintegrated.

But Heydrich clambered out and came toward them, blazing away with his pistol.

Reinhard "Hangman" Heydrich, "protector" of Bohemia and Moravia, had been whipped about like a rat in a terrier's mouth. Pieces of seat-back spring protruded from his back. His spine had been shattered.

Yet he stood there and fought back.

It wasn't his appointed time to die.

As they fled through their smokescreen, with Heydrich's

slugs hunting them, Gabiek said over and over, "I can't change it. But it's *different*."

To effect their escape they were supposed to place themselves in the hands of a priest at Karl Borromaeus Church in Prague. There, among scores of Resistance fighters hiding from the insanity of the security police, Gabiek encountered another time traveler.

The nun was so aged and feeble that she had to perform her limited duties from a wheelchair.

"Dunajcik!" Gabiek gasped.

He didn't know how he knew, but he did. It hit him like a thunderclap. There remained not a shred of doubt.

Kubis gave him a strange look.

"I'll wait here." Gabiek slid behind a pillar, afraid Dunajcik might react as he had. The old woman seemed popular. She might send someone after him. . . .

The conviction grew more absolute. Inside that crone was the man who had caused all this by his treachery at the programming theater. . . .

Gabiek backed from the church, his head shaking. It was a mystery. How *could* he be so positive? And how could the lieutenant have become a priestess? The man had always been weak and effeminate, and a bit too mystically oriented—but this vast a failure in one educated by the State?

He, as Neulist, had failed, he realized. He had not extinguished the spark of Uprising. It persevered, and had thrust its insidious evil into his own office. . . .

The idiot was so happy he almost glowed. Was do devoted that he had done nothing to apply twenty-first century common knowledge to the retardation of the aging process in the body he wore.

Was the fool in such a hurry to get to Heaven?

Or had that ugly body been too old when he had arrived?

At least some laws of chronological conservation appeared to be in effect.

The Hangman, despite his ruined spine, would not die till the historically appointed moment. He lingered till the fourth of June.

Meanwhile, the Protectorate (and Reich) rapidly deteriorated toward chaos. Gabiek, ignored in all his efforts to betray the Resistance fighters in the church, and to link Lidice with the assassination attempt, suffered frustrations equaling those of his dealings with the Zumstegs. Damn it, the security police *had* to move. Fian Groloch was bound to remember his history soon. This fuss had to alert him.

But the timetable continued rectifying itself back toward historically established precedent.

Heydrich finally died.

Something clicked. The engine of history ceased sputtering, began to hum.

The security police closed in on Karl Borromaeus Church.

There were no survivors when they finished.

But this time there was no one named Josef Gabiek among the dead.

Next morning, carrying papers identifying himself as Dr. Hans-Otto Schmidt of the SS-Reich Economic Administration Main Office (the incongruously named bureau responsible for the death camps), in transit from Theriesenstadt to Mathausen, Neulist-Hodža-Gabiek was on the move, destination Ostmark, the Austrian province of the Greater German Reich. In the false bottom of his physician's bag lay stamps massing less than half a kilo, yet worth millions of Reichsmarks. They would be his means till he could reach his Swiss deposits.

There was no easier way to move a fortune.

He was in Linz, preparing yet another identity, when the sword of this vengeance finally touched a Zumsteg.

That was the morning of June 9, 1942.

The massacre at Karl Borromaeus Church hadn't seen enough blood spilled to satiate Heydrich's avengers. For days all the Protectorate had been waiting, treading a razor's edge of fear, not knowing where the inevitable blow would fall.

Early that morning ten trucks rolled to the outskirts of Lidice. Captain Rostock ordered his troops to surround the village. They were hard-faced men, *Totenkopf* men, ready for murder.

Their first victim was a twelve-year-old boy, shot down as he ran to warn his father, who worked in the mines at Kladno.

The next was an old peasant woman, shot in the back repeatedly as she fled across a plowed field.

The men they drove into Mayor Horak's cellar. . . .

And the killing began in earnest.

One thousand three hundred thirty-one people died at Lidice, including 201 women. And it wasn't over then. More would perish in the camps. The babies of pregnant women would be murdered at birth.

Among the 1331 was Fian Groloch, who didn't realize what was happening till far too late. His final remark, to Horak, was, "Ignorance can be a capital offense too," which puzzled the mayor for the few minutes he remained alive.

Groloch spent his last minutes trying to reason out why the Heydrich-Lidice scenario differed from what he vaguely remembered. In the absence of knowledge about Neulist, he erroneously concluded that his own presence had affected the changes. He made admonitory notes in his diary, buried it in a box beneath Horak's cellar floor. The construction crew excavating the foundations of the agency building might find it.

He tried to compose himself.

But he died terrified for the State.

Then Rostock burned the village, dynamited the ruins, and leveled the site. The surviving women went to the camps. Their younger children went to racial experts for determination of which were worthy of adoption into good National Socialist families.

And for three and a half years, in Vienna, a Dr. Schramm smiled, awaited the Russians, and considered how he would pick up his mission in America after the war.

XXI. On the Y Axis; 1975

Cash was reasonably impressed with the Tran family. The boys were a handsome pair, he thought during the introductions. Taller than their parents already, and not at all uncomfortable with American ways.

When he mentioned it, Tran replied, "They spent several years in the company of American children in Saigon. Children are more adaptable than us old folks anyway."

"That's the truth. That's why they turn them into soldiers. Well, let's get your stuff upstairs, show you your rooms. The boys are going to have to share, I'm afraid."

The Vietnamese hadn't brought much with them. Annie asked if the rest of their things were being shipped.

"This is it," Tran replied, almost apologetically. "We weren't able to bring much out." Then, to ease Annie's embarrassment, "Something smells good."

"Supper. It's just spaghetti. I didn't know what to fix."

"You won't hear any complaints from my sons. They were ecstatic when they saw how near that pizza shop is."

"Imo's?" Cash asked. "I know it well. Michael and Matthew damned near kept the place in business when they lived at home. This's it. Your room." He hadn't been into it for weeks. Annie had done a job. New curtains, new sheets, new bedspread, some plants in the windows, everything squeaky clean.

Once it had been Michael's room. She had cleaned out every scrap that had been the mark of their son's personality, even patching the plaster where the framed centerfold of a favorite

Playmate had hung till he and John had pulled it down while clowning.

Cash slipped his arm around Annie's waist in a congratulatory hug.

"It's very nice." Tran seemed as much at a loss as they. His wife said nothing at all, and the boys, in the hall, confined themselves to whispers.

"The bathroom's right here," Annie said. "I'll show your sons their room, then we'll let you settle in. Supper will be ready when you are." She took Norm's hand and led him downstairs.

The wine she served with supper helped everyone relax. It was a native Missouri pink catawba; they made no pretenses in that direction. Soon all but Tran's wife were chattering like old friends. The major didn't seem to mind that his sons were heard as well as seen.

The phone rang while Annie was dishing out homemade butter pecan ice cream.

Cash answered it. "Hi. No. Yeah. You tried the station? Yeah, he was working on something for me, but I figured he'd get done in time for supper. Guess he must've hit a snag, eh? Would you tell him to call me when he gets there? Sure. Bye."

Annie raised a questioning eyebrow when he returned to the dining room.

"Carrie. Looking for John." How long could he keep this Teri business to himself? Annie had an annoying habit of putting odd numbers together to get four. Came from reading those damned mysteries all the time.

"Your partner?" Tran inquired. "I meant to ask, how did you do with that case? The one with the old lady and the mysterious corpse."

"Still going. We keep digging things up. It just gets spookier." He brought Tran up to date.

"And not one body turned up? Very strange."

"No lie. Don't know for sure about the bodies, though. Tomorrow we start checking back, to see what's on the record."

"Norm," said Annie, "I thought O'Lochlain told you they just disappeared. If they'd ever turned up anywhere, his people would have known. Wouldn't they? And he'd have told you, wouldn't he?"

"Maybe. Tommy's a little strange."

As Cash drifted toward sleep that night he realized that John hadn't called. It didn't matter that much this time, but he was going to have to get onto the kid's case. Otherwise this thing with Teri was going to cause problems.

Cash reached work a half hour late because he had driven Tran in for his first day of work and had gotten talking with the man's boss.

Tran seemed to have timed his arrival to his job, to avoid the appearance of freeloading.

"Where's John, Beth?" he asked as he pushed in. Smith and Tucholski had the squad room thoroughly fogged already.

"Not in yet."

"His car's in the lot."

"Maybe he's downstairs."

"Maybe. I've got some research to get him started on. Tell him to see me whenever he shows."

He spent ten minutes reviewing the activities of the previous shifts, then leaned back. It wouldn't be such a bad year after all. The first quarter had been an anomaly. The heavy casualties had been primarily drug-related. That war seemed to have settled out now. Even the papers had found more interesting fare.

The remaining nuts, too, seemed firmly attached to their trees.

Next thing he knew, Beth was shaking him awake. "Your friend from New York just called. He says the Rochester place is a complete bust if you're looking for something illegal. There's one old man who's lived there forever, and that's it. Just like your Miss Groloch, only this one's never been in any trouble. He said it'd help if he knew what the hell you were looking for."

"Ah, the heck with it. Should've known I was wasting my time. What about John?"

"Not here. Hang on a minute." The phone was ringing.

A moment later, "It was that judge. He said he still hasn't made up his mind, but you're getting closer. You've got him interested."

"Okay." He eyed Smith, who was stalking around with one cigarette in hand while another smoldered in his ashtray. The man was talking to himself.

Everybody had problems.

The temptation to run across to the liquor store after a pack of his own was, suddenly, horribly powerful.

"About that dinner I owe you. Would you think I was welshing if I invited you over to the house?"

She was several seconds answering. "No, that's okay." She didn't sound enthusiastic, though.

"Hey. Come on. I owe you. I'll do whatever you want." He had thought that bringing in another shy person might liven Tran's wife. The woman behaved like a lost soul.

Beth brought a cup of coffee. "I know. Doctor says *verboten*. But you'd better get it inside you. Hank's grumbling about whipping the outfit into shape again. What if he catches his sergeant sleeping on the job?"

"It'll blow over by Monday. It always does. You want to slow him down, just look at his old man like he's the first change you're going to make."

"Damn!" It was the phone again. "That thing's been jumping off my desk all morning." A moment later, "It's for you. Your wife."

He took it on his extension. "Yeah?"

"Did John show up this morning? Carrie just called again. He never came home last night."

Suddenly, Cash was back in that shack in the Ardennes. The Tigers and Panthers were clanking past with all the sound of hammers pounding the anvils of doom.

The *panzergrenadiers*, all tough, hard-eyed veterans of five years of warfare, were closing in.

His guts cramped with the fear.

"Norm! What's the matter?"

Two voices said it. He looked from the phone to Beth.

"Oh . . . nothing. Just . . . for some reason I was remembering the war." Now he was more puzzled than frightened.

"Is John up to something?" Annie demanded.

"Not now. I'll tell you later. Tonight. Okay? I'll find him. Bye." Teri. Damned, it had better be Teri. "Beth, would you get ahold of the *Post*'s classified ad department for me?"

Those grim *panzergrenadiers* stalked forward under the low gray sky, their silence a dread contrast with the squeal, clank, and roar of the armor. The young Cash turned the crank on the abandoned field phone, round and round and round. No one answered.

Who was he calling, anyway? Hitler himself?

He was dead meat. He knew it.

"Norm?" Beth was offering the phone.

"Teri Middleton, please," he croaked, hoping the girl was using her maiden name again, or that there was only one Teri employed there. "No, dammit! This isn't a personal call. This's the goddamned police department."

He waved Beth out.

The girl was on the line in seconds. "John?"

"Shit," he muttered to himself. "Teri? This's Norm. I don't want to pry, but have you seen John?"

"No."

"Look, it's important. I want to make sure he isn't in some kind of trouble. We haven't been able to locate him since yesterday."

"Well, I haven't either."

"You're sure?"

"I said so, didn't I?"

"Shit. Oh, shit."

"Swear to God. Really. He was supposed to meet me after work yesterday. He never showed up."

"He didn't?"

"No."

"Okay. Thanks." He lowered the receiver slowly. "What the hell am I going to do?" He looked right through Beth, who had ignored his directive to withdraw.

"Norm?" She sounded frightened now. "What is it? What happened?"

"It's John. He . . . no. I can't tell you yet. I've got to check some things before I tell anybody." His ass was going to be in a sling. He was, voluntarily, going to confess to an illegal entry. "I'll be back in a little while."

He first checked John's car. It seemed to be in the same parking space as yesterday, though that wasn't remarkable in itself. Still, no one had seen Harald. He hadn't signed in, nor had he called in.

A half hour later Cash was cruising past John's home. Harald's children were playing in the yard. He scrunched down to avoid recognition.

Carrie's Plymouth Satellite stood at the curb. And John's Honda stood inside the open garage, leaning against one wall.

John hadn't gone off to live on the beach at Malibu.

"Shit." His vocabulary had grown terribly limited today, he reflected.

His guts were cramping again.

The *feldwebel* with the Winter War patch spun through the door of the shack a second after another grenadier smacked it with the heel of a field boot. His submachine gun looked like an eighty-eight. Cash hadn't believed his fear could grow stronger.

Honking horns and squealing tires yanked him out of the flashback.

He had run a stop sign. Death's greedy claws had missed him by inches.

The brush calmed him.

He drove past the Groloch house twice. It hadn't changed, yet it now seemed somehow both deadly and dead.

Annie would tell him what to do.

"What're you doing home?" She had been trying to explain macrame to Tran's wife. The boys were watching television and playing chess. Cash had already discovered, to his embarrassment, just how good they were at the latter.

"Honey, I . . . I think I yanked the tiger's tail one time too many." He collapsed into a chair. "I don't know what to do." He rubbed his forehead with his left hand.

"What is it?" She was alarmed now.

"It's John. I . . . I had him sneak into Miss Groloch's place while she was at the funeral yesterday."

"Without a warrant? Stupid. You want to blow your retirement? Norman, I think you've become obsessed. When you start cutting corners—"

"Annie. Please. I know all that. That's not the point. It's already too late to worry about it." His breath came in quick, shallow gasps. "It doesn't look like he ever came out."

Her jaw hung slack for fifteen seconds. "What?"

"John went in and never came out. Just like O'Brien and O'Lochlain's hoods and that Colin Meara kid."

"Oh. Oh, no. Lord, no. Norm, what're we going to do?"

"I don't know. God. I don't know. I wish I did. But all I can think about is what I should've done. I've got to talk it over with Hank, got to do *something*. . . ."

Annie sat on the arm of the chair. "Poor Carrie."

"Poor everybody." The shit was going to hit the fan in a big way. A lot of people were going to get hurt.

"Whatever you do, don't go charging in there after him. Okay? Promise?"

"Honey, I don't think I've got the guts to go in there again, ever. Under any conditions. I'm scared. I mean, like I haven't been since the war."

The German sergeant relaxed, laughed softly, dragged the pale youth from behind the heap of broken peasant furnishings. His smile was neither gloating nor malicious. He removed the M1 from Norm's trembling fingers, handed it to a *landser*, patted Norm's shoulder. "Be okay, Yank." He pulled the ration cigarettes from Cash's pocket, passed them around to his men, stuck one between Cash's lips, put the remainder back where he had found them. He and his men took turns lighting up and warming their hands at the stove whose smoke had given the American away.

And it had worked out. Six days later Cash was holding the rifle and passing out the smokes when counterattacking American troops caught up with them.

But the terror had never let up.

What was Joachim Schleicher doing these days? The stone mason's apprentice who had run away in thirty-eight, at sixteen, to enlist and make his contribution to the New Order, had been a bitter old man at twenty-three. Danzig was in Poland now, wasn't it? Had he even bothered to go home? Might be interesting to trace the sergeant someday.

"Norm?"

"Huh? Oh. Sorry. Funny. I keep getting these flashbacks to the war. It's almost like I'm living it over again."

"You'd better get ahold of yourself."

"I know. I know. I almost had a wreck today. I still don't know what to do."

"There isn't a whole lot you can. You just go see Hank. Before you do *anything*."

"I told you, I'm not going in there again. Not without an army, anyway. You've got me wrong if you think I'm a hero."

Le Quyen appeared from the kitchen with a hot cup of tea, which she offered shyly.

"Thank you, Le Quyen. This'll help." And a few sips did. "That reminds me. I invited Beth Tavares over for supper. Been working her pretty hard. Thought that might help make it up."

"Maybe. She'd probably appreciate a dinner out more."

"You think so? Would you mind?"

"No. Why should I?"

Because she had Monday, when first he had mentioned it. Very much. He didn't comment on her reversal, though. Over the years he had grown accustomed to her inconsistencies, however much they confused him.

"Okay. You're probably right. I'll talk to her. Poor girl. She's put up with a lot this week."

"I think you better go talk to Hank."

"I know. I'm stalling. What the hell's all that racket?"

Tran's sons sped outside. Quang returned long enough to announce, "Fire trucks." He dashed up the street.

It was Dr. Smiley's house, at the west end of the block. The one with the junglelike yard. It looked like a bad fire.

It was the first fire on the block since Cash had moved in.

"Hope he saves his sweaters," Annie observed laconically. "What would he do if he had to go around out of uniform?"

Cash chuckled. Other than for the wilderness state of his yard, Dr. Smiley was known for wearing sweater on sweater, year round, all of them in shades of navy blue.

"Maybe you should see if he needs anything," Cash suggested. The man wasn't a friend, but they had known him for nearly thirty years.

Cash headed for his confrontation with Lieutenant Railsback.

The urge to put it off was so powerful that he drove himself straight into Hank's office. Beth tried to stop him, but he ignored her completely. This had to be done before his nerve collapsed.

"Christ, Norm, what's up? You look like hell."

"I feel like it. I fucked up. I mean all-time, royally, chocolate-covered, in spades fucked up."

Railsback slid around his desk and gently closed the office door. "Bad?"

"The worst. For all of us. The whole department, maybe. But especially for me. And John." He told it all at a machine-gun pace.

Hank surprised him by not blowing up. Beyond agreeing, "You're right. You screwed up like a grand champion."

But Railsback could be that way. When it was too late, when the situation was too serious for yelling, he sometimes didn't.

"Dad!"

Cash had to repeat it all for Hank's father.

"You gotta go in after him," the older man told them.

"I know that," Hank replied. "What I'm wondering is how we can cover ourselves."

"Say you went in after a burglar reported by an anonymous caller. I'll go over to the liquor store and make the call."

"That won't mean shit if the inspector's office starts digging." He was furious behind the calm exterior. There would be hell to pay later. "The first question will be how come Homicide responded to a B-and-E."

Cash stared at the worn oak flooring, tracing the dirt-filled cracks. Why hadn't he let go of this thing?

John. Gone! . . .

"You ain't got no choice."

"I know, Dad. I know." Railsback opened the door. "Tavares! Smith! Tucholski! In here!"

Once they arrived, packing the room painfully tight, till body heat and increased humidity made the place a torture chamber, Railsback explained. "Our idiot friend here, the ghost hunter, the flying saucer man, the part-time time traveler, has managed to lose his partner in his favorite haunted house. We're going in after him. And you ain't telling nobody anything about it, not now, not never, unless you get my say-so. It ain't going to be legal, and so I mean *nobody*, or I'll cut your hearts out and have them on my Wheaties with brown sugar. Do I make myself clear?"

Everyone nodded.

"Good. Tavares, call downstairs for a couple extra shotguns; tear gas; handy-talkies; vests; the works. Tucholski, you, Smith, and Dad will take the backdoor. Me, Norm, and Beth will go in from the front."

"Me, too?" Beth asked from the doorway. She had not yet been permitted into the field, though technically she was a detective in training. Railsback was that kind of boss. Had she had any gumption, she could have forced him to stop using her as a secretary.

"You heard me. This's a family matter. . . . Cash!"

"Eh? Sir?"

"Where's your piece?"

He had to think about it. Contrary to regulations, he almost never carried his weapon. Though there was the riot gun in the trunk of his cruise car. . . .

"In my desk."

"You'll carry it today. And every day from here on in. Hear this, everybody. This's going to be a model squad room starting now. When the inspector's office gets onto our case they aren't going to find a thing. I make myself clear?"

He didn't make them sign in blood, but the thought was there.

There were problems with the equipment, but Railsback lied and bluffed. In ten minutes they were moving, a car for each group. Cash drove and kept his mouth shut. He wasn't about to antagonize Railsback. Not even by observing that his having deputized his father was outright illegal.

Smoke hung heavy over the neighborhood. "Looks like that fire is a real bitch kitty," said Cash.

"Don't want to wish anybody misery," Hank replied, "but it'll help. Everybody for blocks will be over there rubbernecking."

Cash parked. Hank was right. There wasn't a soul on the street.

"That the place, Norm?"

"That's it."

"Spooky," said Beth.

They donned protective vests.

"Me and Norm will go in," said Railsback. "You hang on at the door, Beth. And for God's sake holler if you have to." He handed Cash a shotgun.

The fear was there again.

Beth checked her service revolver, a little frightened, a lot awed. Hank used a handy-talkie to tell Smith and Tucholski to break in the back simultaneously, leaving his father to guard the rear.

When everyone was in position, Railsback ordered, "Go!"

Both doors were unlocked.

Cash went in first, low, just like in training. Hank whirled in behind him.

Norm hadn't known what to expect. Anything but what they did find, which was a whole lot of nothing and no one on the ground floor.

"Smith, watch the stairs. Tucholski, cover us from the basement door while we go down."

Nothing again.

"Okay, we go up."

The second floor looked as though it had just been cleaned for the benefit of company. Gone were the bits of dust Cash had spotted during his previous visit. Hank looked puzzled. Cash's fear began welling up anew. It was too late. Way too late for John. . . .

"Third floor now. Be damned careful."

Cash began shaking. Once again he crouched in a dark and dusty corner while Death stalked him across a cruel French December morning. . . .

He didn't know he had fired till Hank grabbed the shotgun. "What the fuck's the matter with you?"

Feet pounded up the stairs.

Smith shoved past, hurtled into the room ahead, yanked curtains aside. "Ah, shit. A cat. You offed a goddamned cat, Norm."

Old Tom, Miss Groloch's sidekick, was splattered all over the bronze-flowered wallpaper.

Cash threw up.

What else could he do to screw up?

"Hey, you guys," Beth called from below. "You all right? Come on down."

"What're you doing in here?" Railsback demanded. "Get back down there and see if anybody heard that shot."

"We've got an emergency call."

"Nothing in the attic," Tucholski reported. "Looks like she's cleared out. Took the body with her."

"We'd better get out too. Hope nobody's noticed us yet."

That would be too good to be true, Cash thought.

"What is it, Beth?" Railsback demanded.

"Dispatcher called. They want us at that fire. They turned up some bodies, and the fire department says it looks like arson."

"Bodies?" Cash asked, finally calm enough to talk and think. "Doc Smiley lived by himself. Didn't have any relatives or anything."

"Another one?" Smith asked.

"Another what?"

"Old loner."

"Naw. This guy was weird, but he was okay. A doctor.

Refugee. Came over from Europe someplace when the Russians took over. . . . Hmmm.''

"What is it?" Railsback asked.

"Just wondering if there *is* a connection. The old lady disappears just when Smiley's house burns down. . . . Nah, couldn't be. That's too far out. She was a lot older than him. Been here eighty years longer. . . .''

"Worry about it later. Let's show over there before somebody starts wondering what we're up to. Hey, Dad. Come here a minute." He had everyone turn in their raid gear. "Put that stuff in Tucholski's car, then move it around front. Then keep an eye on the place till we get back. Let's go, you guys. We might as well walk. We won't get a parking place much closer.''

He was right. The fire-chasers had parked up everything from Russell on south.

It was bad.

The firemen were still hosing the rubble to cool it. Though most of the brickwork remained standing, the house was a complete loss.

The battalion chief led them around to a basement entrance his men had wrecked. "In there.''

Half the wooden parts of the structure had collapsed into the basement, carrying with them furnishings from all three floors. Charred floor joists and wall studs lay tangled like giant pickup sticks. Smoke and steam still rose, and the bricks still held a lot of heat. A man couldn't spend much time close enough to look inside.

There had been cities in Germany and France that had looked like this.

Had Cash not thrown up already, he would have now. Smith did. Iron-gut Tucholski, who claimed to have seen it all, gagged. Hank refused to let Beth close enough to see.

Parts of two bodies, burned till little but steaming skeletons remained, protruded from beneath the wreckage. One seemed to be that of a child.

"Smell's enough to gag a maggot," Hank observed. He held a wet handerchief over his face. To the battalion chief, "How long before you can start digging them out?"

"Going to be a couple hours before we're sure it's cool enough, and that it won't flare up again. And we'll have to scare up a crane. . . . Jesus, it's going to be a job. Somebody really torched it. Whole place must've been soaked down with gas, it went up so fast. We're just lucky this was a corner lot and the one next door was vacant.''

"You sure it was arson?"

"Positive. Smell the gas?"

Railsback sniffed. So did Cash. Both wrinkled their noses. The stench of burnt flesh seemed to override all other odors. "Must take a trained sniffer," Cash gasped.

A creak and groan came from above. A half-dozen rafters plunged into the basement, kicking up a cloud of ash.

"Back!" someone shouted. "Get back! The whole damned thing's going."

He was wrong. It was just a chimney, but the crash was enough to scatter the crowd. Hose teams rushed to soak live coals exposed by the falling bricks.

"Better keep your people back, Lieutenant," said the battalion chief. "The whole thing might collapse. Or we might not have the natural gas all the way off. . . . Wish the tourists would go home."

Cash thought they were well behaved. Awe seemed to have held all but the boldest at a safe distance. The youngsters were the troublesome ones.

He and the other officers formed a little skirmish line clique before the ruin, staying out of the fire department's way, asking neighbors their opinions about what had happened. More police, hospital, and civil defense types kept showing up. The arson squad descended like a swarm of locusts.

Ten o'clock came. Railsback and Cash were still there. Annie, Tran, and Tran's sons had done yeoman service running coffee and sandwiches. Tran had even pitched in to help excavate the bodies. The work didn't seem to bother him. Plenty of practice, Cash supposed.

There were four of them. Not enough remained to tell much just by looking, but they seemed, by size, to have been young.

"You know," said Railsback, "I'll bet they're the ones who started it. I been talking to people. They say this Smiley was always having trouble with kids. They might've been going to show him with a little fire that got out of control and trapped them."

"Yeah? Where's all the mothers crying, 'Oh my baby?' The only trouble he had was kids using his yard for a shortcut."

"What kind of guy was he?" Hank asked, watching the last

plastic bag disappear into the last ambulance.

"I don't know. What do you mean? I knew him for thirty years, but not very well. He was a private sort of guy. Saw him more at the neighborhood association meetings than any other time."

"I just wondered. Can't tell what it was anymore, but he had a lot of strange stuff in his basement."

Cash shrugged. He hadn't noticed. But he hadn't done much looking. "He says he was a doctor in the old country. I don't think he ever practiced here. Never did anything but hang around his house and go to stamp-club meetings. He was some kind of expert on rare stamps. The whole third floor of his house was filled with stamp albums and books about stamps. Like to drove me crazy talking about it the one time I went over there."

"You see anything strange?"

"No. Except for the stamp collections the house was the same as any other place on the street. I never went in the basement, though."

"Hospital-type stuff. Yeah. That's what it was."

"Now you mention it . . ." The basement had looked a lot like a ruined intensive care ward.

"Think he might have been in the abortion business before it was legal?"

"Without us ever getting a hint?"

Railsback shrugged. "I'll believe anything anymore. Not much we can do here now. Shit! I forgot about the Old Man. Smith or Tucholski say anything about taking him in?"

"I don't think so." Cash was too tired to think. And he still had to go back to the station for his own car. He handed Hank the keys to the police vehicle. "Why don't you get the car, check on your dad, then pick up me and Beth at my house?" Beth had fled thither after her first glimpse of a burned corpse.

"Okay."

As Cash strolled homeward with Tran, the major asked, "What became of your partner? His wife and your daughter-in-law were at your house when I returned from work. They were upset."

"Oh, I don't need that."

"Pardon?"

"I'm wiped out. I don't think I can cope with Carrie tonight." He quickly explained what he and John had done, and that John had vanished. Just like O'Brien, four hoods, and a twelve-year-old detective.

"And now the woman's disappeared too?"

"Slick. But I got a good idea where she went. Hank gives me fifteen minutes tomorrow, I'll find out for sure. She's got a brother or uncle or something in New York that she doesn't know we know about. She'll go there."

Annie had managed to get rid of Carrie and Nancy somehow. He didn't ask, just collapsed into a chair and listened bemusedly to Beth and Le Quyen, who were carrying on an animated conversation. Friday would be another along day, and during it he would have to tell Carrie the truth.

And Teri, too.

His life was closing in. His job was polluting it, and he was losing his zest.

He didn't get to bed till one, and then only with Hank's hard, "Be in bright and early, Cash!" still ringing in his ears.

XXII. On the Z Axis; 1969–1973; Huang's Academy

Michael had been there for two years. His teachers had succeeded. He now could not remember ever having been anything but a Maoist. Once, maybe, an unawakened Maoist. But never an enemy of the people. It had been his awakening social conscience that had driven him to enlist in the imperialist army. So he could learn its ways against the day the Revolution came.

He could scarcely wait for the war's end. He dreamed of carrying the truth to family and friends.

He gloried in having been the first American graduate student, and the first of his class chosen to instruct his countrymen. He was now the official greeter of new classes, and one of the senior American staffers. From his humble beginnings here he might one day rise to command an army of liberation.

There wee signs that the potential had begun to develop at home. The marches, the excitement at last summer's Democratic Party National Convention, seemed so promising. It was time for a man, an American Mao or Ho.

Michael believed Huang was grooming him for big things.

The school had a name so typically, so Chinese communistically, hyperbolic that Michael found it embarrassing to repeat. In English it came out resembling: Institute of Imperialist Recidivist Reeducation for the Purpose of the Establishment of a Peace-Loving People's Guided Democratic Republic of the United States of America. It sounded better in Chinese.

Michael suspected that the director himself found the name

both tedious and ludicrous and had chosen it in hopes the fascist intelligence agencies would discount it as a fraud or red herring.

The academy's mission was to produce agent-larvae who would, eventually, devour the rotten fruit of capitalism from its core outward after their repatriation. Only an honored few men were to be reserved, at war's end, for later special employment on behalf of the director.

Michael's dream of bearing the light to his near and dear was pure fantasy. He already knew that he was one of the elect stay-behinds.

What he didn't know was that his selection wasn't an honor. He hadn't been chosen as the American Mao. Those chosen to remain forever MIA were the moral weaklings, the personalities incapable of withstanding the heat of the forges of pre-Revolution. Michael had been singled out as a loser, as a blade good for but one stroke. In the long run he was as expendable as a hand grenade.

Let him dream his dreams of becoming mighty among the socialist mighty. They did no harm, and kept him usefully eager.

The academy's population was never large, and the lot of a confirmed collaborator was loneliness. The weakness of character that made shifting allegiances easy was such that even defectors secretly loathed it in one another.

Michael Cash didn't have a single friend inside.

So it was that he awaited Snake's arrival with rising excitement.

But people change. Time, separation, and hardship devour the commonalities that form the bedrock of friendship. Michael and Snake had lived out two years in radically different environments. They had worked toward radically different goals. They were no longer the two pained, frightened, bewildered GIs who had shared the march up the Ho Chi Minh trail.

Snake wanted nothing more than to get the essential spark that was his *self* through this purgatory unconquered.

"Hey, man!" said Michael as Cantrell came toward him, down the ramp, beneath the cold-eyed desert stars. "Hey! Two years."

His pleasure was genuine and absolute. He had missed Snake's stubborn strength. "Really good to see you. How have they been treating you? I heard they gave you to Chico and Fidel for a while. They tell me those guys play rough. That's why I been busting my ass trying to get you here. Things are better here. You'll see."

While Michael's mouth motored, Snake limped along beside him, following the other new students. The bone hadn't set properly. The two Cubans, who operated out of their country's Hanoi embassy, had refused to let the camp doctor see him. Their specialty was breaking spirits. Sometimes they shattered bones trying to shatter hope.

They had met their match in Snake Cantrell. Snake hadn't had a hope to lose, nor an illusion to kill, for a decade.

He regarded Michael from the edge of his vision. His expression remained unreadable. Sometimes it threatened to become amusement, contempt, compassion, or sorrow, but always it faded before taking real life. He spoke only in response to direct questions.

Even there in the night Michael's apparel betrayed him. Spartan, a curious hybrid of Chinese Army and American work clothing, it did not resemble POW wear at all. The shiny new first lieutenant's insignia were a dead giveaway.

They passed through a camouflaged entrance into a long, steep stairwell illuminated by dull red lights which came to life only after the door closed. Posters and pennants clung to the pale green flaking paint on the concrete walls, sad imitations of college dormitory decor. Each proclaimed some gem of genius from Chairman Mao. Two years of study hadn't made the meaning of most any less impenetrable to Michael.

Snake broke step, frowned at one especially foggy quotation.

"I think you have to *be* Chinese," Michael observed. He felt euphoric, daring. "I guess the first thing should be to show everybody where they bunk. Then you and me can go down to the cafeteria. Shoot the shit about what's been happening. How long since you've had a cup of coffee? Or bacon and eggs? Or a real American cigarette? We've got it whipped here, Snake."

It took only minutes to settle the new class. It consisted of just twenty men, and Cash had done most of the work beforehand. He had tagged bunks and lockers. Issue clothing—sized according to information received from the Vietnamese—and study materials were in place. Soap, towels, blankets, and so forth, he had placed in the lockers. It was an inspection-ready barracks. Occupants were all it needed to bring it to life.

Michael worked hard, wanting to impress his new masters as much as the minions of his old.

"Gentlemen, my name is Michael Cash," he announced after the men had located their bunks and lockers. "I'll be your platoon leader during your first week here. The setup is pretty much like your academies, OCS, or basic. But there'll be no saluting. Your ranks will have no weight. We're all equals here.

"Now, today is a free day. Tomorrow we begin orientation. You'll find a daily schedule posted on the bulletin board. It'll be your responsibility to be at the right place at the right time. The schedule consists of the usual mix of physical fitness, classroom instruction, and testing. In addition, there will be daily periods of self-criticism. At the end of the week you'll be assigned individualized courses of instruction.

"During free time you can wander around, use the library, the rec room, or the cafeteria, as you see fit. The Chinese have gone to a lot of trouble to make us comfortable. Keep their facilities orderly and clean.

"In that vein, you'll find a duty roster posted with the daily schedule. It isn't rough. Comes to about an hour per man per day. Nor is it rigid. If you want to trade off, it's all right with me. Just let me know so I can pass the word to your supervisors.

"Do the same thing with any problems that come up. Most of them I should be able to handle in a few minutes. This is a quiet, efficient institution, geared to your wants and needs. You'll find it a welcome change."

Michael had worked hard on his speech, shaping it on the past half-dozen classes. He was proud of it. Its reward was the doubt and surprise he saw in his audience. Each minim of uncertainty was a bridgehead for their reeducation.

"Lieutenant."

"Yes?"

The speaker showed traces of gray at his temples. He was, probably, the senior officer present.

"Where are we? What the hell is this place?"

The man was less calm than he pretended. Michael remembered his own distress on arriving. Though the process was smoother these days, the new students were given no more idea as to their fate. Having seen fellow prisoners disappear forever, they would be in terror for their lives.

The contrast between violent expectation and apparent pacificity were part of the academy's program to generate uncertainty.

"You'll get most of your answers in your first class tomorrow. I couldn't tell you where we are. I don't really know, but we're in the People's Republic of China, somewhere in Sinkiang province. Closer than that, only the director knows. And he wouldn't tell you.

"As to what the place is, it's a school." He said no more. They would learn soon enough.

There were more questions in the same vein. He evaded them. "I suggest you shift into the uniform you'll find in your locker. Shower if you like. Then wander around. Get to know the installation. Signs or the Chinese staff will let you know—politely—if you're headed into a restricted area. I'll be in the cafeteria with Sergeant Cantrell if anybody needs me. If you smoke, cigarettes can be obtained there, on request. One of the rules, though, is that you have to smoke them there. Same for food and drink. In the interest of cleanliness and sanitation. Sergeant Cantrell?"

"Let me grab a shower first, eh, Mike? You been here two years. Maybe you forgot what it's like, smelling yourself all the time."

Michael was full of talk, bursting with words. He waited impatiently. A Lieutenant Vlassic tried to pump him, but retreated with an expression of horror when he suddenly realized Cash's true status. His reaction didn't faze Michael. He knew his truths better than any new student. Vlassic would be around to his way of thinking sooner than he believed possible. Very few men were difficult, and none of those were ever written off by the director.

In its grossest, simplest form, the academy hinged on positive and negative reinforcement. A bell rings. Salute, get a treat. Fail to do so, receive a shock.

Michael had been a good boy. Snake was one of his treats.

All men are lonely. Each battles the loneliness in his own way, comes to terms with it in his unique fashion. Michael's means of fending it off was to befriend newcomers, taking one or two from each class under his wing. The relationships never endured, though. He seemed to consume them. Within weeks his "friends" began evading him, began finding ways to detach themselves from him.

He never learned that the fault was in himself, that he approached the relationships as a spider approaches a fly. He sucked their substance and gave very little in return. Just material things, or the few little privileges within his power to grant.

That he was a chronic whiner, and absolutely refused to risk any self-responsibility or initiative, didn't help. People got tired of listening to him.

"Christ, that felt good," said Snake, clomping from the shower. "Have to wear anything special to this cafeteria? I'm ready for coffee and a smoke. Going to grab all I can before they bring on the thumbscrews."

"No special uniform. We only have one, a working uniform. And it isn't that way at all."

Snake gave him his most cynical look. "Who are you trying to snow?"

Michael shuffled nervously, embarrassedly. Some students did have it bad. But they made it tough on themselves.

Cash hadn't always been a sorry nebbish, nor would he always be one. Not to his present neurotic extent.

The long march to prison camp, entirely at the mercy of brutal captors, dodging the bombs, shells, and ambushes of his own side, while suffering dysentary and the ravages of tropical diseases, had shaped him more than any five years of prior life.

Snake it had only made more the way he was.

Of the twenty-three prisoners who had begun the trek, only Michael, Snake, and three others had survived.

In his way, Cash was tougher than most men. But he couldn't suffer in silence, nor could he take an uncompromising stand.

For six months he had devoted his whole being to survival. And he had managed. At the cost of having had his personality hammered to a shape suited to no more noble purpose.

Evangelic espousal of the Maoist faith was another reason friends didn't last. Americans tend to isolate and shun zealots.

Michael, initially, was as abrasive as a brand new Jehovah's Witness, by damned going to bring salvation to the unbeliever even if he had to manage it at bayonet point. Later he learned to pursue more subtle paths to conversion.

His evangelism suited the director. New students needed a focus for their hatred. Diffuse, undirected emotion remained hard to tap, to channel, to control.

Snake said little till they had filled their meal trays and had seated themselves. He sipped coffee, smoked half a Marlboro, stared at his tray. "Makes you light-headed after doing without for so long. And more food than we used to get in two days."

"They take good care of us here. You can go back for more if you want."

"Why?"

"Try those pancakes. Like Mom used to make."

Michael had just begun to appreciate the investment that had gone into this place. Where, in Red China, did you find a cook able to whip up a midwestern breakfast and make it taste Iowa on a frosty autumn morning? Where did you get ham, bacon, eggs, sausage, grits, biscuits, gravy, cornbread, cereal, to prepare to each man's taste? Twenty-four brands of cigarettes. Coke, Pepsi, and Seven-Up. Bud, Busch, Burgie, Coors, Hamm's, Miller's, Pabst, Schlitz, and a dozen others, in a beer cooler that was open two hours every evening. . . .

All the comforts of home. But no *Playboy* in the library. No newspapers or periodicals from home, except the like of the *Daily Worker*, and especially selected excerpts from editorial columns.

Snake didn't press. He downed half his meal before noting, "I thought there'd be more people around. They kept taking guys out of every camp I was ever in."

Only two Americans not of the new class were around. Like Michael, they were graduates.

"This is just the orientation center. Only gets used when there's a new class. The main installation is huge. And getting bigger every day." Chinese life-termers, condemned to see the sun nevermore, provided the labor digging the academy ever deeper and larger. "We have six national divisions, all separate, all broken up into as many independent sections as are necessary. The American division is the biggest right now, but the Russian and Burmese are pretty big too." He frowned, wondering why that should be. Nobody knew what the hell was going on outside. The isolation kept you from finding out from anybody who had been there recently. Guys from the camps only knew what had happened before their capture.

It was like living on the moon, trying to follow current events through a telescope.

He shouldn't be telling Snake anything. It wasn't his job. "Most of our graduates go back to special camps."

That hadn't always been the plan. But the threat of commando raids aimed at rescuing POWs had made the director decide that someone should be available for recapture.

Then, too, he was unsure of the extent and efficacy of the CIA networks in the North. He feared a constant, unexplained depletion of prisoner populations would alert the enemy. As it was, the operation limped, crippled by balky, obstinate Vietnamese officials. The middle echelons, it seemed, cooperated as little as possible.

Security was the reason, of course. Only Ho and General Giap had ever been in the know.

Graduates were kept quarantined, doing post-graduate work, being brought ever more into line. The hypnotic treatments, needed to make the majority ignorant of what they were, was delicate, took ages to perfect, and occasionally needed reinforcement.

Michael spent another hour introducing Snake to his new world.

"Mike, I've had it," Cantrell finally protested. "I've got to sleep."

Cash harkened back to his own long, harrowing plane ride. "Sure. I understand. Go ahead. I'll see you in the morning."

Michael retreated to his own room, a bedroom-office off the dormitory. He lay on his bunk a long time, staring at the concrete ceiling.

Snake was still Snake. He was still Michael Cash. But Time had been nurturing one of its infamous treasons. The old bond, wrought between men who had helped one another survive a prisonward hell march, had worn.

He hadn't been there to share and ease the pain when Snake had taken the injuries to his leg and soul. Snake hadn't been here. They just hadn't shared in too long.

A single tear dribbled from Michael's right eye. He brushed it away irritably. Then he moved to his desk, to lose himself in his language studies.

Little of his graduate work was Marxist. The director wanted his special men to have skills making them suitable for the widest possible employment. Michael was pursuing a curriculum ranging from hard science to the softest liberal arts. It was more intense than any he had known in college. And he had his duties as well.

This was higher education without the beer parties and football. And girls.

Michael hardly remembered what a woman was anymore.

In that way the institution mirrored its director thoroughly.

The first class Monday was a simple and honest, if incomplete, lecture describing the academy and its purpose. Michael sat at the back and made notes. Each little reaction went down. A committee of instructors would review them before making course assignments.

The next session was an introduction to Marxist thought. The twenty students fidgeted under a barrage of ideas they found offensive. A navy flier named Jorgenson thundered "Bullshit!" during a cataloging of the crimes of American capitalist-imperialism.

The instructor peeped over round-lensed, wire-framed glasses quizzically, glanced at Cash, continued.

Jorgenson came to Michael during lunch.

"Lieutenant, you said tell you our problems. I've got one. The Chink cocksucker on the chow line won't let me have any coffee or cigarettes. How come? He let everybody else."

Cash glanced at the man's tray. Standard meal. Water to drink. Good. He nodded, ignoring Jorgenson's defiance. "So I see."

"Well, how come? Why me? You said—"

"Mealtimes make good times to reflect on our shortcomings. On our egoisms and willful errors. Reflect while you eat."

Michael caught Snake's thoughtful look. He understood.

Jorgenson ate in silence. He had figured it out too.

These early lessons would be gentle, subtle. Resistance, the director felt, could be more easily disarmed that way.

From that luncheon on Snake was the worst offender. And Cash knew he meant to ease the pressure on the others. He could handle the shit. It had nothing to do with any feud with the Chinese Communists. He loathed them no more than other Statists.

Orientation week dragged.

Michael had a tough night Saturday. His assignment recommendations were due.

Snake was his best friend in this half of the world. Not once had Cantrell condemned him for his change of faith, nor had he been less friendly than in the past, despite the new distance between them. But the man wouldn't let their friendship shape his behavior.

Therefore, Michael decided, neither could he.

And he had to protect himself. . . .

He finally signed that last bitter recommendation.

Snake now faced what the staff called Intensive Reeducation.

Snake, being Snake, would understand. And probably not hold a grudge. He was, himself, a disciple of the doctrine of doing what had to be done.

He was still in Intensive when, a month later, on the eve of the arrival of his next class, Michael finally found the nerve to check on his friend.

They had put Snake into the Crystal Palace, a hexagonal, furnitureless, featureless cell where all the surfaces were mirrors. One-way. Snake couldn't see out but his tormentors could see in. Powerful kliegs pushed enough light through to keep the interior blindingly bright. Sometimes the technicians added deafening white sound, though they preferred recordings of Snake's own mad ravings. Sometimes they turned up the heat, or starved him, or made him do without water. They never actually touched him, let him see them, or did him physical harm. Harm was forbidden by the director. The goal was a broken will, not a broken body.

He had to be made to feel alone. Naked and alone. Not a stitch of clothing, never a human touch or word. That had pushed many a stubborn man past his limit.

But Snake had been alone all his life.

While he was on a no-sleep program the technicians would give him an electric shock if he threatened to drift off. Or they might set the gimbled cell slowly spinning and tumbling.

He was supposed to lose his belief in the fixity, the predictability of his environment, and in elementary concepts of fairness. He was supposed to begin hating the men he saw reflected wherever he looked. Once he wanted rid of the old Snake, the academy staff would begin building him a new one. In a more useful mold.

But Snake had been through all that before, on his own, and had put himself together in his present form.

"How's he coming?" Michael asked the technician on duty.

"Slow. Can't seem to reach him. He just takes it. You know him. Any ideas?"

"I never knew him under normal conditions. From what he told me, he never lived normally. His father was a wife-beater, child batterer, and child molester. He just hid back inside himself so far that nothing could reach him. Before he ever got to high school, let alone the army."

"Is he afraid of anything?"

"Not that I know of. I don't think he even cares if he stays alive. If you kill him, he figures he's beaten you that way too. He's never had anything to lose. How do you get a handle on a guy like that?"

"Every man holds something too precious to lose." The technician consulted his charts, pushed a button. The Crystal Palace began tumbling slowly. "Next time he passes out I'll move him to the Closet. See how he likes that. He's got me ready to start experimenting."

"Why not bring him out, shape him up, and run him through orientation again? See how he reacts to a chance to get into a less rigorous program. Let the contrasts sink in. If he doesn't reform, give him the Closet at the end of the week."

The Closet was a cell sixty centimeters by sixty centimeters by two meters high. Not absolutely impossible. But all its faces were featureless, and there was no light or sound once its door closed. It had broken some tough men.

Michael hoped Snake wouldn't have to go in. He dreaded the Closet so much himself that he willingly risked compromising himself to save his friend that hell.

"It might help. All right. Pick him up tomorrow afternoon."

Michael scarcely concealed his relief.

He owed Snake. Maybe his life, from the march. . . .

"What're his interests? His politics?"

"Music was the only thing he cared about. Only time I heard him complain was when a Vietnamese soldier stole his harmonica. He could play the guitar, too, and, I think, the piano. He was in a band before he joined the army. Politically, you'd have to call him an anarchist."

"Bakuninite?"

"No. Nothing that nihilist. He just wants government to

leave him alone. Not to tax him, or draft him, or to do things to him for his own good. I really don't think he can understand the differences between Marxism and capitalism. All he sees is that states *are* states. They all impose on their citizens."

This was dangerous stuff. For his own welfare he shouldn't be saying it, even to express Snake's beliefs.

But the technician just looked bewildered. The ideas were too alien. Cash didn't go on. It would be like explaining color to a man blind from birth.

"I'll fix a bunk for him then. Tomorrow afternoon, right? Well, I'd better get moving. Got things to do before the plane gets in." He wanted out before the technician got to thinking that Snake might contaminate the incoming class.

Michael stared into the Crystal Palace for several seconds, though, before he left. His guts tightened into a walnut of agony. Snake, why can't you just go along? he wondered. Fake it if you have to, dammit.

He put the thought to Cantrell the following Friday, once it became certain that he faced Intensive again.

Snake was spacy all week. He needed guiding through anything he didn't know as old military routine.

"No," Cantrell replied, eyes fixed on some distant illusion of peace.

Cash, perhaps wishfully, had expected Snake to be eager to please after the Crystal Palace. But obstinance possessed the man. It kept tearing through his remoteness all week.

"Why the hell not?" Try to help a guy . . .

"I can't."

"Snake, please!" He fought to keep his voice soft, his expression neutral. There would be observers.

A thin, weak smile stretched Cantrell's lips. "Thanks, Mike." For an infinitesimal fraction of a second his fingers touched the back of the hand Michael held squeezed into a bloodless fist. His touch was light as a spider's kiss. "You don't understand. You never will. You can't. Not without being me."

It took Cash two years to figure out what Snake had been thanking him for. For Snake's sake that was just as well. It would have been used against him earlier.

He was thanking Michael for caring. No one in his past ever had.

Cantrell did his month in the Closet. Then they dusted him

off and ran him through orientation again.

And he failed again.

And they did it all over again.

For Michael's sake.

Other Intensives were not so favored. Few proved as stubborn.

The pilots talked a good fight. They arrived believing they could hold up. But they didn't have the background, the experience, the stamina. A comfortable middle-class American upbringing prepared no one for the overwhelming psychic pressures of the director's program.

Huang and his minions quietly humored Michael's friendship for purely pragmatic reasons. Converts, even flawed, were going to be too few, too precious, in proportion to the population of their native land. Statistically, it looked like the institute would be lucky to produce a hundred fully employable agents for each year the war dragged on. Many students, though not as recalcitrant as Snake nor as weak as Michael, just could not be programmed reliably. This large group, therefore, would be activated only in an extreme emergency.

And of the prime graduates no more than a handful could be expected to reach critical policy-making positions. The director couldn't program a man for competence.

So no chance was being overlooked. Especially as Michael's evaluators had begun to detect a genius for administrating the conversion of his countrymen in their subject, a genius they intended to test to its limits.

A leader he was not. He lacked all charisma. But, after four years of training, a better pillar for a throne, or a puppet master pulling strings from behind a throne, Huang could not have asked.

Yet Michael was never so devout a Maoist that maltreatment of his friend might not alienate him. That was one face of Marxism-as-practiced that he just couldn't internalize. He couldn't abandon a friend for the good of the state.

By then, because of his talents, he loomed so large in the director's plan that he might one day be in a positon to destroy it.

Snake's education, therefore, remained wholly under Michael's control.

Nevertheless, Snake endured it all—for his own good. Michael shed his tears, but hit the man with every psychological assault ever devised, every nonlethal persuasion ever invented. Only torture and death were tools forbidden the technicians.

Not only did Snake resist the Maoist faith, he refused to recant any other.

So they finally discarded him. But, like a cracked cup that might come in handy someday—perhaps as leverage on Michael—not completely. The director kept him on a back shelf.

Two years later Snake Cantrell was just another tunnel miner, fed, worked, and ignored. He had won. The staff had given up on him. His only service could be to help the academy grow.

While Cantrell hauled baskets of broken rock, Michael studied, trained and administered. He became a brilliant marksman, superior in hand-to-hand, and, in exercises, revealed a strong sixth sense for personal danger. He rapidly soared to the top of the academy's heirarchy. As the years marched, he, and the elect stay-behinds and men who would be repatriated as "live," aware Chinese agents, gradually took command of the American division.

In July 1972, Michael assumed the post of director of curricula for the entire institution. He was the senior officer inside, answerable only to Huang himself.

His cozy little world began fraying almost immediately. The director called within the month.

"Damn Henry Kissinger!" he exploded after breaking the connection.

What was he going to do?

He had known it was coming, someday, but had hoped the petty bickering about table shapes and such would delay the inevitable a lot longer than it had.

Without the war he would be out of a job.

He summoned his administrative assistant.

"Dwight, I just talked to the Old Man," he told Jorgenson. "He said get ready to close up shop. Peace is going to break out any day now."

"We're going home?" The man seemed to glow.

"That's the word. Maybe as soon as six months. So we've got to close the American division down, get everybody back to the camps, and clean up the evidence." He never mentioned that some two hundred men would be staying. That would be the most carefully guarded secret of all. Only those staying would know. No one had more potential usefulness, the director felt, than a man who didn't exist.

"Physical plant shouldn't be much problem," Michael mused. "We'll just turn off the lights on our way out. Personnel, though . . . bring me the lists. I'll have to work out who goes where in a way that'll maximize security."

"Aren't you excited?" Jorgenson couldn't hold still.

Michael could only think of a wife and children he would never see. . . . Well, he had made his choice. It was as much for their sakes. . . . He hoped Nancy would find herself a good man. The kids would need a father. . . . No. No need to worry. Mom would make sure. . . .

He shoved them out of his mind. Remembering hurt too much.

"Of course. My kids . . . they'll be in school by now. . . . But it's so sudden, and there's so much to do. Find me those lists, then go see who wants to claim some of our American space. Samarov has been bugging me since I took over. Give him anything he thinks Russian division can use. Check with Burmese and Indian, too, for sure. They're doing a lot of business. We'll have a staff meeting this weekend. I want to carve up the pie before Peking cuts the budget or moves some other operation in here."

Michael studied the personnel lists the rest of that month. Men had to be placed precisely, according to their preparation and how knowledgeable they were. The least little error . . .

Time and again his treacherous eyes stopped at:

37. CANTRELL, A.O. 314 07 54 E-5 US Army 8 July 67 05 3 Jan 70
38. CANTRELL, W.J. 05798-69 0-3 US Navy 19 Dec 71 02 12 July 72

An accidental transposition . . . ?

And Snake went home while a young lieutenant from the last class admitted disappeared among the excavator crews.

XXIII. On the Y Axis; 1975

Old Man Railsback was prancing like a kid in desperate need of a visit to the bathroom. Cash didn't ask why. He had arrived fifteen minutes early, trying to beat everyone in. But Hank had gotten there ahead of him anyway.

"Come on in here, Norm," the lieutenant called from his lair.

Cash entered on tiptoe, perpetually poised to flee.

"Sit down. And settle down. The shit ain't going to hit the fan just yet." He shoved the door closed. "Purely business."

"Well?"

"First, soon as Gardner comes through with a warrant, we start taking the Groloch place apart. Brick by brick. I got a feeling we're in for some surprises." He kept fingering the edges of something that looked like a very old, hand-drawn, extremely complicated circuit diagram.

"Huh? Why?"

"Well, I not only got idiots in my squad, I've got them in my family. After we left for the fire, the old man tossed the place."

"But . . ." He wanted to ask why he hadn't been told last night.

"Yeah. After I warned him. After what happened to the Kid. After all the time he spent on the force. But he has a mind of his own. And he wants to help, you know what I mean? To be useful, to impress the rest of us. This time it paid off." He rolled his chair back, opened a side drawer, tossed two large, stringbound bundles onto the desktop. "He thought these might be important. He's probably right, but not as right as he

192

wants to be. A few more nails in her coffin, maybe."

One bundle consisted of gold notes. Twenties. Cash suspected he knew the amount without counting. The second bundle, far larger, was made up of old letters still in their original envelopes. There were more than a hundred.

"The counterfeit?" The bills looked fresh, despite their age. Even if they were real, only a bank would accept them.

He picked up a handful of envelopes after Hank cut the string with his nail clippers. The lieutenant admitted that he had been through them already. Hadn't the man slept at all?

"A nice collection of covers." They sketched eighty years of turbulent postal history clearly, beginning with envelopes franked with stamps of the Austro-Hungarian Empire, then stamps of Austria and Hungary overprinted *Czeskoslovenka*, several dozen regular Czech issues of the prewar period, and, on the last few envelopes, Sudetenland provisionals and stamps of the German puppet-protectorate, Bohemia and Moravia. Scattered among the predominate PRAGA postmarks were several indicating that Miss Groloch's correspondent had on occasion wandered into Germany, Poland, Hungary, Austria, and Romania.

"Nothing since the war."

"Since before we got into it, really."

A December 17, 1940, postmark was the most recent. The envelope had been rubber-stamped with censor marks and numerous backstamps indicating the circuitous routing followed by mail coming out of the Greater German Reich. The St. Louis backstamp, indicating date received, was March 6, 1942.

Cash opened that one.

"Your old man can read German, can't he?"

"Yeah. Only these aren't in German. I seen enough when I was a kid to know that."

Cash looked again. "You're right. Czech? Or Slovak?"

Railsback shrugged. "Whatever they talk over there, I guess."

"There aren't any American letters."

"From what Dad told me about the place he found these, there might have been. He said it looked like somebody had taken another bundle out of there."

"She took them with her." Cash smiled. "Because she didn't want to give Rochester away. She's crafty all right. Except that I've already got the angle on her there. I already know."

"Which probably means there's nothing in these we can use. Maybe she even left them to distract us." Railsback tried to put a rubber band around the envelopes. It snapped, stinging him. He cursed. Next try he broke the pile into several bundles. "I'd have you check those bills with your friend the hood, only I want you checking the airport, bus station, and what not."

"She went to Rochester."

"Maybe. Check it. Use Beth if you want. Smith and Tucholski are tied up with this fire thing."

"Hank, I want to go up there."

"Where?"

"New York."

"You've got to be shitting me."

"I mean it. She's old. She'll go by train. I could take a plane and be there waiting for her."

"And then what?"

He hadn't thought about it. "I don't know. Maybe bluff her. . . ."

"Aren't you a little scared? I mean, she's burned seven or eight guys already."

"No." He said it with surprise. "No. You know, I think the house made the difference. I feel like I've won just by getting her out of it."

"Yeah? Well, get on the road. I want to know how she left and where she went."

"I'm going up there, Hank. If I have to pay out of my own pocket."

"Yeah. Sure. Meantime, get on the job I just gave you."

Beth had arrived while they were closeted. Cash whispered with her for a minute, then turned to Old Man Railsback, who was grinning. "Bad as me, eh?"

The elder Railsback chuckled.

"You're not doing anything this morning, you can do me a couple favors."

"Such as?"

"Make it down to St. John Nepomuk Church, Twelfth and Lafayette, and see if the priest can put you on to anybody who could translate those letters for us. Then take one of those bills down to the Feds and see if it's kosher. Only one. We don't want them grabbing the whole damned pile yet."

"Okay. It's something to do."

Damned but it was going to be rough learning to do without John. He was going to have to do his own legwork.

Cash followed his railroad hunch and visited Union Station first. And yes, the ticket agent remembered the little old lady with the foreign accent. But he didn't remember where she had gone. The Amtrak ticket records—of course—were screwed up beyond hope.

"That's what you get when you let the government fuck around with things," Cash grumbled as he walked back to his car, a rail schedule in hand.

She had pulled out Thursday morning. Assuming the usual foul-ups and delays, a plane should get him into Rochester well ahead of her.

He paused to call Beth. "Norm. Yeah. I was right. She took the train. No. Hold off telling him. I'm going to slide home and talk it over with Annie. And I've still got to tell John's wife. You make my reservation? Good girl. Talk to you later."

"You get suspended?" Annie demanded when he popped in. She had been watching Tran, who was to work the evening shift today, engage his elder son in a game of chess.

"No. I just snuck away. Wanted to tell you that I've got to go to New York."

"New York? When?"

"Tonight."

"What the hell for?"

"Because that's where Miss Groloch went. She took the Amtrak. I'm going to be in Rochester waiting when she gets there."

Annie's eyes narrowed suspiciously. Her mouth tightened into a severe little red scar. "This Hank's idea?"

"No."

"I didn't think so. Are you nuts? Just have the Rochester police pick her up."

"I know. I could. But I can't. It's something I've got to do. I don't know why. Call it an intuition."

"I'll call it what it is. It's a damned fool obsession is what, Norman."

"Look, dammit, that witch probably *killed* John. John Harald. Remember him? Michael's best friend? And it looks like she'll get away with it, just like all the others. Into her house and good-bye world."

"Calm down, Norm."

"No. I won't. I'm pissed. At me, at her, at a damned system that can't keep her from doing it again, at everything. John was my friend, Annie. The least I can do is save Carrie from having to go through the same shit as Nancy."

"Come on. Be reasonable. You can't go roaring off up there like some Wild West bounty hunter. They only do things that way in Clint Eastwood movies."

"I know. I know. Beth's making arrangements through Frank Segasture. The guy I met during the FBI course back when. You remember. We went clubbing with him and his wife after we graduated. The one who always talked about his uncle in Miami. I've got it all worked out."

"I'll bet. You're always jumping in without looking."

"I just wanted to tell you so you could get my things together: clothes; traveler's checks; my checkbook; some cash. . . ."

"You've got it all worked out. Sure. Sometimes you're worse than a ten-year-old."

Oh, she sounds bitter, Cash thought.

"You bothered to tell Carrie yet? That's your job, you know."

"I haven't. Not yet."

"What about his girl friend?"

"Huh? What girl friend?"

"Don't be coy with me, Norman. I can still figure things out for myself sometimes."

"Yeah. Well."

" 'Yeah. Well.' We'll talk about it sometime. Right now you'd just better get back to work and forget about going any-where."

The phone rang. Annie turned to answer it.

Cash headed for the door. This battle he would fight later, when the odds were better.

Tran followed him.

"Sergeant?"

"Uhm?"

"I wanted to tell you that I understand. About your need to go to this place Rochester. I'll try to explain if you like. And will go with you if you wish."

"What? Oh. Thanks. Don't bother. Nothing gets through when she's in that mood." He paused. Their eyes met.

Tran smiled. "I would pay my own way. I'm not destitute, just without possessions."

Yes, Cash thought. Like many of his compatriots, Tran had managed to bring some gold out. No great fortune, but a fair stake for the new life.

"Why?"

"Call it curiosity. This woman intrigues me. Your wife allowed me to read the papers you have here."

"She did, eh?" Cash shrugged. "You'd be wasting time and money. Annie's probably right. The whole idea is crazy."

"I don't think so. There are so many strange facets to the case. The denouement is sure to be interesting. And unexpected. I would like to be there when the pieces finally fall together."

"What about Le Quyen?"

"She will understand. She knows me. I won't be surprised if she packs for me without my saying a word."

"Norm, you'd better take this," Annie shouted from inside.

"Can't stop you from coming. You want to throw your money away, too, I'll be glad to have you. Folly loves company as much as misery does."

"Norman!"

"I'm coming. Who is it?"

"That flaky nun. She's been trying to track you down. I can't make any sense out of what she's saying. Something about teeth and the body wasn't her brother after all."

Cash took the receiver. "Sister? Sergeant Cash."

"Sergeant, it just came to me when Sister Magdalena said she had to go to the dentist because she had a toothache."

"What?"

"That dead man wasn't Jack. I know that now. What should I do?"

"Easy now. What made you change your mind? You were so sure. . . ."

"I know. I was positive. Till I thought about teeth. I just remembered when Sister Magdalena said that. The dead man had perfect teeth."

"Yes?"

"Jack's were terrible. He had toothaches all the time. Lots

of cavities. He always smelled like cloves. But he wouldn't go to a dentist.''

Cash felt no elation. He no longer much cared about O'Brien. He was preoccupied with John and Miss Groloch.

"Thank you, Sister. My lieutenant will be glad to hear this. It's the kind of proof he's been wanting.''

"But what should I do?''

"About what?''

"That man. I paid for his funeral. I had to borrow from the convent.''

He didn't think there was anything she could do. She had claimed the body. "Let me ask some people who might know. I'll call you back as soon as I know anything.''

Hanging up, he announced to no one in particular, "Back to square one. We don't know who the dead guy is anymore. Shit.''

"Norman!''

"Get off my back, will you?''

Annie backed away. Cash seldom lost control. She didn't know what he would do.

"I'm going back to the station. I want my stuff packed when I get home.''

He knew it would be ready. And he knew there would be a battle royal all the way to the airport. He left without another word.

Tran joined him. Cash said nothing, just waited while the man fastened his seat belt.

Beth raised an eyebrow when they marched in.

"Volunteer,'' Cash explained.

"Norm?'' Railsback called.

"Yeah. What?''

"Want to come here a minute? Ah. Hello, Major. You get anything, Norm?''

"Like I said, she took the train.''

"Where to?''

"The ticket records were screwed up.''

"That figures. Let the government run something . . . I got about seventy leagues of legwork for you. We came up with something interesting from that fire.''

"Fire? Shit. Let Smith and Tucholski handle it. I've got my own case.''

"Looks like the same one now.''

"What?" Cash slumped into the one extra chair.

"The coroner's office was on the horn while you were gone. They were raising hell about us trying to run the same corpse through twice."

"Huh?"

"One of those four bodies was in halfway human shape. The coroner claims it's the guy we already had so much fun with: O'Brien."

"Can't be. I was there when they planted him. I even got a look at him in the casket before they put him down."

"I know. And you're going to make sure nobody dug him up again. And then you're going to run down this list and find out how and why your doctor friend was spending so much money."

Cash accepted a wrinkled sheet of typing paper covered with tiny, difficult handwriting. Business names with dollar amounts beside them. Large dollar amounts.

"Looks like he had money up the yang-yang," Railsback observed.

"Yeah. I figured he had some. He had to be able to afford some of those stamps. But not where he could lay out a hundred grand in one chunk. . . . Where'd you get this?"

"Some kid found it in the parkway. Must've blown out during the fire somehow. Kid tried to give it to Tucholski. Thought it might be important, on account of the numbers were so big. Tucholski did like he always does when the peasants get in the act. So Smith took it so the kid's feelings wouldn't be hurt. He got to thinking it might give us a clue after he looked it over."

"There's a pattern, I think. The places I know here all sell hospital stuff."

"That's what Smith thought. But what about the others? Can't figure out who half of them are."

Beth leaned in. "I just talked to Smitty. He's been digging around in the garage behind that place that burned down."

"So?"

"He found this thing he says would look like a zeppelin if you blew it up."

"A zeppelin? What the hell does that have to do with anything?"

"You're the lieutenant. I guess he figured you'd know what he was talking about. He didn't tell me."

"I know," Cash declared.

"So spill it," Railsback grumbled.

"Oh, no. It's so simple it's beautiful. So simple we never thought of it. You figure it out for yourself. When you do, you'll have a big chunk of the original puzzle." He slipped the list into a shirt pocket that still felt empty without its pack of cigarettes. "I'm on my way to the cemetery."

"Bastard."

"Not anymore. Mom and Dad got married last week."

Tran followed Cash. In the parking lot he asked, "It was a zeppelin?"

"Or something enough like one to make no difference."

"One rational explanation, then. Perhaps more will follow."

"I hope."

The grave hadn't been disturbed.

"Well, I expected it. This thing always seems to take the least likely alternative," Cash grumbled. "One mystery solved, so we get a bigger one."

He began his rounds of the identifiable businesses on the list.

Again and again people made him wait. Once, for an hour. The records, where they existed at all, were buried deeply.

Smiley had made the most of his purchases during the period 1957–1964.

Yet the noted pattern proved out. Medical supplies, advanced surgical equipment, life-support systems, big stuff, expensive.

"What the hell does a retired doctor do with an electron microscope in his basement?" Cash asked at one point.

Tran could suggest no reasonable answer. The saleswoman just looked blank.

Yet Cash began to suspect something underneath, began to catch whiffs of the spoor of a quarry that was a shaggy old beast his detective's nose just couldn't identify. Vague sketches of its silhouette formed and unformed in the cutting rooms of his mind. Something Annie had talked about? Something from an article he had read? The harder he chased it, the more easily it eluded him. This was going to be like fox-hunting without hounds. The only way he was going to catch it was come stumbling over it accidentally, when he was looking for something else.

But he couldn't ignore it. It lured him on, capturing his imagination the way that one special perfume does when worn by the right woman.

It was getting near shift's end when they returned to the station. They ran into Hank outside.

"Got anything?" Railsback asked.

"Nothing to take to court. I don't think. Just about every outfit I could track down sold him stuff that had to do with medicine, surgery, biochemical research, like that. Except this tent and awning company. That must have been the balloon. And this electronics supply outfit. The entry there has to be a long-term sum. They didn't keep records, but the guy knew Smiley when I described him. Said he's been coming in for twenty years. But he didn't know what Smiley was up to. Thought he was some kind of crackpot inventor trying to build a perpetual motion machine or something."

"Yeah," Railsback grunted. "Smith has a nut theory. . . . Tucholski found out from Arson that they think the guy torched the place himself. He bought gas and gas cans right there at that station by your place. Meaning he didn't give a damn if we found out. Meaning getting whatever got burned up burned was more important than having us after his ass for arson."

"Hard to burn a body bad enough so nobody'll know it was one."

"I've been thinking about that. A doctor would know that, wouldn't he? Wouldn't that mean he was trying to cover up on something else? Anyway, we got some more on the bodies. Except for age, they could all be the same guy."

"No." That nagging scent again, that glimpse of the shaggy beast rustling the brush in the distance.

"Everything says so. A fingerprint, teeth, bones. . . . None of them guys ever broke a bone."

"Teeth. That reminds me. I talked to that nun this morning. She called me. She said she just realized that the dead man couldn't be her brother after all, because her brother had rotten teeth. The dead man's were perfect."

"They all have perfect teeth. That's got the coroner's office wondering too. Four guys, all alike, and none of them ever had a cavity."

"Maybe they were brothers. Maybe it's heredity. I knew a guy in the army. . . . Look, you think there's any way Sister

Mary Joseph can get her money back from the city?"

"For what?"

"For burying the wrong man."

"Shit, Norm."

"I didn't think so."

"She shouldn't have claimed him. She should've known better. It's her own fault."

"Okay. You don't have to get hostile."

"I'm heading for the Rite-Way. You want anything?"

"I'll grab something when I get home."

"Home? Who's going to have time to go home? We're staying on this till—"

"But I've got to catch a plane."

"Yeah?" Railsback turned and trotted into the street, dodging the afternoon traffic.

Cash watched, temper rising. Who the hell did Hank think he was shoving around? . . . He stamped into the station.

"What's the word, Beth?"

"Your wife called. She said to remind you to go see Carrie Harald. Hello, Major."

"Ah, shit. I keep forgetting. Now I'm going to be late to the airport. She's going to carry on all night, and make me feel like shit every time I try to leave."

"Wasn't going to be any trip anyway."

"What?"

"Hank made me cancel it."

"He what?" He was shouting. "Sorry. The son of a bitch."

"He made me do it. Made it an order."

"Annie have anything to do with it?"

"I don't know."

She was lying. He could tell.

"I'm getting goddamned tired of people deciding things for me. It's been a long time since me and Hank had a knock-down drag-out."

"Better be careful. He can have your badge any time he wants. Anyway, I made new reservations for Sunday. At four-twelve in the morning. I'm sorry. That was the best I could do."

His anger weakened. "Okay. Thanks. At least I've got you on my side. What's been going on?"

"He's got a whole mob of volunteers coming in. He isn't fooling around. He's out for blood."

Old Man Railsback came in. He looked dead on his feet.

"Sergeant," said Tran, "I have to go. Since we're not going to Rochester, I'd better go to work."

"Sure. Give me a couple minutes, then I'll run you out."

"No need. I'll call a cab. You have too much to do here."

Cash felt obligated to argue, but couldn't work up much fight. He had too much on his mind. He forgot Tran the moment the door closed behind the man.

Norm wheeled on Old Man Railsback. "What have you got?"

The man heaved a sigh, opened one eyelid. "You were right. The money was homemade. The priest says he'll dig up somebody to read the letters. They *are* in Czech. And the house looks clean. So far."

"House?"

"Henry's got me over there as ramrod emeritus. We ain't found much, except that she was awful interested in doctoring. There're medical books and journals tucked away all over the place. They go back a long time."

"More medicine? That the connection with Smiley?"

"Got me. I've got the feeling the answer's there, though. If we recognize it when we run into it. I guess with fifteen, twenty experts tearing the place apart, somebody is bound to."

"Hank's pushing awful hard, isn't he?"

"Can't blame him, can you?"

"Guess not. Beth, can you get me the *Post* classified department? Ask for Teri Middleton. And tell Nosey Parker it's police business."

"Right."

As she dialed, Cash added, "When you get a minute, hon, see if you can add another reservation to mine. Major Tran wants to go with me."

For an instant she looked shattered.

What the hell? he thought.

Lieutenant Railsback backed through the door, arms full. "Dinner on the boss," he announced, dumping his load atop Beth's work. "Got at least one of everything here. Grab whatever you want. How'd it go, Dad?"

"Not much yet. But we haven't really gotten going."

Beth offered Cash a phone as he was about to jump Hank for having messed with his reservations.

"Teri? Sergeant Cash again. I know you haven't seen him. Look, can I see you after you get off? Yeah. It's important. No. No problem. My lips are sealed, as they say. Okay. I'll pick you up then."

In the background, Hank was telling Beth, "You'd better go home, Tavares. Get a good night's sleep. I want you to come in tomorrow, and it might be a long day."

"I want to go with Norm to see John's wife. It'd help to have a woman there."

"Suit yourself." Railsback was too preoccupied to growl about being contradicted. "Dad, I don't like it when my people get shit on."

Cash hung up, grabbed something from the food heap, slipped into his own cubicle to ponder how best to break the news to Carrie and Teri.

"Henry, you can't drop everything because John disappeared." To Cash this sounded like the resumption of an interrupted argument. "You know there's a chance he just took off because he's having trouble with his wife."

That old man sees and hears a lot, Cash thought. And it's hard to tell what he knows. He just sits there like he's sleeping, and never says anything.

"You said that before. And you told me about the girl, too. And she ain't got nothing to do with it. You heard Norm talking to her."

"Maybe. And maybe she lied."

Cash took a savage bite from a cheeseburger. Suddenly, everybody seemed to know everything about everybody else's business. What do they have on me? he wondered.

Just thinking about it made him feel naked.

"Look," Railsback continued, "I ride these guys like a bronc-buster. And they put up with it because we get results. That makes me feel like I've got obligations to them. I've got responsibilities."

His father chuckled. "And that's why the captain calls you The Prussian. You think these are the Middle Ages? *Noblesse oblige*, and all that? One of your tenants is in trouble, so you drop the king's business while you save his ass? John's past saving, Henry. He's just another piece of the king's business now."

"Who taught me?"

"Touché. But I'm just a burned-out old has-been. You ought to know better."

"Pop, I can't call it off now. We've come to the narrow passage. We can't turn back."

"I know. And I'm proud of you. But somebody has to play Jiminy Cricket around here."

"And somebody has to do the tilting at windmills. Norm can't carry that load by himself anymore."

"I just want you shouldn't forget what happened when Pandora opened that box."

"Sure. There's going to be a stink. Bleeding hearts up the yang-yang. The inspector's office on us like a snake on shit. Well, I'll give them something to sink their teeth into. I just hope those guys who make careers out of handcuffing us get an idea how hard they make it for us to protect them."

"They won't even see it."

"Yeah. I know."

Poor Hank, Cash thought. His city, his empire, is under siege. He's just like poor old Belisarius, rushing hither and yon in a frenetic, foredoomed effort to beat off the barbarians. And he doesn't doubt for a minute that his Justinian, the public, will reward him as kindly for his faithful service.

The Emperor had had Belisarius's eyes put out and had left him to beg at Constantinople's gates.

And John and I, his centurions, have been wasting ourselves for months, chasing Miss Groloch. What harm could one little old lady have done the general welfare? If we had left her alone, John would be here now. . . .

We just had to keep on till it caught up with us, didn't we?

"What do you think really happened to the Kid, Pop?"

"The truth? I think he's dead."

"Why?"

"Because he wasn't the first. Otherwise, I'd put my chips on the girl friend."

The phone rang. A moment later Beth announced, "Sergeant Kurland says there's a man from the government on his way up here."

"What kind?" Hank asked.

"He didn't say. Except he wants to talk about Dr. Smiley. And he doesn't look like he's from the FBI."

"Shit, what're we into now?"

"No imagination, that man," Harald had said of his boss. But he had been wrong. Dead wrong.

Henry Railsback's problem, in Cash's opinion, was a surfeit, not a paucity, of imagination. Norm had been acquainted with the man since high school, when Hank had come in with one of the police public relations teams. Norm had expressed an interest in getting into police work. Hank had taken him around on a few of his patrols.

Cash knew things he had never told John.

Hank's hadn't been a happy youth. His mother had been a violent alcoholic. His father, so much like the man he himself had become, had been too timid to spend much time in the bitter trenches of the home front.

It had taken the death of Abigail Railsback, in a wrong-way auto crash, to bring father and son together, watering a grave with tears, raising a late-blooming relationship.

The boy Henry, even as a young officer, had hidden in the worlds of comic books, pulp magazines, serial movies, and daydreams. He had gone adventuring across landscapes of illusion because, for him, reality was a colorless desert. By taking to wife the first woman willing he had firmly established a marriage that soon had become a Sahara of misery.

He had dreamed great dreams then, had Henry Railsback, and within his mind he still conquered nations and continents, pitched no-hitters, outdrew the fastest guns. . . . Though now he no longer possessed a shred of hope that such things could come to be. Time pulled down hopes and optimisms like wolves coursing round the flanks of the herd.

And in real life he seldom risked his precious *self* by testing the limits of his competence. He feared it would not measure up even to his low expectations.

Cash knew, and understood. Because Hank's story was not much different from his own. Just longer and a little more up and down.

In externals Hank had learned to cope by becoming an arch-conservative, a champion of null-change, a messiah of don't-rock-the-boat.

He didn't want challenges. He was afraid he couldn't handle them.

But he could face them when he *had* to, or when he became angry enough.

He was angry enough now. Harald's disappearance had set

him to flailing out in every conceivable direction, to calling in favors due, to pursuing every theory, no matter how much it might pain his prejudices and preconceptions.

It was, in great part, an overresponse to years of frustration.

The "government man" arrived, after having wandered half the station in search of the Homicide office.

XXIV. On the X Axis; 1975

Dr. Smiley fit his name that chill March evening. He hummed as he pottered around his basement, hunting that last over-looked detail. It was the little thing that always proved critical.

So many years of work finally coming to culmination. So much patient investigation. So much money. He admitted it: he had had a lot of luck: the discovery of the woman's letter when he was a boy; the chance encounter with Fian in Prague, and the equally unexpected discovery of Dunajcik. And now, despite the crudity of his equipment, his first clone had come to term perfectly. It had been out of the amniotic bath only a week, yet was taking baby food already. It was a strong, healthy beast.

Smiley peeped through a curtain.

Snow for sure. Maybe there was a God after all. If so, he must be a security man at heart. He was certainly bringing everything together perfectly.

Smiley had feared he would have to put up with an adult-sized infant till next winter.

This was going to be sweet. Much more subtle than that clumsy business at Lidice. Definitely worth the wait.

He stared at his creation. It was a work of genius. Sheer genius considering the quality of the available hardware. The years and changes hadn't robbed him of his talent.

He applauded himself almost constantly. By damned, he was going to pull it off! A plot so delicate and complex that he was constantly awed by his own temerity.

Finding the man's nearest living relative. What a hunt that had been. Then he had had to become a respected member of her church. Finally, the time had been right to offer his medical services to the convent. . . . He lacked a license, but there hadn't been many questions. It was a poor parish.

Such joy he had known the day he had brought home the blood-stained paper towel she had used to stop a nosebleed. Cells enough for a thousand clones. With a little ingenious gene sculpture using a half-million dollars worth of equipment, he had produced a male embryo.

Ah, the fortunes he had had to spend. But it was worth it. Definitely worth it.

The corpse would cause an uproar so mighty that she would *have* to run to Fial.

It had come to that. He had gotten nowhere in his search for the last Groloch. If only he could have gotten to Fian's things at Lidice. . . . But the security police would have cut him up for fish bait.

Spooking Fiala was the only way left. She would know where to find the man—if he were alive at all.

Smiley could not accept the possibility that one of his enemies might have escaped him through death. No. There was order and justice in this universe. The man was hiding. When the fire got intense enough, Fiala would bolt for the same cover.

Smiley was enjoying himself hugely. For the first time since the Uprising, he was having fun.

He heaved the clone into the power wheelchair. The other four . . . well, he would have to do something. After he saw how this worked out. He wouldn't need them if it clicked. He began whistling while he dressed his homemade stalking horse.

The wheelchair could climb steps. It was the fanciest available. He had practiced leaving the basement with a sandbag as passenger, but never with a human body. He anticipated snags.

There were none. The chair climbed slowly but perfectly.

He opened his garage and dragged the uninflated mini-blimp into the alley. The clone sat silently, motionlessly, the only sign of life an occasional shiver.

Smiley had come to the tricky part. It was still early. If anyone spotted him, or his airship, before the snowfall cut visibility and stopped traffic . . . If he erred during his two block flight and crashed the damned blimp . . . If there were lightning in the storm . . .

He shouldn't have used hydrogen. Too dangerous.

But he wouldn't have gotten enough lift from helium. The airship was too small.

It would work out. It had to. He had invested too much time and money and energy, had taken too many risks, to have it sour now.

It hummed along smoothly. The gas bag filled. He man-handled his unnatural child into the gondola, clambered in himself. Everything was in place. The little single stroke engine began purring first try. The breeze fell off to nothing as the snowfall grew heavier.

He took the ship up. It responded as perfectly as it had during test flights on the small farm he owned a hundred miles south of the city. There was one minor mishap, when the ship nudged the sky-clawing fingers of a gigantic sycamore, but the incident scarcely slowed him. He navigated by the lights of the houses, clearing their rooftops by a scant ten feet.

Soon he was over the alley, anchored to an elm. He lowered the clone. The snow was so dense he could hardly discern the ground, though a streetlight stood fifty feet to the west.

Excellent.

The clone tried to walk, as its muscles had been taught. But when the breakaway harness cut loose, it collapsed.

Smiley aimed his crude sonic weapon. The clone twitched, squirmed, died.

They would think it had been shock.

He flew home to await developments.

But it didn't work out the way he hoped. After momentary excitement, everyone lost interest. Even Fiala misinterpreted the message he had thought implicit in the body's appearance.

Maybe he was being too subtle.

Well, he still had four soldiers sleeping in the womb. He would put them in one by one till the police *had* to lean on somebody. An apparently endless column of O'Briens *had* to break things open.

Meanwhile, his detective agency watched the woman around the clock.

The break came only after months of waiting. The warning that something unusual was in the wind came when she left her home to make a phone call by daylight. Smiley fired up his cranky old '53 Dodge and listened on CB channel nineteen.

His detectives did the tailing. He allowed them to guide him in.

A funeral. For the clone.

He acted on impulse, allowed himself to be seen.

He hadn't wanted to do it that way. But she just hadn't gotten the message of the time-traveler corpse.

He felt the electricity. She had recognized him as surely as he had recognized Dunajcik. Maybe there was some sort of personality field which grew more intense with time. . . .

Smiley began moving the moment he got home. There wasn't much left to do. He had been at it for months. He boxed the remnants of his stamp collection and sent them out by UPS. He watched the truck leave with a feeling of emptiness. It might be years before he found time to relax again. It could be a long chase, police wolves nipping his heels all the way. And he had had to sell so much to finance his work.

Those little bits of paper with their quiet story of human communication were the thing he could love, the one thing he could worry about, cherish and preserve. It was an odd sublimation, though not unusual, and even he recognized that strange twist in his character.

The crisis had come on unexpectedly. Now there would be no time to dispose of the redundant clones, nor to dismantle and disperse the lab. He had planned to bury everything on his farm. But the detectives said the woman was in a panic, shipping out boxes and bags already. He would have to take drastic steps.

He had the nearby service station deliver a hundred gallons of gasoline in a variety of gas cans purchased from the auto parts shop next door. A big, hot fire should erase the most important clues.

All he needed was a head start anyway. Two days and there would be no way they could track him. He had been a step ahead for ages.

He was in a hotel in New York City when his agency informed him that his quarry's final destination appeared to be Rochester. She had stopped making transfers there. Within the hour he was headed north in his chartered Lear jet, nerve ends tingling.

The final reckoning was at hand.

XXV. On the Y Axis; 1975

The government man resembled those always seen in the company of presidents. Not the politicos but the hired guns, the bodyguards. Hard. Late thirties to early forties. Conservative suit and haircut. A Teutonic solidity of build, like the man on the SS recruiting poster. A face that might shatter if forced to smile. He had a string of degrees, certainly, and as certainly was more intelligent than ninety percent of the population.

But there was a cold about him, a permafrost beneath a surface that thawed only to order.

How come they never pick wimps? Norm wondered. You can spot these guys a mile away. They have that hard, Germanic look even when they're as black as this clown.

The visitor's character, however, didn't match Cash's prejudgments.

"Lieutenant Railsback?" he asked uncertainly.

"Here." Hank raised a hand.

"Hi. Name's Tom Malone. Central Intelligence Agency." He extended his hand.

Railsback said, "Huh?" as he shook.

Interestinger and interestinger, Cash thought, changing his attitude. Must be an upfront guy. Pretending a need for another cheeseburger, he moved out to Beth's desk.

"FBI says a man we're interested in, the one called Smiley, is on the move."

Hank didn't seem quite able to get a handle on what was happening.

"Maybe you could fill us in a little?" Cash suggested, glancing at the letter the man offered as identification. Did it mean anything? Agency people wouldn't carry membership cards.

But why on earth would anyone come here pretending to be one? "Like why you're interested?"

"There's been a tag on his file for twenty-five years. Suspicious alien. When you requested the records search, their computer whistled. The word drifted over to Langley that he was up to something. The timing was interesting, so my boss sent me out."

"We want him for arson and murder," Railsback said. "That's not spy business."

"Could be. I'm here to find out. If I can."

"How come you?" Cash asked. "I mean, with all the stink about you people sticking your noses into the public's business. . . ."

Malone shrugged. "I don't make policy. I'm just a gofer. I go where they send me."

"Henry," Old Man Railsback observed, "this looks like the time to play one hand washes the other." To Malone, "We may be able to help each other."

Cash agreed. "Tell us about Smiley."

Malone examined each of them closely. Checking for Russians? "We've got a fat file. Mostly speculation. It goes way back.

"See, he did some work for us in Austria right after the war. It didn't turn out. There's a chance he sold us out to the Russians. We do know he did some work for them too.

"Anyway, when somebody found out he was over here as Smiley, they started a file. It's grown. It's interesting, too. Especially if everything's true."

Cash looked expectant. Then Railsback stirred, anticipating.

"Mostly it's odds and ends skimmed off the edges of other investigations. For instance, something somebody may have come across while we were backgrounding people in our nets in Eastern Europe. I can't show you the file, but I'll hit the high points.

"We're pretty sure he was born Michael Hodža, a miner's son, at Lidice, in Czechoslovakia, in the late eighteen eighties. We got that from a Viennese who roomed with him before World War One, and who worked for us during the occupation."

"That makes him awful old to play James Bond," Railsback grumbled.

"We've got older Czechs, Hank," Cash reminded.

"He does seem to age well. Around nineteen ten he turned up in Vienna. The man who knew him said he lied his way into medical school. In nineteen twelve he got defrocked, or whatever they do to med students, for performing an abortion."

"Aha!" Hank exploded. "What'd I tell you, Norm?"

"For a while he bummed around with Hitler. No, really. And during World War One he seems to have deserted from both the German and Austrian armies, and may have been involved in the Czech nationalist movement. There is also a hint of a connection with the Czech Legion, which kicked up dust in Russia during their civil war. Then he turned up as a doctor in Prague. A good one, too. This Dr. Hodză is pretty well documented. If he's the same man. Anyway, he was so respectable he was one of the team doctors with the Czech contingent to the Berlin Olympics.

"When Germany invaded, though, he reverted." Malone sketched a tale of a man playing both sides.

"And when the Russians came, he worked for them. And us.

"The reason we're interested is he might still be on the Reds' payroll. Even though the Czechs have him on their wanted list."

"How'd you get all that?" Cash wondered aloud. "I mean, I couldn't even find out where he came from. And I knew him personally for twenty years."

"We have our ways," Malone replied. "Easy. Just playing my role there. Some we got on our own, some from the British, some from German records, some from the Czechs back when they wanted us to hand him over. Sometimes we were lucky. Like finding the man who knew him and Hitler in the old days, and getting hold of the diary of the priest who taught him when he was a kid. We've had a lot of years, and some good computers, to work on it, too."

"And money," Cash added softly.

"True," Malone replied.

"But why come looking for him now?" Cash asked.

"It's not the crime. We're not interested in that per se. It's the timing. There's something going on in Czechoslovakia. The Dubcek wing and the Chinese are up to something. We think it might involve us. So we're watching all our suspicious Czech immigrants."

"Who'd have thought it?" Cash mused. "Old Doc Smiley. Hard to believe."

"Not if you read his file. He was a bad dude. A lifetaker. Left a lot of bones behind him. The one thing we can't figure is why. But motivations of agents are always hard to pin down."

"Been a model citizen here. Till now. Then he suddenly torches his house, with the basement filled with bodies and a million bucks worth of fancy hardware nobody can figure out."

"Hardware?"

"Yeah. Looks like it was mostly medical stuff."

"Strange. Excuse me a minute." Malone rummaged through his briefcase, blocking Cash's view with his body. But Norm caught glimpses of piles of hastily typed papers. "Ah. I though so."

"What?" Hank asked.

"Just wanted to check one of the German reports. One of the houses in that town they destroyed had a basement full of hardware. They couldn't figure it out, so they just blew it up and bulldozed it with the rest."

"Smiley was up to the same thing then?"

"No. He lived in Prague before he ran to England. The house belonged to the local electrician."

"Let me guess," said Cash, smitten by inspiration. "It was a man named Fian Groloch."

"Ah, Norm . . ." Railsback started.

Malone looked bewildered. "How did you. . . ?"

"How's that for a connection, Hank? The old witch *has* been hiding out from somebody."

"The guy was born twenty-some years after she left. You got to be shitting me. I don't buy it." But he spoke without conviction.

"Can somebody explain?" Malone pleaded.

Everyone chattered at him.

Once he had let it sink in, Malone mused, "My boss will really want to lay hands on the man now. But he'll probably give us the slip. He's good at changing identities. And he's had a long time to get ready."

"Pop," said Hank, "get over to the old lady's place. See if you can speed things up."

Cash said, "I know where he went."

"Where?"

"Same place as Miss Groloch. Her brother's place. He followed her. To get them both at the same time."

"Don't start that shit again!"

"Don't you start. I'm up to here. . . ."

Beth gripped his arm. Cash forced himself to calm down. "Who's the resident Groloch expert? Maybe I haven't done so good, but you have to admit I know more than anybody else. And I was the only one who realized it was important back when you wanted to push it off on somebody else."

"He's got a point, Henry," Old Man Railsback said from the door.

"At the top of his head."

"Where do you think he went?" Malone asked. "I didn't catch your name, by the way. Nor yours," he told Beth. He turned, but was too late to catch Old Man Railsback.

"Norman Cash. A sergeant in this chicken outfit. That's Beth Tavares. She's a detective too, only she mostly gets shafted into being a secretary."

"Norm's got the fastest mouth and gun west of the Mississippi," Hank snapped.

"You're the jerk who makes me lug a piece. . . ."

The strain had begun to tell.

"Norm, please!" Beth gripped his arms again, wearing an expression so pained and pathetic that he could not help but desist.

He glanced at his watch. Still a half hour before he could collect Teri. He wasn't sure he could handle Railsback that long.

"Sorry, Norm," Hank told him. "You're right. It's as much my fault as yours. I should have listened when I talked, especially . . . just bear with me, okay? Going to be a job getting out of this one."

Cash was flabbergasted. A Railsback apology? They were as common as hen's teeth.

Beth poked him.

He gabbled something. Enough to satisfy Hank and Beth. He turned to Malone. "I think Smiley went after a woman I've been investigating—a Fiala Groloch. The daughter of the man who lived in that house in Czechoslovakia. She has a brother in upstate New York. She doesn't know we know that. That's where they'll both end up. In my opinion."

Railsback opened a Styrofoam cup of coffee that had cooled to lukewarm, began pacing. "What did you want from us, Mr. Malone?"

"I think I have most of it. At least an idea of why he's moving. I'd like copies of the pertinent reports, and a chance to talk to a few people. Also, a look at what's left of the man's house. And I'll want that New York address if you have it."

Cash felt a stubborn streak coming on. "That's *my* baby. I'm going up there personally." He expected smoke to roil from Hank's ears.

Railsback spent a few seconds staring out the window. Reasonably, he asked, "You think you'd be any safer going after her there?"

Norm hadn't considered the risks. "Tran's going with me," he blustered.

"That's good. I hear *he* can take care of himself. But maybe you need reminding. She took out four of Egan's thugs."

"Two at a time. And they weren't ready for her."

"Dammit, Norm, I don't want to lose you too."

Beth interrupted with an explanation for Malone's benefit.

Cash checked his watch. Still a little early . . . no. Downtown traffic would hold him up. "I've got to leave. Got to break the news to a couple of ladies."

Beth overtook him at the car. "I almost left my purse."

He hadn't invited her. Didn't really want her along. And Teri wouldn't like it. But he couldn't find the nerve to say no.

"She won't like you being there."

"She'll change her mind."

Lord, the girl's getting assertive, he thought.

The surprises were piling up.

Teri certainly wasn't pleased.

"Who's she?" she demanded, as Beth got out and moved to the back seat. "You said—"

"Beth Tavares. She's a cop too. And don't worry. She'll keep her mouth shut. Not that it really matters anymore."

Teri glanced at Beth, who smiled reassuringly, then at Norm. Then she slid in, slammed the door. "I hope you're still a right guy."

"Sure. You're looking good. Like a little white-haired bunny."

"What? . . . Oh." Teri studied him. Then blushed. "Okay. You can keep your mouth shut. Daddy-Waddy. God! Don't that sound dumb now?" More embarrassed, "*That* isn't what you want to talk about is it?"

"Oh, no." Now Cash was embarrassed. "Though sometimes I'm sorry. . . . I don't know how to tell you. I guess just straight out." He concentrated on his driving for fifteen seconds. He hated rush hours. "Teri, we think John's been killed."

She stiffened, turned to Beth, saw it wasn't some cruel joke. Her features hardened. She stared straight ahead. "What happened?" Her voice had become very soft, very flat.

When he finished, she reached over and took his hand. "I'm sorry."

"Huh? For what?"

"First Michael. Now John."

For a moment he couldn't see through the tears, couldn't breathe through the tightness in his throat.

Teri cried while Beth made soothing sounds and provided Kleenex.

"Norm," Teri said a few blocks later, still in that voice from which the brass had vanished, "can I come to your house for a while? Just for an hour or two, while I get ahold of myself? I won't be any bother."

A covey of panicky excuses fluttered across his mind. But he understood. And compassion was more important than appearances right now.

"Sure. Annie will understand. What about your kids?"

"They're at my aunt's. She's used to me showing up late. And I won't stay long. I promise. . . ."

"Don't worry. You've always been welcome."

He hoped she would be now. Annie had been getting blue-nosed the past few years.

There was a Rexall drugstore coming up across the street. He and the pharmacist had known one another for years. "Just remembered something I was supposed to pick up." He parked, ran over, borrowed the phone.

Annie was less difficult than he had anticipated.

She was a good woman, his wife.

Forewarned, she would make Teri feel at home, would soften her grief. Teri had cried on her shoulder before.

He bought some Listerine as his excuse for going in. Probably won't fool the girls, he thought.

Once they were on their way to Harald's house, Beth asked, "Why did she want to go to your place?"

"Once upon a time, so long ago that it seems like it was during somebody else's life, she was one of our extra kids. Like John. I don't know what it is. We always attract the strays.

Cats and people. We've got kittens under the back porch right now, and refugees upstairs. . . . Anyway, Teri and John and Michael's first affair. They almost stopped being friends. . . . It's funny when I look back at it.''

"I didn't realize you'd known her before.''

"Her father hit the road when she was eleven. After raping her. And her mother never gave a damn. She got to be a pretty tough kid. I guess she liked us because we were about the only people who treated her decent.''

"Sad. She's such a pretty woman.''

"You should have seen her then. When she cleaned herself up. Before she looked so hard.''

"What was that bunny stuff?''

"The white-haired bunny?'' Cash blushed.

"My God. I can't remember you being embarrassed.'' She giggled. "Daddy-Waddy.''

Cash laughed, but strictly from nervousness. "I don't guess it matters now. Long as you keep it to yourself. She used to bleach her hair. White.''

"And it looked like hell. I tried that once too. It didn't make me a different person.''

"Anyway, we were talking one day, about her plans, and I asked her what she thought about modeling. Or being a *Playboy* Bunny, after she graduated. . . .'' Another little hiccough laugh ripped itself free.

"She had the looks. . . . She was pretty loose then. We were at the house alone. Annie had taken Michael, Matthew, and John to their Saturday afternoon hockey practice. . . .''

"And she tried to seduce you?''

"Liked to drive me crazy, being my 'white-haired bunny.' You'd have to be a man to understand. There's something about a girl that age . . . innocence? Maybe it's just instinct. Get them started breeding.''

Beth snorted derisively.

"What do you do? The girl says she's willing. She throws herself into your lap. She starts playing kissy-face huggy-bear with you. Blows in your ear. Puts your hand . . .''

He felt eggs could be fried on his cheeks.

"But you didn't give in.'' Merriment flickered round the edges of her words. "You're so noble, Sir Norman.''

"No. I didn't. And I was always sorry. That was an archetypal middle-age fantasy come true. And I chickened out. God, I wanted her. . . .

"We were closer afterward. Like she could respect and trust me because I told her no. Probably the only guy who ever did. She never pulled that again, but she made it clear I could collect any time."

"I should meet a guy like that."

Cash ignored that wistful remark. "Then Michael and John went away to school. After a while they stopped coming home weekends. And Teri got pregnant. She married the guy and we didn't see her anymore."

"John did."

"Yeah. I don't know much about it. It hasn't been going on long."

"Didn't he brag? I thought men always kissed and told."

"Some do, I guess. But I don't know any. Guys I know don't talk about a woman till a relationship is over. Well, that's high school stuff anyway."

John's place seemed strange. There was an air of gloom about it, as if the structure knew, as if its heart had been ripped out. Nancy's decrepit Datsun stood behind Carrie's Satellite.

"This could get to be pure soap. Michael's wife is here."

Carrie had red, hollow eyes and wore an air of total despair when she answered the bell.

She stepped aside without speaking, apparently able to respond with nothing but a stare.

"Who is it?" Nancy called from the rear of the house. "News?" Her voice betrayed false optimism.

"It's Norm. And . . . " Carrie struggled for the name.

"Beth Tavares," Beth told her.

Nancy came from the kitchen. She was pale, tense, had a tall drink in hand. Cash glanced around. There had been a lot of drinking and very little housekeeping here since John's disappearance. "Dad? . . ."

"It's news all right." Carrie sniffled. "Bad news."

Where are the kids? Cash wondered. Farmed out to a grandmother? "You'd both better sit down."

"I told you!"

Beth moved nearer Carrie. The woman was on the verge of hysteria.

"Shit!" Cash swore. The grief was creeping up on him too.

Nancy made Carrie gulp half her drink, forcing her head back till she choked. "Calm down, Carrie. We expected bad news, didn't we? Dad, get it over with. Did he really go this time?"

"Go? This time?"

"He's threatened to before. He even started out one time."

"Not this time. I wish that's all it was."

Nancy sat down on Carrie's feet. In an instant she had become as haggard as her cousin.

"We think he's been killed." Christ, wasn't there a gentler way?

"Oh my God!" Carrie moaned. And visibly pulled herself together, becoming more sober, more alert, more intense.

"How, Dad? What happened?"

"We're not sure. . . ."

Beth interrupted. "Norm, let me. You've torn yourself up enough. Make yourself a drink."

"There's Coke in the fridge," Carrie told him. "I think there's still some Bacardi Dark in the liquor cabinet." She had changed radically. Already she was straightening everything within reach.

How long before she breaks? Cash asked himself. As soon as she runs out of laundry, dirty dishes and dusting?

It wasn't a response that could be maintained indefinitely. He knew. He had tried it.

He mixed a weak, water glass full and downed it. Belching, he mixed another, stronger drink. The wall phone began ringing. It went on and on. Should he answer it just to get it to stop?

It did so as he sipped and stared through the kitchen window into the backyard. The swing John had bought his kids last spring creaked in the breeze, abandoned. Grass grew where little feet should have dragged the earth bare. The children just hadn't been interested. To the swing's left stood the brick barbecue pit he had helped John build two years ago. He smiled weakly, remembering how often they had screwed up.

Yes. John might as well have been his son.

"Norm!"

Beth sounded hysterical.

He ran, expecting to find Carrie dying of self-inflicted wounds.

Beth shoved a phone at him. She stared at the thing as if it had turned into a snake.

"Cash. What is it?"

He listened for fifteen seconds, then slammed the receiver down, grabbed his coat. Beth barely kept up as he ran to the car.

It was the first time he had had occasion to use the siren. He flipped the switch, expecting nothing. But the banshee voice began moaning its death song.

They had begun digging for the bodies by the time he reached the Groloch house. Marylin Railsback had gotten there somehow, and was seated on a rubble-strewn lawn one door east, holding her husband. Hank was crying. Marylin couldn't get him to stop.

The explosion had shattered windows for blocks around. The facing walls of the nearest flats bore pocks and scars. One door west, firemen and neighborhood volunteers were shoring a wall that threatened to fall.

The Groloch house had been powdered.

Cash looked for someone calm enough to explain.

"What happened, Smitty?"

"Huh? Oh. Hi. I wasn't here. Ran over from the other place. From what I can make out, they broke through a false wall in the basement and found some kind of electronic rig. Nobody could figure it out. Old Man Railsback decided to fire it up to see what it did."

"Booby-trapped?"

"Looks like. Smell the dynamite?"

"Yeah. Poor Hank. He's taking it hard."

"Poor lots of people. There were eight men down there."

Tucholski and Malone had their heads together a short way away. The agent kept his briefcase clamped between his ankles while he studied a half-dozen sheets of green paper. Tucholski had a handful of photographs.

Cash went over. "What's happening?"

Tucholski expelled a blue cloud. "One of the evidence technicians took these. Polaroid."

Cash studied photos of something from Tom Swift. Bloody fingerprints smeared most.

"He was lucky. Got out with a broken back." Murder burned in Tucholski's eyes.

"What is it?"

Tucholski shrugged. "Maybe the time machine you were looking for."

Cash turned to Malone.

"Don't look at me. I don't know either. But it's something like the thing the Germans found at Lidice."

"Just a bunch of wires and old-time tubes. Look at the size of some of those babies. But she booby-trapped it. With enough dynamite to do this." Cash's sentences were as much puzzled questions as statements.

Tucholski muttered something about the basement being walled off for ages, and what would have happened if the explosive hadn't been old?

"I've got a whole different case from last March," Norm continued. "And I just get more confused. There's got to be some sense in it somewhere. Mr. Malone?"

"Don't look at me. I'm no conjure man."

"Resource-wise you are."

"Maybe. I called my boss. He's going to research everybody connected with this."

Tucholski growled, "Bet you five he don't come up with nothing."

"No bet."

Cash considered the ruin. "We won't get a thing out of that now. Whoever these people are, they sure do make a habit of burning their bridges before anyone else can cross them."

Streetlights flickered to life.

"Getting dark already," Cash observed.

"The days are getting shorter."

"I just meant that it's been a long day."

He was emotionally and physically exhausted. Nevertheless, he helped a uniformed officer hustle the overaggressive Channel Four news crew back to their own side of the barricades. He couldn't muster a smile when the reporter tried questioning him.

The pop of flashbulbs irritated his eyes and wakened his temper. Why the hell wouldn't they go home?

He spied Annie, Teri, and Tran's wife and sons, waved. Annie and Teri appeared to be getting along.

Back to the Groloch house. The workers had opened a passage into the basement.

They brought Old Man Railsback up first. His clothing had been shredded. His hair was gone. He had lost a hand. His skin was one solid bruise beneath a crust of blood.

The buzzing of the flies stopped only after they zipped the old man into the plastic bag.

Cash giggled half-hysterically at an image of the rescue

workers setting him in the alley for the next trash pickup.

That's all we are anyway, he thought. Animated garbage. . . .

Hank and Marylin followed the body into the ambulance.

This is the longest they have been together, without fighting, since they got married, Cash thought. It's a pity that it takes something like this to make them lay down their arms.

He soon wished that Hank hadn't gone. The lieutenant's departure left him responsible, at least for Homicide's interests.

Christ! All he wanted was to go home and crash.

Subsequent hours formed a surreal parade. They left just one memorable impression, near the end. That was the lift he got when somebody below shouted, "Stand by! This one is still breathing." The medical people moved in with their bottles of blood and glucose.

Tran had returned from work by then, and was on hand to walk him home. Neither man spoke. For Cash it was enough to have somebody beside him during that weary march.

He found he had company. Beth was asleep on the couch. Carrie and Nancy were asleep on the parlor carpet, surrounded by their children. Annie snored in a chair. His son Matthew and Le Quyen were talking quietly in the kitchen.

"Matthew! Where'd you come from?"

"Stork brought me, Pop. No. Mom called. I thought I'd better come down."

"Thank you, Le Quyen." Cash accepted a mug of spiced tea. After serving her husband, Le Quyen began fussing over the stove, warming some leftover macaroni and cheese. Norm dropped into the chair she had vacated. "God, what a day."

"You all right?" Matthew asked. "You don't look too good."

"Nothing a week's sleep wouldn't cure. I'm just burned out. Totaled. Don't expect me to make any sense till tomorrow."

XXVI. On the Z Axis; 1973-1977

The days and weeks, though sometimes leaving a brackish taste, flowed swiftly into swamps of years. Four slid past. Michael became convinced he had gotten away with it. He hadn't noted a glimmer of suspicion on the part of any of his associates.

There was no shortage of work, of study, of training. From his Peking office he now commanded the director's entire American operation. It was growing, perfectly, into a gem of the spymaster's art. Webs were being spun tight about an unsuspecting fascist America; the crisis was coming on almost too swiftly for belief.

At Huang's insistence Michael undertook one foreign field operation each year, under deep cover. The missions were supposed to keep him in touch with his Occidental roots. He suspected they were intended to test his reliability more than as training or to accomplish anything.

Twice he ventured into the Soviet Union, first to Kiev, to confer with radical elements in the Ukrainian Party, then to Moscow itself, where he helped transfer certain damning Soviet documents to the custody of the U.S. Embassy. He did his work quickly and carefully, and made the most of the opportunities to see strange lands and peoples. For security reasons he didn't get much chance to see Peking. Caucasians attracted too much attention.

His third venture took him to Prague. It was the spring of seventy-five, and this was a more significant mission. He was supposed to collect a lengthy document outlining anti-Soviet feeling in the Czechoslovak Party. Certain officials, admirers and adherents of Alexander Dubcek, were preparing the report in hopes of enlisting Chinese support for an anti-Soviet move.

Michael's contact was a young woman from Interior Ministry, a comer in the Party. While he fretted through countless delays—the streets seemed curb to curb with KGB—and wrestled anxieties about how his office might be managing in his absence, the lady showed him Prague. And in the shadow of the castle of the Bohemian kings he fell in love with both.

Old Prague was a beautiful city, a fairy-tale city. Ilse was a beautiful woman, a fairy-tale princess, a socialist Cinderella. And the most remarkable wonder was that she fell as madly as he. That he could be loved that way, without reservation, as madly as he himself could love, would amaze him as long as he lived.

The hopelessness of their affair only intensified it. They tried to cram an entire relationship into a few short weeks.

Michael was tempted to betray his trust. And Ilse offered to go to Peking. But once the report changed hands, once the moment for decisions arrived, neither could abandon an appointed pathway. They made violent love throughout a night. Michael made promises he had no hope of keeping. Then he took the report to Peking.

He nursed a hope that, soon, he would feel safe enough to ask Huang's intercession in behalf of his romance.

Moves had to be made. His past had to be secured. The Snake thing couldn't be left ready to hang him at any instant.

Michael's office occupied a backwater of a bureaucratic niche midway between Huang and Sung's more orthodox intelligence command. While he suffered interferences from both, Michael enjoyed a great deal of freedom. His department wasn't on the table of organization; no one knew quite how to handle him. Moreover, his small MIA corps were more loyal to him and one another than to their adopted masters. Michael had the elbow room and means to undertake small actions on his own initiative. And now he had initiative.

Within a month of his return a routine report from Sinkiang noted the passing of prisoner A.O. Cantrell. There had been a mining accident.

The director called with condolences, suggested a few days off. He understood. He himself had had a boyhood friend who had never seen the light, who might even now be on Taiwan.

Michael flew to Sinkiang for the funeral. He took a black wreath. He even made a sad little speech honoring an old comrade who had found peace at last.

He did it very well, very convincingly.

His next mission took him to West Germany, with a license to kill, under instructions to test a possible double agent in Hamburg. He resolved the matter in two days, making a friend of the relieved suspect. But he stole the rest of the month.

His report never mentioned the three-week love vacation in Czechoslovakia.

Ilse's feelings hadn't cooled either. Between them, those few days, they concocted enough wild schemes for a dozen spy novels. But when the moment of decision came, both still couldn't help trudging right on down those roads already programmed.

Michael returned to Peking determined to enlist Huang's aid. But he stalled, and stalled, and the days rolled into weeks, which rolled into months.

He felt secure the day the director summoned him. So secure that he was sure Huang had a positive response to the request he had finally gotten around to making. It had to be good news. Huang sent some hard-eyed flunky around with a handwritten note when he turned you down.

The director had grown fond of him, he knew. He was walking, talking, irrefutable evidence of the soundness, of the value, of the man's work. In private Huang treated him like a favorite son.

Sung, who outside the inner circle wore another name, was there too. Michael was surprised. There was no love lost between Sung and his mentor. Sung's presence made the Spartan little office seem overcrowded.

"An operation?" Michael guessed. "Something important this time?"

"The most critical we've ever faced," Huang replied coolly. "A termination."

Michael trembled. "Me?" His guts cramped. "I've never handled anything like that."

Sung stared like a cobra about to strike.

"You've had the training," Huang countered. "It should be simple. In, do it, and get out before the police know what's happened."

"Out of the country?"

"England."

Who, in Britain, could possibly need killing? "You lost me. There isn't anybody there." Could the target be a renegade agent? The trip to Hamburg had been a police mission. "Anybody important would be buried in security."

"Not this man. Not the kind we're used to—or who are used to us. The British don't know he's important yet. But his life or death could mean the life or death of everything we've been trying to accomplish. We think you're the man to handle it."

Michael's guts tightened more.

"You'd better tell me the whole thing."

Huang pushed a file folder toward him.

Michael need read but the first of the fascist editorials. Sweat beaded on his face. They knew it all. Had known for some time.

So much for Huang's backing in the Ilse matter.

He was so terrified that he just read on, delaying the inevitable confrontation. Finally, he could stall no more. He met Huang's eye.

"So," said Huang.

Michael didn't respond. He couldn't.

"You have your choice. Rectify your error of egoism. Or don't. You remain sufficiently valuable, though compromised, that, if the plan survives, we will consider the trauma of the corrective action ample discipline."

The director's voice was hard now. He was angry and dismayed. He had been betrayed by his masterwork. His words came carefully measured, set alone, as though a period belonged after each.

Sung smiled wickedly. He was enjoying this. He enjoyed anything that discomfited Huang.

Michael was, as he remembered his father saying, between a rock and a hard place. This was one hell of a choice. His life or Snake's.

What could he do?

Snake would be terminated no matter what. The director would go to any length to salvage what he could.

"How do I do it?"

Huang thawed a degree. To the temperature of liquid helium.

This would be hard to survive.

But he would manage. And he would make these men pay.

Time and success had been working changes. Michael was more confident now, more daring. . . . Snake would be mourned. And avenged.

"Tuesday you leave for Prague. Interpreter with a cultural mission. The embassy will put you into Austria with good German papers. You'll go to the man you met in Hamburg. He's already working on it. He'll have new papers for you. He'll relay last-minute instructions and provide the information you'll need to locate your target. You'll be on your own once you leave Hamburg. You'll have to arrange for anything you'll need beforehand."

On his own and alone, Michael thought. And forevermore a target himself if he didn't kill quickly and get himself home. There would be an unspoken and uncertain deadline. Once it passed, the hounds would hit his trail. And they would get him someday.

Remember Leon Trotsky.

Oh, the goddamned, Olympian stupidity that had led him to join the army.

The affair had its bright moment. He was unable to leave Czechoslovakia immediately. His keepers let him see Ilse and their son. Probably as an incentive to come back.

He told Ilse the whole thing. She, too, had trouble reconciling personal feelings and needs with the demands of the State.

With one human being behind him, that one special woman, Michael was certain he could cope. He knew he would someday reach a position where he could extract a savage retribution from the men compelling him to cannibalism.

Then it was down the toboggan run of fear: Hamburg, Bremerhaven, Hull, London. A shop in Bond Street, where a wordless man named Wilson gave him a fat attaché case and a look that said he hated dealing with such sordid people.

Michael wondered what they had on the man, but only momentarily. He had but one goal now, to survive till he could see Huang and Sung roasted on spits.

He was on the Hamburg office expense ledger. Credit unlimited. He picked up a thousand pounds at the firm's London bank. He would live in style. He started with a suite at the Mayfair.

There he examined the case's contents.

One Weatherby .227 bolt action varmint rifle without markings. Monte Carlo stock in hand-rubbed walnut. The weapon had been drilled to mount a starscope, a nightsight that made use of ambient light. The scope shared cheesecloth wrappings with a long tubular silencer, five rounds of target ammo, and five explosives rounds. The latter were the kind that had had a hole tapped down the centerline, filled with a drop of mercury, and resealed. The kind that would rip a man worse than any dumdum or hollow point.

There were two sets of identification. He could be Llewelyn Jones, lorry mechanic from Cardiff. Or Thomas Hardy, insurance executive, on holiday from Ottawa, Canada.

"Too big a hurry," he muttered. How the hell could he fake a Welsh accent? And he didn't know shit about insurance, though that identity would be manageable as long as he didn't have to answer business questions.

It looked like Spuk would have to get him back to Hamburg.

There were flyers for the rock concert. Just two performances remained. Tonight and tomorrow night.

He didn't like it.

The man in Hamburg had called the mission a widowmaker. He had been right.

Haste made wasted agents.

Speed, surprise, and the complacency of the English would be his advantages. He had to make the best possible use of them.

At least someone had bothered to do a preliminary study. There were freehand drawings of the hall layout, and confirmation of earlier reports on the habits of the Danzer group.

They could not be reached outside the hall. The group traveled in dense security, which existed entirely to hype their reputation.

It wasn't working. They hadn't yet played to a sellout audience.

The moment of maximum vulnerability would come while they were on stage. Therefore, the rifle.

Michael sprawled across his bed, eyes closed, for ten minutes.

This could get rough. He wouldn't have a friend in the whole damned country.

Above all else, he concluded, he had to secure his line of retreat.

Thoughts of Ilse and the baby intruded. God, what a woman. . . . He didn't understand her. How could she love him so much?

He had had a dozen lovers before Ilse, but not a one had he needed the way he needed her. Maybe it was a response to his total expatriation. And the little guy . . . He was such a quiet baby, almost spooky with those big, blue, intelligent eyes. Ilse insisted that he was going to be a great man someday.

He tried forcing them from his mind. That only created a vacuum into which Nancy and his first brood stole.

Nerve was the key, he reminded himself. He had to start getting himself up for it now. He could not be the old Michael. He couldn't let fear make him do something that would get him killed or caught.

Damn! There just wasn't time to do it right. They wanted Snake dead quick.

Did Sung have an observer on his tail? Probably.

He rose, turned to the rifle. Why this weapon? With its flat trajectory it was superb for small game at extended ranges, but. . . . For this job Michael would have preferred something heavier, something with a lower muzzle velocity. The slower projectile had more time to break up inside its target. Nor was he familiar with the weapon. He assembled it and broke it down twice, feeling for economy of motion. Speed practice would have to wait. He had things to do, alternatives to establish, before the shops closed for the day.

Cash checked the Canadian papers again. They might do.

He selected a vanity case, descended to the lobby.

"Yes, Herr Spuk?" the clerk asked as he approached.

Michael forced a slight accent as he asked, "Would it be possible for the hotel to obtain entertainment tickets?"

"Of course, sir. A show, sir? They recommend—"

"The Danzer concert. A box. For this evening."

"Danzer, sir?"

"Erik Danzer. The rock singer."

"Very well, sir." The man's nose went up.

"The young lady, she is fond of Danzer."

It was a red herring that Michael hoped would produce multiple rewards. The clerk would adjust his present opinion. And in future should report that Herr Spuk had had a female companion when the police came asking their questions. They might waste valuable time trying to find the woman.

"Ah, I see." The clerk winked.

Michael smiled, then asked the doorman to hail a cab. He tipped generously.

It was Huang's money.

He studied the Hardy identity during a brief journey. And within a half hour was in a second cab, studying again, after having taken a small room as Thomas Hardy.

That afternoon he obtained wigs, theatrical makeup, and new clothing. And surgeon's gloves.

They should have provided the latter with the rifle.

Wigs were a must for the concert hall. His military-style haircut stood out like the sex of a male interloper in the girls' locker room at showertime. He was lucky he was traveling German. The English expected Germans to look like soldiers on leave.

Then he tried pushing his luck, and the calm, talent, and training of the man within him.

"What's the matter, Mr. Hardy?" the rental officer asked.

He had been frantically rehearsing his driving. And had forgotten that the British did everything bass-ackward.

"This is my first trip to England. I forgot all about right-hand steering. On the Continent—"

"I should have realized, sir. I'm sorry. We do have a little left-hand Simca automatic."

"Fine. Perfect. The Jag really wasn't me anyway." What had made him choose that beast? This was no time for doing a Walter Mitty-playing-James Bond number.

"On the expense ledger, sir?" The attendant began processing the new papers.

"Yes. You know how it is."

"I wish I did, sir. I wish I did. I didn't ask before. Not polite, you know. But I wondered . . . you're from Ottawa . . . ?"

"Yes?" Michael's heart crept toward his throat. He didn't even know where in Canada Ottawa was.

"I wondered if you'd ever heard of a Mr. Charles Allen Underhill, sir. That's me mum's brother. He emigrated after the war."

"I'm sorry. No."

"Ah, I expected so. And him always writing Mum what a big name he is over there."

"That's human nature."

"Aye, sir, that it is. Just sign and we're ready to go."

Michael slid the Simca into traffic without giving himself away, then spent two hours puttering around like an old man, relearning his driving. He did so in mortal terror of an accident. If the police noticed him now . . .

He survived. To rent another room and another car—a Volkswagen. He took them under the Spuk name. The room included garage privileges. He moved the Simca there, then drove the Volkswagen back to his original base.

He was leaving tracks, he knew. But time was tight. Corners had to be cut. The important thing was to keep the trail just obscure enough to give him a reasonable chance of reaching Hamburg.

The maid had been in during his absence. He panicked, rushed to the attaché case. But it hadn't been disturbed. He sighed.

"Got to get ahold of myself," he muttered.

He began calling travel agents, scattering a dozen Bremerhaven reservations in three names, and air passages to Hamburg, Cologne, and Munich. And made a mental note to get a road map so he could study the approaches to Dover. As a last resort he would try for Calais.

He threw himself on the bed.

"Why don't I just tool over to the U.S. Embassy?" he muttered to himself. "I could turn myself in. They'd take care of me." He thought of his children, Michael and Tiffany, and one whose name he didn't know, one unborn till after his capture. Little Mike ought to be ready for junior high . . . so many years. So soon gone.

Then he thought of Ilse, and another son, and the debriefing the Americans would put him through.

It would be easier just to go on.

The desk clerk called. His tickets had arrived. He thanked the man and instructed him to obtain the same box for the final performance, then asked not to be disturbed before noon tomorrow.

It was time to commence the evening's adventure. He began by taking two aspirin.

He took his attaché case along, after emptying it of all but innocuous papers. He drove the VW to the garage where he had left the Simca, switched, went on to where he had registered as Hardy. There he changed clothing.

Imitative of the era of George III, his outfit was an eye-grabber. He added makeup and a long-haired blond wig.

Finding a parking space near the hall proved impossible. First point of adjustment. He would have to position the car during the afternoon, and arrive by cab for the critical performance.

There was no trouble with the case. No one paid any attention. His clothing, the limp caused by the stone he had put in his shoe, the winestain birthmark painted on his cheek and throat, proved sufficient distractions.

Inside, he reflected that he should have brought the weapon in now and have hidden it. . . .

But that would have aborted his two A.M. practice session on the bank of the Thames.

That didn't begin encouragingly. He used all five target and two killing rounds before he trusted his weapon. He selected the sternlight of a moored barge for his final check shot.

It shattered. He departed to the muted, mystified curses of a river man.

Two rounds remaining.

He would need just one.

He would use it right up front, while they were spotlighting the members of the band, while the audience was still mesmerized by the show. Three to four seconds exposure for each musician. Plenty of time. If he timed his shot, his target wouldn't fall till after the spot had traveled on. There would be mild confusion at first. Twenty to thirty seconds would pass before anyone realized there was something badly wrong. He would be down to the side exit by then.

The lights would come up. More confusion. Time to reach the Simca. Panic. Screams of "Murder!" and "Police!" He should have the Simca off the street before it began settling out. He would become Hardy, aging himself with makeup, and be on the road again, in the VW, before the police showed any real life.

Would they seal all exits from the country? It seemed unlikely. They would have no reason to believe it a political killing. A grudge killer would just go home. Anyway, they wouldn't want to antagonize thousands of travelers when Britain needed every tourist mark and dollar. He didn't think that they would develop a reliable description before the unavoidable traces he had left had begun to surface. He would have a damned good chance of being over the Czech border, or at least into Austria, by then.

And the exposed trail would end at Hamburg.

Only bad luck could stop him. Or his own weakness.

He began to feel optimistic in spite of the haste of the mission.

But would he squeeze the trigger when the moment came?

He slept. And dreamed a nightmare in which his pursuers had run him into farm country resembling that surrounding the city where he had been raised. He lay exhausted, behind a treeline, near the top of a low ridge. They were coming toward him across a newly harvested cornfield, spread out in a broad skirmish line. They wore dress-blue police uniforms. Some were close enough to make easy targets. But when he laid the crosshairs on the nearest, he found himself looking into the face of his father.

He woke in a sweat, shaking.

And immediately began practicing assembling his weapon.

He kept at it till he could do it without thinking, while concentrating on something else. Then he packed, went over the room till he was sure he had left no fingerprints, and checked out. He drove to the Spuk hideout, repeated his erasures. Then he took the Simca and parked it within a block of the concert hall.

A cab delivered him to his third address, where he changed into the Georgian costume, worked on the rifle, and scrubbed fingerprints again.

What a stir those would cause if found and identified.

And how unhappy the director would be.

Michael waited till he could enter the hall with a surge of young people. Again no one challenged the attaché case.

Only the starscope, a baggy American leisure suit, a wig, and his makeup lay within. Not one person in a thousand would have recognized the scope. The rifle barrel was down his left side, beneath his shirt. Its breach he held clamped in his armpit. The silencer he had tucked inside his waistband at the small of his back. The rifle stock he had cut off at the handgrip. The rest wouldn't be necessary for this shot. What remained he had thrust down the tight pants over the "bad" leg. The long coat concealed the bulges.

He wouldn't have fooled anyone watching for weapons smugglers. But gunrunners don't do business at rock concerts.

And people don't see anything they don't expect to see.

He hurried to a balcony level rest room, locked himself into a stall, quickly changed clothing and makeup. The rifle parts went into his bag. Everything else went into a waste can, beneath used paper towels, while the rest room was momentarily empty. He emerged looking a shopworn forty-five and faggoty, a man people would move away from without knowing why.

Trial chords reverberated through the auditorium.

The worst would be over in minutes.

"Snake, Snake, why the hell did you have to be so damned stubborn?" he muttered.

And thought, Mr. Director, how long do you expect to last if I survive this?

He moved to his box. As the house lights dimmed he assembled his weapon. He was cool, calm, without fear or thought. Training had taken over.

XXVII. On the Y Axis; 1975

Norm would have slept through a good chunk of Saturday if Lieutenant Railsback had let him. But the man was on the phone by eleven. By noon Cash was on his way to the station, his car loaded.

Tran and Matthew chattered in back. Beside him, Beth was being Miss Efficiency.

"I called your friend last night. Frank Segasture. He said he'd meet us at the airport."

The "us" slipped past Norm. "What? What did you tell him? He's one of those people who think that if you cross the New York City limit you fall off the edge of the world."

"I just told him what happened. He's really a pretty nice guy."

He saw the huntress's gleam in her eye. "But very married, babe."

"They all are."

He glanced at her sharply, then leaned, whispered, "What happened to Teri last night?"

"I took her home after John's wife showed up."

A ball of snakes began wriggling in his belly. "What happened?"

"Nothing. Your wife was cool. Just introduced her as a family friend who hadn't been around for years. I guess John didn't tell his wife about his premarital adventures. She didn't react to the name."

"Good for Annie. We've got troubles enough already."

For a moment he listened in on Tran and Matthew. Matthew was making pronouncements on Vietnamese issues with all the authority of a self-taught expert who had been in grade school and high school during the U.S. involvement. He just didn't know. Though some of his assertions came right off the wall, Tran didn't seem offended.

"I think your wife is on your side now," Beth observed. "I saw her packing your things this morning. And she said she'd just gotten back from the bank when I woke up."

"Good. Must have been the explosion that changed her mind. She'd already rung him in on me by then." He jerked a thumb at Matthew. He knew damned well that Annie had asked Matthew to come home to talk him out of going to Rochester.

"It's not hard to understand."

"I know. It's because she cares, because she's scared. But she makes me feel trapped sometimes."

The station was anything but normal for a Saturday morning. There were people everywhere, including some brass from downtown.

The Homicide office was besieged. Reporters recognized Norm as one of the principal investigators, began plaguing him for a statement. They filled the hallway.

Tom Kurland had come upstairs to stand guard on the office door. "Should have accepted Andy's confession," Cash told him.

"Should have." Kurland grinned, opened the door.

"What the hell?" Cash grumbled after he had shepherded his group inside and helped Tom close the door again.

"We made the network news," said Smith, passing.

There were more people in the office than at the height of the last Christmas party. Beth's desk had become a command center. Cash felt an urge to throw people out. But everybody appeared to have more right to be there than did either of his guests.

"That Norm out there?" Railsback called. "Tell him to come in."

The captain was there with Hank, but had nothing to say. He greeted Cash with a curt nod.

"Norm, we're getting it from downtown. Both barrels. They want some answers, and some arrests, yesterday. Must be an election coming up, the way City Hall is bitching and moaning."

"So? We knew it was coming. We've lived through it

before." But he didn't *feel* confident. There was too good a chance that he would lose his job. The best he hoped for was a demotion to patrolman.

"Captain?" Hank said.

The man nodded, left. He closed the door behind him.

"Norm, I did some plain and fancy talking this morning. The division has permission to reimburse you for your travel, meals, and lodging. So get receipts. We'll pay off when we get next quarter's LEA funds."

"Huh?"

"For your trip to New York."

Once again Hank had taken him by surprise.

In a soft, cold voice, Railsback told him, "There wouldn't be many questions asked if it looked like self-defense."

Cash shook his head slowly. "No."

"I don't mean . . ."

"I know exactly what you mean."

They glared at one another for twenty seconds before Hank's gaze drifted to the window.

"Okay. But I'm telling you up front. You'd better come home dragging some coyote skins to hang on the gate."

"I will. That's a promise." Or I won't come home at all. Not on my hind legs.

He had a touch of that Ardennes feeling.

After another twenty seconds, during which he fidgeted with rubber bands and paper clips, Hank muttered, "Good enough. Pick up your loose ends. Give Tucholski anything he can use. He'll be in charge here. Then go home and rest up. You should get there fresh."

"If they haven't hauled ass out of there while we've been farting around," Cash replied sourly.

"Why should they? You said she didn't know we knew about the brother."

Cash shrugged. "Murphy's Law. It's been going strong up till now. Why should my luck change?"

Railsback dipped into his desk for a colorful handful of pills. He took them dry, closing his eyes and grimacing as they went down.

"Try to get back by Wednesday. That's when we're planning the funeral." Hank took a deep breath, sighed.

Norm stared at the man's hands. They shook almost too much to manipulate the paper clips. "And be careful. You're taking Tran? Good. Listen to him. He's a pro."

"I will. I'm no hero. You know that."

"Okay. Get moving."

Cash started toward the door.

"Wait. Norm? Good luck." Railsback half rose to extend a hand.

Surprised, Cash shook. Hank's palm was moist and cold. "Thanks."

He left Hank staring out the window.

It was suppertime before he got home. There was so much to do, so many people to talk to. Time fled as if some light-fingered thief were stealing his life-hours while he was preoccupied.

Malone. He was the worst chrono-bandit. Every time Cash turned around, the agent was, pushing him for that New York address. The man wanted the stalk for himself. Apparently there were points to be tallied with Langley.

This was the downhill side. The big slide to the brink of the pit. Time seem to flow at an ever-increasing pace. . . . He couldn't relax, couldn't rest. He kept remembering the shot-gunned cat. This was no good. He was working himself into another state of nerves. . . .

Carrie, Nancy, and their offspring didn't help. They made his home scene seem like there was a Sicilian wake taking place amid the goings on at Little Big Horn. He finally fled to his bedroom, to lie staring at the ceiling, reviewing the insignificance and disappointment of his life.

It hadn't been much. Wouldn't become much. He hadn't contributed anything. History wouldn't have noticed at all if he had never been born. The highs and lows, the goods and evils, those hadn't touched but a handful of lives.

Not much of a bright side, thinking that, if you hadn't saved the world, at least you hadn't helped destroy it.

The next thing he knew, Annie was shaking his shoulder.

"What time is it?"

"Two." She eased down beside him.

"I have to leave pretty soon."

"I know."

He rolled toward her, pulling her close.

There was a gentle sorrow to their loving, an expression of unspoken fears. For Norm there was a thirty-year-old *déjà vu*. There had been another such night early in 1944, before he had marched off to war.

They hadn't been married then. Had not been lovers till that final night. . . .

Alpha and Omega?

Annie refused to go to the airport, just as she had refused to go to the railway station back then.

Le Quyen watched her husband depart with the same sad eyes.

Matthew did the driving. It was a cool, silent morning. They had the freeway almost to themselves. There was a heavy dew, and the air smelled of rain.

Cash didn't notice Beth till after they had boarded the plane. She couldn't hide there. There weren't a dozen passengers to get lost among.

"Beth!" he exploded. "What the hell do you think you're doing?"

"Going to Rochester."

For half a minute he was too confused to say anything. Then, "Girl, you just march yourself right back home."

She sat down, buckled her seat belt.

"Come on, Beth. This isn't any job for you."

She ignored him.

He started to summon a stewardess, to have her put off the plane. Then he realized that people were staring, realized how foolish he would look and sound. He plopped down, angrily fastened his own belt.

Tran stared out a window with a bemused smile.

"I don't think it's funny," Cash told him. "This isn't some vacation trip."

"I was reflecting on the paradoxes in chains of command."

"I don't follow you."

"How many times have you threatened to crucify your lieutenant because he wouldn't let you do things your way? How many times have you ignored him? You set the example for her."

Cash looked at Tran sharply. He wanted to claim that these circumstances were different. But he couldn't. That would have been pure hypocrisy.

He grinned. "You got me dead to rights."

Having listened to the conversation, Beth remarked, "It's too late anyway, Norm." The engines began to whine. "So let's get on with the job."

He gave her a look that promised he wouldn't forget, but said only, "What else can I do?" He sighed, closed his eyes.

"Wake me up when we get there."

He wouldn't sleep. Flying frightened him too much. Every little creak from the airframe would be sandpaper across raw nerves. Safety statistics didn't mean a thing to the primitive cowering at the back of his skull.

Frank Segasture, true to his promise, was there to meet them.

Cash embraced the man. "How the hell are you, you runt wop? Getting a little chunky there, aren't you?" He jabbed a finger into the man's spare tire.

Segasture was short, broad, and swarthy. He looked more like a movie Mafioso than a detective. He took the insults with a grin. "When you going to wake up and start wearing a hat? What the wind ain't bleached it's blown away. Kids started calling you chrome-dome yet?"

"Hey, Frank, when the dust settles let's go out and get plowed. I haven't gone clubbing since that time in D.C."

"In Rochester? You got to be shitting me. Man, people around here go to Cleveland for excitement." He eyeballed Beth while he talked. She reddened, tried pretending she didn't notice.

"Oh. This is Major Tran. And Beth Tavares."

"Ah. The lady on the phone. The one with the sexy voice." He ogled her. "Maybe we *can* learn something from you guys in the sticks. I never had a partner like this."

Beth blushed more deeply, moved nearer Cash.

"Tran, did you say? The Viets are in on this, too?"

"Just personal curiosity," Tran replied. "I was a police officer myself. I find this case extremely interesting."

"That it is. You guys had breakfast yet? Didn't think so. With that outfit you're lucky the plane even got here. Come on. Let's get your bags and go. I've got us set up at the Holiday Inn. It's only a couple of miles from the house."

"I'm not hungry," said Cash, puffing as he tried to match Segasture's pace. "Let's just go out there. . . ."

"Down, Sherlock. There ain't no rush. She hasn't showed yet. Might as well take it easy till she does."

"She hasn't?" Sudden fear rolled over Cash. Had he guessed wrong? "But she's had plenty of time. . . ."

"Hey! Don't get an ulcer. Okay? We'll know if . . . *when* she comes in. And where she goes."

"Huh? How?"

"Think about it." Segasture grinned as he helped Beth claim her bags.

Christ, she must plan on a long stay, Norm thought.

"I give up, Frank."

"Ah, Norm, you never were any fun."

"Taxi drivers," said Tran.

Segasture spat to one side. "Yeah. Norm, your friend is too damned smart. Yeah. What I did was get to the cabbies working the stations. I told them there was a twenty for the guy who spotted her and let us know."

"Isn't that a little cheap?"

"There's guys would cut your throat for that much down in the city. Anyway, they're going to be your bucks. I'll up the ante if you want. Hey, pretty lady, I'll carry them."

"Don't worry, Beth. This old dog is all bark. He's the last of the faithful husbands."

In a tight voice she remarked, "That's what I was afraid of." She wasn't at ease with that kind of banter.

"You're blowing my mystique, Norm. Come on. I've got a car. Hey! You remember the time we booby-trapped old Handley's microscope?"

They relived similar hijinx all the way to the motel, till Cash was sure Beth and Tran were convinced that his FBI course had been waste of the taxpayers' money.

Over breakfast Beth became Miss Business. "Norm, did you forget Dr. Smiley?"

He halted a forkful of pancake halfway along its arc to his mouth. "Damned near." He explained to Segasture.

"Okay. I'll put the word out for the drivers to watch for him. You got any other rats going to come out of the woodwork back here?"

Cash shook his head. "You know, I wish I could get out and prowl around the countryside. My mother came from a place called Johnstown. I think it's around here somewhere."

"Nah. It's almost over to Albany."

"I remember, back in thirty-four, we drove all the way back there in a twenty-six chevy. For my grandfather's funeral. Only time I ever saw the man. Laying in a casket."

Cash's mind drifted into the past. It was hard to believe that he had ever been that young. "He had two wooden legs. That's all I remember about him. He was some kind of mechanic on the railroad. One day he fell asleep under an en-

gine he was working on. Somebody got in and drove it off. . . .
You know, the only other thing I remember about that trip is
playing on a barge on the Erie Canal.''

"Maybe you can go over there after we close this thing up,"
Segasture suggested.

"No. There won't be time. We've got to get back. Fu-
nerals.''

And that was the story of his life. Always there was something that had to be done. Twenty-six months in Europe, with
Uncle Sam footing the bill, and he hadn't seen a damned thing
but the cathedral at Cologne.

Later, in Norm's motel room, Segasture opened a briefcase
and passed out weapons. "I hope we don't have to use these.
Try not to. Especially you, Major. They're legal, but we might
have to do a lot of explaining. So wave them around if the
feeling grabs you, but don't shoot. Norm, you want to ride
out there? Look the place over?''

What he wanted was to go lay an ambush at the railway station. "What if she comes in while we're gone?''

"Christ! Don't be so damned anxious. We'll find out. If the
cabbies can't get ahold of me, they know who to call at the
Rochester P.D. They've got to be in on the edges of this thing
anyway. It's their turf.''

"Sure. You're right. Let's go take a look.''

Segasture drove past slowly.

"It's a goddamned mansion,'' Cash muttered.

"The old boy is worth a mint. And the feeling around here
is that he didn't come by all of it legit.''

"What do you mean?''

"Koppel. . . . The local cops think he's connected
somehow. Little visible means of support. And he has some
pretty strange visitors. Mainly foreigners. The couple who
work for him are German.''

"Who's this Koppel?''

"The guy who owns the place.''

"But . . . the man we want is Fial Groloch.''

"Then you're out luck.''

"You're sure that's the right house?'' All he needed was to
have to go back to Hank and admit that he had gone on a wild
goose chase.

"That's the address you gave me. Hey! Calm down. It did
belong to Fial Groloch. He sold out to this Koppel about forty
years ago.''

"But she got letters from here!" Cash protested. He shuffled mental files, dredging up everything he had learned about Fial Groloch.

"Perhaps only the name of the owner changed," Tran suggested. "The man in residence might be the same."

"Of course!" Cash jumped on it instantly. "That'd be the perfect way to cover up the fact that you're outliving all your neighbors."

Segasture's expression was dubious. "I vote we go back and party till we get word that she's here."

"What I'd like to know," Beth said, "is why, when we asked you to check the place out, back when, you didn't let us know these things. If Koppel isn't Groloch, then we're out time and money for nothing."

"She always like this, Norm?"

"She doesn't let much get past."

"Yeah. Well. It's like this. I didn't get into it as deep as it might have sounded on the phone."

"I don't think you got into it at all," Beth retorted.

"You faked it?" Cash demanded.

"Well, sort of. I called some people. In the state police, up here. . . ."

"I get the picture. They didn't want to be bothered either. You just wanted me off your back. I'm going to remember this, Frank."

"Hey, I'm sorry, Norm. It just didn't look very important at the time. You know what I mean?"

"I know what I think. But it's too late to cry now. Come on. Let's get back. I need a drink."

Two hours at the motel were all Cash could take. He left the others with the impression that he was going to take a nap, caught a cab to the railway station.

At ten P.M. he finally admitted his folly to himself. He was just working on an ulcer. At the motel, at least, he could share the waiting with friends.

But he had this damned overpowering urge to *do* something.

It almost conned him into a solo recon of the local Groloch establishment.

For once terror did him a favor. It stopped him.

By sheer chance, as his taxi pulled away, he glimpsed someone through a blindless window. The man was crossing the waiting room, toward the rest rooms, at a trot.

"Damn!" Norm growled. "That Malone is stubborn." He hoped the man's bladder was choking him. Serve him right, hiding, spying on people.

He didn't get upset. There wasn't a thing he could do about it.

He went looking for Frank right away. The bartender told him that Segasture had gone to bed. Tran had turned in too. "Hell, it's still too early. Mix me a rum and Coke in a water glass. Two shots. No ice."

Maybe it was just as well. He wouldn't have to take any crap about sneaking off.

He went through three drinks before announcing, "I might as well sack out too. Ain't nothing else to do." He was dog-tired, but not really sleepy. Too keyed up.

He was about to become more keyed up.

He stepped into his room and ass deep into a "situation."

Beth was in his bed. She had fallen asleep while reading.

She didn't have a stitch on beneath that sheet. One bare, large, dark-nippled breast peeked out at him.

"So this is why she came." He closed the door gently, quietly seated himself in the room's one chair. His knees missed brushing the bed by a scant half inch.

As nervous as she was, how could she have fallen asleep? She should have been too scared to think.

Maybe she had reached the point of emotional exhaustion.

His thoughts went round and round, pecking at the situation from a hundred angles.

It boiled down to a choice between *should do* and *want to do*.

God, she looked good.

A half hour passed. The alcohol gradually caught up. He felt on the verge of collapse. He had to get to bed.

He would have to disturb her or stay awake.

He didn't want to endure the inevitable confrontation.

God damn it, it was his bed.

A disinterested fraction of his mind observed, with amusement, that, whenever he began to relax, he reacted in healthy male fashion. The resulting tension invariably caused a detumescence.

He rose, stripped to his shorts, switched the light off, slid into bed.

Beth wakened instantly, sat upright. "Norm? I'm sorry. I don't know why—"

"Shut up. Lay down. Shut up," he said again. He pulled her toward him, cuddling spoon fashion. She remained stiff, but her skin was smooth, soft, warm. She shivered, tried to pull away. "Lay still. And go back to sleep."

They didn't drift off quickly. There was too much tension, too much waiting for someone to make an advance. But the forced silence gradually sapped the fury of the emotional storm.

Cash slept, but awakened with the dawn.

Beth snored fitfully beside him, sprawled on her back. Obviously she was used to sleeping alone.

Cash touched himself. He had one of those throbbing morning erections that a cat couldn't scratch.

He lifted himself onto one elbow, eased the sheet off the bed.

"Nice," he whispered.

She really did have a dynamite body.

His heart hammered. He shook all over. It was like the first time ever all over again.

He was going to do it.

He bent to one of those magnificent breasts.

Frank came pounding on the door shortly after ten. "Hey. Norm. Come on. Get up."

They came out of bed grabbing for clothes.

"In the bathroom," Cash whispered. "What do you want?" he growled.

"Come on. We've got to move."

Norm dragged his shorts on and stumbled to the door. "Man, what's all the racket for?" he demanded as he opened up.

"She's here. Your target. Cabbie just took her out there. She sent him back for a bunch of luggage."

"We've got to grab that. There's a trunk I want."

"I'll call the Rochester P.D. while you get dressed. Want me to get Beth? Tran's already over at the café."

Cash's heart hammered. "No. I'll take care of it. Just get somebody on to that trunk. That'll make my case."

"Ah. I see." Segasture hurried off.

What had he meant by that? Cash wondered. And by that sudden little grin?

He understood the instant he turned. Beth had missed her purse and bra in her rush to the bathroom.

"Oh, shit."

But what could he do? The horse had escaped. Better play it cool, say nothing, and hope that Frank did the same. "Hey, babe, I need the shower."

Blushing all over, Beth came for her bra.

They were even more impressive when she was standing.

"Male chauvinist," he murmured.

"See if there's anybody outside," she said softly. "I have to go change."

Cash peeked out. "It's okay."

She started to leave. He stopped her, lifted her chin, kissed her lightly. "Thank you, Beth."

She clung to him momentarily, head against his chest. "Thank *you*." She left.

He didn't think it would happen again. Her need had been filled. As once he had filled Teri's need with a refusal.

When would his turn come?

Norm found breakfast awaiting him. "Beginning to look like you're hooked on this one, too, Frank."

"It was the major's idea. He was afraid you wouldn't eat unless you were put under obligation."

Tran smiled. "We have to care for ourselves first."

Cash drained half a cup of coffee, pushed it aside so the waitress could refill it. "I'm looking forward to today. But now that I'm here, and she's here, I don't feel any big rush anymore. Did you order for Beth?"

"Yes. But I assumed she would take longer. Women usually do."

"Frank, you were right. He's too damned smart." Cash wondered if Tran were smart enough to have figured the night's happening. Not that it mattered. The man would keep his mouth shut.

It had been ages since he had felt so relaxed, so fulfilled, so at peace. He had Beth to thank.

She arrived looking bright and cheerful and not the least bit guilty.

Cash felt no guilt himself, to his surprise. Maybe it would set in after the euphoria passed.

The waitress quickly arrived with Beth's breakfast.

I'm getting close to it now, Cash thought, visualizing Miss Groloch's elfin face.

"Here's how I figure we should do it," Segasture said, and began outlining a plan.

XXVIII. On the X Axis; 1975

She paid the cabbie, tipping generously, then added twenty dollars and asked him to recover her baggage from the railway station. She watched him pull away, then marched up the winding, rose-flanked walk to the door.

He responded almost as if he had been waiting.

"Fiala! What are you doing here?" He spoke German. His English remained as broken as hers. "Come on in."

The house was old, rich, dark. It had changed little with the years.

Fial had. He had aged.

But sixty years separated this meeting from their last.

A woman of sixty, confused and embarrassed, rushed from the rear of the house. "I'm sorry, Herr Koppel. I was in the bathroom." She, too, spoke German, but with a northern accent.

"That's all right, Greta. You and Hans take the car into town, will you? Catch up on your shopping."

The woman withdrew with a slight, stiff, Teutonic bow. She seemed accustomed to disappearing when strangers arrived.

"My God, that woman is ugly."

"But the perfect housekeeper. Absolutely close-mouthed. She and her husband have been with me since forty-nine. They're refugees. I think they were involved with the SS. Whatever, they don't attract any attention."

"Koppel?"

"I changed names during the Depression. My business connections were beginning to wonder about my longevity. It seemed like a good time to disappear. Financial empires were

249

crumbling right and left. But you haven't told me why you're here."

"I had to run. I had to, Fial. After I saw him, and the policeman. . . . I couldn't stay there anymore. It was all closing in. . . ."

The old man guided her to an overstuffed chair. "Sit. I'll make some tea. You settle down. Get your thoughts organized."

One familiar with Fiala would have guessed Fial to be as fussy and old-fashioned as his sister. The interiors of their homes were almost interchangeable, though Fial's place was larger and more carefully maintained. He didn't fear carpenters, electricians, or plumbers.

Fial had two cats and a dog. The beagle, a bitch, was seventeen and so feeble she could barely move. She had lost so many teeth that Greta had to spoon-feed her baby food. Yet Fial refused to have her put to sleep.

Fial returned in ten minutes. "Now tell me about it. From the beginning. I really didn't understand your letters."

"First I'd better tell you. I saw Neulist."

"What?" Fial sprang from his chair, began pacing. "How do you know?"

"I can't tell *how*. I just knew who he was when I saw him. Maybe because I was unconsciously expecting him."

"We're supposed to have orderly minds," Fial reminded her. "Minds forged and honed by the State. Let's apply them. Go back to the beginning."

He was worried; this lack of pleasantries, this minimization of the amenities, indicated a fear that something critical was in the wind, that they might have to act swiftly.

"It started with the body in the alley."

"I don't understand why the police were so excited. In this country the alleys are carpeted with corpses."

"Because the dead man was the double of Jack O'Brien. Because two detectives found that out and turned the investigation into a crusade. They just wouldn't stop digging."

"But . . ."

"I know. But it *was* O'Brien. To perfection. Even to the clothing. I know there had to be differences, but after fifty years I couldn't put my finger on a thing. I was too upset the one time I saw the body, though I remember saying it looked smaller.

"I finally figured it out on the way here. Because I saw

Neulist at the funeral. *He* planted the body. How, I don't know.''

Fial paced. "What about why?"

"To stir up the police? That would be his style, wouldn't it?"

Fial stopped abruptly, peered at her. He dropped into his chair. For two minutes he steepled his fingers before his face and stared into nothing.

"Yes it would. Exactly.'' He paused again.

"There's something I haven't told you, Fiala. Fian's dead.'' He described the circumstances.

"I went over there personally. In forty-six and again in forty-eight. The Russians weren't much help.

"I always thought there was something fishy about it. But Neulist? No. I didn't suspect that. The informer, Josef Gabiek . . . in the history I learned, he was a patriot. He was killed in a police raid on a Resistance hideout. But this one wasn't. He disappeared instead.

"I've spent a million dollars trying to find out where he went. I think I know now."

"You should've told me, Fial. I don't need protection from the truth.'' She had suspected Fian's death for a long time. He would have gotten in touch after the war had he been alive.

"I didn't want you to worry. You always overreacted in emotional situations. Anyway, this one didn't seem that suspicious then. There were fifteen hundred other people in the village, and the raid was identical to the one in our own history—except that Fian was there. There wasn't a shred of evidence against the colonel. I wanted to find Gabiek to satisfy my own curiosity as to his motives, as a check against history as we know it. I certainly couldn't go ask Hitler why the bomb didn't kill him in his bunker and stop the war eight months earlier than it ended. I thought I might uncover some pattern to the changes we've seen. That I might find a way to abort them, or neutralize them, or soften their long-range impact.

"Well, if Gabiek *was* Neulist, he shouldn't be able to trace *us*. I don't see how he found you. Unless he got it from Fian somehow. And that's impossible. It had to be dumb luck. I mean, the Czechs let me do some digging where he died. I found his journal, that he kept right up to the minute when the security police started shooting. He never mentioned Gabiek, nor did he have a word to say about Neulist, except a warning about what happened in the programming theater. . . .

"Oh! He didn't follow you, did he?"

"No. Nobody could have. Not without being ten people. We're safe. I don't think anyone even knows you exist. And I took time to make sure they didn't find out. I cleaned the house top to bottom."

"But . . . Neulist. You should have let me know. I could have come in and surprised him. I could have. . . . I've got contacts. Hans knows people who would have loaned us an assassin. As a favor."

"I didn't know till it was too late. I didn't run from him anyway. I could have handled him. He's vulnerable. But the police aren't."

"But we took care of the O'Brien thing back when." A wrinkle of distaste marred Fial's expression.

"Back when isn't the problem."

"Fiala? Don't tell me. Not again? Not another one?"

"A policeman this time. And I had no choice, Fial. It wasn't like before, just madness and meanness.

"I went to the funeral for the O'Brien doppelganger. And Neulist showed up, like I said. That left me in a state, not thinking very good. Otherwise, I might have handled it differently.

"While I was out, one of the detectives got into the house. He must've lost track of time. He was still there when I got home. He left the door open a crack. Because I was upset, I was ready to be suspicious of anything. I snuck in. He was in the little west parlor going through my journals. I did a lot of them in English, to practice. He was so preoccupied that it was child's play to slip up with a hypodermic. . . . It just didn't occur to me that I didn't have to kill him, not if I was going to run anyway. What I should've done was sedate him while I scoured the house and got out. Nobody would have believed him. But at the time I just didn't see that there was any choice."

"Okay. I understand. I don't like it, but I understand. What about the body?"

"I shipped it in a trunk again."

"I'm running out of room in the basement." He smiled weakly. "You're sure you can't be traced? The police are more sophisticated now."

"I made it as complicated as I could. I bought a railway ticket to Indianapolis. The police sergeant looked the type to think me too old-fashioned to travel any other way. Then I went to the airport. I spent the last five days hopping from Memphis to Chicago to Detroit, to Cincinnati, Pittsburgh, Philadelphia, Cleveland, Detroit again, Buffalo, then here. Sometimes I used the bus, the railroad, or went by plane. The luggage I sent by bus and several other shippers, skipping every other city. I used three different names and paid for everything in cash. I changed my clothes every time, and I wore wigs." She was unable to put into words the fright, the feeling of anachronism that had accompanied her every step of the way. She had kept going on sheer willpower.

"Okay. You used your head. If they can untangle that at all, it'll take a month. We'll get the jump on them in the meantime. It's time we went back to Europe anyway. The international situation is going to get nasty soon. The Chinese are going to start in. I've been getting ready for ten years, aiming for seventy-eight, just before it hit. But now is just as good.

"The route will be as complicated as yours was. We'll use four different identities. They've existed for years, and they've been leaving the necessary paper residue in the files of several governments. They'll keep on, because these people really exist. We'll eventually end up tenants on a little farm near Tirschenreuth, at the edge of the Bohemian Forest, just on the Bavarian side of the Czech border, in West Germany. We can cross over whenever we want. Hans handled the arrangments. He knows some ex-Nazis who can manage things like that. I've done them a few favors over here.

"When Hans gets back I'll have him contact his people. I'll contact my brokers in New York and tell them to start moving our money. To Beirut, not Zurich. They always look in Switzerland first these days. After that, we can leave as soon as your body is buried. For my part, I'll apparently die and be buried here. I made the arrangements a long time ago. Seemed the best way to disappear. Hans will get this place. He'll cover our backtrail."

Fial chuckled. "Now we've even got a body to put in my coffin."

"Father couldn't have done better, Fial."

"He couldn't have done as good. That's why he always left me the staff work."

For ten minutes they said little, just sipped tea and contemplated the dramatic tricks fate had played with their lives.

"Eighty-one years to go," Fial muttered. "It'll be one colossal drudge."

"And no way of knowing what we'll face when we get there. Things are so different."

"Not so much. It's our perspective and revisionist educations. more than anything. The real difference peaked around nineteen fifty. Since then history has been undergoing a normalization. It's as if the fabric had been stretched, but now it's going back to its normal shape. But, still, I sometimes wonder why we bother."

"What *are* we doing here, Fial? A surgeon and a physicist playing secret agents in somebody else's time."

"It's no game. Not with a crazy colonel out there somewhere, willing to shuffle history all over again. Not with Fian killed. . . ."

"Don't forget an angry St. Louis police sergeant named Norman Cash. He'll get me if he can, Fial. He's another Neulist. You'd think the young policeman, the dead one, was his son, the way he acted toward him."

"Cash? Norman Cash? A homicide detective? From St. Louis? In Missouri?"

"United States of America, planet Earth. Yes. So?"

"Fiala, think! Christ, how bizarre is this thing going to get? Girl, there *has* to be a God. Not even a dynamic of historical restoration can explain this. Don't you see? He *has* to be Michael Cash's father. Just has to be. There couldn't be two policemen with the same job in the same city with the same name."

"You think so? Really? I never thought of it. But you might be right. His wife said they lost a son in Vietnam. Her name was Ann, and I think she said her son's name was Michael. Or Matthew. . . ? I just never made the connection. You see how stupid I am sometimes?"

"No. You've never been that interested in history or geneology."

"Grandmother told me all those stories when I was little. . . . About the old days, before the State. . . . It *is* a coincidence as big as the Great Pyramid. But does it matter? Michael Cash would still be in China. He won't come over for years yet, will he? By then we'll be gone."

"I was thinking about his visits to Prague. But I guess you're right. It doesn't matter. Still, it gives me the queasies, having to live through the same times as these people. . . .

"Things have changed, but history is sliding back into its old groove. It looks like the State will be born right on time. The way we learned it, with Grandma and Grandpa colluding to make it happen. What scares me is that we might still change it. One slip. Anything that would keep Cash out of Prague, or from coming here to take over at the right time. . . . This United States would survive. Cash wouldn't dump his Chinese allies during their Russian adventure, because he hated that man Huang for what he did to his friend. He wouldn't fix it up with the Czech leadership while the Russians and Chinese are smashing each other. Prague would remain just another capital of an occupied satellite, not the European hub of the new order. . . ."

How critically important this one man would be, Fiala reflected. He would shape the future as surely as Adolf Hitler had shaped the past.

Yet what she had heard about him, so long ago in her own future-past, made him seem a pretty ordinary man. Not at all a megalomaniac. Her grandmother had talked about him ceaselessly.

Michael Cash's driving forces had been a neurotic love and a devouring hatred, each targeted on one woman, one man. He would become powerful only to satisfy the two emotions.

And having done so, he would abdicate. . . .

When had a dictator ever yielded his power voluntarily? Or forbid his family to have anything to do with politics afterward?

Even his wife. And she, chairing the European Party, had been as powerful as he.

That tangled skein fled her mind.

"The doorbell," Fial observed nervously.

"Must be the man with the luggage." Fiala squirmed in her chair, unaccountably nervous herself.

She would like to meet Michael Cash sometime, while the opportunity existed. The memories of a grandmother who had passed away nearly twenty years before their translation into the past, and a father who had seen little of the man, satisfied few of the questions she had today, when she could finally recognize and understand the issues of Cash's day.

Fial had known him too, though only as a child. Maybe he would want a look from an adult perspective. Maybe he would let her tag along.

Fial peered through a curtain. "It's a woman."

"A woman?"

"Yes. Late twenties, I'd say. Dark hair, long and straight. Dark skin. Attractive. Know anyone like that?"

"No. Maybe she's selling something."

The bell rang for the fourth time.

"She's sure determined."

"Well, get rid of her before the man with the luggage shows up."

Fial opened the door. "Of help to you I may be?"

The woman yanked the screen door.

And from a crouch against the outside wall a man lunged inside.

He had a gun.

Fiala swore murderously in German.

"*Danke schön.*" His grin was broad and evil.

XXIX. On the Y Axis;
1975

"Back door, Beth," said Cash, unable to stifle that terrible grin. "Watch yourself."

Pistol in hand, she drifted toward the rear of the house.

Norm backed up to a paisley-upholstered chair. He gestured with his weapon. "I *will* shoot. I have instructions to do so at the slightest excuse. We've stopped being polite. Whoa. Right there. Miss Groloch, move a step away from Fial."

Fial stared without expression. "This is which, Fiala?"

"Ca-Cash."

Fial regarded him with disconcerting intensity.

Beth returned with Segasture and Tran. Frank observed, "They don't look so mean, Norm."

"That's why they're so deadly. Especially her. Major, you want to look around? I haven't seen the servants."

"Greta and Hans, they have gone to shop," Fial said. Cash ignored him.

"Move a little to your left, Beth. We don't want to turn this into a Polish firing squad."

Neither prisoner tried to bullshit him. Fiala seemed too upset. Fial was, apparently, busy thinking.

Segasture and Tran soon returned. "Place is clean," Frank said.

"You see a phone anywhere?"

"No. Why?"

"Impulse. I wanted to call Railsback. To tell him I've got her."

"You've found her, you mean. You haven't gotten her yet. Now the legal hassles start. Extradition. Malone."

"Malone can have this one." He indicated Fial. "But the bitch is mine."

"Hey! Hello!" someone called from outside.

Cash whirled. A man in police blue leaned in the door. Norm relaxed. "Come on in."

"Frank Segasture?"

"Right here."

"Okay. I'm supposed to tell you that warrants and the wagon will be out when they're available. And to treat the prisoners right. Somebody from Washington wants to see them."

"Shit. That damned Malone again," Cash grumbled.

"And a cabbie just spotted the man you wanted to know about. Came over the radio when I was pulling up."

"Smiley?" Cash asked.

"Calls himself Augsberg. As in the Augsberg Pickle Company. Came in on a Lear jet with a couple other guys. Three more were here to meet him."

"That don't sound like my man."

"He fit the description."

"Watch him," Tran suggested. "You know what Malone said about him shifting identities."

"Good idea," Cash replied. "Frank, you think it'd be worth the trouble to find out where the real pickle king is?"

"We'd better. Officer, you got that?"

"I think so. Tail him. And find out if he's the real magilla."

"Check."

"I'll go call it in."

"This man, he would be from St. Louis?" Fial asked.

"That's right, Pop," Segasture told him. "Seems to have what you'd call an abiding interest in you people."

Fial wheeled on Fiala. "You said you weren't followed. You swore. . . ."

Cash laughed. "She wasn't. Not by me. I was here waiting for her."

Fial glared at him.

"You blew it when you changed your name. You kept your newspaper subscription under Groloch."

"I see. And then to Colonel Neulist you sold us."

"Never heard of him."

Cash exchanged glances with Segasture, said, "Looks like Malone might have been on to something." Then he frowned.

The name Neulist agitated Miss Groloch more than ever.

The patrolman returned. "They picked up your trunk. It's on its way to the morgue."

Cash's stomach flopped. "There was a body?"

"They're waiting for a warrant. But they said it's heavy enough. Oh. There's some spade out there who wants in."

"Might as well let him. He's the Washington interest."

Malone let himself in. "Sergeant Cash. Miss Tavares." He wore a broad grin. "They don't look so terrible." He circled the Grolochs. "You turned up anything?"

"Not much," Cash replied. "This one's calling himself Koppel. He's got a couple of Krauts working for him. And he's scared shitless that somebody named Colonel Neulist is going to catch up with them."

"Neulist? I don't know that one. Have to run it through Langley. Koppel, though . . . I think I've heard that one. In connection with the ODESSA. Fits having Germans working for him."

Cash nodded. "I'll make you a deal. We split. Down the middle. You take him, I take her. Oh. Did Smiley ever use the name Neulist?"

"It's not on the record. It might be a workname, though. We'll find out."

"Excuse me." The patrolman was back again. "They've lost the pickle guy."

"Already?" Cash demanded. "How the hell did they manage that?"

"He had a chopper there. He took off in it."

"A planner. It must be Smiley."

"Who?" Malone asked.

"A man who calls himself Augsberg but who looks like Smiley. Maybe he's their Neulist."

Miss Groloch jerked as if slapped every time she heard that name. She was now spookier than Cash had ever seen. Something apocalyptic was going on inside her head.

"Interesting," Malone observed. "You. Fial, is it? Tell me about it."

The old man ignored him.

"Well, we'll find out later."

The officer outside shouted, "Hey, you guys. There *was* a body in that trunk."

Cash closed his eyes, silently counted while the earth

dropped away. There it was. The death of his last hope.

The whickering sound of helicopter rotors grew in the distance.

"Officer! Get in here!" Malone yelled. To the others, "Let's make it a trap. Any reason he should be expecting one?"

"He had people here," Segasture replied. "Probably the ones who followed *her*. They might have noticed we were watching, too."

"He knows we're interested," Cash added. "He had somebody watching her back home. I'd say he's trying to beat us here. If we hadn't gotten the break with the newspaper subscription, he would have."

Malone parted a curtain. "That damned gumball parked out there. And your car and mine. The crowd will scare him off."

The whickering passed overhead, began a slow revolution around the house.

"Guess it isn't the real pickle king," said Segasture, ending with a nervous little laugh.

They waited in silence. The helicopter circled twice.

"He's landing in the garden," Tran called from the kitchen.

"Okay. Everybody out of sight," Malone ordered.

Cash rebelled. This was his show. Neither Malone nor Smiley were going to steal it from him. "I'm staying here. So are these two."

"Suit yourself."

Fiala sobbed. Fial held her, defying Cash. Norm let it go. "Got to meet nightmares toe to toe," he told Fial. His voice betrayed his own fear.

The helicopter's engines died.

Tran called, "They're armed. AK47s. They look professional."

"How many?" Malone asked.

"Five, plus the pilot and old man. The pilot isn't armed. He looks like a conscript."

"Okay. Everybody hang easy. Don't start anything. They've got a firepower advantage." Satisfied with everyone's hiding places, Malone slithered into the tight shadow behind a massive Victorian-style couch.

Cash was scared shitless. His pistol grip was slick. His face was pale. His stomach had become a tiny, aching knot. He

ground his teeth to prevent chattering. He adjusted h.
so he could watch both the front door and the Grolochs.

It was his show, damn it! Fear wasn't going to rip it
his control.

For an instant he saw snowy brush where rosebushes sto
He heard the squeal of tank tracks, the footsteps and bre;
ing of shadowless *panzergrenadiers*. . . .

A real shadow splashed across the porch. Norm slipped l
revolver beneath his leg, prayed he wouldn't do somethin
stupid again.

Fial still held Fiala. She babbled continuously in Czech. Fial
patted her head and murmured in the same tongue.

His eyes, on Norm, remained hate-filled, angry.

You would think, Cash reflected, that he was the wronged
party.

He glanced toward the door. The shadow was gone.

Why were they taking so long?

Miss Groloch shuddered, groaned. Fial spoke to her in a
hard, urgent tone, shifting to German when she did. Cash
couldn't pick out one word in twenty. Most were *nein* or *nicht*
something. Comprehension grew. Fial was telling her, over
and over, to shut up.

Cash wished he could record them.

He glanced at the door. The shadow had returned.

They were playing a game of nerves out there.

Glass shattered in the kitchen. A door slammed. There was
a shout, sounds of a scuffle.

Cash sweated, fearing he would have to carry bad news to
Le Quyen, too.

Within a minute Tran steered a groggy, linebacker-sized
gentleman into the room. He hit the man again, smiled Cash's
way, started back.

And stopped, stared down the bore of an assault rifle.

Cash was tempted. Hitting the interloper wouldn't be difficult.

A cat yowled upstairs. A pair of the beasts hurtled downstairs, disappeared.

And Norm spotted a second man beyond the head of the
stairs.

No point in gunplay now. Too many automatic weapons
around.

The shadow still stretched across the porch.

Where were the others? What were they up to?

Miss Groloch's shakes and moans took on the violence of a seizure. Fial's efforts calmed her not at all.

The man's emotional agony was so obvious, so deep, that Cash couldn't help feeling compassion. Compassion tainted by anger. The old witch was going to get off on an insanity plea.

There would be another feint before the real move, Cash decided. Something to distract them for one critical instant.

Neighbors who had known the man better than he had described Dr. Smiley as an excellent, unorthodox chess player.

He did the unexpected now.

He walked in the front door. Unarmed. With just one bodyguard.

Cash was beyond surprise. "Good morning, Doctor. I've been waiting."

If having been beaten to his prey had disappointed Smiley, he hid it well.

"Norman. You're more efficient than I anticipated." He was no longer the quiet, retiring, bookish neighbor. He had gained a commanding, frightening presence. His clothing, too, had changed. No longer was he the little old man in second-hand. His suit must have set him back four hundred dollars. He turned slightly. "Stefan. And little Marda. It's been an interesting chase. Let me savor the moment. There was no chance with Otho and Dunajcik."

Fial nodded slightly. "Colonel. You, too, are more efficient than anticipated." His hatred was palpable.

"Norman, we could get to butting heads here," Smiley observed. "But you should know that I'm invoking a prior claim. If you accept it we can work this out." He glanced at his watch. "Our goals are nearly the same anyway."

"Afraid not."

"Excuse me?"

"I could never want somebody so bad that I'd get a couple thousand people killed just to nail them. Like you did when you were Josef Gabiek. So I don't recognize your claim. Not here. You should have caught them over there."

Smiley's face flashed several successive reactions.

"Yeah, we know, Dr. Hodză. You just caught us with our pants down." Cash was stalling, hoping reinforcements would arrive. That paddy wagon showing now would be like the cavalry charging over the hill. "Now I have to arrest you, too.

Suspicion of arson and murder. You have the right to remain silent. . . ."

Smiley glanced at his watch, shook his head. "You do amaze me, Norman. I never would have thought it. You seemed such an unimaginative fellow. But we're wasting time. These people are enemies of the State."

Cash caught the odd intensity of the remark. "So are you. Of my state. By the way, what did they do? I've read about some of the off-the-wall crimes you clowns nail people for over there. Conspiracy to defame the State. Jesus!"

"Who speaks for the State?" Fiala demanded suddenly, strangely calm. "Agency Colonel Neulist? The man who destroyed his State's future out of wounded vanity? The man who is poisoning its past? The man who will, without doubt, be remembered as its greatest villain? Colonel, do you know *who* you're talking to?"

Smiley raised an eyebrow. Cash stared.

"He is Michael Cash's father."

Norm's heart leaped into his throat.

"Yes. I know. Does that make him a saint? I'm no simple-minded peasant. . . ."

"Michael is still in China, Colonel. Certain key events can still be aborted."

Cash's mind was collapsing into utter chaos.

"You wouldn't."

"You destroyed my future. What use to me, then, your past?"

"That great a treason . . . you wouldn't dare . . . would you?"

Fial muttered something, apparently agreeing. Fiala glared at him. Something wild and primitive animated her. She seemed much younger, much harder. And her English, Cash noted, had improved markedly.

Fiala snapped, "You, Colonel, are the traitor. The kind Marda's grandfather called the worst. The kind who abuses position, who betrays a trust, to satisfy his ego."

"What the hell is all this?" Cash asked. "You people know something about my son?"

"Too much talk. Norman, I want these people." Smiley gestured. The movement became a slap. Fial backed away, rubbing a stinging cheek. "Or do I have to take them? Bitch." He moved again. Fiala evaded his swing. One foot tried for his groin.

"Doc, I wouldn't try anything if I was you. Too many guns around here. All we can do is cut each other up. Prize goes to the last man standing up. That wouldn't be you." He revealed his weapon. "You might say I've taken a dislike to you lately."

Believing Malone's allegations about the man's past had become easy.

A ghost of a smile teased Smiley's lips. But he was less calm than he pretended. He kept glancing at his watch. With his left thumb he kept fidgeting with his wedding band.

"All right. Your point. A draw." To Fial and Fiala, "But we still have eighty years. We'll meet again." Smiling wickedly now, he backed toward the door.

How do I stop him? Cash wondered. Hank wants him, too.

There was no way. Not without a shootout.

Too late, Norm noticed the absence of the stairway and kitchen gunmen. Tran now lay in a heap beside the man he had subdued. Cash had missed whatever had happened there.

The helicopter chugged to life.

Cash whirled.

Smiley was gone, too.

"The sonofabitch is going to get away!"

Fial collapsed. Moaning, he clawed at a bright purple mark on his cheek.

"What the . . . ?"

"The bastard foxed us," Malone spat as he crawled from behind the couch. "He was wearing a poison ring. . . ."

"Norm, look out!" Beth shrieked.

Guns boomed.

Bullets parted Cash's hair as he plunged to the floor. Polish firing squad, he thought.

He saw slugs tear at Miss Groloch's clothing, saw Smiley vanish again before anyone could hit him. The old woman silently sat down beside her brother. Feebly, she reached for his hand.

Cash scrambled toward the doorway. He looked out, got back an instant before fragments of brick, wood, and metal started flying.

The helicopter sounded ready for takeoff.

He joined a rush to the kitchen.

Through a window he watched Smiley's behind vanish into the chopper. Malone grabbed the downed gunman's abandoned AK47 and broke the pane.

XXX. On the Z Axis;
12 September 1977;
Final Program

Total darkness. Near silence broken only by whispering and restless audience movements.

Suddenly, all-surrounding sound. A crossbreed, falsetto yodel/scream backed by one reverberating chord of the bass guitar. A pillar of red light waxes and wanes with the sound.

Erik Danzer is on.

Nude to the waist, in hip-deep vapor, he rakes his cheeks with his fingernails. He looks like an agonized demon rising from some smoldering lava pit of hell.

Light and sound depart for several seconds.

Sudden light reveals Danzer glaring audience right. Light and sound fade. Repeat, Danzer glaring left.

Harsh electric guitar chords, with the bass throbbing up chills for the spine. Mirror tricks, flashing, put Danzer all over the stage, screaming, "You! You! You!" while pointing into the audience. "You, girl!"

The lights remain on, though dimly, throbbing with the master chords. Danzer sometimes seems to be several places at once. The pillar-spot jumps from band member to band member.

The man whose forged German Federal Republic passport bears the joke-name Spuk neither understands nor enjoys. His last encounter with British rock was the Beatles' "Penny Lane." He does not know that Harrison, Lennon, McCartney, and Starr have gone their separate ways. He has never heard of "Crackerbox Palace," Yoko, Wings, "No, No, No." . . .

Nor does he care.

The pillar moves from man to man. The spook lifts the silenced Weatherby .227. Through the starscope the once familiar face looks like a stranger's.

The curtain masking the door to the box stirs. A shoe whispers on carpeting. A hand reaches from the darkness. The rifle barrel goes down.

The spook turns pale as he stares into another face from the past.

"Dad."

"Michael."